THE CRACK AT THE HEART OF EVERYTHING

FIONA FENN

A Tiny Fox Press Book

ISBN 978-1-946501-71-4

Library of Congress Control Number: 2024947028

Tiny Fox Press and the book fox logo are all registered trademarks of Tiny Fox Press LLC

Tiny Fox Press LLC
Parrish, FL

For every villain who died while trying to become better.

The Labs
The Gilded Palace
The Wasteland
The Stack
The Keep
The Pit

The Empire
The Rim

CHAPTER I
THE EMPIRE

The siren rose from the night, a warning and a herald.

She was coming. Lore was nearly home.

Orpheus took to the halls alongside the rest of the court. Night had descended hours ago, but the Gilded Palace never really slept. Too many people filled its walls for Orpheus to not fondly recall when it had been his and Lore's footsteps echoing through empty corridors. Now, hundreds of courtiers bustled towards the receiving hall, donned in costumes of colorful silks and embroidered brocades like the regal courts of old. Orpheus didn't think it possible for these *nobles* to appear any more absurd, but someone must have circulated a message that they were to wear their most ostentatious finery because that was definitely an aide dressed as a swan and the man in the corner looked one breath away from hyperventilating, due in no small part to the mine's worth of gold armor he must have commissioned for just this occasion.

Stupid. Excessive. *Ridiculous.*

Orpheus avoided the crowd, slipping through a service door and taking to the tunnels. The meandering route would have wasted time if not for the court's bloated excess clogging up the main thoroughfares. And, unlike the rest of the court, Orpheus was used to the palace's underbelly—he had lived there his whole life, after all.

That didn't mean the dangers weren't very much real.

Orpheus spent approximately three seconds checking the shadows for anything unusual and only encountered a handful of workers coming off their shift. They trailed him through the labyrinthine maze, tools clinking in their belts as they hustled steadily towards the receiving hall along with the rest of the palace. Pouches of silver and gold hung heavy at their hips, as unassuming as they were ominous. Orpheus chewed his lip and refused to think of what portion of the palace facade they had stripped that day. Which renovations had required the removal of sigils he'd spent his life within the safe harbor of.

Ahead, warm light cut through the shadows of the tunnels, the crack below the service door revealing the receiving hall beyond. Orpheus quickened his pace.

A guard came to attention at the other side of the door, gaze lowering when they recognized him. Orpheus may not have been wearing anything flashier than his robes, but even in their simplicity he stood out. Inky black fabric swept around his feet, his tall figure cutting a narrow shadow out of the glow of the receiving hall. Wordlessly, the guard moved forward alongside him. Reputation was a useful thing when it was born of respect—even more so with fear. Because respect was what compelled the guard to raise his pike and cut a path through the sea of courtiers, but fear was what kept his eyes on the ground when he did it.

One may feel lonelier than the other, but the results were the same, in the end.

Orpheus stalked into the path the guard created and allowed his *reputation* to do the rest. Courtiers stumbled apart, opening a straight line towards the hall's double doors and the courtyard beyond.

Outside, night swallowed him whole, bitter and cold.

The Gilded Palace's courtyard glowed with the same electric lanterns that illuminated the interior halls. Some new kind of tech come down from the northern laboratories that involved gas instead of filaments—or that's what Orpheus had heard. Electricity wasn't their most recent technological development, but the Gilded Palace was remote enough that connecting to the grid had taken some effort. For the last six weeks workers had been running wires behind the walls and now the whole palace was outfitted with the stuff. But as Orpheus ascended the stairs to the ramparts above, darkness returned, lanterns traded for the Netherflame torches he had ignited years ago, before electricity had been more than an improbable dream.

Up here, some sigils remained. Orpheus reached out to touch one, fingers brushing along familiar silver.

Magic sparked beneath his touch. A spell, as ancient as the palace itself, one of many that adorned the entirety of its structure. From its high outer walls to the deepest bowels of its dungeons, a filigree of silver and gold had been inlaid amongst all the layers of stone, a myriad of archaic etchings connecting each one to the next. Sigils for protection. To remain hidden. The mountain valley the Gilded Palace had been carved from just one layer of isolation that had, for centuries, kept everyone out.

Not anymore. Now the spellwork was almost gone, and Lore had invited everyone from her newly won empire *in*.

Dim violet light flickered across the flagstones, guards tipping their heads down as he passed. A few courtiers already lined the rampart walls, leaning out as if the few extra inches could make the darkness of the pine woods any less dense. Their eyes slipped over him as he passed, never lingering longer than the half-second it took for them to recognize him. A group of frilly women clustered together when he chose a spot along the wall that overlooked the center of the courtyard. Their whispers were hushed, words lost to the gentle buffet of the wind, smothered by fingers they held over their lips.

Orpheus ignored them. Barely blinked an eye when they shuffled farther along the ramparts so they didn't have to share the same air with the palace's resident dark sorcerer.

It was all the same to him. Orpheus had long passed the point where he expected to make friends from these people. Lore had always been enough and now she was home—for *good*.

The herald sounded again, and from the darkness of the towering pine woods, soldiers emerged like ghosts in the night.

The army made little sound, the crunch of boots on gravel no louder than the howl of wind through the needly trees. From his place atop the ramparts, Orpheus possessed an unimpeded view of their approach. Weight dragged their steps, pace barely kept, heads hung low against the cold bite of approaching winter. They passed under the Gilded Palace's gates without the fanfare their victory had earned them. Instead, the courtyard's Netherflame lanterns threw strange shapes across their faces, shadows carved so deep that, months ago, Orpheus might have said they resembled ghouls.

Now, he knew what a ghoul actually looked like, and the drawn faces of the men and women who marched were nothing like the hollowed-out visages of the skeletal army that brought up their rear.

Orpheus tugged his sleeves down over his wrists, pulled his collar higher up his neck. Winter had come early, but the skeletons were the source of this cold. They filled the gaps where human soldiers once numbered in the thousands, their Netherflame flesh burning icier than the wind, decay held at bay by bodies that were meant for a world far more poisonous than their own.

It was a small price to pay. Cold traded for ice. Years more of war for a few short months. It had been Lore who had come up with the idea, but Orpheus who had summoned the army, and despite the haggard faces of the human soldiers lining up along the courtyard wall, Orpheus knew they hadn't made a mistake.

A decade-long war, won. An untamed wasteland, united. A lifetime of hoping and planning, of sacrifice and pain, *over*. All because of Lore and the dream she had shared with Orpheus, when heroes were only ever men they had read about in books.

Down in the courtyard a tall, wild-haired figure cut a path amongst the soldiers. The frilly women's whispers rose into a giggle, one of them waving a silk ribbon while the others played demure. Fenrir Rawkner, formerly undefeated General of Lore's human army and the palace's reigning *Most Eligible Bachelor*, did not notice them. He came to a stop before a gray-faced soldier, mouth moving with words Orpheus couldn't hear. Their exchange was a short one, heads bent close and words too soft to carry on the wind. Orpheus stared anyway. Didn't miss when Fenrir clapped his hand to her shoulder, a bolstering gesture any General might bestow upon one of his soldiers.

As if Fenrir hadn't lost twice as many men invading the Pit, and then retreating from it, his final campaign before Lore had come to Orpheus with that fated spell.

He shoved his hand in his pocket, felt for the ragged-edged parchment and clutched at it like a lifeline. Fenrir could rub his victories in Orpheus' face all he wanted—charm Lore into believing he was the key to her campaign's success—but in the end, it had been *he* who'd won this hells-damned war.

He and Lore, as it was always meant to be.

The wind kicked up, tearing the silk ribbon from the woman's hand and carrying it into the courtyard towards Fenrir. When he looked up, the women gasped, then began to squeal, but it was Orpheus' eyes Fenrir met. Orpheus refused to look away.

You can't blame me, he would have said if Fenrir had been standing before him. Instead, he lifted his chin and sneered.

Then, from the depths of the pine forest, a foghorn wailed through the night.

Orpheus looked out to the forest and the shadows that churned outside the palace's electric light.

It was easy to find Lore's herald amongst the reanimated corpses, the bright red of her flag standing strong amongst the violet glow of their carcasses. Donned in steel, dark hair loose over her shoulder, she rode at the center of her honor guard, atop the shoulder of one taller than all the rest.

Hell's General—Ohm himself—carried Lore towards the gates.

It was time.

Orpheus straightened to his full height, shoulders back as he turned on his heel and headed towards the staircase that would take him to the courtyard adjacent to the crowded receiving hall. Eyes followed him as he stalked by, the courtiers diverting their gazes faster than he could sneer, guards parting the pockets of congestion so he had a clear path. Here, at the edge of the upper towers, more workers were gathered, perched upon their scaffolding, tools tucked into their belts, staring openly down at him when he passed them by.

Orpheus ignored them and took the steps by two, dodging the crawling mass of unguent-like slick that leaked across his path.

Another one? Already?

The Acid Gut did not reach for him. It remained tucked into the corner of the landing, leaking slime from its exposed bowels while following him with eyes that Orpheus would be hard-pressed to identify amongst the mass of half-burst boils. Someone would shoo it out later. Hopefully before it found its way down to his workshop along with what seemed like every other hell beast who had wandered into the palace over the last several weeks.

Don't think about it, the voice inside his head snapped, viciously desperate even as Orpheus thought of the Blood Boiler that had tried to kill him that morning.

He couldn't remember what he had been dreaming of, the nightmare wholly inconsequential to the reality he'd woken to. Body in a full-blown sweat, heart racing, blanket saturated, fever lancing from his heart towards his brain at a degree that would have killed a person who didn't have Netherflame flowing through their veins, Orpheus had incinerated the Blood Boiler on the spot. Of course, his bed had been caught in the crossfire. He didn't know which was worse—having to clean hell beast guts from his floor or the fact that he no longer had a mattress to collapse upon once it was over.

There's no curse, you fool. But the Acid Gut watched him still, creeping out from the shadows that contained it, as if it might follow him down the stairs into the courtyard below.

It didn't. Orpheus lost sight of it when he rounded the final landing and stepped onto the gravel of the courtyard. Across the open expanse, the gates groaned against the wenches pulling them open wide enough for the enormous skeletons to pass through. The human soldiers crowded closer to the wall, a hush falling over the ramparts, only the echoing twang of the scaffolding bouncing gently off the stone walls daring to break the silence—a collective breath held as Lore rode in through the gates.

"Our Lady of the Gilded Palace, Conqueror of the Wasteland,

Commander of Hell's Fist, Empress Lore!" the standard-bearer announced, voice warbling in the night.

Applause rose from the quiet, building into a cacophony when Lore lifted her chin and observed the gathered crowd. Courtiers waved atop the ramparts, handkerchiefs and sashes in hand, what should be a colorful array gone gray in the evening light. Not that Lore appeared to care. She sat on Ohm's shoulder, eying the crowd as if the palace were another stronghold to conquer, an idea that hit strangely close to home when Orpheus considered the reality of the future that awaited them.

What would a warrior Empress do with her peace? How could he help achieve it? What was next for them to build, together?

Orpheus held his head high and strode directly towards Lore.

That's when the Acid Gut decided to shamble after him down the stairs.

He heard it before he saw it—the squelch of bursting pustules, the hissing spit of bile singeing the air. A stripe of bubbling shadow splattered over the gravel at Orpheus' feet at the exact moment his shadow fell across Lore's path. Slime oozed underfoot, burping steam into the early winter air while the acid ate through the gravel—and the leather of his boot.

Blood flooded his mouth when Orpheus bit his tongue to silence his scream. Amongst the long shadows cast by the courtyard's lanterns, he skipped out of the path of steaming bile, kicking his boot to the side to dislodge the slime that clung to his sole. The Acid Gut ambled onwards, slow and bulbous as it crept after him, another burp of acid spraying directly at Orpheus' head.

His shriek echoed through the courtyard, the eruption of Netherflame from his hand cold against the sudden heat rising to his face. Ice shattered into crystalline pieces when the frozen acid hit the ground, the courtyard and ramparts agonizingly silent, Acid Gut squelching in a puddle of eviscerated goo where the remnants of his ice spell had struck it. It was halfway towards dead, which was exactly where Orpheus wanted to be when he realized the whole of the Gilded Palace's court just bore witness to the humiliation of his *death curse*.

The court...and Lore, too.

Orpheus swung around, the taste of blood in his mouth suddenly less acrid than the bile rising on the back of his tongue.

From her place atop Ohm's shoulder, Lore's gaze slipped past him without meeting his eyes. Shadows shifted, deep and consuming, Ohm forging a path towards the entry hall that gave Orpheus a wide berth. And there he stood, caught in a limelight that had turned sour—humiliation a heat that spread from his face down towards his feet.

The world felt far away when Orpheus watched Lore's back disappear inside the palace, the feverish buzz under his skin building into a crescendo.

You're not cursed, the voice snarled, even though Orpheus absolutely *was*.

All around, the courtyard broke into a curious murmur. Orpheus stood at the center of it all, staring after Lore while the weight of what had happened threatened to achieve what the Acid Gut had failed to do.

CHAPTER II
THE CURSE

"The Lady is not receiving guests today, Sir," the guard said, voice hollow within her helm.

"Don't you know who I am?" Orpheus snapped, ignoring the gaggle of courtiers standing behind him, all of them also waiting to see Lore. "I demand you personally inform our Lady of my request."

The guard avoided his eyes, instead glancing at the skeleton positioned at the opposite side of the stairs. Cold leaked from the armored husk, a kaleidoscope of ice edging the sheet that hung over the entrance to the throne room. Scaffolding rose in a tangled web around them, workers perched atop the rickety platforms framing the newly renovated throne room entrance, two massive engraved doors propped up on either side of the scaffolding, waiting to be installed.

The skeleton watched Orpheus through hollow eyes, attention unnerving. At least it wasn't attacking him like every other hell beast he encountered.

"She will see me." Orpheus turned back to the guard, voice low enough to carry a threat. Behind him, the courtier's whispers rose into a murmur. Before him, the guard looked out over the crowd.

Her throat dipped as she swallowed, frigid blue eyes slippery when they refused to meet his. She wasn't another Wastelander like most of the soldiers. Her pale eyes marked her as a child of the Rim—east of the Empire, the land at the edge of the world. Her parents would have been refugees, arrived before they'd closed the border. Maybe that's why she had been paired off with the skeleton. She'd be used to the icy cold that accompanied it. More so, she'd be used to brushing shoulders with Hell itself.

"I'm sorry, sir," the guard finally said, her pale eyes lowering. "She was very clear with her orders."

They specifically mentioned you.

Behind him, the murmuring rose in tenor. Surprised. Possibly a little excited.

She won't see him, either—

—Did you hear about the hell beast?

Hear? I was there—

It wasn't the first. I heard there was—

—a curse. It's a death curse—

Red bled into his vision, bloody and thick. Orpheus bared his teeth, pivoted on his heel and snarled at the crowd. Their collective gasp clocked in at about sixty percent of what it should have been.

All hells. This was worse than he'd expected.

Orpheus' stomach twisted, heart hammering as he stormed down the steps and straight into the crowd. At least one person tripped to get out of his way, and Orpheus clung to that, stalking away from the throne room towards the only place in the palace he could think of that might hold a shred of help.

The heavy door groaned on stiff hinges, the air inside stale with age. High above, winter's gray sky bled weakly through the tall narrow windows lining the ceiling, light barely breaching the thick gloom between the aisles of bookshelves.

The library door closed behind him, the soft click of the lock too loud in the quiet.

Orpheus held his breath and stared into the shadows, waiting for the moment one of them moved—a ghost of memory come to haunt him—another hell beast on the attack. At this point, he wasn't sure what would be worse.

THE CRACK AT THE HEART OF EVERYTHING

Don't think about it, the voice inside snapped. *Focus on what you came here to do.*

Orpheus pulled a breath into his lungs, inhaling slowly. Then he did it again. And *again*. Until the sound of his breathing drowned out the thump of his heart, and the shadows churning between the stacks of books became almost welcoming again. It should feel comforting—the Gilded Palace's library. Instead, he felt an impeding sense of doom.

Orpheus turned back to the door, put his hand to the heavy steel and whispered his spell.

Violet fire bled from his fingertips, crawling along the etchings of a sigil he had placed there years ago. Whether he'd been sealing away the knowledge these stacks contained for safe keeping or hiding away his own secrets Orpheus never could say. The library was simply a library, in the end. He may have spent years hiding amongst its stacks, but that didn't mean the books were going to tell his secrets.

That also didn't mean Orpheus just wanted anyone traipsing about the damn place, least of all the court of fools that now called the Gilded Palace home.

Seal back in place, Orpheus closed his eyes and breathed.

A curse. A death curse. He needed to find anything he could that would explain this fucking death curse.

No, not explain—*disprove* it.

He began where everything had started. At the beginning of known history.

The earliest recorded curse Orpheus could recall was that harbored by the mummified remains of an ancient child emperor. The curse had spanned over three millennium, killing all who came into contact with it—including the grave robber who had excavated the emperor's tomb and shipped the mummified corpse back to his homeland far away from the dig site.

That curse had been disproved, however. Bacteria, later texts had claimed, was the simple explanation. Orpheus had seen the effects of a bacterial infection. Even behind the walls of the Gilded Palace, one didn't escape the fallout of a world at war, including the results of an injury turned gangrenous. Lore had dragged the injured back up her mountain often enough that Orpheus had been forced to look after a dying soldier or two before she'd recruited enough surgeons to give one a permanent place within the palace.

Was it a reasonable enough explanation for a whole team of explorers to fall ill, and then dead? Orpheus didn't see why not—all hells, it sounded *logical*. Far more logical than every hell beast within miles deciding he was their next best meal, or—hells forbid—an easy target.

Orpheus shoved the book back into place on the shelf, ran his finger along the spines until he came to another.

This curse originated several dozen centuries later. A sect of holy knights tasked with bringing down a feared king, their own esteemed leader captured when their plot was thwarted. That death curse had been forged from the fires of Hell itself when their leader burned alive at the stake. Death had crept upon the royal family years later, eliminating every male heir until the crown was forced to be handed off to some estranged, ill-known lineage.

It would have been a powerful spell, cast by a powerful sorcerer. Intentional. Not something one simply stumbled upon, and under circumstances that afforded the kind of power not normally seen with average spellcasting.

Could that be a clue? Orpheus had only wielded that kind of power once in his life.

He shoved his hand in his pocket, felt for the carefully folded piece of paper—the spell that had summoned Ohm.

A lifetime of casting—of crafting—of building war engines that ran off the cold fire of his Netherflame had barely prepared Orpheus for the scale of Ohm's summoning. It was his finest achievement. An infernal machine powerful enough to drill straight into Hell and draw its legions into the light of their still living sun. Certainly, that was enough power for a death curse. But where was the intention? The part of the spell that would cause the curse in the first place? A rune or a chant or even a damn warning?

Inside his pocket, the folded-up piece of paper was an ignominious presence. Orpheus slipped it free, held it in both hands and stared down at its torn, ragged edge.

A single page from a book he would not find in this library. Was there more to the script he hadn't been given? Lore had brought the page to him without an explanation. Orpheus hadn't even questioned where it had come from. In that moment, nothing but victory had mattered, and this spell had been their key.

Now, the rest mattered very, very much—at least to him.

Orpheus' footsteps echoed into the library's arched ceiling, dust circling his boots when he rounded a corner and found a low table tucked into the shadows. A kicked-over lantern rolled halfway into the light, glass broken but otherwise intact. He kept his eyes on his hands when he dropped to his knees, ignored the clammy way his palms snagged when he smoothed the paper atop the table. The little runes and inscriptions were smeared with soot, the parchment old and yellowed with a timeless age, the torn edge evidence that he was, in fact, missing something—the very spell book that harbored the kind of magic Orpheus had only ever read about.

A curse seemed a small price to pay for that kind of power.

Right?

Orpheus' chest went tight when he reached for the lantern. Something about it was familiar, an echo of a memory he had shoved away. A little bit of wick peeked out from the reservoir, blackened from past use, the oil long since used up. But when his fingers came together in a sharp snap, the wick caught anyway. Netherflame erupted, a single lick of purple fire that danced across his skin. A vision clawed out of his thoughts when it tumbled off his finger to catch the wick, the shadows around the table receding just enough that Orpheus could—

—Not remember anything worthwhile.

He twisted away from the corner, staring out at the stacks instead. Memories hedged his awareness, old dusty things that put these books to shame, and it occurred to him that he'd locked this place up for a reason, even if he couldn't remember it clearly right then. Death curse or not, there were things lurking in the shadows of this place, dangerous enough to have warranted the sigil he had placed on the door so many years ago.

Maybe that's why his skin crawled when the scratch of metal against stone tore open the silence.

High above, a grappling hook plunged through an old broken window, scraping along stone before catching the edge of the sill.

Orpheus snatched up the spell page, scrambling away from the table and tripping over a leg in the process. The lantern clattered to the floor, cacophonously loud, giving away far more than his position - there was only one person in the Gilded Palace who could ignite a lantern with Netherflame.

Damn it all to Hell, why was he hiding? These were *his* secrets, and he had every right to greet whoever had decided to break into the damn royal library with a fireball straight to the face.

Instead, Orpheus slunk in between two stacks where a tower of old boxes provided a decent place to hide.

Dust tickled his nose, nearly made him sneeze. Orpheus bit his cheek, blinked through the sting and found the window through the gaps in the bookcases. Shadows deepened, something large blocking out the light, window rattling in its frame. The window gave way easier than Orpheus had expected, the fall of rope skittering down the interior wall a precursor to the shadow that vaulted down after it.

Books obscured his view, the packed shelves offering a sliver of opening by which he could almost see—

Shoulders big enough to swing a sword through steel. Hair wilder than an oak tree, growing from a skull just as thick.

Of course. Of course it was *him*.

General Fenrir Rawkner stood tall in the window's sunspot, patting book dust from his knees like he fucking belonged there.

Orpheus bit down on his tongue and resisted the urge to snarl.

Fenrir's footfalls fell softly, the path he took between two stacks slow, but not hesitant. He glanced at the spines that he passed, fingers touching some, tracing others. Clearly, he knew what he was looking for and had some idea of how to find it. Perusing the stacks like he'd...had he...had Fenrir been here *before*?

That wasn't possible. Except...The hole in the glass. The perfect length of rope. The easy way Fenrir hooked a finger in a spine and slid a book free.

Orpheus held his breath when Fenrir opened the cover and thumbed through the pages, the smile on his face fond, the hand cradling the book gentle.

He'd been here before. He'd been here *often*. Fenrir Rawkner, of all people, had spent the last who knows how many years breaking into his library and *reading his books*.

Fenrir shook a pack off his shoulder and placed the book carefully inside.

Wait. He'd been *stealing them?*

Orpheus choked on a snarl, didn't manage to swallow it down before the tiniest bit escaped.

Fenrir's head jerked up, eyes narrowed. "Hello?" he called out into the quiet.

Boxes crushed Orpheus' shoulders, one teetering atop its stack. He shoved back into the corner and prayed Fenrir hadn't seen him.

"Is someone there?"

He could barely see anything now, a glimmer of wild hair catching the light, heading in the direction of the table and the...the Netherflame lantern.

Orpheus could only watch as Fenrir crept forward and toed the lantern with his boot.

"Fifi?" rose out of the quiet. "Is that you?"

Of course it was him, who else would it be? But like hell he was going to come crawling out of his hiding spot for *Fenrir* of all people. He'd rather throw himself off the mountain—or at least out the window. Not that he could reach it. Orpheus stared at the rope, dust motes glimmering high up where the sun shown through—a taunting reminder of the very real differences between his and Fenrir's strengths.

A spell might do the trick, though. Something small, unassuming. A distraction, even if it would confirm Fenrir's suspicions.

Through the gap in the bookshelf, Orpheus saw Fenrir peering in his direction. He was coming. Orpheus didn't have a lot of time.

Abandoning all caution, he scrambled out of the corner and put his finger to the dust covered cement floor.

The sigil was simple, one of the first spells he'd taught himself from the handful of grimoires Lore had given him over the years. Three arcs and two strikes and a series of sharper, smaller marks around their perimeter formed a semi-circle in the thick dust, meaningless shapes until Orpheus hovered his palm over the drawing and whispered the invocation.

It began as it always did: a lick of Netherflame from his palm, the sigil flaring, then catching in a bright violet light. Smoke streamed from the sigil, the marks he'd made directing it towards the back of the library where Fenrir's shadow fell between the stacks. It moved slowly, the spell building, a bubbling cloud that would keep growing.

"Fifi, I know you're in here!" Fenrir fucking *sing-songed*. Orpheus chewed his lip and scrambled to his feet within the knee-high smoke. He had another second, maybe two, before the spell really took off.

Fenrir chose that moment to round the corner.

Their eyes met, Fenrir's grin triumphant, but by then it was too late.

A self-satisfied smirk split open Orpheus' face. "Hello, Rawkner."

Then smoke simmered into a boil, erupting from the sigil and cascading between the bookshelves to swallow the aisle—and Fenrir—whole.

From the dense gray-black curdle of smoke, Fenrir began violently hacking.

"Orpheus— you— *asshole!*"

As much as he would have liked to stay and watch Fenrir choke on his own breath, Orpheus took off for the door. Something big banged against something bigger and Orpheus got the distinct impression that Fenrir had knocked over a whole bookcase, but by the time he skidded around a corner and got a clear shot for the door, his eyes were already on something else.

The broken window, and the rope that hung from it. It swung gently in the cool eastern wind, too tempting to ignore.

The spell breathed past Orpheus' lips, a little ball of Netherflame shooting from his hand—small and concentrated and *sharp*—sharp enough to sever the rope three-fourths of the way up the wall where it swung.

Not far behind him, Fenrir choke-shouted, "Oh, *come on!*"

Orpheus knew better than to turn around and gloat in the face of Fenrir's sudden and unlikely imprisonment. He hit the door running, slapped a palm to the steel and watched the sigil fizzle into sparks, heaving the door open wide enough for him to slip through and then dragging it shut again, sealing spell already rolling off his tongue by the time the mechanical lock clicked into place. Netherflame flared at the precise moment something enormous slammed into the other side, door vibrating in its frame when Fenrir collided with it, seal safely in place.

"That's what you get for the crossbow!" Orpheus shouted at the door while Fenrir banged on it with no small amount of effort. The sigil would hold against even Fenrir's brutal strength, not that Orpheus expected Fenrir to remain trapped for long. The window was high, but Fenrir had scaled the hells-damned palace wall so moving some bookcases around shouldn't be a whole lot of trouble.

For now, though, Orpheus was safe—at least from Fenrir—and that felt more monumental than anything else had in the last six weeks.

A death curse may eventually pull one over on Orpheus, but like hell Fenrir Rawkner ever would.

CHAPTER III

THE SUMMONS

It wasn't Empress Lore's inevitable summons that disturbed Orpheus; it was that he hadn't had a lick of warning it was coming at all.

From the quiet of his dungeon workshop, five sharp knocks echoed down the staircase. Needle in hand and silver thread halfway through a stitch, he had to stare into his bowl of quicksilver to gather himself together, replay the knocks in his head before he could be sure—

Three sharp knocks in quick succession, two a heartbeat after, the pattern indicating a messenger of the royal court.

Lore. It was *Lore*.

It was about damn time.

Orpheus bit through the thread and quickly knotted off the tail of silver dangling from his robe, sigils glinting in the violet light of his Netherflame lantern. He passed a hand over the stitching, Netherflame sparking through the thread and activating each spell. It wasn't his finest work, but the sigils would hold against most attacks: protection against fire, against acid, against ice and rot and decay, and—just to be extra cautions—against vanishment.

Waking to a Bone Reaver tapping its needly proboscis against his thankfully not bare shoulder would inspire someone to desperate measures. Having that be the fourth morning in the last week he was woken by a hell beast at all would push anyone straight into the realm of outright panic.

The knocks came again. The same series of five. A little faster, a little less sure. Orpheus pulled the robe over his head, wiggling through the narrow waist and then smoothing his palms down the front, too tired to judge whether he felt safer or not.

Well, there was only one way to find out.

He took the stairs by two, stumbling to a halt for the three seconds required to even his breathing, then reached for the door. It was heavier than it should be, the morning too bright when it flooded onto the landing, Orpheus too tired to wait for his eyes to adjust. He glared down at the messenger, sneering against the light.

A boy stood there to greet him—no, a teenager. He couldn't be more than seventeen.

Lore's personal messenger.

"M—master Orpheus." The boy backed away from the dungeon door, rocking on his heels as if about to launch himself either down the hall or out the nearest window. The morning light was bright enough to inspire a headache even without a stammering teenager at his door, and Orpheus pinched the bridge of his nose, counting his breaths while the messenger did his best to form syllables. "Her—es—esteemed—empress—L—Lady—*Lore*—"

"Yes, yes, the esteemed Empress Lady Lore has sent you with a message, I've already put that much together," Orpheus snapped, a snarl of sleepless frustration. The boy flushed, then cringed, then looked like he might actually pass out when his face turned a concerning shade of gray.

At least Orpheus could still inspire fear in *someone*, panicky teenager or not.

"The message, boy. Tell me and then you're free to go." Unharmed. Alive. Certainly not *cursed*, if that happened to be of concern to anyone else besides him.

"Empress Lore requires your presence in the throne room at your utmost behest. The matter is urgent," the messenger managed in a single breath. Orpheus felt as stunned at the messenger looked when their eyes met.

Urgent?

One of the benefits of living in the Gilded Palace his entire life was that Orpheus always heard the most important news first. He had ears in most places and gossip traveled faster than sneezes—particularly now that the war was over, and people didn't have anything better to do. If it didn't come from the after-hours guard prowling the garden hedges, then it was one of the Empress' ladies who constantly skittered about the palace like a hells-damned infestation. So, most news—when it was finally announced to the whole of the court—was well and truly *old* news.

Except this time.

"Master Orpheus, are you..."

What? *Okay?* Orpheus would have laughed if he wasn't too busy trying not to scream. "Did The Lady task you with escorting me too, boy?"

The messenger turned gray again, shaking his head.

"Well then, why are you still here? Go!"

The messenger took off down the corridor, good sense keeping him running until he rounded a corner and only the echo of his footsteps remained.

Alone in the morning light, Orpheus felt the weight of the summons descend.

Lore wanted to see him. Lore had an urgent matter she needed *his help with.*

So why did he feel so...uneasy?

Orpheus swallowed, stomach clenching, feet heavy when he took the first step away from the dungeon door.

His boots landed heavily atop the polished stone, sound carrying ahead when he turned down the familiar hallway that led to Lore's throne room. Some of the same nobles from the previous day lined the walls, either still waiting for their petitions to be heard or returned for another chance to glimpse the Empress herself. High above, dust motes drifted through the sunlight slanting through the narrow windows, setting aflame the far end of the hallway where the workers picked their way across the scaffolding. One after another, they hauled blocks of freshly carved stone up to where the platforms converged. And at the center of it all, the newly installed throne room doors stood tall, heavy, like they were meant to keep whatever was behind them in, rather than everyone else out.

It wasn't just Lore he'd find inside the throne room.

Orpheus approached the doors, eying the empty places where sigils had once been embedded. At this rate, there'd be little left of what had given the Gilded Palace its name. And the idea gnawed at him, uncomfortably, just like the Hell Rat currently gnawing on the hem of his robe.

Of all times—not *now*.

"Knock it off, you menace!"

Bright violet flames spilled from his fingers, the resounding crack of his snap echoing loudly through the hall. One of the workers atop the scaffolding yelped, then shouted, the guards positioned at the doors scrambling to get out of the way as a massive stone block teetered on its wench.

At any other time, Orpheus would have heeded the warning signs and gotten the hell out of there too, but Fenrir chose that moment to wave enthusiastically at him from his place beside the doors.

Wait—why was Fenrir out *here*?

Too late to stop, the Blood Boiling spell shot from Orpheus' fingertips, heading towards the rat just as the massive stone brick crashed to the floor at his feet. Stone and viscera exploded into the air, the rat making the sound of a popped balloon when all the oxygen in its blood bubbled to bursting, a deadly explosion of macerated flesh that splattered across the hem of his newly-enchanted robes.

Right. Fine. *Peachy.*

He lifted an edge of his robe, face twisting. Blood smeared in a bright arc across the floor where it leaked from the saturated fabric— harmless, thanks to his sigils, but no less *disgusting*.

Fenrir's guffawing laughter echoed through the hall.

"You think this is funny?" Orpheus snapped, spinning back

towards the doors and taking a step forward.

Apparently, the curse wasn't done with him yet.

Blood, guts, and shattered bits of stone slid under Orpheus' boot sole, his leg shooting out from under him, gravity no longer a chapter out of a dusty textbook but an inarguable law of reality.

The only thing keeping him from plummeting into a pool of man-eating Hell Rat remains was the hand suddenly tangled in his collar.

"Whoa there, Fifi." Fenrir grinned down at where Orpheus hung.

Orpheus kept his head high and his mouth shut as he looked into the face of the single person in this whole hells-damned palace who had the actual gumption to *touch him*—to save his life entirely notwithstanding. His robe may be enchanted, but his skin absolutely wasn't.

"Keep your filthy hands off me, Rawkner," Orpheus finally snarled once he was upright. Overhead, the scaffolding creaked as the workers scrambled away. Orpheus considered his chances of successfully dropping it on Fenrir's head before Lore got a good look.

Maybe she wouldn't care. After all, Fenrir was out here, when he should be in there, because Fenrir was always *in there*, grinning toothy needles down at him from his place beside Lore's throne.

Except this time.

"You look surprised." Fenrir took his time releasing Orpheus' collar, staring like he half expected Orpheus to fall over again. To be fair, when Fenrir's Rim pale eyes locked onto his, Orpheus was afraid he might. "You think I was still locked in the library?"

No, he didn't. But a dark wizard could dream.

"So, you admit to breaking into it?"

Fenrir's mouth quirked up into a half smile. "I wouldn't have to break in if someone hadn't sealed it up tighter than a virgin's asshole." For some reason Fenrir wiggled his eyebrows when he said it.

Orpheus bared his teeth and snarled, "I sealed it off for a *reason*, Rawkner."

"Oh yeah? And that reason is?"

Orpheus didn't have an answer for Fenrir. He didn't even have one for *himself*.

THE CRACK AT THE HEART OF EVERYTHING

"Uh huh, that's what I thought," Fenrir said, voice curiously low. "You gonna tell on me? Gonna tell Lore? Because I promise you, Fifi—" Fenrir leaned in close, the quirked up corner of his mouth going strangely flat. "She doesn't fucking care."

Heat prickled his face and Orpheus shoved past Fenrir, stumbling over the shattered stone and heading for the doors without another glance.

"You're welcome, by the way!" Fenrir's taunting voice followed him into the throne room—as if the dark red skid mark of flesh and blood on the floor wasn't embarrassing *enough*. "If you wanted me to roll out the red carpet, all you had to do was a—"

Orpheus didn't have to snap at Fenrir to *shut his hells-damned mouth*; the closing double doors beat him to it.

"M-master Dark W-wizard Orpheus Zon Z-Ziffler of the Empress' Exalted C-court," the messenger announced, voice shrill and nasally as if the more nervous he sounded directly correlated with his likelihood of falling victim to— well— *shit*—

Orpheus' stomach dropped when the messenger's foot descended into his bloodied trail. It shouldn't have been a concern. Most people had lived their lives dealing with hell beasts and Orpheus shouldn't have to warn anyone to watch their step when it came to unidentified blood stains. But despite it all, the messenger's heel slipped through the trail of viscera, the soft-soled—*unenchanted*—slipper sucking up enough Hell Rat remains to chew through the leather and touch the skin and by that point, it was too late.

Shrieks echoed through the cavernous throne room, courtiers scattering as the messenger stumbled towards them and promptly collapsed on the floor, out cold.

Orpheus couldn't look away as the death curse meant for him ate through the teenager's foot and began on his calf, the Hell Rat hungry even in its eviscerated state.

"Should we..." one brave courtier began, coming close enough to get a good look, avoiding Orpheus like he was contagious.

"You'll have to cut the leg off if you want to save him," he said loudly enough that everyone could hear.

The collective murmur of consideration was as surprising as the vicious looks directed his way were not. The messenger must have been well-liked; how unfortunate for Orpheus. More unfortunate was his inability to craft a half-decent healing spell, something that had never really mattered much in his work but sure would have come in handy right then.

Orpheus stared when the messenger began twitching, foam bubbling from his nose and mouth, and then stopped breathing entirely. The courtier's murmurs rose into panicked whispering. *He's going to get us all killed,* bit through the collective hiss.

"Orpheus," Empress Lore sighed, voice about as ephemeral as the klaxon call of an oncoming army. The whole panicked hall went silent as Orpheus approached the throne.

Milky marble stone created a tiered dais at the center of the room, the war table Orpheus had spent countless years hunched over tucked away in the shadow of a half-erected pillar. He could see the pieces positioned on the board, the tall sword that denoted Lore's foot soldiers, the horses that marked her cavalry, the wagons of her supply chain. At the center her mountain rose, a shadowy behemoth second to the gray seam of the Rim, an enormous blight that nearly overwhelmed the eastern half of the board before terminating at the edge of the known world.

The toppled-over figure of a white-robed invader remained swallowed by the rows of trenches that had once been the Rim's front line. But it was the figure placed at the southernmost tip which drew Orpheus' attention. Standing tall amongst the shattered pieces of the resistance's leadership, the most recent addition to the board possessed an uncanny likeness to the creature before him.

Atop the raised marble dais Lore sat perched not on a throne, but on the shoulders of the skeletal warlord Orpheus had, six weeks ago, summoned from the deepest pit of Hell.

The soft violet tint of Ohm's glowing carcass bled through the seams of his armor, setting the gauze of Lore's gown alight so she looked all the world like a goddess rather than an Empress.

To him, she may as well be.

"Exalted One." Orpheus lowered his eyes alongside his knee, feeling Lore's attention follow him to the ground while Ohm's cold, freezer-like aura stripped the heat from his skin like he was a hot drink to savor. He caught a flash of red where the rat's viscera still trailed behind him. Thinner now, the danger fading alongside the color of the blood. It'd become harmless in minutes, though the curse would try again. It always did. Orpheus was coming to terms with the fact that it always would.

"Are you...?" Lore asked, eyes drifting to the trail of Hell Rat mess. She was a woman of few words, always had been, but they'd known each other too long for Orpheus not to understand what she asked.

"I am fine, Empress. My enchantment will hold," Orpheus said, rising again. He looked at Lore and his heart swelled, honored, if not prepared, for whatever task she set upon him.

"Your death, Orpheus—what would that mean for me?" From atop Ohm's shoulder Lore breathed the question. Body draped over the sickle-sharp crest of Ohm's helm, cheek pressed soft and comfortable in the cradle of her arms, Lore gazed down at him, eyes no more or less warm than they normally were. It was impossible to read her thoughts, but Orpheus suspected he could make a pretty good guess.

"This power is yours alone, my Lady. Even if my corpse is delivered to the bowels of Hell itself, your power will reign." Orpheus bowed his head again as he spoke. If she thought his death would result in her losing control of Ohm and his demonic army, she was luckily mistaken.

"Truly..." Lore murmured as she shifted, hand sliding over Ohm's helm. Orpheus lifted his head when she rose, dark hair slipping over her shoulder until she sat upright. From the change in position Orpheus could see the shadow of her facade shift. Gone was the lazy ease of her lounge, replaced with a sternness that he'd only seen in the moments before she'd ridden out the Gilded Gates into battle. Her armor might not be donned but she held herself as if it were, and Orpheus noticed himself responding in kind.

He stood taller, straighter, shoulders back and head held high. He was ready. Whatever she asked of him, he would give it.

"I need you to leave, Orpheus."

She...*what?*

"Your curse, Orpheus," she continued, addressing the concern everyone in the palace but him must have had. Amongst the courtiers a murmur rose and fell; there was no mistaking their excitement. "It has become...cumbersome."

Damn these courtiers. Damn them all to *Hell.*

All decorum fled as he said, "Lore—"

She cut him off. "You've been faithful, Orpheus, that should be rewarded."

Rewarded? By sparing his life, rather than setting Ohm upon him and ending his nuisance here and now? The room spun, gravity giving way, like someone had ripped the world open around him, and the void left behind was deep enough to swallow him whole.

"I gift you a loyal steed and the day to prepare for your departure. By dawn, you will be gone."

There were moments in his life he thought about often. Commemorations of the milestones he had achieved as both a mage and a servant to the Gilded Throne. Good memories that had gotten him through the sleepless nights of his now cursed existence, when everything he had traded for Lore's power caught up to him, demanding a price he would pay, but *not yet, not today,* because there was still so much he could offer her.

"Farewell, Orpheus," Lore continued, pale eyes hooded so not even Ohm's ghostly aura could set them alight. "This is our goodbye."

CHAPTER IV
WORKSHOP

His workshop was a familiar comfort, turned foreboding farewell.

The dim light of Orpheus' Netherflame cast long shadows across the contents of his life: Tomes of magic he'd spent a lifetime studying; a shallow pot of liquid silver he used for casting sigils; and the smallest of his archanics, meticulously crafted with the tools of their lost ancestors, now pushed into a lifeless pile, empty of any magic they might have once held.

These were his tools. Familiar enough to feel like extensions of himself: the brush between an artist's fingers, the sword in a soldier's hand. Without them—without his magic—his life would be very different, but Orpheus couldn't imagine what the alternative looked like because for as long as he had magic, he'd had the palace longer. His life was here. It had always been *here*.

Not anymore.

Exile. Banishment. A death curse.

Orpheus snarled, letting the Netherflame die in the cradle of his palm and shoving back from his workbench. The bowl of quicksilver teetered dangerously close to the edge of the table, and he reached for it, liquid catching the light and then his reflection. His pale skin was sallow, black hair hanging limp, his once neatly kept beard now a mess of kinks, and the circles under his eyes were deeper than he could remember. This man was a stranger, and Orpheus pushed the bowl away before he could get to know him, burying his face back into his arms lest he do something embarrassing like *cry*.

"Good morning, Fifi!"

A familiar voice punched through his thoughts as Fenrir, of all people, came gallivanting into his workshop.

"What in all hells—" Orpheus staggered upright, Fenrir emerging from the shadows of the stairwell, all wild hair and a toothy grin. "What are *you* doing here?"

"It's almost dawn," Fenrir stated, like it was a simple observation and not the harbinger of everything in Orpheus' life falling apart.

"The Lady needn't send *you* to fetch me. I am well aware of what time it is!"

"Actually..." Fenrir's grin turning a little vicious. "She sent Ohm. He's waiting upstairs. Figured I'd come snatch you for myself first."

Orpheus' ears went hot beneath his hair while his stomach sunk into the floor.

Ohm was waiting for him?

"So, you ready to go?" Fenrir stared over Orpheus' shoulder, likely at his *unpacked* stacks of tomes. And raised an eyebrow. "Doesn't look like you're ready."

What do you care? Orpheus didn't say aloud, but Fenrir rolled his eyes like he had.

"It's not the end of the world, Fifi. Fresh air and sunlight never hurt anyone before," wasn't the comfort some might interpret it as. Orpheus knew Fenrir better than that. And Fenrir knew Orpheus better than to think anything about this was—hells forbid—*good* for him.

"Spare me your opinion, Rawkner. You may think you've finally rid yourself of me, but Lore is only bending to the will of the court. She knows my curse could never hurt her, not with Ohm as her bodyguard." He hadn't meant the dig, but there it was, the truth of it a loose thread between them, somewhat like that damnable rope. Orpheus narrowed his eyes. "That's why you're here, isn't it? To gloat?

Because I toppled you from your place at her side?"

Fenrir said nothing as he stood half-cast in Netherflame, Rimpale eyes glowing in the cool light. Even here he was unfairly attractive. Large, looming, and arguably cut from the same stone the Gilded Palace was forged from. There were some laugh-lines around his mouth and a new scar severing his cheek, but Orpheus would be hard-pressed to admit any of it didn't suit the blasted warrior—the best in Lore's army, at least until that infernal Ohm had come along.

Outclassed by an undead warlord or not, that didn't mean Fenrir wasn't still *dangerous*.

Slowly, Fenrir approached. Slower yet, their eyes met. Orpheus silently cursed the scant two inches of height difference separating them.

"Is it revenge you want?" Orpheus asked, voice gravelly. "I'd sooner let this curse get me than you, Rawkner."

Fenrir cocked his head, face untenable in the low light.

"Would you really, Fifi?" Fenrir asked, voice low. "I guess there's only one way to find out."

Against his will, a shiver prickled under Orpheus' skin. Maybe it wasn't the greatest idea to antagonize Fenrir. Not here and now when Orpheus wasn't in any shape to defend himself—not with the curse constantly at his back, whittling away at him, waiting for its chance to get lucky and *strike*.

Fenrir's fist snapped out, Orpheus' eyes screwing shut as he braced for the punch. It took him a second to interpret that the terrified screeching he heard was not his.

He cracked an eye open and saw...Was that? Oh hells, it *was*.

"A Brainrotter," Fenrir said. "It's been here since I walked in."

The Brainrotter twisted in Fenrir's clutch, leaking a thread of pale purple that barely tickled the tiny hairs where it entered Orpheus' ear.

It wasn't an excuse because Orpheus didn't *have* an excuse—he should have noticed—he should have *known*.

"What wretched creature!"

"—Do you have to do something? Cut it out or—"

"Yes, don't kill it." He felt around for something, *anything*—ah, yes, that would do.

The enchanting knife balanced lightly in his hand, delicate and silver but sharper than any sword. "I have to sever the connection first, or risk—" he cut off, remembering this was *Fenrir* he was talking to and that he didn't need to know more than he already did.

The Brainrotter could have killed him. Orpheus recognized the feast he presented: the spiral of indecision he hadn't been able to shake, the sleepy lethargy that had been plaguing him for weeks, and the last twelve hours, time passing in a limitless loop, dawn no closer than the next minute, let alone nearly arrived because he couldn't wrap his head around what was happening to his life. The Brainrotter had feasted upon all that—could have kept on until he dozed off into dreamless unconsciousness.

After that, it would have been a matter of hours before his memories were drained, then his knowledge, the electrical pulses that controlled things like muscle memory and the will of his body to so much as *breathe* fading. Death coming quietly, like a thief in the night.

Orpheus reached up, knife in one hand, the thread in the other, and sawed through the sensation of his brain on fire.

In a flutter of violet embers, the thread dissolved. Orpheus slumped over, panting.

At the peripheral of his awareness, Fenrir waited, close enough that Orpheus could feel the ebb of his body heat chasing away the cool dampness of the workshop, the smell of sweat and leather and something unidentifiable settling on the back of his tongue. It wasn't the closest he'd been to Fenrir, much to his dismay, but this time it was voluntary. Mostly. And neither moved away. Fenrir still clutched the Brainrotter, waiting for permission Orpheus was half-pressed not to give.

Loathed as he was to admit, Fenrir had saved his life again. More so, after weeks of successfully thwarting each of the curse's attempts, it had nearly *gotten him.*

"Kill it," he breathed, voice like venom. "Crush it into *ash.*"

One tiny, pathetic little squeal and then the Brainrotter was gone, a sad poof of dissipating smoke leaking through the cracks of Fenrir's damnably capable fist.

If Orpheus didn't make eye contact, he could use that as his reason for not surrendering his thanks. So he collapsed back against the table, squeezed his eyes shut, and waited for the moment Fenrir finally went away.

Too many breaths later he was still there.

"Rawkner," Orpheus breathed through clenched teeth. "Is there a reason you haven't left yet?"

Fenrir sighed, too loud in the dark little dungeon.

"I'm not leaving without you."

A hand pushed into Orpheus' chest, something rough shoved between them: an empty traveling pack.

"Pack up. It's time to leave this tomb behind."

Only then did Fenrir move away, the pack slithering down Orpheus' body to pool lifelessly on the ground.

Orpheus stared at it like it was the real curse come to claim him.

CHAPTER V
PALACE GATES

"When you said *we*," Orpheus managed to say around the dry discomfort of his closing throat. "I hadn't thought to take you so literally."

Fenrir stood off to the side of the palace gates tacking out two horses, the ancient steel doors opened to the vast slope of pine forest beyond. In the pre-dawn light, the gate's filigreed sigil-work glowed, silver and gold stretching up doors that nearly reached the height of the tallest palace turret.

Orpheus stared up at the doors, then at the courtyard, unable to believe this was the last time he may ever see either.

All around, the electric lanterns hummed, warm yellow light creating shadows out of the darkness. Workers were already assembled, scaling the scaffolding, the *cling-twang* of their picks melodic as they peeled away at a portion of the sigil work closest to the stables. Orpheus looked away before his staring was noticed. Lore hadn't listened to him six weeks ago and she wasn't going to now that he was leaving.

Maybe that was why she'd kicked him out. Maybe she'd simply grown tired of his constant contrarian comments and his critique of her stripping the palace of everything that gave it its name.

Someone had spent a lot of resources hiding this place from the public eye and while the war may be won, Orpheus didn't think now was a great time to dismantle the spells that had protected them this long.

Not that it would matter for him much longer. In a few minutes he would be gone. In a few days or weeks… he would be dead.

Wind bit through his robes, stinging his skin, and Orpheus hunched into himself. High above, the gates caught the light of the eastern sun, golden dawn luminescent against the dark sky.

This is it.

"Got us enough fuel to get through the southern pass," Fenrir stated loudly, breaking Orpheus from his thoughts. "Any idea where you wanna go after that?"

"Is that a joke?" He diverted his face so Fenrir couldn't see his flush. Fenrir had already seen him at his lowest and here he was, tagging along on Orpheus' banishment like it was some grand adventure.

Orpheus should let the curse have him, just to make Fenrir deal with the inevitable mess.

"We'll get through this *pass*—" he spat the word out so that Fenrir didn't ask any more stupid questions, "—Then we'll part ways, obviously. The Lady does not need to worry about me disobeying her orders."

Fenrir rolled his eyes while his jaw worked, chewing over whatever he wanted to say and then deciding to remain silent. Orpheus didn't want Fenrir to be quiet, however. To be honest, he wanted a *fight*.

Dust kicked up as he stomped over to where Fenrir stood, the two horses snuffing, eying him as he crowded into Fenrir's space, nearly chest to chest.

"What's your goal, Rawkner?" he asked softly, mocking curiosity. "A loyal dog like you doesn't abandon its master, but here you are, following me around instead. Is it possible you have outgrown your usefulness too?"

Fenrir did not take the bait. He cast his eyes downward, staring at the little void of space that remained between them. Orpheus pushed closer, because the emptiness inside him was too vast to be filled by his own lonely, impotent anger.

No. He needed Fenrir to *say* something. Something cruel. Something that would make everything make *sense*.

"Is it an apology you're after? Or revenge? I hadn't *meant* to put you out of a job, Rawkner, but I can't say I'm disappointed, either," Orpheus pushed, watching Fenrir's expression finally break.

"Orpheus," Fenrir said, and then he put a hand on Orpheus' chest.

It was a promise of all the pain and hate that should exist between them and Orpheus closed his eyes while he waited for the blow. It never came. The pressure against his chest was too gentle, the hand too warm and lingering for the violence Orpheus wanted. And he must have given himself away because when his eyes flew open and met Fenrir's, the commiseration he saw felt oddly shared.

"Just get on the hells-damned horse, okay?" Fenrir said, voice low and deep—like a mother talking a child out of tantrum, or a lover to his sweetheart.

Then the hand retreated, cold left in its place, taking all the hot anger inside him with it.

No. That wasn't *right*—

The emptiness flooded back, vast and consuming, growing deeper while Orpheus watched Fenrir walk over to his horse, leaving him alone.

Alone. Abandoned. *Banished.* His only companion a man who he hated, the world beyond an unknown he wasn't ready to face. And what future he may have had already been prematurely claimed, by a death curse he didn't even remember casting.

He was completely *fucked*.

Wind bit through his robe, cold enough to make him stagger. Orpheus put a steadying hand on the horse's flank without thinking, leaning into it while a low drone filled his head. Only once his breathing calmed did Orpheus realize what the sound really was: the low whorl of mechanics at work, a familiar monotonous whine.

His horse. It was an amalgam. His horse was an *amalgam?*

THE CRACK AT THE HEART OF EVERYTHING

Orpheus snatched his hand away. Something about the convergence of creature and mechanical left a sour taste in his mouth, an unnatural rhythm to the way the horse's fuel-filled heart chugged away without a single sigil holding it all in place. Or, perhaps, it was the realization that the rest of the world had finally adopted the technological advancements that came with a decade-long war, Netherflame engines replaced by an energy source that didn't depend on one lone sorcerer's ability to harness magic.

Sustainability, some would call it. Maybe Orpheus' usefulness had truly worn out.

Orpheus looked at the horse, meeting the single black eye that stared at him and he swore it looked just as scared. Its artificial pupil contracted, and Orpheus imagined he could hear the optics whine, whatever information it gathered filing away in its hard drive of a brain. Still, there was no outward evidence of its unnatural mechanics. The amalgam shuffled nervously in place like any wholly natural horse would, and Orpheus tried not to think about how seamless the impression was.

"Gonna assume you've never ridden before?" Fenrir stood beside his tall black war horse, head cocked to the side. Orpheus glanced at him in time to catch the pair of leather riding gloves Fenrir tossed to him. He fumbled them into his chest, face turning red.

Of course, he had never ridden a horse before—he didn't need Fenrir pointing that out to everyone within earshot.

"I haven't, but if someone with a brain the size of a slug can, I can't imagine it's difficult," Orpheus snapped, but if Fenrir hadn't risen to his bait before, there was no way he would now. Orpheus pushed his hands into the gloves and ignored how they were too big for his hands, too soft to be new. Castoffs. Just like him.

Out of the corner of his eye he saw Fenrir take a step towards him. "I can show—"

"I don't need your help!" Orpheus snapped. Lore may get away with writing him off as incompetent, but he would burn the Gilded Palace down before he allowed anyone else to, at least *out loud*.

Fenrir looked at him in quiet contemplation, choosing silence over words like he was trying to keep a non-existent peace.

Orpheus wanted to scream. This wasn't their usual dynamic. No, their usual dynamic involved trading barbs like currency and then moving onto spells and sometimes knives—or that one time, in Fenrir's case, a crossbow. Not whatever *this* was, which stank suspiciously of pity.

If there was one thing worse than Fenrir's presumed incompetence, it was his *pity*.

Glaring at Fenrir, Orpheus reached up, grabbed the saddle horn, shoved his foot in the stirrup, and tried to remember what all those soldiers he watched from the ramparts did when they mounted up before battle.

It was no small feat to haul himself upright while balancing on one precariously holstered foot, even less so to ensure his leg cleared the horse's sizable rump when he swung it over, but he managed both without much struggle. It wasn't the smoothest maneuver ever, but he mostly ended up where he was supposed to be and Fenrir— Orpheus gleefully noticed from the corner of his eye—stared in surprise.

Then the gates opened, and there was nowhere else Orpheus could look.

Snow-covered peaks arose in the not-so-great distance, gray capping the ridge in a jagged saw of hewed ice. An abrupt severing of the sky from the earth as if the two were never meant to meet. But it was the mist that swallowed the pine forest that set his heart racing. It bubbled between the trees like a broth, a veritable stew of the unknown waiting to boil him alive, unnerving with how *untamed* it looked, who-knows-what hiding in shadows Orpheus had spent a lifetime thinking were his to haunt.

Face tight, he gripped his reins and sucked in a breath. He couldn't make his horse move towards the gates any more than he could guess what lay beyond them, but it turned out he didn't need to do either. Fenrir clicked his tongue, and then both their horses were moving, agency traded for an unlikely quiescence.

For once, Orpheus was relieved not to be in control.

He kept his head high as he followed Fenrir into the world beyond the palace walls. The differences were sudden and immediate.

A blanket of frozen lichen muffled the clop of their horses' hooves, different from the variety he knew to grow along the lower garden flagstones. There was a knife-like sharpness to the wind that bit through his robes, something the enormous palace walls had always tempered. And there was a lonesome feeling growing in the pit of his stomach. A strangely weighted absence that he'd never felt before, because for as long as he'd lived, he'd only ever had Lore to lose—not home itself.

By the time they reached the first divergence in the road, the sun had cleared the horizon.

He told himself he wouldn't look back, but then they crested a steep incline and the vantage it afforded was undeniable. Morning bled golden and brilliant from the eastern hemisphere, a halo of radiant light so bright and the Gilded Palace so black it was like staring into the totality of an eclipse. It sat upon the valley ridge like a sentinel, a watchful guardian overlooking a lost domain, history etched in the silver-gilded turrets and the smooth edge of the outer cinder block walls.

It occurred to Orpheus that he'd never seen the palace from outside the walls before. From here, it looked more foreign than it did familiar. Another person in his position may find that revelation comforting, but Orpheus only experienced an acute sense of loss.

He watched until he no longer could. Until his eyes stung and his body shivered, and the palace disappeared behind a copse of spindly trees, his path taking him down a road he had no map for, into an unknown world he had built his legacy conquering from afar. Justice had always seemed too slippery of a concept for him to grasp but now it poisoned his thoughts—like the curse wasn't so much payment for his spell as it was the balancing of scales he'd tipped too far out of place.

It wasn't until hours later, once Fenrir led their horses over the ridge of another incline, that Orpheus was confronted with why that idea struck so close to the truth.

He felt it before he saw it, a tug on his soul, impossible to ignore.

Desolation spread out across the valley below, blighted and angry where the seam of the world split asunder. Netherflame frothed in the early morning mist, consuming miles of dense pine trees now blackened into needles, the ground hammered shiny like the earth had turned molten and then been forged into steel. There were still traces of an army's former encampment. Toppled-over tents and the half-crushed fencing of a stable recognizable because it all looked so out of place—though not as out of place as the machinery sunk into the scar of the world.

The archanics loomed, enormous strikes of black against a violet-tinged sky. Hell beasts crawled from the cracks, their shadows contorting within the already dense darkness. And fluttering at the heart of it all was Lore's herald, the red smear of her flag catching the sun like a still-bleeding wound.

This was where Ohm and his army would have emerged. This was the damage Orpheus had wrought when he'd built his machines, carved his sigils, and then sent them off through the palace gates into a world he only knew the name of, yet dared to think he could shape.

He shoved his hand into his pocket, felt for the folded up page through the leather of his glove.

"I was there when the spell went off." The words nearly jolted him from his saddle.

"What?" Orpheus snapped, barely hiding the shake in his voice.

"I led the execution team," Fenrir continued, voice strangely calm despite how Orpheus assumed his heart must hammer. If Fenrir had been there during the execution, that meant he had nearly died in the cataclysm that followed. It didn't make sense that Lore would have sent her favorite soldier off on a suicide mission, but here they were, reality laid bare before them, the scar on Fenrir's cheek ominous in the late morning light.

The wind kicked hard against his back, spearing through the darning of his robes; Orpheus hunched against it. "I'm not going to apologize," came out weaker than he intended, but his words were probably lost anyway, the wind rising in a distinct howl, building like a foghorn in the wide-open expanse below.

THE CRACK AT THE HEART OF EVERYTHING

"We should keep moving," Fenrir said, turning away.

Orpheus remained silent while he made to follow. He kept his eyes on his hands, gripping the reins because looking ahead seemed impossible, and looking behind... looking behind had become painful.

As they left the valley behind, the sounds of the forest closed in: the rush of wind through the reedy pines; the soft crunch of hooves on loam; the ancient, animistic thrum of magic in a place it shouldn't be, leaking through the crack in the world he had made, the crack he had also made inside himself.

INTERLUDE
THE LIBRARY

The sun filters thin and gray through the high filmy windows, the library dreamlike in the gently dispersed light. He picks his way between boxes and bookcases, eyes on the uppermost shelves where the light reaches best. He can't read the spines from here, but he can count, and by the time he reaches one-thousand the boy has realized he probably won't be able to read every book in this library, no matter how much he may want to.

There's so much here. Lives bound into stories from a world that no longer exists—that maybe never existed. He's not sure if that matters. Everything feels like a fantasy, whether that's a historian's account documenting the world before The Incident or King Arthur riding into battle against the Saxons.

The boxes hold more. More books. More of that musty, strangely sweet smell and a cake of dust that was already old well before they arrived here. The newest publications—a term he learned early on, when reading dates was easier than reading words—are three-hundred years old. These are what he's most familiar with. The hermits had used these when teaching him how to read, and while the accounts are many, they tell the same story. Maybe that's why they stopped publishing them. Why, after the turn of the twenty-fifth century, there aren't any new books to read.

A large box blocks his way, the stacks beyond drowned in shadow here at the back of the Library where the light doesn't reach. The books on the shelf beside him are sorted strangely—not by author, but by size and color. Stranger are the tracks through the gray dust. Someone has been here recently, and he knows for a fact that the hermits don't come to the library. It's why he's come here, after all. They will be looking for him soon, and he knows they won't think to search for him here.

"Hello?" he calls into the quiet, just to be sure. Just to be safe.

He doesn't anticipate that one of the books would *move*.

He leaps back with a stifled gasp, heart pounding in his chest as a gap emerges between two large green tomes. Darkness fills the crack, but then something else. He has to blink his eyes to make them adjust, but when they do, he sees an eye peering back at him.

A *human* eye.

Words fail him. He stares into the eye uncomprehending. It's large and the pupil flooded black in the shadows, focused and unblinking upon him, as if it's he who is the curiosity here rather than this stranger hiding in the stacks.

He swallows once, feels how his throat has closed up and his stomach has crawled into his chest. He's looking around before he can stop himself, suddenly sure that this is a trap, that the hermits have found some new way to test him. To push him. To make him hurt and then—and then make him—

"Stop." A small voice breaks through the quiet—knives through his mind.

More books move, dragging trails through the dust, until a rectangular black void appears, and then a little girl's face.

He sinks to his knees. His hands are shaking when he clasps them before his chest. He looks into her eyes and it feels like falling.

"Who are you?" he asks.

The girl shrugs, one boney shoulder rising up through long, dark hair. She can't be much younger than him but she is smaller, thinner, paler despite how wholly those descriptors suit him. All at once, he feels they're cut from the same cloth. He only knows he's right because of the band on her wrist. It matches his, the silvered filigree of the hermit's sigils a mirror to his own.

He's always been alone but suddenly, he's not. There's another. Someone he never knew about. Two children the hermits must have intended to keep apart.

Not anymore. Now, they've found one another, and there is nothing in the whole world that will separate them again.

CHAPTER VI
PINE WOODS

It occurred to Orpheus once the sun had reached its zenith and Fenrir called for a break that this was the longest he'd gone without the curse making an attempt on his life.

Orpheus knew better than to assume something stupid like the curse was tied to the palace and couldn't follow him out here. Or *worse*, that witnessing the ramifications of his crimes against nature had planted a seed of remorse in his soul and goodness in his heart and now the curse couldn't find a foothold against him. No, Orpheus may be naïve, but he wasn't an *idiot*. As if to prove him right, from beneath the layer of packed needles covering the forest floor emerged the tell-tale rattle of a Spinemouth nest, mere inches from where he'd put his hells-damned foot.

Everything happened in the span of an instant.

Needles crunched under his boot, and beneath those, a slippery *nothing*. A rattle of warning sounded off but Orpheus was too slow, lifting his foot just as the ground erupted beneath him and a gnashing nest of teeth came chomping for his foot—the Spinemouths, writhing with hunger. His horse reared, his hands slipped, and then he was falling. One moment of suspended gravity later, his collar went taunt, choking off whatever embarrassing sound he was definitely *not* about to make.

Orpheus got a split-second of watching Fenrir stomp around like some enormous man-child throwing a tantrum before he abruptly went weightless again. The world tipped over as he was tossed over his horse's saddle and *held there* by a large, entirely unwelcome hand in a place he refused to mention, while Fenrir crushed the Spinemouths into paste beneath his feet.

Orpheus didn't allow himself the indignity of squirming. He laid limp over the saddle, fighting the heat of his face turning not red, but magenta, thinking of all the ways he could kill Fenrir and coming to the disconcerting conclusion that none of them would probably work.

He was beginning to understand why Fenrir was Lore's favorite. Mainly, he was beginning to suspect that Fenrir was entirely immune to death and *that* was why he was Lore's favorite, dashing good looks and big muscles be damned.

"You okay?" Fenrir actually had the nerve to ask while his hand was still—well—*there*.

"Take your hand off me this instant!" Orpheus snarled, finally succumbing to the urge to squirm.

He slid off the saddle and hit the ground hard, steadying himself against his horse, the coat under his palms softer than it had any right to be. The strangest sensation of relief prickled his mind, and he seized it, leaning into the horse's bulk for a brief, desperate moment. Fenrir remained where he stood, offending hand half-raised as if burned, and Orpheus thought: *If only.*

"That was a nest of Spinemouths—"

"Yes, I know what Spinemouths are!" Orpheus spun around to put his back to his horse, refusing to look down at where said Spinemouths were leaking liquefied entrails through the layer of pine tips. "And I'm perfectly capable of taking care of a nest of them myself!"

Fenrir frowned. "You dismounted right on it."

Orpheus definitely didn't appreciate him pointing that out. "To kill them, of course!"

"But they could have—"

THE CRACK AT THE HEART OF EVERYTHING

"—I would have been *fine!*" Orpheus shrieked, whole body shaking. "I don't need your help, I definitely don't need you *saving* me, and I absolutely don't need you tagging along on my banishment and rubbing it in my face every chance you get!"

Silence descended, heavy and suffocating. Orpheus refused to meet Fenrir's eyes even though they were so close it was hard to look anywhere else. He stared down at his boots instead, watched the way the pine needles clumped together under his soles, sticky-slick and leaking red from the crushed Spinemouth remains.

"I know you can protect yourself, Fifi," Fenrir eventually said.

But that didn't explain why Fenrir was *here*.

Fenrir Rawkner was supposed to be Lady Lore's favorite soldier. He was supposed to be the shield always at her side, a position he had earned by leading an army in her name. Not relegated to palace guard. Not positioned outside her throne room doors, an undead magical skeleton taking his rightful place.

Certainly, he wasn't supposed to be escorting the Empress' newly banished dark sorcerer towards his inevitable doom.

"I'm going for a walk," Orpheus managed to say, dismissal left unsaid: *Don't follow me.*

It took several dozen paces to create enough distance for Fenrir to be hidden from sight. It took several dozen more for the tight feeling in Orpheus' chest to begin to loosen. Here off the trail, the forest grew dense, limitless and empty. They must be at a lower altitude than the palace because the biting cold of oncoming winter had lost its edge, the atmosphere strangely comforting despite Orpheus not knowing where in all hells he was. He continued walking anyway, boots sinking into the spongy loam of the forest floor, pine tips traded for moss out here where the forest had been left untouched.

It helped, the walking. It always did. When Orpheus' thoughts became ill-suited to his mood he had a habit of pacing, and his cluttered workshop hadn't always been the ideal location. So, he'd flee to the lower gardens, their high walls and well-tended hedges providing a privacy that Orpheus was hard-pressed to find within a palace at war. Walking helped him put his mind together, and right then, his mind was in as many pieces as his life.

One piece in particular refused to be walked away from.

Why was Fenrir here?

A better person might have confronted the likelihood that Fenrir was just as fucked as he was, even sans a banishment, let alone a death curse. But Orpheus was not a *better person*. He absolutely wasn't a good one. And if Fenrir was dealing with his own sense of loss or abandonment, Orpheus didn't see why that had to become his problem. They'd never had the kind of relationship that lent itself to talking unless it was to insult or outright gloat. Orpheus wouldn't have called it a rivalry but it was no secret that the two of them had been the closest of Lore's inner circle, and to keep that position they'd made a habit of trying to outdo one another, in whatever way they could serve her best.

Fenrir had led Lore's armies into battle, and Orpheus...

Orpheus had built her a god machine.

Ahead, light streamed through the trees in a strange scatter, the mossy groundcover churned up in a dark stripe, as if something enormous had tunneled through the forest. All around, the evergreen of the pine trees traded for an ashy, deadened decay. And at his feet, tiny violet cinders breathed amongst the shadows, immortal Netherflame blackening everywhere it touched, burning—always burning—for centuries or eons or however long it took to eat away the mountainside and then move on to whatever lay beyond. Orpheus followed the unnatural trail the damage made, footsteps light as he skirted the edge of a small clearing. He wasn't prepared for what he found.

Erupting from the earth in monumental proportion was a piece of his machine. Twisted and looming, it caught the light in a sparkle of pale metal, the enchanted silver coating still gleaming in the places where sun touched the frame. Below, Netherflame leaked from the churned-up earth, the husks of pine tips shriveled, like what little life remained in them had long been eaten up.

He recognized the shape of it, the spiral of the drill-head that would have pierced not bedrock, but the literal seam between worlds.

He'd forged three of these heads, one primary and two backups for an incident such as this. This was a long distance for it to travel. The Netherflame had released a testament to its success just as much as the spray of earth and shattered trees were. It must have burrowed miles through the mountainside, severing rock alongside the fabric of the world itself, although Orpheus never could have conceptualized the actual force necessary to tear open Hell. A scratched-out equation in his grimoire was one thing; seeing the physical evidence of the power he had wrought was entirely another.

He stopped inside the copse of dead trees, following along the shape of the drill while his heart beat a strange rhythm in his chest. It wasn't pride coiling in his throat, it was the nascent tenements of horror.

He'd done this. He'd *created* this.

Is that why the curse followed him? Maybe it wasn't payment or balance fate sought, but revenge.

All at once, Orpheus wished he were back in the palace. Out here, the world was too big, too overwhelming, too much and too broken for him to ever find his way within it. There weren't any high walls to protect him. No underground workshop to shelter him. No Empress or army or even a guard between him and the vast nothing of a world he'd only ever observed from the parapets of a dream that hadn't even been *his*.

Heat prickled his skin, spiraled up his spine. Suddenly, vertigo sent the world spinning, made him sway where he stood and then stumble, his heel catching a root as he took a step back—a step *away*—like retreat was an option when he already knew it wasn't. Then he was falling, tumbling backwards onto the mossy forest floor to stare up at the same sky he'd spent his whole life looking at, from a vantage he'd never before achieved.

There, alone with himself and the brutality of the power he wielded, Orpheus began to cry.

Sobs hitched his chest, bare and breathless. He couldn't even explain why he was crying. He couldn't get his thoughts straight let alone something as intangible as his feelings. All he knew was that he'd lost something more important than his home when he'd ridden through the Gilded Palace gates, and the void it had left behind felt large enough to swallow him whole.

He didn't know how long he laid there. Time passed in the slow angle of the sun through the trees, the cast of shadows lengthening cool and dim around him. Spots of Netherflame burned close enough he could feel the ice cold sting of their fire but he remained where he was, laid out amongst the detritus of all his mistakes, Lore and her dreams and her Empire no more than an excuse for his own selfish, stupid choices.

He never meant to fall asleep. Didn't think it possible to find any sort of peace out here, let alone rest. Hell beasts were territorial of the places in the world they crawled out of, so to be this close to one meant he was a sitting duck. But as his body went lax and his brain went buzzy and his face tipped up into the warmth of a slow-moving sun that dared to shine down upon him, sleep came, and Orpheus didn't have the strength to fight it.

Instead, he closed his eyes, and he surrendered.

CHAPTER VII

LOYALTIES

He woke to the strangest sensation of wet velvet smacking against his cheek.

If someone asked Orpheus what he knew about horses he'd only be able to tell them that they looked one extra meal away from being crushed by their own body weight, and they smelled like shit. He would have forgotten all about their need for community, their susception to loneliness, let alone their ability to read human emotion. But as the world came back into focus and he found himself face to face with the beast of an amalgam that had, as of that morning, become his companion in an unforgiving world, he was uncomfortably confronted with all that and more.

"What are you doing here?" Came out more like a scratch against a chalkboard than his own voice; Orpheus flinched.

Above, his horse stared down at him, big brown eyes dewy in the dreamy light of the dying forest. He couldn't tell how much time had passed, but the heaviness in his limbs suggested enough for him to have slipped into a deep, dreamless sleep. An hour then, perhaps two. Orpheus closed his eyes for one more second, gauging the absence of his will to stand, let alone sit up.

Maybe he didn't have to. Maybe he could stay right here, make a home in the forest foraging berries and fighting off the inevitable decay of the Netherflame. Maybe the curse would forget about him, and he could lead a life as a *real* hermit, find some dirt hole to be his hovel and become the subject of court rumors—the bone-reader who lived deep in the pine woods, telling fortunes in exchange for bottles of gin because the hooch he'd brew from all these fucking pine tips would inevitably taste like piss.

Another snuff of warm air against his cheek broke his ill-fated fantasy. He was almost grateful for it. How much further could he fall when the daydream of life as a homeless drunk felt like an escape? Orpheus wasn't particularly keen to find out, and his horse didn't appear to have the bad sense to let him. A drunken hermit couldn't care for a horse, could it? It was probably hungry. Or lonely. Likely, Fenrir had given up waiting and returned to the palace, left the horse behind and, if Orpheus was lucky, most of the supplies.

"Did Fenrir abandon us, then?" Orpheus asked when he finally, painfully, sat up. Sleeping on the ground had done little for his exhausted body. Pine needles pricked his neck where they'd slipped under his collar. He pushed a hand through his hair to dislodge what he could.

The horse remained silent. Not that it could answer, let alone *understand*. Obviously, it was waiting for Orpheus to do more than have a conversation with himself. Like stand up and find it an apple or figure out how to put fuel in its, well, *gas tank* or something equally ridiculous. But when Orpheus finally regained his feet the horse's ears flicked at him in what Orpheus interpreted as satisfaction. If he had to guess, all the horse actually wanted was for Orpheus to get up off his ass.

"So, you came all the way out here to find me, is that right?"

The horse flared its nostrils and gave him a huff.

"I don't suppose you have a name, do you?"

Asking that came incredibly close to talking to himself, but the horse didn't seem to mind, and it wasn't like Orpheus didn't spend a lot of time enjoying his own company anyway.

Orpheus touched his fingers to the horse's bridle. There wasn't any trace of an identifying tag like some of the dogs at the palace wore. Something about that sat sadly with Orpheus, too impersonal for a creature that would wander off in search of another, when no one had ever cared enough about it to give it something as simple as a *name*.

"I must call you something, wouldn't you agree?" Orpheus asked, half rhetorical; he swallowed when the horse gave a powerful snuff. "How about Ears, or Tank, or—" the horse chewed on its bit, exposing a set of large white teeth that could probably bite his finger clean off. It wasn't threatening but neither was it the easy satisfaction from before. "Okay, fine, I understand, none of those!"

Again, the horse tossed its head, but before Orpheus could retreat, it began walking—presumably in the direction it had originally come from. It didn't look back to make sure he was following. It simply walked on, leaving Orpheus exactly where he stood.

"Excuse—" Orpheus cut off mid-breath. Like all hells he was going to politely bargain with a *horse*. "Now hold your—" what, *horses?* Orpheus ignored the sound of his teeth grinding to stumps and decided, just this once, that he would chase after the damned amalgam.

He caught up alongside its flank, slowing from a jog to a trudge, so they could pick their way around the towering pines together. Maybe the horse was annoyed, but Orpheus couldn't ignore the way its ears kept flicking towards him, the swing of its head as if to make sure he kept pace, and the swish of its tail against his side every time Orpheus lost it, a gentle reminder to *keep up*. Steadfast and stalwart, the horse actually seemed to be looking out for him, and what a strange, impossible impression *that* gave.

"Achates," he blurted out, the name coming to him as any other long-forgotten memory might.

Dark nights spent by dim lamplight, a young child scouring the shelves of the hermits' library, the palace asleep except for the guards who kept to the walls of the gardens, the peaks of the watchtowers. And that small waif of a girl who had met him there between the shelves, wide-eyed and silent, orphans, the two of them, akin in more ways than Lore would ever admit—*had* ever admitted. Even back then she'd been a strange person. Quietly presumptuous. Expectant. Like she already knew how Orpheus' mind ticked—the desire inside him to be of worth to someone, anyone, even if that person was a shade of the Empress she would one day become.

She'd been the one to hand him the ancient book of poetry, a leather-bound tome that had taken him weeks to read. The same one he'd chosen his own name from, all those many years ago.

"Achates, that was Aeneas' friend, his loyal companion when he was forced to flee his home of Troy. How is that, for your name?" he asked the horse. They came to a stop, the horse swinging its head around to look at him, dark eyes fathomless, the chug of its engine an even, rolling rhythm. "Achates," Orpheus repeated, touching his palm to the blaze of white between the horse's eyes. It made a soft sound, not quite a whinny, and Orpheus presumed to have his answer.

The horse—Achates—began walking again. Something in his chest unclenched as he kept pace.

When the trees broke into a small clearing ahead, Orpheus realized how little distance he'd actually put between him and the road. But that didn't explain why Fenrir was still there, sitting in front of a campfire, head bent over his knees, looking, all the world, like he was waiting for something—for *him*.

Not abandoned, then.

Relief coiled inside him, leaving him wrung out and exhausted. Seeing Fenrir shouldn't have that effect, but there it was, uncomfortably overwhelming to the point Orpheus wanted to turn around and walk right back out into the forest. Unfortunately, Achates was in the way.

And Fenrir had already spotted him.

Orpheus chewed his lip as Fenrir swept to his feet and abruptly spun to face him.

"You're alright," he said without the familiar annoyance that could have made Orpheus feel better. No, Fenrir sounded *relieved*.

Orpheus swallowed, coming to a stop several paces from where Fenrir stood.

He saw it, then. What Fenrir had been bent over.

THE CRACK AT THE HEART OF EVERYTHING

A book. Orpheus recognized it. Some darkly romantic story of a man and the ghost of the woman he had loved, who he'd driven to grief-stricken illness, then death. Orpheus gritted his teeth when he saw the dog-eared page Fenrir had marked, knew the book well enough to recognize he'd reached the part when the man had left home to make something of himself worthy of the woman he loved.

His mouth tasted dry when he said, "I needed to walk." Avoiding Fenrir's eyes, he stared at the book, then at the fire. It crackled quietly, the flames warm, natural, so unlike the Netherflame he was used to.

Fenrir had broken into the library to *read*. Not for anything more nefarious than the simple pleasure of curling up with a good book.

"But the curse—" Fenrir cut himself off. Orpheus looked up, found Fenrir's mouth twisted in a strange display of self-control. It wasn't like Fenrir, just as the impression of pity Orpheus felt was unlike Fenrir—just as the *book* set aside before the fire wasn't what Orpheus ever would have expected from *Fenrir Rawkner*.

Nothing made sense. Why did nothing *make sense?*

"I can take care of myself." His voice sounded weak in his own ears.

"It killed that messenger."

He finally met Fenrir's eyes when he asked, "And why, exactly, do you care?"

Fenrir might be mostly muscles, but there was obviously a brain somewhere in there too. It wasn't just the book, because when Fenrir held his eyes and said, "Because Lore's a cold-hearted bitch," a whole world very different than the one he'd been punted into opened up around him.

It was too much. It was too different. No—it was all too *strange.*

Orpheus couldn't stop himself from *laughing.*

It tore through him, a violent sound that erupted out of his chest and then wouldn't stop. His stomach tightened to the point of pain, until he hunched over, arms wrapped around his middle, face contorting while his laughter grew louder, and then thinned, dissolving into what could be called a giggle and still, he couldn't *stop.* Because Fenrir was right. He was *right,* and Orpheus, up until today, probably would have torn him a magical new one if Fenrir had ever said that to him before. But now the truth of it struck with about as much absurdity as everything else in his life.

Lore may be his only friend and the woman he'd sworn his loyalty to, but like the man in the book who had driven his own lover to death, Lore was—simply put—a *bitch*.

Orpheus began laughing all over again.

CHAPTER VIII
THE TRUCE

This recent development of Fenrir treating him like a friend was as new as it was unwelcome, because Orpheus, as a rule, did not have friends.

Fenrir was doing a great job reminding him why.

"Do you want combination meat patties over broccoli stalks or stuffed peppers with rice and sausage-like substitute?" Fenrir asked while sorting through a pile of—Orpheus had to get a second look to make sure—meal replacement rations.

"I'm not eating any of those." Orpheus made a face where he sat, close enough to the fire that the warmth had grown to a heat.

"You've gotta eat something. How about sweet and sour pork byproduct with pickled hundred-year duck eggs?" Fenrir lifted the packet up alongside an eyebrow, dangling it out so Orpheus could see for himself. The gesture came out honest and intentional like Fenrir ate this shit not because he had to but because he wanted to. Orpheus thought he was going to be sick.

"What do the horses get to eat?" he asked around a mouthful of saliva.

"Gasoline." Fenrir finally grinned. "And grass."

"I'll take my chances on the grass." Orpheus turned back to the fire to stare into the white-hot center of the flames. It was either that or watch Fenrir squeeze a package of unspeakable contents into his wide-open maw.

Past the ring of firelight, he could see their horses. Fenrir's big black beast barely cut a shape out of the shadowy pine forest, ears back and head high, at attention while its companion stuffed its face with—exactly like Fenrir said—every blade of grass within reach.

"You get a taste for them after a while." Fenrir rolled the packet up from the bottom, so every last drop of sludge squeezed out the other end. "Better than anything considered fresh when you're on a front line."

If Orpheus thought he was going to be sick before, now he actually tasted bile. "Please, don't elaborate on what that means."

Fenrir grinned again, ripping open a second packet and holding it out towards him. "Come on, try it. When was the last time you even ate?"

Thirty-six hours ago, right before Lore's summons had come. It didn't make Fenrir's offer any more appealing. But by virtue of the human condition, Orpheus *did* need to eat.

Reluctantly, he took the packet from Fenrir, held it close to the firelight, and tried to judge what level of desperation he'd achieved in the last day and a half.

"You gotta squeeze it," Fenrir continued with his one-sided conversation. "Into your mouth."

"Into my mouth, you say?" he snapped. "As opposed to where else, I wonder?"

Across the fire, Fenrir blinked, both eyebrows raising.

Orpheus flushed. He'd always been shit at conversation but with Fenrir that had never been a problem. However, that also meant Fenrir wasn't supposed to look at him like *that*—like Orpheus was anything other than something to be laughed at. Not that Fenrir was laughing. For once, he remained uncomfortably silent.

The ration packet barely possessed a flavor. Nothing compared to the banquets the palace had frequently held. Maybe that was for the best considering how empty his stomach was. Orpheus took another taste before sucking down a third of the packet, hunger rearing to life now that he'd been reminded food existed at all.

It wasn't...awful. And he might have said as much to Fenrir except then the firelight caught right and there was no way Orpheus could ignore the string of letters and numbers imprinted on the bottom of the packet.

Expiry: 9.9.2059

All at once, nausea bubbled back to life.

Did he eat food that was three-hundred-and-fifty years *expired?*

"Rawkner," Orpheus hissed through clenched teeth, lobbing the packet back at Fenrir who, unfairly, caught it out of mid-air. "Please tell me you can't count." Because at least that would explain the *why*, if not the *what the actual fuck—*

"Count?" Fenrir mocked, turning over the packet before setting it aside in favor of bringing his sword into his lap. "Does that have something to do with all those numbers you love?"

If Orpheus wasn't so busy keeping himself from violently expelling the contents of his stomach, he may have paid more attention to the way Fenrir pushed his thumb against the sword's hilt to expose a bit of blade.

"I know they're old. It's fine, I've eaten hundreds of them," Fenrir said, tossing his hair, something between an eye-roll and a dismissal.

"Well, that certainly explains a lot!" Orpheus reached for his canteen of water and drowned out the sickly sweet-sour taste of unidentified pork parts and—he did the math quickly—four-hundred-and-fifty-year-old eggs.

"I'll make you a deal." Fenrir's smile turned darker than the surrounding forest. "You finish off your food and I'll finish off the pack of Jackdogs that's been stalking you for the last thirty minutes."

Rigid cold straightened Orpheus' spine, one icy vertebra after another. He forced himself not to look when Fenrir's beast of a horse began stamping its massive, heavy steel-toed hooves, ears tipped towards the shadows at its back. Beside it, Achates chugged along steadily, oblivious to the danger beyond the black veil of the pine woods.

Jackdogs always hunted in packs of three. Orpheus knew because at the beginning of the war Lore had lured several home with her. Back then, soldiers were hard to come by, and Jackdogs weren't all that different from other dogs if kept exercised and well-fed. Obedient too. Orpheus remembered how they'd sat before him, ears perked and heads cocked, curiously staring up at him from the center of the courtyard. But if the last day had proved anything, it was that these woods were barren of anything alive, let alone that could be prey. If the curse hadn't drawn the Jackdogs here, their inevitable starvation would have.

Please kill them, he didn't say aloud.

Panic curdled in his stomach, worse than the expired rations packet Fenrir once again held out. Orpheus looked up and met his eyes.

"Eat up," Fenrir said expectantly, as if he knew Orpheus wouldn't disobey.

Like the Jackdogs on the hunt, Fenrir also had him cornered.

His hand shook when he snatched the packet. He kept his focus on the fire and the slippery sensation of the food on his tongue instead of the echo of drawn steel, the soft crunch of pine tips under heavy-booted soles.

Screams peeled off into the night, desperate and panicked. The Jackdogs, dying one by one.

When Fenrir re-entered the clearing, Orpheus was shivering.

"You cold?" Fenrir asked, thumbing a spot of blood from the leather cuff of his bracer. Orpheus shook his head, refusing to meet his eyes. Fenrir made a breathy sound he couldn't identify—a laugh or just as likely exacerbation—and sat back down. "Wanna get closer to the—"

"Don't treat me like glass!" he lashed out, empty ration packet crumpling in his fist. "I'm perfectly capable of taking care of myself!"

"Orpheus, it's okay to need—"

"*Help?*" Heat flooded his face, chasing away the cold. He was still shaking, but now it had nothing to do with the temperature. "I don't need help; I need my life back! I've lost *everything* Rawkner, has it occurred to you that perhaps I don't need to die in order for the curse to succeed?"

Fenrir kept quiet, but his expression said enough; it hadn't occurred to Orpheus, either, not until this very moment.

"The palace was my *life*," Orpheus continued, voice quieter but no less sharp. "And maybe Lore was a bitch, and maybe the court did hate me, and maybe I spent too much time locked away in my workshop putting my energy into other people's success but it was still *mine*, and it was *something*."

Something awful and horrific but at least he had made an impact on the world, however cataclysmic.

"And now what?" he asked. "I start over? Spend my life surviving each day so I can do it all over again the next?" His voice wavered as he said it, the real impact of what was happening settling over the pall of disbelief that had followed him since yesterday. "Forgive me if I fail to jump at the chance to prolong that particular brand of torture!"

Fenrir leaned forward, like he was trying to memorize everything Orpheus had said because there was going to be a test on it in a week's time. The fire drew shadows out of his expression, a miasmic shift that made Fenrir impossible to read.

"You can't break it? The curse?"

No, he couldn't. He'd never been very good at fixing things—Hell Rat-rotted legs or curses or his own fucking mistakes.

His voice cracked when he said, "There's no counter curse."

"It didn't even mention a curse? The spell that summoned Ohm?" Fenrir confirmed, much to Orpheus' festering dismay. "The one that—"

"—that started this whole mess? You mean *this* spell?" Orpheus snapped, shoving his hand in his pocket to pull out the page and wave it towards the fire—towards Fenrir's face. "There is no counter curse, there isn't any mention *of* a curse in the whole hells-damned spell!"

"That's where we go," Fenrir said, eyes on the spell, alight with the white-hot flames of the fire. "To the Keep where I found the spell book."

Time slowed, trickling through the narrowed funnel of his perception as Orpheus stared at Fenrir, his arm lowering until the page was safely in his lap.

"You found the spell?" Orpheus asked from somewhere outside his body.

"Yeah." Fenrir broke eye contact to stare down at his sword. "When I found it I knew it was powerful, but I had no idea it would do—" he cut off, glanced away, towards the scar and the palace and devastation Orpheus, and Fenrir, had *both* made. "—That, to you," Fenrir finished lamely.

Was *that* why Fenrir was here? Did he feel *guilty?*

Orpheus stared at Fenrir, the firelight playing across the planes of his face. Everything Fenrir said felt like the scratch on the surface of a story only he could tell, like what little he'd seen outside the palace had been a beginning, the opening verse of a song Orpheus had never heard before. The sensation of being more out of his depth than he could fathom prickled to life under his skin.

But...there *was* hope, despite how lost he felt.

"The Keep," he said. "I have to get to the Keep."

Fenrir dipped his chin, eyes Rim-pale in the firelight.

The night grew colder as the hours passed. By the time sleep dragged at Orpheus' eyelids, he'd moved closer to the fire than was probably safe. Heat licked at his bare palms, gloves tucked into his pocket alongside the spell, the icy bite of an eastern wind creeping through his robes.

Orpheus watched Fenrir while he tended the fire. The energy between them wouldn't stop shifting. A budding friendliness traded once again for that strange, immutable tension Orpheus struggled to define. Maybe that was why he held his breath when Fenrir finally approached him.

Their eyes met, unreadable in the flickering firelight, but it was what Fenrir had in his hand that inevitably caught his attention. He held it out like a peace offering: a blanket.

"Ice queen is definitely a look, but you're making me cold just looking at you." The words barely held a hint of Fenrir's typical teasing. "Think you can get some sleep? I'll keep watch."

Orpheus ignored how his hands shook and reached for the blanket. But when Fenrir's skin brushed his own, he couldn't ignore how warm he was, or how some of his warmth continued to cling to the blanket well into the coldest hours of the night.

CHAPTER IX
THE EDGE

Like the start of every bad day worth remembering, Orpheus' began with rain.

The pine trees did little to protect them out on the ridge at the edge of the mountain. Loam had been traded for dirt, and it made the journey down the narrow switchback pass slow-going, their horses carefully navigating through puddles of mud that grew slippery where it sloughed off the steep incline. Orpheus clutched his reins for dear life, keeping his eyes on Fenrir's back as he gave Achates the lead, no matter how insistent the urge to drag them to a stop became.

Orpheus understood why he'd never seen much of Lore's army. The procession of troops through the palace gates had been a fraction of their real numbers. Orpheus always assumed that was due to a sort of elite classicism that discluded most men. Now he knew it was logistics that kept them stationed at the base of the mountain. That, and perhaps the defensible position of guarding the two paths that fed into the pass. Not that anyone unfamiliar with the route could easily make the journey. Or, at least, not while hauling the equipment necessary to stage a siege.

The Gilded Palace, Orpheus began to realize, had spent its life more sheltered than him.

THE CRACK AT THE HEART OF EVERYTHING

Gray clouds hung low and bloated, the morning's mist lingering well into early afternoon. It wasn't quite pouring but the steady trickle was enough for him to feel soaked through. Orpheus eyed Fenrir's coat greedily. The single source of heat he had was Achates, the gentle warmth of his quietly chugging engine bleeding through the saddle. He hadn't thought to pack anything heavier than his outer robes, not that he owned anything that would've worked. When you spent your life at the same place, you simply stayed inside when the weather turned foul.

He lacked that luxury now. Orpheus wasn't sure he would ever have that luxury again. It had been two days since his and Fenrir's conversation around the fire, and the world had kept growing while he had struggled to keep pace.

Looking out past the ridge was difficult for reasons that had nothing to do with the rain.

Beyond the mist stretched a tangled wasteland, an expanse of ruin Orpheus struggled to find words to describe. He'd read about cities in books before, seen drawings of towers that numbered in the dozens, tall scaly structures that looked too fragile to exist at all, let alone stand up to the entropy of time. Perhaps they weren't meant to, because what Orpheus could see certainly looked like those towers, only if the massive hand of God had come down and swept them all aside.

Fires still smoldered inside each, skeletons of what he assumed were support structures clawing at the sky like blackened bones. And the ground...the ground glowed with the heat of a forge, molten red cracks belching thick smoke in the places where they converged, other veins branching off into thin threads of glimmering orange, all of it collapsing upon itself, an enormous crater that shadowed the land with so much more than smoke. Orpheus wondered if Fenrir had seen this place before it fell—wasn't sure if he should ask, not after the last time they'd passed a ruin like this.

I was there when the spell went off. The admission hadn't left Orpheus alone. He didn't know if it was guilt he felt, or desperation to share his own burden.

"Watch the path."

Fenrir's voice broke through his head, the thread of his thoughts severing at the precise moment Achates' hoof slid out from under them.

For one precarious moment the whole world tipped. Orpheus' throat closed and he choked on his scream, gripping the reins as a handful of rocks went skittering over the ridge right before he did. The world opened up beneath him, a drop into nothing, the vast open sprawl of a shattered wasteland ready to swallow him whole.

Then he was jerked back, Achates righting itself in the last split second before they both went tumbling over the ridge.

Orpheus was shaking by the time one big brown eye rolled back to meet his. Wide-eyed and blown black, Orpheus stared into an uncanny mirror of his own fear. He patted a hand over the horse's twitching neck. Something about that seemed to calm them both, so Orpheus kept his hand there, hunched over the saddle, slowly petting Achates' neck, keeping his eyes on the play of his glove through the brown-black strands of the amalgam's mane.

It was the excuse he needed to not look at the wasteland. If the curse was going to push him off this fucking mountain pass, he'd rather not see it coming.

"You okay back there?" Fenrir asked.

"I'm fine," he snapped, half-hearted. "Is that where we're going?" He didn't bother indicating what he meant by *where*.

"We'll make a quick fuel stop, but no, we're still a few days out from the Keep."

"Fuel stop?"

Fenrir glanced out at the ruins before meeting Orpheus' eyes again, then gestured. "See that smoke?"

No way was Orpheus taking his eyes off the road. He swallowed, then frowned. "What of it?"

"There's a lot of oil and natural gas out there, and that refinery has been burning for centuries, but there's some pockets isolated from the fires, and we built a refinery to access it. Army's been using the place as a fuel depot for a while now. We'll re-fuel there."

"Centuries?" Was that even possible?

"Most of what's burning is natural gas," Fenrir said simply, like Orpheus understood what that meant. He must have realized his mistake when he saw his expression. "Oil's deeper. Comes up from underground, somewhere there's a big deposit. Coal too, unreachable now because of the fires. They'll burn for as long as there's gas, probably another few hundred years if it's broken through to the coal. This refinery processed it all, back when it was originally in use."

"That refinery, is it a..." Orpheus trailed off, liking the feeling of foolishness even less than he did the impression of being out of his depth.

"What?" Fenrir asked.

Orpheus looked up to find Fenrir watching him from his saddle. Rain had slicked Fenrir's wild hair straight, long sticky streaks that clung to his cheeks and hid his scar. Even water-logged he was handsome, and Orpheus couldn't help but notice.

"Is it a city?" he asked, praying the cold rain kept his flush away.

"Cities are a lot bigger."

There wasn't any judgment in the statement—a simple fact made plain, like Orpheus wasn't the complete imbecile he suddenly feared he was.

But...bigger? How was that possible...

Fenrir met his eyes. "You've really never been outside the palace before, have you?"

Again, there wasn't any judgment in Fenrir's voice, but that didn't stop Orpheus from finally feeling heat reach his face.

"Is that so strange? To live in one place your entire life?" Orpheus asked. "Why would I have left when everything I needed was there?"

"Well, sure, but what about as a kid? Your parents? You remember anything from before?"

Before, Orpheus thought, *did not exist*. Because he had no idea where he'd come from, who his parents were—had always assumed they'd dumped him there, right at the Gilded Palace gates before he was old enough to make memories. If there was anyone in a person's life who were at least obligated to care about them, it was their parents, and Orpheus hadn't even been given that much.

"No," he finally answered, ending the conversation before he said something stupid like: *How many parents want a dark wizard as a child?* Because that had been the conclusion he'd come to so many years ago, when he'd asked himself the same question.

"I got sold to a mine when I was ten," Fenrir said as simply as if he were talking about the weather. "By the time I turned fifteen I'd worked off my debt and left to join the war. Lore paid well. More than enough to get out of the mines for good and get my parents out of debt too."

"Your parents?" Orpheus asked. For as long as they had known each other, Orpheus only knew a few facts about Fenrir. Such as how he was complete shit with a crossbow, apparently preferred to eat centuries old rations rather than be reduced to cannibalism on the front line, and now that he'd been sold into slavery as a child. All of which seemed like too much when placed within the small scope of everything else Orpheus knew about this hells-be-damned planet, which was next to nothing, much to his increasing dismay.

"They're refugees from the Rim. Family fled here when I was a baby, though I grew up in the wasteland. Moved to a small town a day's ride west of the northern pass sometime after I joined up with Lore. Got two brothers and a sister who haven't left the nest yet, and a couple others who moved back in recently. They have their own families now, last I heard. I should probably visit them but..." Fenrir trailed off into silence, which was almost as disconcerting as the story he was telling.

"But they sold you into slavery and then you sent them all your money and you somehow feel a sense of guilt for not having a better relationship with them yet don't really care enough to change that?" he finished unhelpfully.

"Got it in one."

Orpheus looked away when Fenrir turned to him and grinned.

"Is that why you're helping me? Out of a sense of guilt?"

"Maybe I'm just a helpful guy?"

"Says the man who's slaughtered half the population."

"Half the *soldiers* of the population," Fenrir corrected, as if everyone weren't a soldier fighting something to simply survive. "And don't talk as if you're not responsible for the rest."

It hit like the punch Orpheus had spent the last several days expecting, and he couldn't help but look at Fenrir and wonder...

"Was it..." he didn't know how to ask any other way, "Was it that bad?"

"Ohm didn't leave survivors."

A ringing rose in his ears, high and tinny.

He'd always known there'd be grim results to his work, but the palace had done more than shelter him from the scope of his impact. It had allowed him to become utterly *detached* from it. It was too easy to paint an enemy in flat colors when you held the vantage of power, to overlook the humanity of what you destroyed and see simply a means to an end. Orpheus didn't have the altruistic excuse of fighting his way out of poverty or supporting a family. He had made his choices, and the only motivator he could claim was the echo of Lore's dream in his head.

By the time they reached the bottom of the ridge, the ringing had turned into a sharp, aching throb.

Too late, Orpheus realized why.

"My pack," he gasped, screwing his eyes shut. Ahead, Fenrir pulled his horse to a stop, Orpheus could tell by the scraping sound of gravel sliding beneath heavy hooves.

"What's wrong?" came too late.

While Shriekers could be physically dangerous, the insanity they inflicted by the sound of their tinny white-noise was their preferred brand of attack. They fed off mental anguish, the tinnitus a short-cut to madness, and Orpheus was probably enough of a feast without much effort on the Shrieker's part. Still, as unhinged as he could be, Orpheus knew he wasn't actually crazy, so when the ringing in his ears kept growing and pressure began to follow, he knew something was wrong.

He grabbed his pack, hands shaking as he tore through the contents, several of Fenrir's precious ration packets tumbling over the edge of the hells-damned ridge. He might have mindlessly leapt after them if the pressure between his ears hadn't reached the point of excruciating agony.

His whole body seized, then twisted, pack falling to the ground a moment before he did. Pain lanced through his skull and Orpheus clawed his way onto his side as he stuck his fingers in his ears, trying to reach the source of the pain and encountering nothing but cartilage. Someone shouted his name in the near distance, but Orpheus couldn't care about anything but making the pain go away.

He wiggled his fingers in further, navigating a tight tunnel and finding the angle he needed to shove in *deep*.

Hands grabbed his wrists, ripping his fingers from his ears a second before he punctured his own eardrums. Orpheus screamed with the loss, pain pulsating through his head, Fenrir's profile a swimming vision above him while he curled atop the gravel, kicking his feet, trying to break free.

He felt his wrists come together over his head in a bone-grinding resistance and then, all at once, the pain extinguished.

"Orpheus, you're safe."

The world slammed back into place. Orpheus sucked in a sticky gasp with the force of it, saliva and dirt smeared across his cheek, the crushed Shrieker twitching in Fenrir's lap.

His hands shook, wrists still trapped in one of Fenrir's big, infuriatingly strong fists.

Slowly, Fenrir released him. Slower yet, Orpheus shoved up into a seat. Time slowed while Fenrir's hands hovered over him, whether to comfort or to restrain him again Orpheus didn't want to think about. He kept his eyes on the ground, refusing to look at Fenrir until a hand descended to rest atop his knee.

Rim-pale eyes met his. "You okay?"

Orpheus' mouth was too dry to swallow, his throat too tight to breathe, let alone speak. He nodded his head instead, hoping that was enough. It had to be enough.

They spent a long time like that, side by side in the gravely mud, words there but unspoken, just like the comfort Fenrir seemed determined to give, his hand a warm weight atop Orpheus' knee.

THE CRACK AT THE HEART OF EVERYTHING

Orpheus focused on his breath when Fenrir eventually turned away. Time slowly crept back to speed while Fenrir searched the rest of their supplies for any other castaways, Orpheus wondering whether the things he felt were rooted in madness or if the world was more strange and elusive than he could have ever predicted.

INTERLUDE
NAMES

He's the first one to ask, but she's the first to decide.

Names. It occurs to him after months together, that neither of them have *names*.

"Lore," she replies, voice reedy with disuse, like wind through ancient stone.

"Lore," he repeats, testing it out. It rolls off the tongue, feeling strong, but mysterious. A name built of legends, and he says: "I like it. It suits you."

The girl—Lore—does not react. She's sitting crossed leg in front of him, the book he has splayed open to a page he'd earmarked two nights ago, when he'd been up here in the library, reading by lantern light, stacks upon stacks of poems and history books and legends and folk tales surrounding him like towers of possibilities—names upon names for him to consider—so many men and women and creatures that he wondered if he shouldn't let Lore choose for him, because how was he supposed to pick for himself?

Yet, he kept coming back to one.

"Orpheus," he tells her, voice wavering over the syllables. He should have practiced it more because Lore frowns. Did he say it wrong?

"Who's Orpheus?"

It's me, he doesn't say. "He's a Grecian bard. Well, Thracian. But he was a poet and a prophet and when his beloved died, he went to Hell to find them and bring them back, which I think is very romantic."

"Romantic," Lore repeats, inflection even lower, slower, like she's trying to make sense of him.

Orpheus feels the blush rising and there's nothing he can do to stop it.

"Daedalus would be better," she says, and Orpheus is too wrapped up in his surprise that Lore knows who Daedalus is. He wasn't always sure she was listening when he read to her from the history books.

"But he's so boring," Orpheus argues. Nobody liked Daedalus. He was useful, sure, but there weren't any stories of him going on adventures because he spent all his time inventing stuff. "I want to be someone people like. I want to make people happy. I bet Daedalus didn't have any friends."

"Friends," Lore says. "You want friends."

Don't you? But Orpheus doesn't say that. He looks down at the book and flattens his palm to the page, eyes the silver circling his wrist and the dull etchings inscribed there, the burned ring underneath that is dull and gray—the skin cold, his wrist too thin.

His stomach grumbles as he tugs his sleeve down.

"Orpheus had an impact on people," he settles for when the silence stretches on. "Lots of people loved him."

"I don't want to make an impact on people," Lore says, the most words Orpheus has ever heard her use at once, and with a vehemence that feels unexpected—important. "I want to make an impact on the world."

He realizes then, how much bigger Lore dreams. That for how little she speaks she is thinking on a scale far grander than he has ever conjured. Big, luminous, *enormous* dreams that put the heroes hidden away in these books to shame. A tale that the Orpheus of old would have written poems about, passed down for millennium, generation after generation, until the story of Lore becomes something of legend—a hero for the people to remember, when their lives grow hard and hope feels lost.

Orpheus likes the idea of that. Likes that people might remember him the same way. Love him, for time immemorial, after his bones have become dust but his songs are still sung, the memory of him living on in the very heartbeat of the world.

"I can help," he breathes, leaning forward. "Let me help."

"Okay," Lore says after a breath, staring at him from behind her veil of dark hair. "You can help, *Orpheus.*"

His name sounds like spears when she says it, piercing as deep as her eyes, needling him open like Orpheus has offered up so much more than his simple cooperation. Suddenly, there's an expectation hanging between them, a commitment and a choice so vastly encompassing that Orpheus is sure that, if anyone is going to change the world, it will be Lore, and he should be so lucky to help.

CHAPTER X
THE STACKS

After all the years spent in his workshop, he should be used to the acrid scent of soot by now, but as the smokestacks spewed dense black clouds into the sky, Orpheus admitted he'd barely gotten a taste.

The Stacks were a tangle of twisted metal tubing surrounded by a sprawling collection of brick buildings and colorful, glowing lights, the field adjacent to the settlement dotted with over two dozen hammerhead oil pumps, scattered across the horizon in a haphazard array. Across the distant ridge at the edge of the field, little pinpricks of what Orpheus assumed were people stood stationed like sentinels, a vigilant guard overseeing the operation of the oil field. Of the six or so operational pumps, each moved slowly, the steady rise and fall of their massive steel weights taking as long as fifteen minutes to complete a rotation.

Orpheus watched with ill-contained wonder, and not a small amount of jealousy. He'd already driven off one refinery worker with all of his questions. It was only a matter of time before he drove this one off too. At least she seemed interested in what he had to say, or possibly amused.

Orpheus hadn't completely shaken the impression that he was as much a spectacle to her as those pumps were for him.

"Magic is much cleaner fuel, you know." The worker chewed through a handful of dried fruit and nuts, blinking dully at him, like she was bored. She had yet to speak a word, so Orpheus moved on from asking questions to giving a lecture. "According to the surgeon general, smoke inhalation is likely to lead to increased heart failure and decreased lung capacity. Netherflame engines pose no such risks."

Despite his best efforts—twenty minutes of him extolling the virtues of magic over their ancestors' machinery—the woman didn't crack. She watched him from across the massive pipe they both sat upon, foot bouncing while she poured another handful of fruit and nuts into her mouth. If small talk was the death of friendly conversation, Orpheus finally had an explanation for why he had no friends.

"Sugar is the leading cause of tooth decay followed by nuts," he continued. "I won't presume you don't know the basics of oral hygiene, but if you always eat that rubbish, you do know to floss after every meal, don't you?"

That, at least, got a reaction. She held his eyes and seemed to consider something. The bouncing foot stilled, then planted, taking her weight as she leaned forward and lifted her hand. Orpheus cocked his head and looked down at it.

The pile of the dried fruit and nuts were a medley of reds and oranges and yellows, the salted scent of nutty sugar hitting his nostrils in a tempting mix and setting his mouth to water. Orpheus didn't think he was drooling but something of his effort to swallow must have shown on his face.

"Maybe," the woman spoke for the first time, voice deep, words slow. "Some of this *rubbish* will finally get you to shut up."

Orpheus stiffened. *Well*, if she was going to be like that...

He snatched the pile of fruit straight out of her hand.

It took him an embarrassingly short half-minute to chew through the salty sweet mix. The fruit must have been dried recently; the nuts newly shelled. Both melted across his tongue in waves of flavor, as natural and whole as Fenrir's ration packets were not. He closed his eyes when he finally swallowed, his stomach making a grateful rumble.

THE CRACK AT THE HEART OF EVERYTHING

If Achates were here, Orpheus imagined he'd be nipping at his ear to get at the fruit and nuts, but he was with Fenrir at the stable and Orpheus had no one to share the food with but himself. He took a second handful from the woman, noticing for the first time the hip pack she wore, how heavy it looked, spilling over with an abundance of *trail mix*—that's what she called it—when she offered him a third helping.

"Thank you," he finally remembered to say when he turned down a fourth.

"Three minutes and twenty-six seconds," the woman said. "That a new record for you?"

Orpheus allowed himself the indignity of turning red. *You're going to have to learn to laugh at yourself someday*, a voice that sounded suspiciously like Fenrir piped up inside his head.

"So, you're Fenrir's friend, huh? The magician?"

Orpheus frowned. "I am Master Dark Wizard Orpheus Zon Ziffler of the Exalted Court," was an even bigger mouthful than the trail mix had been. Out here, amongst the smoke and wreckage of the war Lore had waged, the title sounded ostentatious. Pretentious. Maybe a little ridiculous.

"Right, the magician." Orpheus clenched his jaw. *Magician*—like something out of some children's book. "So then, let's see some, show me what all the fuss is about."

"Excuse me?" his voice raised, shrill. "I'm not some performer of—of *tricks*." That would be an insult to every wizard he knew. Which weren't many, but Orpheus knew they existed—they had to—because what did the world run off of if not magic? At least in the places where things like this refinery weren't publicly accessible. Once, technology had lit the lanterns of the world, now Netherflame filled the darkness, and Orpheus refused to be made into a joke by some no-name refinery worker. He crossed his arms and sneered at her, then looked out across the oil field and the long lines of shadow arcing in time with the pumps.

This low, the sun set the field ablaze, a fire across the horizon.

"Ah, so that's how y'all repay a stranger's kindness up in that mountain fortress?" The woman's voice grew louder when she leaned towards him, trying to catch his eye. "Just never met one of your kind before, is all. Always wondered if Fenrir's stories were true."

Orpheus kept his eyes on the horizon, the rise and fall of the pump heads keeping a slow steady rhythm, anathema to the hammering of his heart. He didn't linger on why using magic suddenly seemed wrong. Maybe it was the ruins of the scar he couldn't stop thinking about, or the curse he knew slept underneath his skin. Or maybe it was that, in the face of this ancient technology raised from the deathbed of history like some savior come for humanity, he felt acutely inadequate.

"Go on, you owe me," the woman urged, nearly pleaded.

His fingers prickled when he rubbed the tips together. He knew the moment the Netherflame kindled, the cold sting of purple fire a familiar comfort. Something inside him unraveled with the release of it. He watched it grow, rolling his fingers so the flame danced between them.

"All hells," the woman breathed, leaning in close. "That's the dark flame alright, you ain't joking."

Out of the corner of his eye he saw the moment her hand lifted— to touch the flame—touch *him*—as second nature as her need to breathe. He snatched his hand away before it could happen. Netherflame sputtered out in a crackle of sparks between them.

"Don't touch it, unless you have a wish for immediate death, that is."

"It's really that dangerous?" she asked, eyes meeting his. Orpheus nodded. Netherflame came straight from the infernos of Hell; dangerous was an understatement. "And you can just make it—simple as that?"

"I don't make it," Orpheus clarified. "I summon it, and then I refine it, through sigil work and archanics, so it becomes safe for anyone to use."

"You're an engineer," the woman said, gruff voice brightening ever so slightly. She met his eyes again and, this time, they caught with a friendly possession.

Orpheus couldn't look away.

"I'm an engineer too. The name's Red. Got this place up and running after the grid was partially restored, been in charge ever since."

"*You're* an engineer?" Orpheus asked, unable to keep the surprise from his voice.

Red grinned, smile wide, teeth bared. "One of the best."

"And you...run this place?" Orpheus looked away from Red long enough to glance at the pumps. It wasn't possible, but they somehow seemed even more foreign now. "You repaired those pumps?"

"Took a few months of studying some half-corrupted schematics, but once I got my team to tear one of 'em down we were able to make sense of how they worked. The refinery was the real challenge. Who knew how complicated turning slag could be, at least if you want to actually use it and not fuck up every piece of equipment you've got. Had to take some shortcuts there which explains all the smog, but I got everything working well enough in the end. Told myself I'd have the chance to refine the design once we were up and running but it's been all business ever since. Well, business, and..." Red leaned back, hands planted on the pipe behind her, looking at Orpheus as if judging if he'd earned hearing whatever she was about to say next.

"And?" Orpheus gambled.

Red shrugged. "Everyday things: dying orchards, poisoned ground water, and..." Red trailed off, lips pursed. "And defense, I suppose."

"The war is over, who's left to defend against? Brigands?"

"It's not thieves we're worried about," Red sniffed, tossing her head. Gold glinted in the deep auburn shadows of her hair, catching fire in the brilliant sunset, but it was her eyes that burned when she looked at Orpheus. "Pretty sure we got ourselves a dragon sniffing around. We think it's made a nest in one of the collapsed gas lines out in the ruins. They like the fire, you know, and as you can see, we've got plenty of it."

"A dragon?" Orpheus had never seen a dragon—well, not outside the books in the Gilded Palace's library. They were rare even down in

Hell where they came from. "Are you certain?"

"Showed up around the same time the orchards started to die. Got some pictures supporting the theory, though nothing's confirmed. Hard to keep the cameras up and running reliably in the fields, and no one's gotten snatched yet so at least there's that. But some of the pumps have been damaged, and those scratches—" Red cut off to make a whistling sound, low and swooping like Orpheus' turning belly, "—don't know what else could make those."

Orpheus knew of several hell beasts that could, but he didn't think Red needed anything more to worry about than what was already on her plate.

"Have you petitioned the throne for help?" He asked instead, genuinely curious, because if there was a dragon threatening the refinery Orpheus couldn't imagine Lore would ignore that.

"Sent two messengers up the mountain," Red said, voice a little different. Strange, though Orpheus couldn't pinpoint why. "Still waiting for a reply."

There were excuses he could make—viable reasons Lore wouldn't have dispatched a team to take care of a dragon which Orpheus couldn't fault her for. The fact that, as of yet, the dragon hadn't made any trouble was a start. Nor did they know where its den was located, or its hunting grounds. They didn't really know for sure there was a dragon at all, and it wasn't just one lonely little fuel depot Lore was responsible for now, it was a whole empire of people.

"I'm certain the Lady will send help when the time comes," he said diplomatically, excluding the fact that her most capable *help* was currently gallivanting across the countryside with *him*.

"Fifi!" Speak of the devil. "Wow, you're actually making friends?"

Something small and tight inside him loosened at the sight of Fenrir. Orpheus shoved the feeling away while sitting up straighter, barely remembering to force out a gravelly, "Rawkner," in greeting.

Fenrir beamed and clapped Orpheus on the shoulder. He rocked with the strength of it, Fenrir's touch heavy but fleeting, lingering long past the brief moment his shoulder took the weight.

"Been a minute, Fenrir," Red drawled, eyes sliding from Orpheus' slowly. "Didn't think I'd see you round here for a long while, figured you'd be too busy running an Empire and all that."

Orpheus looked between the two, confronted with the confirmation that Fenrir and Red knew each other. Of course they did. Why wouldn't the general of Lore's army know who was supplying their fuel? But what hadn't become apparent until now was that their relationship wasn't just professional, it was *friendly*.

"You know nothing could keep me away from you too long, Red," Fenrir said with a grin. "Oh, I almost forgot, I got you a gift!"

Fenrir reached into the pack slung over his shoulder and dug out a book—one of *Orpheus'* books—what he recognized as an almanac several hundred years old.

"Excuse you, that is stolen pro—"

"A farmer's almanac?" Red snatched the book out of Fenrir's hand, flipping through the water-stained pages, eyes narrowed.

"Latest I could find. It doesn't quite go far enough forward but—"

"There's always a pattern," Red breathed, pausing at a page two-thirds of the way deep, on what Orpheus identified as a weather table. "This could help, Fenrir. Thanks." Orpheus watched her eyes scan the page, the thumb she ran down the book's spine slow, gentle. Reverent.

Something cold inside him warmed hot. Like him, Red appreciated books, so he didn't understand what compelled him to say, "That's property of the Exalted Court."

Red met his eyes, her own dark, dangerously narrowed.

Orpheus sneered. "Books are precious and not to be carelessly lent out."

"Thought you were a mage, not a librarian."

"Protecting the integrity of the palace library is—"

Suddenly, Fenrir's arm came around him, drawing him in close. Any words Orpheus meant to say were forgotten in the face of the warm solid body pressed against his.

"Don't mind him, Red. He's got a thing for books. You should have seen his face when he caught me in the library. You'd have thought I'd walked in on him having an illicit affair with an encyclopedia."

His face went from warm to outright *hot*.

"Books aren't—That's not—*funny*," Orpheus uselessly sputtered.

Red laughed, eyes bright while Fenrir's arm hung around him like a weight. But before he could snap at Fenrir to get his hands off him, he slipped away. The heat fled with him and for some reason losing it felt even more disconcerting than the fever of Fenrir's touch.

Orpheus kept his eyes diverted when Fenrir leaned a hip against the pipe beside him, casually, as if friendly touches were a thing that existed between them, rather than barbs and insults and spells and crossbow bolts.

"I'll take good care of it." Red's voice cut through his thoughts. Then, "He's the real deal Fenrir, you were right."

Wait—had Fenrir been talking about him?

"What did he tell you?" Orpheus snapped. "Why was he talking about me?"

Red didn't reply. She crossed her arms and cocked her head, lips pursed, and eyebrows lifted as she looked curiously at Fenrir.

"So, uh—did he show you that trick?" Fenrir punctuated with a wiggle of his fingers. "That snappy flame thing he does?"

"Don't ignore—" Orpheus choked off, then sputtered, "—that flame thing is not a *trick*."

"Yeah, he showed me. Says he's an engineer too." Red and Fenrir fell into conversation as if Orpheus—their very subject—wasn't sitting right there between them. That hells-damned sword-for-brains was ignoring him. And now Red was too. "And he likes my trail mix, so I guess you could do worse."

Fenrir beamed so brightly he put the sun to shame. "I knew you'd like him too, Red."

Then Fenrir went and laughed, belly deep and earthquake low. Orpheus didn't miss how he looked at him when he did, a softness at the edge of his smile, in the cadence of his voice. And when Red gave Fenrir what Orpheus could only describe as a knowing look, there was an entirely different conversation happening, one Fenrir and Red were having with all the words they didn't say.

Orpheus didn't like it. He didn't *understand* it.

"So," Red said, smile brightening into a grin, dark eyes glimmering, "Y'all ready to see our hotel?"

Hotels, Orpheus soon learned, were somewhat like palaces, except that instead of intending to keep people out, they were meant to welcome all types in.

Wealth limned every surface, from the brass light fixtures to the polished mahogany front desk. Richly woven carpets created a path through the soaring lobby, little couches with floral printed fabrics tucked between big leafy palms Orpheus was shocked to discover were made of wire and waxed fiber. A bar curved out of a dark alcove, the big man behind it polishing glasses that looked too delicate to stand up to his hands. And above it all, marble columns held a towering ceiling aloft, the elaborately carved tiles converging at the point where an enormous crystal chandelier hung.

"The chandelier was a gift from the labs. You been there before? Up north? Weird place, don't recommend it. There's magic and there's tech and then there's whatever the hell they're up to. It's not natural, I tell ya. Won't catch me dead near an amalgam, let alone replacing my pre-frontal cortex with a circuit board."

Orpheus stared out at the lobby, not understanding half of what Red rambled on about, let alone caring. Was that a stuffed *bear?* They'd been extinct since the twenty-second century, where in all hells *was he?*

"Tried to get us the honeymoon suite but apparently it's booked." Fenrir appeared with a pair of key rings swinging lazily around his hooked finger. "Guess we won't be sharing a bed after all, Fifi."

"Don't you know dogs sleep on the floor, Rawkner?" Orpheus snapped instinctively, not intending to make anyone laugh, but Red burst into a gut-clenching guffaw.

"Oh, he's *good*, Fenrir," Red said through her grin, all teeth. "I can see why you—"

Fenrir drowned Red out with an obnoxious yawn. "Well, I'm absolutely bushed!" He stretched when he said it, sidling up to Orpheus so that when his arm came down it was around his shoulders for the second time that day. "Fifi needs a shower, I'm sure you agree.

And I need my beauty sleep. Until tomorrow, yeah?"

Red rolled her eyes, making a gesture with her hand that couldn't have been polite.

"Coffee. Eight A.M. sharp. Don't make me come find you."

"She's nice, right?" Fenrir said after Red left them in the lobby. When Orpheus didn't reply Fenrir kept on talking. "Red's been a good friend, I think you'll like her, just give her a chance."

"She's smart," Orpheus said, following along as they ascended the grand staircase, plush red carpet soft beneath his bootsoles. "I can't understand why she likes *you*."

The rumble of Fenrir's laughter moved through him like a tremor, the weight of a hand sliding across his shoulders balanced precariously on a moment Orpheus tried to tell himself didn't exist. Unlike the first two times, Fenrir did not move away. Breath hit Orpheus' cheek when Fenrir drew him in close.

"So," Fenrir's said low in his ear, "you warming up to us yet?"

Heat fanned not across his cheeks, but his whole body.

"You know I don't have friends," came out strangely breathless.

Fenrir's arm tightened. "So, what does that make me?"

Orpheus didn't have an answer for him. Not in any words that made sense.

Maybe that was why he didn't ask questions when Fenrir led him into a single room with two beds. Why he didn't throw a fit when Fenrir gestured at one of them while dropping his sword on the second. Why Orpheus sat on it, and then remained there, silent even when Fenrir shucked off his leather armor and then sauntered into the bathroom in nothing but his underpants.

Why he was still there when Fenrir returned, a little wet, mostly undressed, Rim-pale eyes finding his in the quickly darkening room.

Orpheus looked at Fenrir as if the key to clearing the pollution inside his head was right here, staring him in the face.

All he had to do was figure out why.

CHAPTER XI

JOY RIDE

For the first time in recent memory, Orpheus slept the whole night through.

He'd almost forgotten what it felt like to get a solid eight hours of sleep. The curse had made it impossible, but Orpheus hadn't been sleeping well long before that. Despite the safety the Gilded Palace afforded, war still festered like a spreading disease in the back of everyone's minds. Not even a fortress could save someone from starvation, or disease, or any of the myriad of extenuating circumstances a protracted war risked. The Gilded Palace may have outlasted the literal end of the world, but the original inhabitants hadn't, and there had been too many incidents during the last three decades when it became clear why.

Food hadn't grown easily on the mountainside. The soil had been too astringent and the ancient ice caps feeding the aquifers were mostly poisoned by the Incident's fallout. Rainwater had been safe but during the summer they'd depended on the barrels they'd fill during the spring, and then later, the tablets Lore had brought back after each expedition down the mountain. And that didn't even take into account the threat of a siege. Siege engines wouldn't have had to make it up the mountain to put the Palace into desperate peril—they'd only have to camp at the mouth of the passes to disrupt the chain of supplies they had grown to depend on.

Now that Orpheus knew more about the terrain surrounding the mountain and the part the Stacks played in supporting the war effort, he didn't feel any less validated than he originally had, when Lore's court had insisted upon their lavish parties and excessive plunder of the Palace's food stores. He'd been called an "Enemy of Fun" often enough to have begun questioning his instincts. Maybe he hadn't realized exactly how close all of them had been to starving, but he also hadn't ever stopped worrying he was one bad turn away from it happening again.

Needless to say, the stress of starvation had kept Orpheus awake as often as the death curse had. But here in the Stacks with Fenrir in the bed beside his, Orpheus discovered he didn't have to worry about either.

"Good morning," Fenrir said from where he sat cross-legged atop his mussed-up blankets, chewing on a crispy stick of still-warm bacon.

Orpheus dragged himself out of a pool of drool saturating his pillow. He wasn't sure if it had to do with the sleep or the scent of freshly cooked food.

"Want some?" Fenrir continued when Orpheus' answer was to stare at the plate Fenrir currently cradled in his lap.

Fenrir offered it up without further comment, and Orpheus took it. The sticky taste of sleep was immediately overwhelmed by the flavor of scrambled eggs and sweet fruit and greasy bacon as Orpheus devoured everything he could. Where had Fenrir found the eggs? How had he managed to make them so light and fluffy? Expired meal packs didn't hold a candle to *this*. Orpheus would have said as much except the way he caught Fenrir watching him made him feel a little unsettled.

A smile tugged at Fenrir's face, small and satisfied, as if watching Orpheus gorge himself inspired within him some unidentifiable measure of pleasure.

"What?" Orpheus finally snapped when all that remained on the plate was a bit of buttered toast and jam. "Why are you looking at me like that?"

Fenrir grinned.

Orpheus narrowed his eyes. "Is the food drugged?" It was possible. He felt strangely...good, which could just as well be from a full stomach as it was some deftly disguised narcotic.

"What!" Fenrir squawked, laughing, "Why would Jack do that?"

"...Jack?"

"Big guy behind the bar downstairs. He made breakfast. Does more than sling drinks, ya know?" Of course, Fenrir hadn't made him breakfast. How could Orpheus be so— "Hungry still? Want some more?"

Orpheus shook his head as he forced himself to chew.

"So...Red came by the hotel earlier, asked if we could stick around for a couple days. I think it's a good idea."

Suddenly, the toast tasted foul, his saliva drying up like his mouth was a desert; Orpheus struggled to swallow.

"But the Keep," he finally managed, voice scratchy with dried toast. Fenrir gestured at the shared bedside table where two paper cups of coffee sat, and Orpheus reached for the one closest to him. The coffee tasted stale, bitter, but cleared his throat and softened the hard knot beginning to form in his stomach.

Fenrir wanted to stay in the Stacks, which could mean any number of things, the most important being that getting Orpheus to the Keep wasn't actually at the top of his list.

You actually thought he wanted to help? How wrong had he been. Lore had abandoned him, after all. Why shouldn't Fenrir too?

Orpheus felt like that little boy again, hiding in a fabrication of his own making because anything was better than the reality of the world. His hand slipped into his sleeve, fingernails finding his wrist. He dug in, blunted and painful.

"We don't have to."

Orpheus jerked his head up and looked at Fenrir. "What?"

"We don't have to stay here, if you don't want."

"Why?" He couldn't stop himself from asking.

"Just thought it'd be nice for you to sleep in a real bed for a few days. Eat real food. Get a plan together before we head to the Keep."

We, Fenrir had said. *Together*, he had implied.

So, he wasn't planning on leaving Orpheus behind. Not yet.

"Fine, okay," Orpheus breathed, apparently surprising them both.

Fenrir blinked, eyebrows raised, mouth half open. "Okay," he repeated, like he was trying the word out on Orpheus, making sure it would stick.

The sun had nearly reached its zenith by the time Orpheus showered and dressed. He felt more like himself than he had in weeks, but when he looked into the hotel room's mirror, he saw precisely how the curse had caught up to him. Freshly shaven, his short beard trimmed to delicate points, the man in the reflection still appeared exhausted. There were shadows under his eyes and his cheeks were a little sunken, his mouth severe, his skin sallow.

So, he absolutely wasn't expecting Fenrir to appear in the mirror and announce, "Lookin' good, Fifi!"

He should have had some kind of snappy retort, but Orpheus stood frozen in place. His eyes caught Fenrir's before he finally broke off and headed for the door. By the time he made it down to the ground floor his breath was coming in short and shallow; he wasn't sure if it was the ten stories of stairs he'd descended or the uncanny awareness of Fenrir following closely at his back.

The lobby wasn't any busier than it had been last night, but a few people were seated at a long, curved counter of deep mahogany where the bartender—Jack—served coffee. Orpheus didn't slow when Fenrir waved at him, heading straight for the rotating door and the Stacks beyond.

Cold hit him like a slap when he finally stepped outside of the hotel.

The first thing he noticed was the lack of smog in the air. A brisk wind came down off the mountain, bringing with it the nascent bite of deep winter, a trade Orpheus would happily make again and again when he inhaled deeply and didn't feel his lungs revolt. Beside him Fenrir did the same. Their arms briefly brushed as Fenrir's already substantial chest expanded, his leather armor creaking in weak protest as all those muscles shifted.

He didn't flee this time. Orpheus stole what he intended as a glance but found himself lingering. Sunlight dappled, bright and golden, a halo of light behind the wavy mess of Fenrir's hair. In profile Fenrir was even more striking, cutting a bold shape out of the backlight, taking up space he had every right to claim. Orpheus couldn't help but compare himself to that. His own lanky body resisted any sort of weight he tried to put on it, and his skin was permanently pale from decades spent out of the sun. The only possible thing he had going for him was his brain but even that wasn't anything to write poems about nowadays, and Orpheus didn't even know why he was comparing himself to Fenrir at all, because it wasn't as if he—

"Red said she was looking into something out beyond the orchards, asked that we come meet her. That okay?" Fenrir asked and Orpheus nearly jumped out of his skin for the second time that day.

"Yes, alright," he managed to say.

Fenrir looked down at him, all two inches separating them an ocean Orpheus would drown in if he dared try to swim. Particularly when Fenrir stated, "You're strangely amenable today. Remind me to put you to bed early every night."

That heat came back, and Orpheus did everything short of summoning an inferno of Netherflame to smother it.

"Amenable," he spat instead, voice dripping with all the substantial vitriol he could muster, "that's quite the vocabulary for a brain-addled sword jockey."

"Phew, there he is!" Fenrir grinned, laughing, "I was almost worried something had happened to my angry little flame thrower."

"Your—" Orpheus cut off, sputtering, then choking, "—your *what?*"

Fenrir grinned wider. "My angry little flame thrower?"

"I'm not little. I'm nearly as tall as you!"

Both Orpheus and Fenrir didn't miss how he hadn't bothered to deny the rest.

All around them, the Stacks arose as their namesake predicated.

The hotel was one of the tallest buildings, a respectable eleven stories and a cellar tucked amongst the low brick warehouses that populated this part of the district. The rest of the buildings were shorter, squatter. Glass storefronts lined the street level while apartments filled the vacancies above, and several blocks north the refinery took shape, the tangle of tubes and smokestacks bellowing out a steady cloud of gray smoke and dense white steam.

The Stacks may not be a city, but it was larger than anything Orpheus had seen before, and he stared up at the buildings as he followed Fenrir along a pre-determined path called a sidewalk. The street itself was dedicated to vehicles, gasoline engines chugging by on steel frames and wheel axles—a few archanics glowing a dull purple from their own Netherflame engine compartments.

But as strange and curious as he found the Stacks to be, he must have been of equal interest to the people that lived here. Eyes followed him as he passed, people watching openly despite the way Orpheus would meet their gazes and sneer. Most everyone wore what he assumed was their work attire. Soot-stained pants and heavy leather boots, waxed cotton coats offering more protection from the harmful elements in the air than the actual cold. His own dark robes stood out, the delicate silver filigree of his embroidered enchantments displaying a wealth that would have set him apart even if the sheer difference in style had not.

Orpheus hadn't failed to notice how out of place he looked. Thankfully, Fenrir looked equally distracting. His armor and sword and the scar across his cheek were certainly unique, but it was the way he carried himself that set him apart in a way not even Orpheus' robes could achieve. Like the space he claimed by simply existing, the world seemed to shape itself around Fenrir in a way that belied something greater than reputation or power.

These people knew Fenrir. More so, they respected him.

A man greeted them when Fenrir guided Orpheus into a building he realized was a garage.

"General!" The man snapped alongside a salute. "It's good to see you again, Sir. I wasn't aware you were back in the Stacks."

"It's good to see you too, Farris. I don't believe you've met Master Orpheus, the Empress' court mage?"

"Sir," Farris breathed, eyes wide. They were pale, like Fenrir's. Another refugee from the Rim. "It's an honor to meet you. Your work is an inspiration, most of the vehicles here ran off archanic power before the refinery was even a thought in our heads. Thought my life was over when I joined the force, just lookin' for an excuse at that point. Then I saw your work. Learned to become a mechanic on your engines, I did. Got a couple still sitting around here, antiques at this point but working like beasts!"

Farris was an older man with at least two decades on him and Fenrir, well past the average age for a military officer. Like Orpheus, Farris looked out of place in the Stacks. A meticulously tailored surcoat over leather pants and tall boots made him seem like an alien amongst the workers—similar to the uniforms the palace guard wore, a thread of familiarity he found himself strangely displaced by, even without the expression of fearful awe Farris currently wore.

Orpheus didn't like it. He didn't like any of it. His sneer emerged, harsh and twisted, and as if by command, Farris straightened into a well-oiled salute.

"Forgive me, Sir. I've spoken out of turn."

Before Orpheus could say anything upsetting, Fenrir cut in.

"It's alright, Captain. Orpheus is getting used to life in the Stacks, you know how it can be for those palace types." Fenrir tossed Orpheus a surreptitious wink. "Got a truck we could requisition?"

"Not headed east by chance, are ya?" Farris' face went strangely stiff.

Fenrir cleared his throat. "Just out to the watchtower to meet Red."

"Of course, Sir," Farris sputtered, somehow straightening further, "right this way."

Farris turned on his heel and hurried ahead, Fenrir taking the opportunity to lean in close.

"Don't like having fans?"

"I don't care to hear my archanics be called *antiques*," Orpheus snapped. "What's out east that he's so afraid of?"

Fenrir grinned, whispering, "*Ghosts*," then smothered a bark of laughter behind his hand.

"*Ghosts?*" Orpheus exclaimed. The absolute *absurdity*—

Fenrir's grin turned into a grimace, glancing over at where Farris stood frozen at his workbench. And rolling his eyes. "I tried to warn you." The hand he clapped onto Orpheus' shoulder landed strangely heavy.

"Ghosts are the only explanation for what I've seen, sirs." A stray sunbeam caught the clipboard Farris clutched to his chest, his eyes distant, far away in a memory. "Back 'fore I moved my family from the Rim and the border closed, I seen them all the time. Tall like a man, but moved like a wisp, coming out at night, silent like, eyes as big as an owl's. Took my little girl with them, they did. Never saw her again."

"They took your child?" The world around Orpheus weighed strangely, cold fingers crawling up his spine.

"Straight from her crib, they did." Farris nodded sadly, meeting Orpheus' eyes like the grief he felt was shared.

"Farris, ghosts aren't real, and your daughter died from an infection, remember? That's why you moved your family from the Rim in the first place."

"I suppose," Farris said, unconvinced. "Don't change the fact that east ain't fit for no man, alive or dead. Can't trust anyone that walks it like a ghost."

Orpheus stared at Farris like *he* was the ghost.

"You okay?" Fenrir asked, suddenly close.

Orpheus jerked around to face him. "Is *he* okay?" he hissed under his breath.

Fenrir laughed, low enough only Orpheus could hear. "He's fine. The stories have gotten worse over the years. No one pays them any mind."

"Is that normal?" Orpheus glanced over at where Farris sorted through a ring of keys. "To be serving at his age?"

Fenrir's eyes held his. "By the end of the war, we were lucky to have what soldiers were left."

THE CRACK AT THE HEART OF EVERYTHING

"The casualty reports—" Orpheus cut off when he saw a flicker of discomfort cross Fenrir's expression. "—I suppose they didn't paint the full picture."

"No," Fenrir said simply, anathema to the play of emotions Orpheus read in his face. The urge to push Fenrir into a greater explanation caught in his throat. Something small and intangible inside Orpheus insisted now was not the time.

Which wasn't exactly an excuse for why he blurted out, "I'm sorry."

Silence swelled, a strange elasticity threading this moment to the last. Orpheus didn't know what else to do beside panic. But right as his pulse was about to kick into overdrive, he looked up, and Fenrir smiled.

"Thanks, Fifi," shouldn't have inspired the kindle of heat in his gut, but there it was all the same.

He followed Fenrir at a distance, looking around the garage first as an excuse to avoid whatever had just happened, second because the vehicles truly made what he'd worked on feel archaic. If someone had told Orpheus he'd stepped back in time three-hundred years, he'd have been hard pressed not to believe them.

Vehicles of every shape were parked in neat lines, massive trucks with bulbous headlights and grated fronts and tarp-covered beds that stood taller than he and Fenrir. There were smaller vehicles, two-wheeled bikes with armored shielding and something Orpheus wanted to call a tank but couldn't quite wrap his head around whether that was the correct term. And far in the back where the bay door stood halfway open, a stitched-together quilt of tarps had been thrown over something so enormous he couldn't begin to identify it. And then there were the racks. Hundreds—no, thousands of firearms were secured behind the metal caging of a trig-level gun rack, more than enough guns to outfit the entirety of the Stacks in case of a dragon attack. Certainly, enough for an army, but Orpheus knew the armory in the palace was where most of their guns were stored.

Fenrir must be thinking the same thing. "You've got quite the collection, Farris."

"It's what you requested, sir."

Fenrir cleared his throat and Orpheus rolled his eyes. "Making up for something, are you Rawkner?"

Tears were beading the corners of Fenrir's eyes when Farris handed him a set of keys and a clipboard with a piece of paper, the sound of his laughter echoing through the garage.

"Sign off here, if you would, Sir."

Fenrir scratched out what Orpheus assumed was his signature but actually said: "LADY LORE'S FAVORITE." He dangled the clipboard obnoxiously in front of Orpheus' nose.

"He can't read," Fenrir whispered after handing the clipboard back.

"You're such a menace." Orpheus sneered, crossing his arms over his chest—the place inside where that heat had gone from a kindle to a flame. But he couldn't hide how his sneer quirked up into a smile, a fact not lost on Fenrir.

"Wanna see something really funny?" Fenrir slid an arm around Orpheus' shoulders like he had the day before. This time, he didn't immediately let go.

Something about it was different now. Orpheus didn't jump like he should have. Didn't push his arm away or snap an ember of flame in his face. And he couldn't help but think of that morning. Waking to Fenrir in the bed beside his, the peace he'd felt, comfortable and at ease.

When he looked up at Fenrir his face was close enough Orpheus could see his pale blue eyes were ringed by a deep shade of indigo. Orpheus swallowed around the sensation of his heart climbing into his throat.

"Keep a straight face." Fenrir continued when Orpheus stood there stupidly saying nothing. Arm around his shoulders, Fenrir walked him around the vehicle to the passenger side seat. "Sit," came out low enough to bottom out somewhere below his navel.

Orpheus didn't protest, he buckled under the pressure of Fenrir's hand on his shoulder, pushing a shaking breath through his teeth when Fenrir didn't immediately move it away.

It was a very strong hand. Fenrir had to feel him trembling. Orpheus was sure of it when Fenrir stared at him for one prolonged moment before turning away.

His hand went with him, though the impression remained burned into Orpheus' memory.

"Orpheus here hasn't ridden in a vehicle like this before, Farris," Fenrir announced. "I think he could benefit from the safety demonstration."

"Oh! Of course, if you let me—I would—over here—" Farris scrambled across the garage to a work table and a toolbox, the screaming whine of rusty hinges loud enough to make Orpheus flinch. When Farris returned, it was with an arm full of supplies and... the smallest, fanciest cap Orpheus had ever seen.

Farris fit it atop his head as if it were Lore's very own crown.

"Gentlemen," he announced, voice carrying a command Orpheus did not think Farris capable of. "If you would please direct your attention to me for the vehicle safety demonstration."

"Rawkner," Orpheus growled under his breath. "What in all hells is he doing?"

Fenrir put a single finger to his lips, a silent *shh*.

"In your passenger glove compartment is your vehicle safety sheet. Please retrieve it now so that you may follow along with the demonstration." Farris paused here and looked directly at Orpheus, face stern and expectant and absolutely nothing like the Farris from three minutes ago.

"I want the other one back," Orpheus hissed as Fenrir leaned forward with a half-smothered snicker. The glove compartment clicked open, and a tumble of papers spilled into Orpheus' lap.

Fenrir plucked a single well-worn pamphlet from the pile and slipped it into Orpheus' twitching hands.

"But look, he's so happy," Fenrir murmured into his ear. "Just sit back and enjoy the show."

"Your vehicle is an F-class off-road armored personal utility transport capable of carrying six fully kitted soldiers and a chassis-mounted weapons array. Each of the six seats is equipped with a seatbelt which you will find at either the right—" Farris made a sweeping gesture towards Orpheus, then a second towards the driver's side, "—or left side of the vehicle. To engage the seatbelt, draw the nylon strap across your body and insert the latch into the lock. The seatbelt will adjust automatically—"

Suddenly, Fenrir reached across Orpheus, crowding so close he could smell the shampoo he'd used on his hair last night. A hand brushed his hip, a mechanical lock clicked into place, then something tightened across his chest. The seat belt.

"Safety first," Fenrir murmured, breath hitting Orpheus' cheek, the strap across his chest cinching him in tight when Fenrir gave it a little tug. By now Orpheus was on fire.

"I hate you," he hissed, despite the heady way his heart pounded.

Fenrir simply grinned and tapped the pamphlet in Orpheus' fist as he leaned away. Blood flooded Orpheus' face. It was clear his options were to look at Farris or Fenrir or the safety data sheet, and because the first two were not actually real options, Orpheus chose the safety sheet, and immediately grimaced when he saw the scribbled-over maze of words and images. Someone had taken black ink to the yellow peeling laminate, and he couldn't decide which was more horrifying: the messy scrawl indicating the safety sheet's updates or the winged-like monstrosity it was originally intended for.

"In addition to the seatbelts, your vehicle is equipped with a roll cage for the case of an off-terrain incident. Please be warned that the airbags are not currently functioning—" Orpheus ignored Farris and shoved a finger at the picture of what looked like a flying metal bird.

"Is that a plane?"

"Yeah, you've seen one before?"

"Yes—no—only in books!" Orpheus sputtered, wondering if Lore had found a fucking plane and then if she had gotten that working too. He looked up at Fenrir with every intention to ask precisely that except—

"Gentlemen!" Farris nearly shouted.

Orpheus and Fenrir looked up in horrified, synchronized tandem.

"May I remind you that this safety demonstration is for your own *safety*," Farris said with an inspired finger pointed at the pamphlet in Orpheus' hands. Orpheus raised it up, mostly to hide how badly his face was turning red.

"Sorry, Captain," Fenrir said through his sharp-toothed smile.

Farris gave them both a pained look and then straightened up again, chin raised and hands clasped behind his back, looking between them as if this were the most important part of the entire demonstration. "Finally, please remember to keep your arms and legs inside the vehicle at all times and enjoy your ride in the Empire's F-class personnel utility transport!"

Orpheus released a breath he hadn't intended to hold, slouching down as far as the seatbelt would allow while ignoring Fenrir's stifled laughter. A hand squeezed his shoulder again, more gentle than before, as if to say: *Good job*, and then Fenrir climbed into the vehicle beside him.

From over the dash, he watched Farris remove the tiny cap from his head, and with it the safety instructor persona. He smiled at them, a big dopey grin that made Orpheus wonder how the fuck Lore had won her Empire at all if these were the kind of people at her disposal.

When the vehicle roared to life, Orpheus got a first-hand reminder.

"Thanks for the demonstration, Farris!" Fenrir shouted over the chugging of the engine, "I'll have this back in a few hours!"

"No rush at all, General!" Farris waved, his smile—and good nature—returned. "If you need anything there's a walkie in the fire box!"

The screech of metal against metal tore through the garage as a massive bay door squealed opened before them, the sudden spill of sunlight drowning out Orpheus' vision in a flood of white. And then they were shooting forward, momentum pushing him into the seat, the cinch of the seatbelt pathetic in comparison to the force of physics compressing his chest.

They tore out of the garage at top speed, Fenrir whooping loudly beside him, voice carrying over the roar of the engine, so much louder than Achates' guttural chug. Beyond the garage door, the wasteland sprawled in a wide swath of dull-stained color, the oil field's pumps rising and falling against a golden-green horizon, smog hanging low and hazy where the land met the sky.

It was beautiful, in the same way the spindly struggle of the pine forest was beautiful—desolate but not empty—a liminal space, where neither life nor death were anything more than a fledgling dream.

Orpheus tipped his head back in quiet wonder, wind tickling his face as the vehicle moved through the world at what should have felt like a reckless speed. It didn't. Maybe the safety demonstration had worked, or maybe it was Fenrir beside him, one big hand steady on the steering wheel, the other on the gear shift between them, eyes blown translucent in the golden sunlight, the whip of his hair soft, the crook of his smile deep.

Orpheus felt comfortable, safe, with Fenrir at his side.

Their eyes met, Fenrir's head tipped gently towards him, the hand on the gear flexing its grip. His knuckles were close, close enough to brush Orpheus' leg if he allowed it, and some wild, animistic part of him begged to do exactly that.

What would happen if you did? a tiny voice inside his head whispered.

Instead, Orpheus let his head fall back and his eyes drift low. Let his leg remain where it was, Fenrir's hand no more than a ghost of a touch, there but not there, an option not yet within Orpheus' reach.

Already, the Stacks were far behind them, the brick buildings and refinery towers less dark and looming under the lens of a cloudless sun. To his right, darkness rose, the southern horizon broken by the massive rise of Lore's mountain, a smear of shadow against the otherwise bright afternoon. Orpheus turned away as if it held something worse than his memories, found Fenrir still watching him— a question in the cant of his mouth, the cast of his eyes.

He didn't ask, but Orpheus heard him regardless, the unspoken, *Everything okay?* that Fenrir had asked often enough at this point to be called a habit. Strangely, had he asked, Orpheus' answer would have been a curious, *I think so.*

A little farther out—farther west—the light bent strange. It took a moment for Orpheus to realize what it was, the orange-red glow of the burning gas pits almost ephemeral beyond the low-hanging smog. Those blackened fingers rose up, a hand forever clawing at a sky it couldn't reach, the inferno it would never escape. This was the direction Fenrir headed towards. West. Towards the fire. Towards the dragon.

"Red asked if we could take a look at some of the stuff they've found out here," Fenrir said without Orpheus having to ask. "Think they're pretty worried about that dragon."

"Have you ever seen one?" Orpheus asked, raising his voice to be heard over the engine, "A dragon?"

"Once, I think." Fenrir didn't elaborate, and before Orpheus could ignore the thing inside him that said this was another one of *those* times—when he needed to leave Fenrir well enough alone—the vehicle jolted over something that threw Orpheus up out of his seat.

He hung suspended in a moment of terrifying weightlessness, before his seatbelt snapped him back into place.

"I believe this is what that safety pamphlet would call turbulence," Fenrir laughed when they jerked again—sideways this time—the ground dipping out from underneath them. "Might want to hold on to something, ride gets pretty rough out here."

The vehicle danced over the rocky terrain, the dips and breaks in the earth increasing the closer they got to that strange fiery glow. Dirt kicked up in voluminous clouds, a trail of dust in their wake that arose in glittering puffs as their tires caught and slid over the cracked-open earth.

Here, the ground had turned brown and arid. Desiccated grass clung to the dirt between the shattered sun-bleached concrete slabs of what Orpheus guessed was an ancient road. A little bit of paint remained on the concrete, stripes of white and the occasional bit of yellow standing out from all the gray. Orpheus wondered where it led, if it had been important, or simply convenient. If their ancestors had known how little of what they'd built would survive—or whether the future had been on their minds at all.

The more he saw, the less he understood—of their intentions, but also their vision. Mostly, he wondered if it was worth dredging back up. Because the Incident hadn't caused this damage. Time hadn't caused this damage. It had existed before. That much he knew to be true.

"There, do you see?" Fenrir called out beside him, pointing to a spot in the distance, a dark little building perched atop a hill where the light limned strangely.

And all at once, he realized he almost missed it. Almost overlooked the smoke seeping through the fractured concrete, the tiny burning embers floating on the wind, the sting of ash amongst the scent of exhaust, and the way the world warmed, almost hot despite the cold winter wind coming down off the mountain.

Fire—an eternity's inferno—here where the world burned, just beneath their feet.

CHAPTER XII
NESTING

Two sentries stood sentinel at the edge of the vast, smoking expanse of concrete and mangled steel. The red-orange haze of the fires shimmered in the distance, fingers of blackened ruins wavering along the horizon, embers catching and flaring, riding the cold wind coming down off the mountain. Where the pine woods had struggled to thrive on the mountain peaks, here those same trees were gray husks—dead things striking marks against the wasteland, earth made unnatural by forces long dead—the men and women of history here in the memory of the fuel lines they'd once worked so hard to lay.

"We set up this outpost to monitor the fires," Red said, scuffing her boot over the broken concrete slab where an Incendiary Beetle kept trying to climb over her foot. Tiny flames crawled across its back in its harmless unlit state. "It's always attracted a fair amount of shit, but the dragon is new. First sign we found was about three weeks ago, I suspect it's been hanging around a little longer than that."

"No signs of it within the Stacks, though?" Fenrir crossed his arms over his chest, squinting out across the cracked concrete wasteland.

"Not yet," Red said simply as she scuffed at the ground again. The Incendiary Beetle finally gave up, trundling over a slope of concrete to disappear into one of the many smoking crevices. Orpheus released a breath he hadn't intended to hold. "I can't take any chances. Not now. Not like before."

Fenrir nodded, fingers tapping atop his bicep, muscles flexing under skin warmed by days spent under a sun just like this one. He stood outside the deep shade the lookout tower provided, the perfect cover for Orpheus to hide from the burning landscape before him. He didn't know what it was about the cracked-open earth that disturbed him so much, but some buried instinct kept him rooted to this very spot.

If there's actually a dragon out there, you won't find it—it'll find you, that awful voice inside his head reminded him.

"—What do you know about dragons, Fifi?" Fenrir asked, and it took him a full two seconds to drag his eyes away from the red-orange glow in the not-far-enough distance, eyes snapping to Fenrir's like the dragon was already here and Fenrir was the only thing standing between him and imminent death. Maybe that explained the soft smile Fenrir gave him. Whatever Orpheus might have said died in his throat, his face turning a brilliant shade of crimson.

"I— well— dragons are— they like— uh— fire—" he unhelpfully stuttered.

"But a lot of hell beasts are attracted to fire," Fenrir filled in when it became clear Orpheus was still rediscovering language. "And from what I understand dragons aren't normally aggressive unless they're provoked, or feel their territory is threatened."

Orpheus shifted from one foot to another, nodding his head when Red looked at him for confirmation. The ground wasn't hot enough to melt the soles, but in the dead of summer, he imagined it'd be close. Heat, in massive, limitless quantity. The perfect nesting ground for a dragon. So perfect that Orpheus wondered how one hadn't discovered it before now. While incredibly rare, dragons had been recorded throughout the last several thousand years of history—that one might make a nest here where the pulse of the planet lay open and exposed not only made sense, but it was also basically an invitation.

"What have you found?" he finally asked Red, relieved that he'd managed to string together a whole sentence. "What kind of evidence?"

"Easier to show you."

Red pulled a device from her pocket, bringing it to her mouth while squinting up at the lookout tower and the two sentries stationed at the top. "We won't be long but let me know the first sign of anything strange. Got it?" she said into the device. Orpheus recognized it now, a match to the walkie Farris had pointed out in the firebox.

His eyes widened when two disembodied voices crackled a reply, "Yes, sir!"

Red must have caught his expression because she gave him a wink. "Come on, follow me."

Over the broken, cracked landscape, along a route that took them around the worst of the smoking pits, Red led them towards the unknown. Fires burned incessantly, the air tinged with the gaseous tang of sulfur, smoke carrying white drifts of cloud high up into the sky. Where the wind kicked up, embers spiraled, flaring and dying like tiny amber stars, their heat never lasting longer than a belated, curious sting against his skin. But it was the ground that revealed the worst of the destruction—the churned-up mess of concrete and earth that reminded Orpheus on some visceral, immediate level of the scar though the mountainside—the smoldering Netherflame that, unlike this fire, would never go out, no matter how many thousands of years the flames burned.

Beneath his feet, the ground shifted, a skitter of gravel going over a ledge Orpheus didn't remember seeing three seconds ago. He felt a hand on his upper arm and a pressure guiding him away before the concrete beneath his shoes sunk into itself, a curl of smoke trailing free in this new, ever-changing hellscape.

"Keep to the bigger chunks," Fenrir said quietly into his ear. Orpheus didn't realize he was shaking until the sensation of Fenrir's hand on his arm lingered past the point of courtesy.

By the time they reached wherever it was Red was leading them, he was outright scrambling over concrete the size of boulders. Fenrir was a constant at his side, offering a hand when he needed it and hovering beside him when he didn't. It didn't help that Orpheus' breath was coming thin enough to make a wheezing sound in his chest, and while he could blame some of that on the smoke and gasses he was breathing, most of it was pure physical inactivity.

He was going to be sore the next morning, that much he was sure of. That was, if he lived to see tomorrow in the first place.

"Here," Red said, "this is some of the worst we've come across."

Etched into the concrete in a half-circle were the claw marks belonging to some kind of massive beast. The immediate area was clear of any chipped-away bits that would have been created by the gouges, but when Orpheus let his peripheral vision take in the whole scene he saw the enormous semi-circle of swept away debris—the clearing the creature had made for itself before it settled down for a long night's nap.

"Could be a dragon," Fenrir said, a frown on his face. "Could also be a gargoyle, or a gryphon."

"Gryphon's aren't attracted to heat, and gargoyles turn to stone during the day. If one was nesting here, your scouts likely would have come across it, or seen it from the lookout. Also, generally they are not dangerous. Most hell beasts aren't, unless you get too close to their feeding ground." Orpheus knew, because of all the people on this hells-damned planet, he was the only one who seemed to stir them into a mindless rage, all because of his damned curse. "Also, the semi-circle clearing suggests a tail swept away most of the debris. A gryphon's tail is neither large nor strong enough to do that."

"Could be a manticore. Killed one of those once, nasty fuckers," Fenrir added as if he were ticking off creatures from a tally he kept in his head. Orpheus narrowed his eyes and considered the likelihood Fenrir had faced down most of the world's various hell beasts at one point in his life or another and was actually looking forward to fighting another.

Not that they were fighting a dragon. Not yet, at least.

"Manticores don't fly," Orpheus ruled out. "You'd have a lot more than a semi-circle of gouges if a manticore was hunting nearby. They also would not thrive well in this kind of terrain. They're large, and very heavy." He thought again of the sinking concrete he'd nearly slipped into, what little weight it took before crumbling into dust beneath his feet.

"So, a dragon," Red said, voice deflating. "Fuck, I was hoping you two would have some good news."

"It hasn't attacked the Stacks, so it likely has an established hunting ground?" Orpheus tried. Red merely gave him what Fenrir would call the stink eye.

"You mean the refugees still hiding out in camps across the wasteland? Or the deer in the southern forests Lore basically hunted into re-extinction?"

Orpheus flinched like she'd directed the question at him rather than the proverbial powers that be—as if Orpheus had anything to do with Lore's irresponsible hunting habits.

"She had an army to feed," didn't seem to mean much to Red, because she scowled deeper and turned towards the scratches with a huff.

"Feed is an overstatement, either that or deer meat tastes suspiciously like week old trash," Fenrir unhelpfully added—a sharp-toothed grin on his face. "Have you ever tasted trash, Fifi?"

"Rawkner," Orpheus drawled, "the only person here I know who voluntarily eats trash is you."

Fenrir made an exaggerated face of confusion, palm slapping to his chest for added effect. "Come on, those meal packets don't taste that bad."

"Would you two stop flirting for one fucking second, I can't think!" Red snapped.

The world went very, very silent.

Flirting. Were they *flirting?*

When he looked at Fenrir it wasn't denial he saw but the faintest tinge of pink across his nose. Orpheus would have thought he was falling backwards through a hole in the ground with how strange gravity felt.

You've been flirting, that voice inside his head viciously sang. *You've been flirting this whole time.*

"I'm not flirting!" he spat in case there was any doubt besides his own.

He refused to look at Fenrir again. Refused to confront his stupid blush and his stupider grin and all those stupid muscles.

"So, we are dealing with a dragon, and we can assume it's simply a matter of time before it shows up in the Stacks." Red ignored him, choosing to confront what was, Orpheus thought, the second most important topic at hand—the first being someone else acknowledging that he was not, indeed, flirting with Fenrir.

"We need to get rid of it," Red snapped, spinning towards them. "How do we get rid of it?"

"Well—" Fenrir began, but Orpheus cut him off.

"You're not fighting a dragon!"

Fenrir raised his eyebrows high enough to wrinkle his forehead.

"No, he's right, it's too dangerous." At least Red agreed. "We need to lure it away somehow." Except...oh, that was worse.

Orpheus' mouth went dry, and his body went buzzy, the eerie silence of the broken hellscape he stood upon suddenly suffocating.

A lure. He could be a lure. He could be their *bait*.

Orpheus looked at Fenrir like he could save him from this spiral he was most certainly going down. The look Fenrir leveled on him was clear: *don't you dare say it*. They were both thinking the same thing and coming to identical conclusions, their only saving grace that Orpheus wasn't some magnanimous self-sacrificing sword-jockey with muscles larger than his brain.

Apparently, neither was Fenrir—at least when it came to him.

He cares about the Stacks, Orpheus' mind whispered, *but he cares about me, too.*

Orpheus shoved his hands into his sleeves and turned away, the fingernails he dug into his wrists enough to drown out the sound of his thoughts.

"I don't expect either of y'all to endanger yourself over this," Red said in a firm voice. "Lore and her ridiculous skeleton should be down here, making sure her hells-damned grid stays up, but she hasn't answered any of my petitions."

THE CRACK AT THE HEART OF EVERYTHING

Orpheus opened his mouth to suggest something even more ridiculous than him acting as bait: maybe he could talk to Lore on the Stacks' behalf. His jaw snapped shut before so much as a breath could spill free.

As little as he desired to become dragon bait, he desired even less trudging back up that mountain to face Lore.

"Let's get back," Red sighed, "I've got time, if not options."

The sun arced high through the sky, well past its zenith but burning down with an intensity that chased winter from the air. Sweat beaded under Orpheus' arms, the wavering horizon just as likely due to the fires as it was his own mounting exhaustion. By the time the lookout tower reappeared, Orpheus was nearly delirious. He needed a break, some water, a cold shower—possibly a nap—and that's where his thoughts drifted when the ground beneath him shuddered, and then began to collapse.

"Grab hold of something!" Red shouted over the scraping rumble of stone against stone, the chunk of concrete beneath their feet lurching sideways.

His boots slipped, his balance tipped, and Orpheus hit the ground with a muffled *whoosh* of breath. He was sliding towards the edge before he could stop himself, hands scrabbling for any handhold he could find, jerking back when a geyser of smoke and gas shot out of the concrete cracking around him. Rotten eggs and burnt iron flooded his nose and throat and he choked—heat flooding his lungs as he gasped for clean air. And as the world shook around him, his body began to slide. He couldn't see. He could hardly breathe. And there was nothing for him to grab hold to, nothing but loose gravel and sun-peeled paint.

Well, at least it wasn't the curse that would kill him in the end.

Something solid slammed into his back and a fist grabbed his collar. Then, the world swept away in a current of wind and air as he sailed—no *flew* over the crumbling concrete—past the danger that had nearly swallowed him whole, towards a safety he kept telling himself he shouldn't get used to, held against a solid barrel of a body—Fenrir's absolute wall of a chest—and every suppressed thought from the last two weeks flooded his head as he descended towards reality again.

They landed with a jolt, stumbling, Orpheus gasping in a breath at the precise moment Fenrir's arm cinched around his waist, holding him close. Goosebumps prickled across his skin, hot and electric. The Orpheus of two weeks ago would have slapped that arm away and then cast a shattering spell on the ground beneath Fenrir's feet, dropping him into that pit full of fire or just straight into hell itself. But when he pressed his hand to Fenrir's chest to do just that...he couldn't. No, he didn't *want* to.

Orpheus swallowed around the lump in his throat—the sensation of his heart pounding out of his chest.

Fenrir held him steady as he failed to find his feet, body shaking too hard to stand upright, let alone take his weight. He shook against Fenrir's chest, staring at the hand he had pressed there, the way his fingertips curled against the leather, scratching or searching or simply trying to hold on to whatever it was about this moment that could possibly make sense.

"It's okay, I have you," Fenrir said into his ear, voice soft, claim bold.

Orpheus believed him. He *trusted* him. And maybe that was why his knees buckled when he finally tried to shove him away.

"Whoa there," Fenrir breathed, Orpheus stumbling right back into his chest. Fenrir did, quite summarily, *have him*, at least in the somatic sense: the weight of his arm around his waist, the sensation of his hand settling on Orpheus' hip. Of fingers curling, and then holding—a pressure building, without release.

Heat that had nothing to do with the inferno raging meters below their feet flared all throughout Orpheus' body.

Kind hands. Gentle hands. Kind gentle hands all over him, all over his body. Making him feel good and safe and happy and lo—

"—Fifi?" Fenrir asked, voice right there beside his ear.

The thin whine of breath passing through teeth started innocently enough, but then it twisted, going lower, deeper, a rumble and a shifting that quaked Orpheus straight down to his soul.

He and Fenrir both froze as they realized in tandem that Orpheus

THE CRACK AT THE HEART OF EVERYTHING
had *moaned.*

He shoved at Fenrir, palms splayed across his chest as Fenrir loosened his arm enough that Orpheus could get some breathing room. Fenrir didn't let go, but maybe that was for the best. Orpheus' legs were still weak, his knees shaking. And Fenrir was looking at him as if he were about to say something—something Orpheus didn't need to hear to understand.

"If you tell me to stop spiraling, I will kill you," he breathed, hands shaking, fingers clawing, leaving little indentured marks against Fenrir's leather armor.

"Well, you should," Fenrir said. Then, as if realizing his own error, "Stop spiraling I mean. Please don't kill me."

The unlikely sound of Orpheus' laugh scratched through his ears, and under his palms he felt the rumble of Fenrir's own.

"You two okay?" Red's voice carried over the thin sound of their hesitant laughter, her head poking up over the edge of one of the collapsed concrete slabs. "Y'all didn't fall in, did ya?"

"We're fine!" Fenrir called out over his shoulder, "think Fifi's a little shook, give us a sec?"

The look Red threw Fenrir made it clear she saw through his ruse, but she played along anyway, turning away and giving them something close to a shred of privacy, not that they needed it. Because nothing was happening—

"Take your time," Fenrir continued, talking like Orpheus wasn't going on thirty seconds of hanging off him like some ill-swooning damsel. Then a thumb slid along his hip, and Orpheus realized Fenrir was outright touching him in a way that no longer had anything to do with keeping him vertical on this hells-damned planet.

Whatever little bit of decorum he'd held onto dissolved.

"*Fenrir,*" he said for possibly the first time in his life.

"Okay, who are you and what have you done with Fifi?" Fenrir joked but it sounded tense, the fingers on his hip flexing, then relaxing, over and over, like Fenrir was fighting to restrain himself.

No, that wasn't possible. None of this was *possible.*

Not Fenrir touching him. Not him holding him. Nor that Orpheus was allowing it—was in fact doing nothing within his power to stop it. And that wild, animistic part of him that had begged to touch Fenrir's hand in the ride out here sang alongside the voice in his head, the one repeating—over and over—that Red was right and Fenrir had been flirting with him for years now, and Orpheus could only now see it for what it was.

"I'm—" Orpheus choked, struggling to remain standing. Fenrir gripped him tighter, holding him up when Orpheus might have crumbled, only his head tipping forward onto Fenrir's shoulder. The heat of his skin burned close, his scent heavy on his tongue. And when he felt Fenrir's nose brush his ear, heard the slow draw of a long inhale and everything inside him turned to fire, Orpheus confronted what had been weeks or months or possibly years building between them— a deeply-rooted connection that had nothing to do with hate or rivalry but simple infallible chemistry.

You're attracted to him, that traitorous voice accused, *you're attracted to Fenrir Rawkner.*

Oh.

Oh—

"*Shit*," stuttered through his mind for two full terrifying seconds before he realized it was Fenrir who had spoken aloud and not the hells-damned voice inside his head.

He noticed it, finally. There at the back of his boot, a glowing hot ember chewing a path of fire through the leather—the Incendiary Beetle, ignited into a walking ball of flame.

Fenrir was already moving—dropping to his knees and batting at the beetle in his best attempt to knock it away without blowing himself up—Orpheus felt the moment break. Felt the world spiral back into place as his mind caught up to his hells-damned body and a crushing wave of confused disappointment slammed into him like a brick to the face. If Fenrir weren't currently busy figuring out a way to crush an Incendiary Beetle without the use of his hands or feet Orpheus would have likely grabbed the thing and blown himself back up Lore's mountain, gone straight to her throne room and begged her to take him back for how utterly lost he suddenly felt.

THE CRACK AT THE HEART OF EVERYTHING

"You're doing it again," Fenrir said, a little breathless, when he swept upright. Several yards away, a burning carapace belched smoke into the air. In front of Orpheus' face, one tiny flame chewed its way up a wavy lock of Fenrir's tousled hair. Orpheus gave up at the same moment he gave in, reaching out with a flick of Netherflame to smother the ensuing blaze.

His fingers touched Fenrir's hair, fire sputtering out in the face of that strangling cold, and Orpheus watched something in Fenrir transform. *That* smile slid over his face, the soft small one he only used on him.

Orpheus again imagined Fenrir falling through the crust of the earth, but for some reason, this time he was there too, falling together, and they both seemed pretty damned pleased about it.

He stood frozen, caught in the moment, hand half-raised as if it was Fenrir's cheek he had meant to brush his fingers against.

You like him, that voice whispered again, less accusatory and more amazed. *I like Fenrir Rawkner.*

Fenrir lifted his hand, touched Orpheus' wrist, carefully, like he knew exactly what he was doing, what he was touching. And as his fingers closed over Orpheus' wrist, the gentle squeeze he gave him said so much more than any words could possibly encompass. Not that Orpheus wanted to hear them. Because he didn't. He most certainly did not want to hear anything Fenrir had to say about any of this—

"You okay?" Fenrir asked.

"Yes," he lied.

The look Fenrir gave him was indecipherable, soft in a way Orpheus didn't recognize, the shift of his body tight, like he was caught between one decision and the next. It occurred to Orpheus that he'd never seen Fenrir like this before and something about that was reassuring—the idea that Fenrir was as out of his depth as Orpheus leveling the cracked-open earth they both stood upon.

"What was that?" Red snapped when Orpheus reluctantly followed Fenrir over the slab of concrete. "What happened?"

"Uh, well—" Fenrir froze and looked at Orpheus, who unhelpfully refused to fill in the blank because he was too busy turning crimson.

"Those things are normally harmless. Why did it blow up?" Red, blessedly, clarified.

"I'm cursed," Orpheus breathed, claiming what had, strangely enough, become the lesser of two confessions. "Hell beasts have been trying to kill me since I summoned Ohm and his army." He figured Red knew that much already. "We think the spell caused the curse. It's why we're headed to the Keep, to try and find a counter."

He held his breath as the panicked expression on Red's face was directed at Fenrir rather than him, but Orpheus supposed that made sense. Fenrir had brought him here, after all. Granted, her, "Should y'all be here?" hit a little harder than he anticipated.

"It's fine," Fenrir assured no one but himself. "Nothing I can't handle."

"That's not what I'm worried about," Red snapped at Fenrir, abruptly turning back to Orpheus with a pained expression contorting her face, "I never would have asked y'all out here if I'd known. I put you in danger, Orpheus."

I'm the one putting you in danger, Orpheus probably should have said instead of:

"I'm sorry."

Red held his eyes, expression unreadable, so different from the frown she gave Fenrir that Orpheus wondered if he hadn't actually said something wrong. Because there was no shaking the impression that this was all his fault—the dragon and the shattered earth and the danger he was constantly caught up in. He might not be the reason the dragon was hanging around but he sure as hell wasn't helping them by being here either. Orpheus was, for lack of a better term, a ticking time bomb, and now that Red knew, she had every right to throw him out of the Stacks.

You shouldn't be here, that voice inside said, *you're not supposed to be here.*

You should already be dead, whispered underneath the rest.

Just like that, whatever adrenaline had been pulsing through his veins was gone, leaving Orpheus drained, all used up. The world grew loud and shimmery as he stared into a spot on the ground where the sun beat down, bright and blinding but no longer warm—the dark flame inside him too cold—the yawning void too great.

Something touched his elbow. Gentle, but brief.

Fenrir.

Orpheus looked up into his face and saw a mirror of his own. Long and drawn, Fenrir looked sad, and Orpheus knew what he wanted to say, even if he couldn't bring himself to do it.

Stop spiraling, went unspoken, but maybe Fenrir understood it was already too late.

"Let's get back to the Stacks," Red said, and Orpheus turned away—breaking their connection. Red remained close as she continued to say, "I think we could all use a drink."

Then she clapped a hand on his shoulder, weight heavy, her grip strong.

"Thank you for helping, Orpheus," she said, "and though I'm not too good at this magic stuff, if there's anything I can do to help with the curse, you say the word."

And it was like Fenrir had his hands back on him, because this too, no one had ever done for him before.

She cares, Orpheus thought. *Without any good reason, she cares.*

As Red led them back to the shadow of the watchtower while making them promise to meet her for a drink at a place called Old Patsy's, Orpheus thought at least two people might miss him, once the curse finally caught up and he was dead and gone.

And as he rode passenger to Fenrir—wind in his hair, sun on his face, hand curled atop the gear shift, tipped towards him like an option he hadn't thought himself able to take—he considered what that meant. If he actually wasn't ready for what was happening between them, or if it was simply fear holding him back. And did he really want to die before getting the chance to know?

That was, perhaps, what scared Orpheus the most—that for all the changes happening in his life, he wouldn't live long enough to see how it could turn out.

At least that made it easier to walk away.

"Fifi, wait!" Fenrir called out from, hand raised and body turned as if he were about to follow him out of the garage and into the street if not for Farris. "Tonight, just a drink, meet me at Old Patsy's—please!"

Orpheus said nothing. He kept walking, eyes low as he slid into the alley outside the garage while Fenrir tried to disengage from Farris' incessant chattering. As soon as he turned the corner, a spell whispered past his lips, Netherflame glittering cold sparks into the sole of his boot, the curl of violet smoke all that was left when he disappeared into the closing shadows and fled.

INTERLUDE
PAIN

The filtered light of the Library has turned everything gray. Raindrops patter the glass windows, a gentle rhythm anathema to the racing beat of Orpheus' heart. He chokes again as his legs nearly give out, the pain in his stomach curdling like the hand of god itself has reached inside him and clamped down on his guts. The trek here has cost him, but he doesn't know where else to go. The hermits usually give him more time between sessions but when he saw the golden light of their lantern passing under the crack of the bathroom door in the direction of his bedroom, he knew he had to go.

They'll find him eventually, but the Library always seems to be the last place they look.

"What's wrong with you?" Lore snaps when Orpheus stumbles into the stack of history books he's been sorting for the last week. His hand hits the floor a second before his face would have, and he pushes a breath past his teeth as his stomach muscles seize and clench.

"Hurts—" he forces out, slipping forward until his forehead touches the blessedly cold floor.

He sees from behind the fall of his hair the way Lore has clutched the silver band circling her wrist. The skin of her wrist is pale, colorless like the rest of her. The skin of Orpheus' wrist is anything but. Tracks of blue-purple streak like poison in his veins, the silver band so tight he wonders how there's any room left for his blood to circulate. His flesh is swollen, the skin distended as to appear like it's swallowing the band whole. That, at least, had concerned the hermits, though they'd done nothing to help him.

The etchings are glowing less, and Orpheus thinks that's a good sign. They'd been a faint purple for the last two weeks, growing brighter with the setting of the sun last night, the moonless sky a black expanse that had sucked the light out of his tiny bedroom, so he'd thought that the reason why the band seemed so much brighter. Now he knows it was something else. Something that now pulses through his body. Something that feels cold despite the swollen heat of his wrist, the fever in his brain.

A hand touches him, and his whole body jerks. Lore flinches away, hissing like she's been stung, and Orpheus regrets everything in that singular timeless instant. If he had held still, she would have kept her hand there—on his shoulder—a comfort he aches for that the hermits have never bothered with. That *no one* has ever bothered with.

"Sorry—" he gasps, rolling onto his side to curl into a ball, "you can—it's fine—"

"I want to see," Lore snaps, short and terse and filled with the most emotion Orpheus has ever heard from her.

He raises his eyes like it's his attention she wants, but instead she snatches his wrist up into her small, pale hands.

Despite the harsh way she handles him, the touch feels good. Warm and real. Orpheus closes his eyes when Lore brings his arm close to stare at the silver band.

He loses track of time, seconds kept in the sensation of Lore's breath over his wrist, the almost pained sound she makes while she holds his arm in her hands. The world shifts in tilting shadows, vertigo clogging his thoughts, a nightmare of a dream taking shape in the *pulsing-clenching-throbbing* of his stomach and the feeling of ice in his veins. He hasn't eaten in days and he thinks of the last meal he'd been given. The bread and broth he'd brought to Lore last night because, for how hungry he may be, she is even more. He doesn't know why the hermits stopped feeding her three weeks ago, only that she told him to bring his meals to the library around the same time his band started glowing violet.

"It's going away," she says after what could have been minutes or hours. His arm hits the ground with a dull thump when it slips from her hands.

He's not sure if she means the light or the pulsing or the pain, but his head is all mixed up now. His body is so cold that it's begun to shut off systems that aren't required to live. His mouth opens to explain but all that comes out is his breath, and then the world goes black. He thinks he's sleeping, but it's possible he's actually dead.

He's not dead.

When Orpheus wakes next, he's back in his room, the sun dull and gray, the pulsing in his body faint, and for the first time in his life, the band on his wrist is gone.

CHAPTER XIII

ACHATES

Achates was warm beneath his palm, coat strangely soft despite how coarse he once thought it had been.

"Has anyone been feeding you, or is it all fuel now?" Orpheus asked while stroking his flank. Achates' eyes rolled back to meet his, big and brown and looking as if he was relieved to have any company that wasn't Fenrir's massive war steed. Orpheus could relate to that feeling. Could in fact admit that was precisely the reason he was here at all. "Should I go find you an apple, or a carrot? Or is it hay that you want instead?"

Outside his stall sat a bale of green hay—the same kind he'd watched the stable hands drag in for the Palace's horses. Orpheus hadn't paid too much attention back then, but he seemed to recall the horses chewing on it, so he reached for some—keeping the gate closed and his movements quick as he snuck some of the hay through the bars of the stall.

He wasn't afraid to be seen, he simply didn't want to be seen *yet*.

Blunt teeth gnashed his palm, snatching up the hay.

"Is that good?"

The snort Achates gave him may have actually been an answer, but Orpheus felt silly enough talking to the beast without succumbing to the delusion that it might talk back.

And yet, he continued.

"That overgrown stallion is a right nuisance, isn't he?" Orpheus said, indicating Fenrir's war horse. Achates said nothing, chewing his hay and watching him, like he was waiting for Orpheus to get at what he really meant.

Orpheus sighed, tucked his hands into his sleeves and held onto his wrists.

"Would you judge me if I said I might be rather taken with his rider?"

Still, no reaction. Achates' gaze was as placid as ever, whether because he didn't understand a word Orpheus said or because he wasn't surprised by any of it.

Orpheus sighed and hung his head. "What if I were more than fond?"

He'd had run-ins with romance over the years. Short-lived obsessions with men that had caught his eye. A courtier who had been fetchingly handsome and strangely good-natured—a young blonde Captain who had come to complete his officer's training never to return again after riding out with one of Lore's deployments. Nothing serious had happened with either. Neither had stuck around the palace long enough for Orpheus to have pursued more than an inkling of attraction. There'd been conversations here and there. An invitation to share a drink the courtier had never taken him up on, and the Captain had never seemed able to get past the implied designation of Orpheus' non-existent rank.

Eventually, he gave up chasing prospects. He had told himself he was okay with that. Had convinced his heart that nothing was amiss. Stolen conversations in dark corners weren't worth the rumor mill the court churned out, and Orpheus was much more content in his solitary chambers where the only whispers were those of memories he couldn't be bothered to dwell on. He didn't need a partner to complicate his life. He didn't want his life complicated at all.

But if talking to a horse who had a hard drive for a brain was any indicator, it was that Orpheus was far lonelier than he'd ever given himself credit for before.

"What's truly terrifying," Orpheus continued, voice low, as if Fenrir's horse might be listening in, "is that I get the impression he might be fond of me too."

Achates whinnied softly, sounding as torn as Orpheus felt.

"I don't know what to do, my friend," he confessed. The fur under his palm bristled as he leaned in close—close enough to tip his forehead against Achates' neck, his mane a tickle across his cheeks. "I feel like my time here is already borrowed. Who in their right mind would want to get to know a dead man?"

Achates didn't have an answer. He looked at Orpheus steadily, big, brown, watery eyes reflecting back all the doubt Orpheus held— his cowardice to confront his limitless ability to deny himself every unnecessary pleasure in life all because it could get in the way of his higher purpose. And how he was still doing precisely that, while his "higher purpose" had blown up in his face.

Even if Orpheus hadn't misinterpreted Fenrir's attraction, whatever Fenrir felt for him was surely a side effect of his playing hero. Not once in all the time they had known each other had Orpheus ever considered Fenrir as anything more than a nuisance. He might be unbearably attractive, and surprisingly adept as a leader, and possessing of at least some amount of wit—a quality Orpheus had always told himself he had a stranglehold on—but to pursue a romantic relationship together? Even if Orpheus weren't one foul step away from death the idea seemed...impossible.

Right?

Orpheus clutched Achates' mane and sighed again. Beneath him, Achates shuffled to the side, out of his reach.

"You think I should go see him?"

Achates snorted, ears flicking, one hoof stomping.

Orpheus sighed. "Fine."

Twilight washed the Stacks in shades of blue, the darkness of a moonless night settling in early with the waning sunlight. Dust kicked up as he walked down the alley, making his way to the mouth of the street and the candy-colored lamplight that filled it. Glass of all shades glowed in long tubular filaments, twining together into signs of scrawled handwriting, decorative baubles on display, and illicit calls to action. As the sky turned to fire and then slowly bled red, Orpheus wandered a world that didn't feel real. He may as well be a ghost of another time already passed—one of those imaginary threats Farris had conjured in place of the brutal reality he lived.

If it weren't for the eyes catching his as he wandered down the sidewalk, he may have believed the tale he spun for himself. A dead man walking was close enough to his own brutal truth. But the people of the Stacks were made of sturdier stuff—grounded in the unyielding surety of what was and would be, rather than the tensile flux of Orpheus' own maybes and what-ifs.

Is that why he felt so small and unspectacular? Like he had blown everything between him and Fenrir out of proportion—made mountains out of nothing, let alone something so inconsequential as his and Fenrir's tenuous friendship.

Old Patsy's emerged from the neon lights like its own kind of ghost.

A comely building of brick walls and golden lamplight, Old Patsy's green and white motif of a beer mug hung from squeaking hinges that had seen better decades. Of all the places to get a drink at in the Stacks, this seemed like the least popular—the drift of voices through the cracked-open windows more of a murmur compared to the cacophony from the other bars Orpheus had passed.

Was it serendipity or chance that had brought him to the place Fenrir had asked him to? Surely it couldn't be fate because Orpheus already knew fate had no interest in working towards his favor. A death curse was hunting him still.

But not tonight. Tonight, Orpheus was already a ghost.

He reached out, pulled the door open, and stepped into the bar.

Light flooded his vision, a wall of sound rushing into his ears, and then the world narrowed in on the only thing that mattered—his doubt and nerves and curse be damned.

Fenrir sat tucked into a booth in the back, Red opposite him, an empty chair there in the void between both. Waiting. Expectant.

Hopeful.

Fenrir turned his head and met his eyes, bright and Rim-pale and glowing with a pleased kind of surprise that Orpheus couldn't help but hope he put there.

Oh hells, he couldn't do this. He wasn't ready to do this.

With a steadying breath, he took a step away from the door, and made his way towards the booth.

CHAPTER XIV
Bar Tricks

Time slipped past him on borrowed seconds, a stretch of infinity he had no right to claim, entropy failing at everything but eating away at his nerves. By the time he actually stepped up to the table, he was in a sweat. Tingles shot up and down his spine, gut churning when he came to an awkward stop outside the light of the low-hanging booth lamp.

"Hey," Fenrir breathed as he stood to greet him.

Their eyes met, Fenrir's gaze level and steady, Orpheus' darting up and down like he couldn't figure out where to look. Barely a breath existed between them when Fenrir sidled around to pull out the empty chair in obvious invitation. Orpheus focused on his breathing while he lowered himself down, cognizant of Fenrir close behind him, the warmth of his body dragging at Orpheus intangibly, making him feel all at once smothered but in a strange, comforting way.

When Fenrir gripped the chair's backrest, Orpheus fought a shiver. When his knuckles brushed his shoulders as he pushed the chair in, Orpheus held his breath. And when Fenrir leaned over him—hair falling around Orpheus' ears, arms a bracket around him—Orpheus had to steel himself from jumping to his feet and fleeing.

I'm okay, became a mantra in his head.

A thumb touched his shoulder, a barely-there pressure, a line of heat that slid down in the most surreptitious of strokes. Suddenly, Orpheus was very much *not* okay. He hunched where he sat, breath coming in shallow, furtive sips, the world feeling all at once too real, too raw, too *much* for him to take. All because Fenrir had touched him. One stupid small slip of his thumb. How little it took to send him spiraling.

Because I want it to mean something, whispered inside him.

Fuck. Orpheus was *fucked.*

This was ridiculous. He didn't even know if this thing between him and Fenrir was reciprocated. He hardly understood the things he felt, let alone what Fenrir must be thinking. He'd never been good at reading people, so he didn't know why he thought he might possess that ability *now.*

With a half-smothered snarl, he shoved his hands in his sleeves and clutched his wrist.

Pain dug in, vicious and searing, grounding him as nothing else could. Seconds ticked, kept by the pulse beneath his nails, sensation drowning out emotion, until Orpheus felt close enough to himself again to open his eyes.

"Welcome back, Sparks." Red said, looking up from his wrist. Orpheus blinked at her and—shit. She'd seen, and Fenrir was gone. Off to the bar, or anywhere else—understanding on some reptilian level that Orpheus needed space. Which, yeah, he absolutely did.

"Sparks?" He said around the dryness of his mouth. Red shrugged, leaning an elbow onto the table, wiggling her fingers in the air as if that was supposed to explain everything.

"Won't anyone on this blasted planet use my name?" But the ridiculous nickname had done something to him—grounded him. Like how when Fenrir used *Fifi* it barely struck a nerve, anymore. A sign of familiarity rather than malice. Red obviously didn't mean anything by it—perhaps Fenrir didn't either.

Speak of the devil.

"I'm back!" Fenrir announced, a round of drinks clutched between his hands—a mug of beer for each of them, offered up like a token of peace, alongside a sheepish: "I don't actually know if you drink."

Fenrir peered down at Orpheus, as if intentionally heading off any apology he might be expected to make—like Fenrir understood he'd crossed a line, even if it had nothing to do with the beer he slid into Orpheus' hands.

A deep, brittle part of him turned to dust when he said, "Only when the occasion calls for it." His voice came out fractured and sandy, edged with emotional disuse. He cleared his throat and tried again: "Like Red said, I think we could all use one after today."

"I'll cheers to that," Red said, holding up her mug. Fenrir settled back into his seat to meet them in a solemn salute.

Their mugs clinked when they came together, beer splashing over the rim to soak Orpheus' fingers.

It was second nature to snap. Netherflame surged over his palm to balance on his fingers, rolling over each and burning away what was left of the beer.

"I'll *never* get used to that."

Netherflame extinguished in an abrupt *poof* of purple smoke. In a different time and place he might have bit out something clever. Instead, he looked at his mug and simply glared.

"Yeah, it's a pretty neat trick, isn't it?" Fenrir said, and the jab made him feel like he was no better than Lore's jester and not the former Master Dark Wizard of her Exalted Court. Except, when Orpheus turned his glare on Fenrir he got caught up in his eyes, gentle and steady and so very blue.

Maybe...Fenrir *wasn't* teasing?

"It's impressive," Fenrir continued, voice quiet, careful, like he knew exactly what Orpheus was thinking.

"It's also not a trick." Orpheus looked away and took another swig of his beer. It was cool on his lips, bitter but flavorful on his tongue, and what could have been unpleasant turned nice, particularly when Fenrir scooted closer and leaned into his space.

Out of the corner of his eye he saw another one of those soft, gentle smiles.

It seemed different, this time. More private than before. Guarded, but not in a careful way—in a searching way. Like Fenrir didn't know if Orpheus would even want it.

I do, that new voice snapped. Orpheus clutched his mug so that Fenrir couldn't see how his hands trembled. *I think I actually do.*

Shadowed by the dim bar light, Fenrir watched him from beneath long, dark eyelashes. If Orpheus had actually read any of those romance novels he'd found in the Palace's library, he would have recognized that Fenrir was making eyes at him. Instead, he chose to ignore him by taking yet another sip of his hells-damned beer.

An enormous bang ricocheted across the tiny booth as Red slammed her empty mug down.

"So!" she said loudly, breaking the moment. "How *does* someone kill a dragon?"

Fenrir made a production of thinking hard, finger tapping his lip while he cupped his chin and propped his elbow atop the table. He gazed at Red as if the answer were a matter of counting the curls growing out of her head.

"We could drug it?" Fenrir suggested like—well, *fuck*. Fenrir was supposed to be the most experienced hunter here.

"That's a terrible idea," he snapped. "Yes, let's get the dragon high. Surely that will make it *less* dangerous."

"Guns?" Red suggested. "One of the automatic machine guns Farris has stashed away in his garage?"

"Not a bad idea," said the person who'd just suggested *drugging a dragon.*

"You're never going to kill that dragon, certainly not with a *gun,*" Orpheus said in a voice Fenrir had previously called *'Mr. Smarty Pants Posh'.* "And even if you do, another is going to eventually come crawling out of whatever hell hole this one came out of and start causing problems all over again if whatever they're attracted to isn't dealt with first. Your best bet, therefore, isn't to *kill* the dragon, but eliminate the reason it's interested in you at all. In your case, that would be the fires burning in the crater."

Or me, Orpheus didn't say out loud.

Red frowned. "We can't put those fires out. If it was possible we would have years ago."

"And you can't move the refinery, either," Fenrir unhelpfully added. "I suppose that leaves luring it away, like you suggested before."

Red pursed her lips, cocked her head. "If that dragon is after fire, I can't imagine anything more alluring than that damned crater."

I am, he thought again, the words right there, balanced on the tip of his tongue—so close to flying off it that Fenrir looked at him as if he'd actually spoken, frown hardening his face.

"Fifi's about to offer himself up as bait and I need the two of us to agree right now that he's an idiot for suggesting it."

"The fuck!" Red shouted, the bar quieting into a peculiar calm as everyone became very interested in their conversation.

"I wasn't, actually," Orpheus said through gritted teeth. "But if you'd care to see how well Rawkner might fare as bait, I've got it on good authority he is rather full of hot air."

"No one is going to be *bait!*" Red snarled. "If either of you even think of doing something as reckless as that, I'll throw you off the refinery tower myself!" Her fist slammed onto the table in punctuation, all their mugs jumping in a frothy leap. More beer splashed over the lip of Orpheus' mug, dripping down his fingers to pool in his palm, and it was second nature to summon his Netherflame again, his whole mug turning white and frosty as the violet flame crawled over his hand and evaporated the spilled beer.

Red licked her lips, hand clenching and unclenching around her beer, eyes following the lick of flame that caught the air and burned away in a puff of purple smoke. She bared her teeth when it was gone, nailbeds gone pale with how tightly she clutched his mug.

"You *sure* I can't touch it?" she asked once the moment had settled, eyes snapping to his.

Orpheus felt sick. "I told you before, it's not safe." He looked at Red with the hope that, this time, it would sink it.

"Remind me why can you touch it, but I can't?" she pushed.

Orpheus chewed his lip. "No one really knows why some people can summon Netherflame and others can't. For most of our history, people denied magic's existence at all, so research is limited to the last several hundred years." He didn't mention the hermits who had been doing most of that research were now entirely dead—nor that he'd been a part of that research to begin with.

"Right," Red drawled, eyebrow lifting, "that doesn't explain why you keep saying it'll poof me if I touch it."

Orpheus pulled his hand down his face, skin still cold from the Netherflame, his breath fogging with his sigh.

When he met Red's eyes, she looked at him expectantly.

Fine. "It's perfectly safe when worked through a sigil or archanic, but exposure to Netherflame in its purest form has been documented as causing accelerated molecular decay in living organisms. Your skin will first peel, then weep, and by the time your body fights off the..." Poison? Rot? Orpheus chewed his lip, then settled on, "By the time it fights off the burn, you may have caused more damage than you can reasonably expect to survive. For whatever reason, my biology is immune to the phenomena, but yours is not. Some level of damage is inevitable, and I'd rather not be responsible for the premature expiration of the people I care—"

He cut off abruptly, mouth snapping shut with an audible click.

Fenrir had gone still beside him, tension in the space between them, building out of all the things they'd left unspoken, this near innocent confession more than anything he'd admitted yet.

A quick glance at Fenrir revealed he was staring. The soft smile he gave Orpheus was growing more familiar than that raucous grin, and that was—preposterous.

Orpheus' body kindled warm, then cold, then back again as their eyes held longer than they had all night. When he finally looked away, his heart skipped into a fluttering, compulsive beat.

"For the record, I wanna know because it's fascinating," Red clarified. "Before we got the grid going this place was a shanty town. We relied on the Dark Flame for all our power, and I need y'all to understand how it feels to be an engineer and then having absolutely zero ability to work with the only reliable energy source you've got."

Red punctuated this by slapping her palm atop the table, leaning in close again as she said to Fenrir while gesturing at Orpheus. "Lore may be a crazy fucking bitch—" Orpheus bristled, but kept his mouth clamped shut, "— but she gave this place something more valuable than anyone else when she made us get that grid going. But it's *nothing* to that damn Dark Flame. Infinite energy from one single hells-damned ember, but the only fucking person who can work with it is this—ah—"

Red abruptly went silent, caught mid gesture, hand half raised towards Orpheus in obvious exasperation.

She cringed. "Sorry, Sparks."

"No offense taken." Orpheus paused, then said, "though I believe the word you're looking for is asshole."

A smile twisted Red's mouth as she tipped back her chair and raised an eyebrow. "Well, I didn't want to make Fenrir randy by bringing up your asshole."

His—*what?*

Orpheus choked and Fenrir sputtered. If either had been drinking their beer, half would likely be sprayed across the table. Instead, Orpheus turned a brilliant shade of scarlet which nearly matched Red's hair while Fenrir burst out laughing.

"Okay, *okay*," Fenrir wheezed, waving a hand at Red while the other clutched his chest, heaving. "That was good. I'll give you that one, that was really, *really* good."

And then they were *both* laughing. Loud guffaws that put the rest of the bar to shame—the clink of their mugs together splashing even more beer across the table. Orpheus sneered when Fenrir pushed his mug into his hands, then, somehow, into a salute, beer dripping all over his hands for the third time that night.

"I'd like to drink my beer, not wear it, Rawkner," Orpheus muttered, holding out his dripping hand.

"Do it again!" Red cut in before Fenrir could do anything more than grin at him, wiggling her fingers around just like Fenrir did mimicking Orpheus' magic.

Orpheus rolled his eyes and let the Netherflame spark, catch, as natural as breathing, purple fire building and building until it engulfed his hand, licked down his arm. A twist of his wrist and little *push* from his mind and the fire contracted, swirling and condensing until a ball of it hovered, right there, over his palm, purple fire contained to an invisible sphere, like the gazing balls fortune tellers in his books used— except, of course, that his was *real*.

One of the first "tricks" he'd learned, shaping Netherflame didn't require a sigil or an incantation. It was pure willpower, a command from his mind that allowed him to sculpt it to his needs. From the smallest of embers to the largest of infernos, however he needed for whichever archanic he was working on. Right then, he had no greater purpose, no machine to power or weapon to forge. So, Orpheus let his mind wander, the simple sphere over his palm contracting until it split like a cell. Two, four, eight and then ten spheres replicated until a whole tiny galaxy orbited over the table, the largest sphere at the center a perfect reproduction of the sun itself, a pretty flicker of arcing flares and churning plasma.

Orpheus smiled to himself. The smaller spheres orbited the sun while he did his best to recall what he'd read in the astronomy books regarding the different paths they followed, the precise number of moons Saturn had, the asteroid belt between Mars and Jupiter, and the major comets that circled further out. He added each as he thought of them, until the solar system was as complete as any drawing he'd ever seen, hovering in space like it wasn't hell-forged flame, but life itself.

Maybe that was why he didn't notice the bar had gone quiet, or that someone had turned the lights down low. Why he didn't see Red's breath fogging with her exhale, or the shimmer of ice where their beer had spilled. It wasn't until he felt the barest touch on his knee that he blinked back to awareness.

His eyes went immediately to Fenrir, realizing at once whose hand rested atop his knee—stroking lightly—gently—like his smile— and the words he spoke, low enough that not even the silent bar could overhear:

"That's beautiful, Fifi."

The solar system sputtered out in poof of smoke, heat engulfing

Orpheus' face, anathema to the cold that had overwhelmed the entirety of the bar.

Conversation erupted into a cacophony of sound as Orpheus' world narrowed down to the sensation of Fenrir's hand on his knee—the smile on his face.

Like a trap sprung, he couldn't escape it: the need to confront this thing between him and Fenrir, but also the need to point out the falsehood that anything Orpheus created was *beautiful*, because Fenrir had seen firsthand what kind of awful devastation his magic had wrought.

Sickness swelled in his stomach, regret a weight holding him down. He tore his attention away from Fenrir and realized that half the bar had gathered around their table, like Orpheus actually was some kind of magician turning tricks for fun.

Shame joined the ill churning in his stomach.

"It's not a trick," he hissed without thinking, hands clenched atop the table, Netherflame rolling over his fist in an ominous, withering crawl.

A few of the people closest must have seen because the tenor of the voices grew strange. Memories of the palace's courtiers crawled from the shadows, but Red's voice severed his thoughts before they could take hold: "Okay, that's enough you drunks, show's over, anymore and I'm gonna ask y'all to pay up. If you want free entertainment, I've got a quarry overflowing with shit you can go swim in!"

The room grew brighter as the patrons disbursed, the clink of mugs on tables and the thin threads of laughter slow-building into normalcy again. By the time the bar had moved on from Orpheus' impromptu performance, it was as if nothing had happened at all.

Except, he could still feel Fenrir's hand on his knee, moving slowly, an anchor of a touch within a world he felt lost in. Then, that pulled away too.

Orpheus stared at Fenrir's profile, his breath shallow. If he had touched him any longer, he didn't know what he would have done. Bolt for the door or...or let him continue.

Let him continue, that voice breathed.

Because only Fenrir had come for him when his whole life began unraveling. Had protected him. Had witnessed the horror of his abilities yet called them beautiful, like he saw—actually *saw*—through the shadows Orpheus hid within.

No one had ever seen that person. No one except a strange girl in a secret library who would eventually turn on him, and because of that Orpheus knew better than to let his heart near anyone ever again.

Except Fenrir—*Fenrir*—

"Okay, that's enough."

Orpheus jumped in his seat, heart clenching, realizing too late that Fenrir was talking to Red.

"What? Not allowed to look? You know he ain't my type." Red caught Orpheus' eyes, then gave him a wink. "As adorable as y'all both are."

"Actually, I'm happy to report I'm everyone's type." Fenrir grinned, turning to Orpheus and wiggling his eyebrows. Teasing back in its rightful place, Orpheus felt flayed open by it, like a nerve exposed.

"Well, I'm *no one's* type!" He burst out, like he needed to remind Fenrir of how unlikable he was. Of course he didn't. Fenrir wasn't some schoolboy pulling the pigtails of the girl he liked. He was a celebrated warrior who could have his pick of any person under the sun. There was no reason he'd ever look at Orpheus. No reason at all. Everything that had happened today? It was all in Orpheus' head.

Right—*right?*

He resisted the moment his tears broke, tipping his head down so he could hide behind his hair, staring at his clenched fists like they held some kind of answer.

"Hey, you okay?" Fenrir's hand slid over Orpheus'. They looked good together. Warm against pale, big against small. Like they fit— were always meant to fit.

Something inside Orpheus twisted to breaking.

This had to be a joke to Fenrir—some button of Orpheus' that was way too fun to push. That's all Fenrir *did*. He pushed Orpheus' buttons because tormenting him was apparently second only to massacring armies on Fenrir's short list of *"Things That Give Me a Chuckle."* He was not supposed to be nice to him, or helpful, or understanding.

All hells, Fenrir absolutely was not supposed to be *attracted* to him.

He hates me. He's always hated me.

He's supposed to hate me.

Orpheus jerked his hand away, breath coming shallow while the bar spun stars around his head.

"Red, I'm sorry, we're pretty beat, I think it's time for us to go," Fenrir said when it became clear Orpheus was not okay. "See you tomorrow, yeah?"

Fingers touched his shoulder, then his elbow. He stood out of habit, detached, following Fenrir with little more than a hand ghosting his waist.

"Come on, hotel's not far."

Cold night touched his face, and Orpheus breathed it in greedily. The scent of smog and soot and the acrid taste of burnt fuel hardly mattered, it was the cold Orpheus wanted—that numbing nothing that could make him feel like himself again.

It almost worked. He almost pushed away the conflicting feelings inside himself and moved forward on a path he'd been following his whole life. A lonely, isolated path where it wasn't a future he worked towards but surviving each day. Where relationships weren't defined by the things he felt, but the needs they met, and friendships were something meant for the weak-hearted—romance nothing more than a fantasy to read about in a book.

Then he thought of the easy way Fenrir found all of Orpheus' soft parts—the pieces of himself he kept hidden—as if he knew exactly what each hid and how to reveal them. But also the kind, gentle way he covered him up again, when it became clear Orpheus couldn't handle being so deeply exposed.

Not teasing. Not hurting.

Encouraging. Supporting.

Because Fenrir...Fenrir *cared* about him. It wasn't all in his head—it wasn't a *trick*.

"I'm—" he tried to speak, but the world was tilting, and when he reached for the wall he found Fenrir instead.

Arms came around him, shadows converging as Fenrir pulled him into the alley, his back hitting the bricks a moment before his cheek hit Fenrir's chest. He sagged forward, the velvet of Fenrir's skin a breath away from his gasping mouth.

If he had half a mind left, he would have tipped his head against the wall behind him, put his hands to Fenrir's chest and shoved him to arms distance. Instead, he dropped his head onto Fenrir's shoulder.

"What's wrong?" Fenrir asked, voice raw—a little scared. "Is it the curse?"

Orpheus couldn't answer, words lost to the churning inside his gut, the shallow breath in his lungs. Hands touched his shoulders, then his waist, careful things, a little perfunctory, sliding along him in their search for a reason why Orpheus was acting so strange. He didn't bother telling Fenrir he wouldn't find anything. Didn't want this moment to end any more than he hadn't wanted it to happen in the first place. Later he could blame the alcohol or his nerves or his fear of the dragon coming after him, but for now Orpheus bit his tongue, smothered his thoughts and sank into Fenrir.

"Fifi?" Fenrir said, voice rumbling through the very heart of him.

"Do it." Orpheus didn't have to say *what*.

Slow as the coming winter, Fenrir pulled Orpheus into a hug.

He released a breath he hadn't intended to hold, gasped in a sob. Tears pushed free, his hands shaking when they fisted into Fenrir's shirt, wrists itching with the urge to feel—pain, sensation, anything to distract him from the impossible reality he faced. Instead, he clung to Fenrir. Burrowed his face into his shoulder and pushed his mouth into his skin and hid his tears with a snarl, hoping Fenrir understood it wasn't him he fought, but everything inside himself.

"Okay," Fenrir whispered, voice shaking, "you're okay."

Orpheus didn't feel okay. Grief rose, a mourning for the person he could have been had the world not gone to shit. He couldn't unsee himself: the little boy with his head in the clouds because reality had been so much harder than anything those heroes in his books had faced. The person Lore had exploited, seeing in him the very weakness that afflicted him now—this need for human connection—affection— someone to simply care, not because he was useful, but because they *liked* him. Just him. The weird, lonely man who lived in his dark little dungeon, head out of the clouds but into the shadows, because at least in the shadows he could hide from all the things that might hurt him.

It figured that Fenrir would be the one to find him.

"I'm sorry," Orpheus hissed, clutching Fenrir tighter.

"Don't—" Fenrir choked off when Orpheus sobbed again, the heave of his chest like a wave crashing in the sea. Orpheus would have drowned if he didn't have Fenrir to cling to. "—don't you dare apologize."

Fingers slid into his hair, slow and careful. A palm settled over his neck, a warm weight. Fenrir held Orpheus there, tucked into the crook of his shoulder, fingertips digging and dragging, a slow circling into his scalp that calmed Orpheus in a way nothing ever had. Fenrir burned hotter than that crater—like there was a fire under his surface that would consume Orpheus alive—and how tempting was it, to have this be the way he'd die, rather than an infernal fucking curse?

"I can hear you," Fenrir tried to joke.

Orpheus sniffed. "I'm not spiraling,"

"Good," Fenrir said, voice ragged, raw in his ear. "That's really good."

There was no bar. No dragon. No curse and no betrayal. There was only Fenrir's breath and the beating pulse of his heart. The warmth of his skin and the weight of his arms. The parts of them most important slotting into place as if they always were meant to fit. And while Lore had tried to drive a wedge between them, it made Orpheus wonder if she hadn't known—hadn't seen—all they were capable of, together.

Fenrir had seen it. Now Orpheus could see it, too.

He swallowed down another sob, turned his face into Fenrir's shirt to wipe away some of his tears. Fenrir hummed low, breath tickling over Orpheus' cheek, the weight of his body an anchor he clung to. The night was cold but Fenrir was warm, and Orpheus felt the moment Fenrir leaned away. It wasn't distance he put between them so much as space, drawing back so their eyes could meet. Color refracted in spectral shards, neon lights filtering through the fall of Fenrir's wild hair, making shapes out of his face that made his expression impossible to read. Except for his smile. Orpheus knew that smile. Was beginning to understand exactly what it meant.

Is this when we kiss?

Orpheus glanced down at Fenrir's lips, felt the hidden places inside him shrink back, already panicked over all he'd exposed tonight, terrified of the unknown that came next. He pushed air past his teeth before he could stop it, a shallow hiss that Fenrir must have heard.

"You're doing it again." Fenrir's hand moved from the back of Orpheus' neck to cup his cheek. A thumb traced a tear mark, a slow slide that set his nerves alight. Distance closed, shadows reconverging, and when their noses touched, it was a gut reaction for Orpheus to press his palm into Fenrir's chest.

Yes, his mind whispered. What he said aloud was: "I can't."

"Okay," Fenrir whispered, and they were so close Orpheus could feel Fenrir's breath shaking past his lips. "That's okay."

Never before in his life had Orpheus wished for something harder—that he could have the strength to take this moment where they both so obviously wanted. But when Fenrir pulled him back into his chest and into another hug, he knew the opportunity wasn't completely lost. It would come again, and next time, Orpheus would be ready.

CHAPTER XV
THE TOWER

Things should have been strange after the encounter in the alley, but when Orpheus woke the next morning, the sight of Fenrir asleep in the bed beside him felt more natural than the Netherflame burning through his veins.

Sun streaked brightly across the skin of his shoulder, through the fall of his hair. Now that Orpheus could see, his hair was less wild than it was wavy, darker at the roots where the sun hadn't yet touched it. And across his cheek the scar stood out. One day it would becoming silvery like the rest, but for now it stood out, pink with Fenrir's sleepy flush. Orpheus wondered what it would feel like to run his finger down its length.

Fenrir grinned before his eyes even opened. They were incredibly blue when they caught Orpheus staring.

"Morning, Fifi."

"Good morning," Orpheus rasped.

Orpheus swallowed, still couldn't look away.

Fenrir made a show of it—his stretch—sheet slipping to the side to expose the bare skin beneath and all those ridiculous muscles. Orpheus' stomach did something embarrassing as saliva filled his mouth, his eyes skipping between Fenrir's face and his chest where he scratched at what Orpheus suspected was an imaginary itch.

Fenrir's expression said it all: *Like what you see, huh?*

He spent a long time in the shower. Cool water ran down his shoulders, dripped from his hair, and Orpheus watched it spiral away down the floor drain, wondering—not the first time that morning—what came next. What did he want to happen? And what did Fenrir expect? More than anything, they probably needed to have a conversation about all this, but unless it was a lecture Orpheus was terrible at talking about literally everything. And something told him most people didn't go around outlining the play-by-play of a budding relationship.

Relationship. Was that what was happening? Were he and Fenrir entering a *relationship?*

They hadn't even *kissed.*

But we could have, he thought. *We almost did.*

How soft were Fenrir's lips? How rough was his stubble? Would he hold his face when they kissed, or let Orpheus lead? They were important questions, his mind insisted, and by the time Orpheus stepped out of the shower, his body was doing things he didn't have the time to deal with. He had to take a few minutes in front of the mirror staring into his reflection just to get himself back under control.

Steam fogged the mirror, but the smear he made with his hand revealed enough. The man staring back at him was the same person he'd always known, but under this new lens he began to wonder—what did Fenrir see? Orpheus had always taken pride in his appearance, inspiration derived from the magicians in the stories he'd read—the elaborate robes they wore, and the dramatic effect they had. But the body underneath had always left something wanting, and it was this that Orpheus looked at now.

Starvation as a boy had left him forever skinny, the fine bones of his wrists and collarbones jutting out from pale, violet-veined skin. His hair was dark but scattered his chest sparsely, thicker near his groin, a dark trail that led to strong thighs but weak knees, bony ankles, the veins in his forearms surprisingly prominent even though there wasn't a whole lot of muscle underneath. His face would be fine if not for those circles he couldn't seem to shake, his beard kept closely trimmed and meticulously styled, the shape of his nose giving him a distinguished, noble look. Maybe his eyes were too severe and his lips too thin, but he had all his teeth and his hair too. He could absolutely look worse, even if he could also look a lot better.

But Orpheus supposed someone could call him striking, and perhaps for a man as impossibly handsome as Fenrir—that was enough.

They ate breakfast together, down at the hotel bar.

He could feel the weight of the staring, the two of them out in the open, seated at the bar eating from a shared plate of food the bartender—Jack—served them, sipping coffee from paper cups stamped with some long-dead establishment's orange and pink logo. The food tasted fresh and the coffee bitter, but their fingers kept touching as they plucked bites from the plate, some strange little dance between them that Orpheus didn't know the steps to because he could have sworn Fenrir went for his fingertips more often than a slice of melon or a bacon strip.

"I figure we can head to the Keep tomorrow, if you're okay with one more day in the Stacks." Fenrir scooped sugar into his steaming cup, spoon tiny in his enormous hand. Jack had taken their plate but refilled their coffee, and they were sitting close together, knees nearly touching, Fenrir leant casually into Orpheus' space.

"What about the dragon?" Orpheus asked. He kept trying to look up from his coffee but every time he met Fenrir's eyes his cheeks started to pink.

"What about it?" Fenrir's face wasn't guarded, but Orpheus couldn't look at him long enough to get a good read.

"Aren't we going to help?" He asked, finally catching Fenrir's eyes.

Fenrir smiled, that soft one, lips pinked by the heat of the coffee. Orpheus dropped his gaze to stare at his cup. The steam made shapes in the air. Nice, safe shapes that looked nothing like Fenrir or his stupid kissable lips.

"I don't think the dragon is a problem yet," Fenrir said, the *yet* hanging like a waiting noose.

Orpheus swallowed. "So why not leave today?"

"So eager to get me alone—"

Jack circled back around and took their empty plate, whistling loudly before moving off again.

Fenrir's mouth twisted into something Orpheus could neither call a grimace nor a grin. Not that it mattered; the damage was done. He could feel his face turning red.

But that was all. Just a single, simple, physiological reaction. Because, after last night, Orpheus knew Fenrir's teasing was innocent, and Fenrir had to know Orpheus' adversity was a front. And when Orpheus looked up and met those Rim-pale eyes, Fenrir relaxed. Orpheus may not know how to talk about what had happened in the alley, but he wasn't denying it either. And for now, that would have to be enough.

"One more day," Fenrir repeated. "You haven't even been to the refinery yet, and I know Red would throw a fit if you left without seeing her pride and joy."

"Alright," he said, spinning his cup between his fingers, enjoying the way the warm steam curled up between them. Enjoying the way Fenrir beamed at him more.

Red jogged out to meet them when they passed through the refinery's gate, gravel crunching atop the asphalt underfoot.

"Morning to ya both!" Her hair shone bright in the sunlight, dark skin a little wet with a sheen that could as easily be sweat or the steam pouring from the refinery tower. Orpheus blanched when she reached for him, looking to Fenrir when her arm hooked through his to drag him towards one of the tallest towers. "Y'all okay? Didn't drink too much did ya?"

"No, no, we were fine. Went to bed early, I want as much time in that hotel bed as I can get," Fenrir said from behind. Orpheus strained his neck in order to keep his eyes on him.

"Hotel's nice, yeah? Not too many people coming through yet but once Lore grows tired of all those bougie bitches in her ivory tower I'm sure we'll get an influx of customers."

Orpheus nearly choked on a laugh.

"You don't count, Sparks," Red continued with barely a pause. "I know you're nothing like those over-grown peacocks playing dress-up that Lore calls a court."

Over his shoulder, Fenrir winked at him, his grin shit-eating.

Red led them through a thick steel door with a wheel for a lock, their footfalls echoing up the massive cylindrical structure of the main refinery tower. If outside looked like a tangle, inside looked like a knot. Piping intersected more piping, some a hand's width wide, others small and soft and of various identifiable colors. Sunlight filtered through a series of breaks in the structure, enough to get by with on a sunny day, but when Red guided them directly to a cage-like contraption Orpheus realized the tower was connected to an electrical system. A panel of lights illuminated at the touch of Red's hand, and then a loud *whir-whine* rumbled through the tower as the cage engaged. Suddenly, they were rising, ascending smoothly up the enormous tower, the gentle hum of well-maintained mechanics a familiar comfort Orpheus didn't expect.

"This is our primary distillation unit," Red said, gesturing at a massive tube erected at the center of the tower, and the very piece of equipment all these smaller tubes connected to. "About sixty percent of all our crude oil gets processed through this unit. It's capable of producing seven thousand barrels of gasoline a month, but we're utilizing twenty percent of its maximum capacity. Once we get the grid connected to the old pit, we'll need to pump out more, but not yet. No use letting barrels rot. Don't have the same stabilizing capabilities those ancient farts did. Our shelf life is getting better but it's still not ideal. It's why those pumps in the field move so slow. I saw you watching them, Sparks. Probably thought we were a bunch of ninnies incapable of getting a simple oil drill right. Well, hah!"

"The old pit?" Orpheus asked, head spinning with everything Red said.

"That one didn't tell you 'bout it yet?" Red jutted her chin at Fenrir, something of an accusation in her voice.

Fenrir shrugged, didn't meet his eyes. "Figured we'd get there, eventually."

"Well?" Orpheus demanded, voice rising, "what is it?"

"The old pit is a city," Red breathed, eyes sparkling. "And we're going to restore it."

A city? There was a *city?*

Orpheus didn't think he'd said that out loud, but Fenrir's expression said otherwise.

"It's still standing, mostly," Red said, voice gone a little quiet. "Didn't get hit like the others. At least, not as badly. Or so I've been told. Never seen another myself, but this one has—" again, Red indicated Fenrir. This time, Orpheus sought out Fenrir's eyes and held them. Something uncomfortable played beneath Fenrir's expression. Orpheus didn't have the information to determine why. "—refused to take me the one time we went to the Rim."

"You don't want to go to the Rim," Fenrir said without looking at Red, as if Orpheus was going to go anywhere that made Fenrir Rawkner, of all people, *scared*—good reason or not.

Plus, the Rim didn't have a Keep with a potential counter curse.

"Is the Keep in the city?" Orpheus asked, and he knew he'd hit the nail on the head when Fenrir turned pink. "The Keep is in a city, and you were going keep that a secret?"

"It was supposed to be a *surprise*," Fenrir didn't say to Orpheus, he snarled it at Red.

"Aw, shit." Red's hand went to her hair, ruffling through it. "Sorry Fenrir, I didn't realize."

Fenrir...wanted to surprise him?

Sunlight dappling through the narrow refinery windows, cage rattling on its mechanical tracks, Orpheus stared at Fenrir as if the blush on his face was supposed to be some kind of explanation.

Fenrir stared back as if, well...it was.

"You're gonna love it," Fenrir said, boldly, like it meant something. Orpheus swallowed down the sensation of his heart climbing into his throat.

Then the cage came to a jerky stop, door clattered open on mechanical tracks, and Orpheus would have hit the button to take them back to the ground floor if not for what he saw next.

At the end of the catwalk circling the cylindrical wall, were two semi-circles of beeping consoles and glowing screens, converged together like something straight from a dream.

Computers. These were *computers*.

"Here we are!" Red announced, and there was nowhere else Orpheus wanted to be.

He crossed the threshold of the cage before anyone could stop him, robes sweeping around his feet as he walked right up to one of the stations and the person sitting at it. Over their shoulder was something like a blueprint, but an interactive one, where the different components of the main distillation unit were highlighted in various colors, the knot of tubes surrounding it laid out in an easy to decipher map. It was similar to some of the plans he had followed before. The archanics he had crafted from their ancestors' very own blueprints. But this was different. This was more. This made Orpheus feel like no matter how much Netherflame he pumped into however much sigil-forged metal, he could never compare to something like this.

"What does that mean?" Orpheus asked, pointing at one of the colored sections of the distillation unit, close to the middle where most of the auxiliary tubes were illuminated as active.

"That's our gasoline production. Crude oil is heavy, so it sinks to the bottom. Gasoline hits mid-levels, and up top are our more refined outputs, mainly petroleum gas, which burns clean enough for use indoors. Most of the petroleum ends up in the labs, but we reserve some for ourselves."

"The labs run mostly off the underground natural gas network," Fenrir added. "Some of the lines are still intact, and the further north you go you'll eventually hit the old lake beds where we got part of the hydroelectric plant online. They've got their own dedicated power source now so that's where the labs are," Fenrir rambled on as if he'd been a part of all this.

Had he been? Had Fenrir been doing more than fighting off the remnants of the world's population? Had he been uniting them, under Lore's banner, but with the real promise of technological advancement?

What else did Orpheus know nothing about?

"Was Lore a part of this?" he asked, looking between Red and Fenrir.

"She...laid the groundwork," Fenrir answered in a way that didn't sound like an answer at all.

"She burned out the resisting settlements and cleared out the bandits and then said to the people doing the real work, 'you've got eight weeks to get this grid up and running or I'll pike all your heads'."

Silence descended, heavy and strange. Orpheus looked at Red, couldn't look anywhere else. He'd never heard anyone talk about Lore like this before. No one in the palace would have dared. He certainly hadn't, but Orpheus had reasons that had nothing to do with the war or the Empire at large. This was one of her subjects. One of the people she'd...she'd *helped*.

"Oh please," Red continued, rolling her eyes, "if you're with this one—" she jerked a thumb at Fenrir, "—there's no way you're one of Lore's loyal dogs—"

Fenrir flinched. "Red—"

"What?" she snapped, spinning on Fenrir. Her expression froze when she their eyes met. "You still haven't *told* him?" She breathed.

"Told me what?" He heard himself say.

Red didn't look at him, jaw clenched, staring at Fenrir as if Orpheus wasn't there.

And Fenrir...Fenrir wouldn't stop staring at him, Rim-pale eyes near colorless in the refracted sunlight, impossible to read.

Something was wrong.

Something was *very wrong*.

The stolen books. The unspoken exchanges. The garage full of vehicles—but also an armory's worth of guns. Red's anger, and Fenrir's smooth deflections, the animosity they both seemed to harbor not towards the Empire, but the person who had built it. But for what purpose? For what goal?

You know what, that voice whispered.

Orpheus swallowed, the world going weightless. "Excuse me."

THE CRACK AT THE HEART OF EVERYTHING

There was a certain quality to the light that made him feel as though he were walking through a tunnel, a darkness at the edge of his vision that blocked out the world and all the truths he'd naively thought he'd confronted. All he could focus on was the gentle clang of one step in front of the other, the scent of unburned petroleum in the air. He didn't know where he was headed, only that he needed to get away, and when a door appeared before him that was all Orpheus could think of.

Sunlight hit his face, bright and blinding.

He blinked to clear his vision, shapes swimming out of focus, pulling in a breath that tasted rotten, like he'd been forced to swallow something old and foul. Maybe it was the smog, or maybe it was something else. Whatever it was, Orpheus choked, sound strangled as he reached for the railing and hung on.

This high up the tower, the Stacks sprawled, a tangle of twisting metal and brick walls and asphalt streets, and then further—bled red by a fire that would never stop burning, a cracked world that would never stop hurting—the oil fields. Somehow, he'd missed it. There, against the horizon, where the massive pumps rose and fell, there were smaller shapes. Ones that had looked so alive, days ago. The men and women Lore had put there, not as committed sentinels over her most precious resource, but as warnings. As threats.

She did what she had to, to unite them, a voice tried to reason, but Orpheus was tired of that voice. Had been listening to it since he was a little boy, and where had it gotten him?

Used. Taken advantage of. Manipulated.

A gust of wind ruffled his hair, pushed at his back; Orpheus swayed with it.

"Whoa there, buddy, not so fast."

A hand closed over his shoulder, drew him back. Fenrir. When Orpheus turned around, he couldn't meet his eyes.

"Fuck," Fenrir breathed. "Orpheus, I'm—"

"Planning a coup against Lore. Yes, I've put that much together."

In the shadow of the tower, Fenrir stood tall, unwavering despite the wind kicking at his back.

"Yes," he said, and Orpheus cringed, as if the word would carry on the wind, all the way back up Lore's mountain and give him away. "But only if she leaves the palace. And only then if she tries to march east again."

Heat traveled up Orpheus' spine, a buzzy electricity sparking beneath his skin. He might throw up. He might *scream*. In the end, he laughed; it was not a kind sound.

"Lore's fabled hero, a traitor in the end." He had to say it aloud, just to make sure it was real.

Fenrir said nothing. His weight balanced, body motionless, his shadow deepening under a passing cloud.

"Why?" Orpheus breathed.

There was a tightness to the lines around Fenrir's eyes that spoke of a buried pain, the kind of wound that didn't leave scars so much as shape the person one became. Orpheus knew what that kind of pain felt like. Knew, without a doubt, that what Fenrir said next reflected the exact kind of pain Orpheus had spent his life running from.

Unlike him, Fenrir wasn't running.

"I met Red fifteen years ago. She was sixteen when we discovered her and her band of Wastelanders living at the edge of the Stacks. They weren't much more than a few dilapidated buildings back then. Red and her friends foraged off the forest and scrapped old tech they found in the ruins," Fenrir said, voice starting soft, growing stronger as he spoke. "They'd been out here a while, and Red had developed a knack for fixing tech. Gifted, all of them were, but Red was the best. Lore saw that, saw the value in someone like that, and pursued her. And Red, she came along willingly, got her friends to follow her too. Easy food and protection and enough crazy tech salvage to keep you busy for a lifetime—what could be better than that? They all joined the war effort together, their own little mechanic team, working on getting us computers and batteries and shortwave radios and all sorts of insane shit I never thought I'd see in my lifetime. And Lore built Red up, bolstered her—groomed her, essentially, for the task she would dump on her a couple years later."

Fenrir paused, brows drawn together, focus inward, as if recalling a memory from the deepest dregs of his subconscious mind.

"I was there when Lore gave Red and her team their assignment. Eight weeks she said, to get the grid up and running. I was also there when she piked everyone except Red at the end of seven."

"All hells, Fenrir," Orpheus breathed.

"Lore's done some good things, created opportunities for a lot of incredible people. But she's done it for the wrong reasons. I've seen the choices she's made, in the name of her Empire. People are pawns to her, pieces to move about, the world a board to be conquered. Not nurtured. Not seeded. Not even to keep the peace. But the people here, look at them. They're onto something without her help. And that war she's been fighting? It hasn't been a war since she cleared out all those Wastelander bandits those first few years. That wasn't enough for her. She kept wanting more. I've seen her steamroll peaceful settlements in the name of expansion and then slaughter them when their resources didn't live up to her expectations. I've watched her abandon the most incredible discoveries we've ever unearthed because there's no immediate use for the technology.

"But for the first time in centuries, we have a chance to fix a lot of what is broken. Rediscover what we've lost. Except..." Fenrir trailed off, eyes drifting over Orpheus' face for a long moment, so he could see the sadness there. The painful, heavy burden Fenrir must have been carrying for years, if not decades. "Except, if Lore decides she wants to march east again, or doesn't like what Red's doing down here, or all hells—if she just gets bored of peace and wants to stir shit up again—everything we're working for will be gone in an instant."

And who had given her the power to do precisely that?

"It's my fault," Orpheus said, voice gone thin. "I cast that spell, summoned Ohm and his army, then handed the reigns right over to her."

Wind gusted, a buffet against his face. His breath stole away with it, breathing becoming a struggle. He clutched his chest as he inhaled, his heart pounding so fast it might crack open his chest. He squeezed his eyes closed and focused.

"Orpheus," Fenrir said, voice closer than it had been. He could feel Fenrir's breath brush his forehead. A hand slid over his shoulder, fingers brushing under his chin. Orpheus looked up and met Fenrir's eyes, saw how close they were, how blue they looked in the clear sunny light. "That wasn't your fault, Orpheus."

Orpheus shook his head. "It is my fault, Rawkner."

It was all his fault. Everything. *All of it.*

"I never meant for Lore to have that spell," Fenrir admitted so softly Orpheus wasn't sure he heard right. "I still don't know how she knew I had it. I made it all the way back to the palace before she came asking for it. It's like she could smell it on me. The magic, or the deception. But in the end..." Fenrir smiled, shook his head, "I always intended for it to end up with you."

Wait...*what?*

"Me?" Orpheus said, voice thin. "What do you mean?"

Fenrir met his eyes and held them. Let Orpheus see how heavy they were. How tired. How exhausted.

No. This couldn't be right. This wasn't actually happening.

"You wanted me to raise that army for *you*," came out of him like a scratch. "You wanted to use it to fight Lore."

Fenrir swallowed, and said, "Not for me. For us. For everyone just trying to survive out here without another catastrophe." But it was too late.

All hells. All fucking *hells.*

"That's—" That was his explanation. The reason Fenrir stood here at all. Orpheus looked up at Fenrir and ached for something to convince him he misunderstood. "Don't tell me this," he begged, voice cracked-through.

"You're not like her, Orpheus." Fenrir gripped his shoulder so tightly it bordered on painful, but it was the look in his eyes that hurt the most. So sure of himself—and of Orpheus. "If given the choice, I knew you'd do what was right."

"Overthrowing a newly won empire that's united disparate people is *right?*" Orpheus snapped, voice high, a little desperate. In the face of everything he fell back on logic, using it like the shield it'd always provided.

Except Fenrir didn't back down. "When it's won with the blood of innocent people, yeah."

"All empires are won with the blood of innocent people!" Orpheus roared. "Read any book and it will say the same! There hasn't been an empire where innocent people haven't suffered for it. Lore did what no one else has bothered to try and it worked. Look at this! She did this! She made this happen!"

He waved at the surrounding refinery, an overly dramatic gesture that he couldn't put his heart into; Fenrir seemed convinced enough.

Anger flared in Fenrir's eyes as he said, "Can you stand there and tell me Lore built this, when we both know it was Red? Can you not imagine another kind of leader who inspired people rather than threatened them, and tell me they couldn't have achieved the same results?" Fenrir's voice dropped low, anger lost, replaced with a plea. "I'm not saying violence doesn't have its place, only that Lore doesn't know what that place is."

"And you do?" Orpheus asked, voice shaking. "The man who led her armies and slaughtered her enemies. You can make that judgment call?"

Without any hesitation, Fenrir breathed, "Better than anyone else."

His legs were trembling, his heart pounding through his chest. If Fenrir hadn't still been gripping his shoulder he might have collapsed.

So, you get to walk away from it all, everything you've done, while I have a death curse hunting me down, he didn't say.

More so, he buried the thought: *So that's why you're here. Not to help me. Not because you care. But to use me, just like everyone else.*

This had nothing to do with right or wrong. He couldn't care less about Lore's empire. He certainly didn't care if Lore dropped dead in a mess of her own making. All he cared about was the growing pit in the core of him, the one Fenrir had put there, when he'd tagged along on his banishment under the guise of helping him, then made him— *made him—*

Orpheus choked out a snarl, squeezed his eyes shut. Accepted, that all Fenrir really wanted was another weapon in his fight against Lore.

Wind kicked up again, colder this time, swirling about his robes, a gentle whistle of warning for the winter storm coming down from the mountain. Orpheus wrapped his arms around himself like that could protect him. He had no protection. He should have learned that much by now. Fenrir had almost made him think otherwise. Had almost, despite his better judgment, convinced Orpheus that someone might actually care about him—magic or not. Power or not.

He was, as always, a naive fool.

A shiver tore down his spine, shaking him down to his very bones, knees weak as the weight of everything he'd done completely overwhelmed him. He needed to sit down. He needed to think. He needed, for possibly the first time in his life, a fucking break.

Instead, he had a death curse.

"Help," he breathed, barely a whisper. The wind picked up again, a hard gust against his chest that pushed, and pushed, and *pushed*. "Please, please I need help."

"Orpheus, I'm sorry—"

Fenrir's voice drowned in the wind, a sudden cyclone of air twisting to life, spiraling up through the grating beneath his feet. Orpheus' boots separated from the rigid tooth of the metal, robes swept up like leaves in a storm as a Wind Sprite darted between his legs and over the edge of the platform. Green skin glowed like acid, the dozen thinly webbed wings and spiny body swelling with gathered air. It hovered out of reach, its dozen slitted gem-like eyes blinking in tandem, tiny glimmering gems staring at him through the holes in the grating, watching as its spell caught and his weight gave way.

He reached for the railing but was too late. A second gust threw him and Fenrir off their feet, and while Fenrir stumbled back towards the tower behind, Orpheus grappled with the disconcerting sensation of tipping over—tipping backwards—flipping over the railing in a tangle of dark robes and then the world opened up beneath him, gravity rushing to take hold.

He fell. Through the web of piping towards the smooth pale concrete, Orpheus *fell*.

"Orpheus!" Fenrir's voice cut through the howl of panic in his head. One massive jolt and he swung upside-down, suspended below the platform, staring into the face of the Wind Sprite as Fenrir clung to his fucking ankle.

"Why are you doing this!" He screamed in the Wind Sprite's face. Fenrir squeezed his ankle hard enough to put tears in his eyes, but it was everything else that hurt the most. He was tired of this. Tired of fighting for his right to live. To have an important conversation without this hells-damned curse coming after him. Tired of having his heart crushed, every time he dared open it up to someone he thought might care. "What in all hells did I ever do to you! What do you want! Why won't you fucking stop!"

Those dozen eyes blinked, immutable of emotion but Orpheus got the uncanny impression that it was thinking, and whatever conclusion it came to wasn't one Orpheus would like. Suddenly, the Wind Sprite shivered, another gust of air slapping him, sharp, like a hundred cold knives slicing his face, then it zipped down, skittering along the edge of the tower before shooting at an angle straight towards where Orpheus hung.

Wind shear tore through him, so hard and so fast he was thrown upwards. He felt the moment Fenrir's fingers slipped from his ankle, counted the seconds between when Fenrir let go and when he began to fall. The platform passed in slow motion, Fenrir's Rim-pale eyes widening when he realized Orpheus had been blown too far past the platform for him to reach.

Despite the lies—despite the betrayal—Orpheus' heart still ached when Fenrir climbed atop the railing and leapt after him.

"You brainless fool!" he screamed, wind and tears and anger stinging his eyes.

Their bodies collided in a weightless tumble, a tangle of panicked flailing that abruptly ended when Fenrir clamped his arms around Orpheus and dragged him into his chest. He snarled into the not-quite embrace, a sore mimic of the alleyway Orpheus was unprepared for. But he didn't have time to dwell in the memory. The Wind Sprite zipped past them in another punch of air, and all Orpheus could think about was how much it would hurt when his body splattered across the concrete below.

He closed his eyes, smothered his sob, and, against all logic, buried his face in Fenrir's neck.

An arm tightened around him, then Fenrir jerked, a bellowing "Gotcha!" rumbling into his ear. Orpheus twisted his head to the side and came face to face with the Wind Sprite caught in Fenrir's fist—gnashing teeth and all.

"What the fuck, Fenrir?" Orpheus screeched.

The sprite twisted, screeching, mouth full of teeth chewing air in vicious opposition, desperately trying to tear itself from Fenrir's hand as the ground hurtled up towards all of them—

Oh. *Oh—*

"Do it," Fenrir growled into his ear, and Orpheus didn't have to ask *what.*

Tears stung his eyes, adrenaline tightened his chest, and like a gun locked and loaded, he lifted his hand, and he snapped.

Netherflame erupted, licked up his fingers. The spell came on a whisper, carrying on his breath as he reached for the Wind Sprite's face. Tiny teeth coming for his fingers, but it was too late, the Wind Sprite convulsed as the blood boiling spell encountered zero resistance, and all the magically hoarded oxygen inside its tiny body burst into a massive acid green cloud.

The impact struck, instantaneous. He and Fenrir tumbled upwards, not high enough to reach the platform—not even close—but enough to break their free-fall. Two seconds later he hit the ground, but instead of his guts splattering across the concrete, it was all the air in his lungs.

But...he was *alive.*

Orpheus reveled in one moment of blazing, breathless relief, before the world slammed--literally—back into place.

Air flooded his lungs, choked in his throat. Orpheus gasped, hacking and coughing his way back to breathing, and beneath him, Fenrir did the same. Orpheus' whole body rose as Fenrir sucked in one greedy inhale after another, all those muscles straining against leather and Orpheus' own not insubstantial weight. Orpheus realized, all at once, that he was splayed atop Fenrir like a blanket, and immediately met resistance when his instincts screamed at him to *get away*.

One arm around his waist, holding him close, another around his shoulders, hand buried in his hair, Fenrir clung to Orpheus like they were still falling. Like he knew the moment he let go Orpheus would be gone forever.

He wasn't wrong. Maybe that was why Orpheus allowed it. Why he let himself feel the weight of Fenrir's arms and the swell of his chest, listened to the adrenaline beat of his heart, the rasp of his breath, and he didn't push it away. He didn't run. He let it happen. Pretended, for one precious, infinite moment, that they were back in that alleyway again, and someone cared enough about him to help him—to save him—without some kind of ulterior motive.

Like all the lies he'd told himself over the years, this illusion didn't last, either.

Heart in his throat, Orpheus shoved away from Fenrir. His feet slipped as he scrambled to stand, his legs shaking, lungs struggling to breathe, a prickling heat stinging his eyes. But it was blind pain that compelled him. That had him spinning on his heel and running away.

INTERLUDE
MAGIC

Like the slow birth of dawn, Orpheus discovers something is different over the span of one long morning.

He wakes after days of fever. The room feels cold but it's not winter yet, the air damp with early autumn rain. Orpheus takes in a deep breath, waits for the fever and the pain and finds both missing. All that remains is an itch in his fingers, and he chases it by rubbing his fingertips over his wrist, images of that pale violet fire in his veins coming and going with each scratch. And while his stomach still clenches, now it's with the empty ache of hunger. The food the hermits have left is piled up in a heap inside his door, the biscuits and broth and canteen of water simple things a sick child should be able to keep down, but even as his stomach growls, Orpheus gathers it all up and heads for the library.

Shadows follow him, hiding in corners and skirting through cracks. He's used to avoiding them—reticent, as always, of the dangers he knows lurk there—but there's a strange tenor to them now. A luminosity that he didn't think existed five days ago.

In the moments between his fevered dreams, Orpheus had kept track. Had traced the veins of violet fire in his arm against a backdrop of ever-shifting light, the cusp of twilight there under his skin as often as it had bled through the barred window of his not-cage. Three times Orpheus had woken to the dim hollow of near night, staring at his wrist and waiting for his band—his manacle—to reappear. The hermits may not have chained him to this place, but the shackles had always been there, and he'd felt that acutely while bedridden in pain. Orpheus thought of the prisoners in his stories who kept track of days with a stick of burnt charcoal or a wedge of chalk—worried the thin skin of his bare wrist with a single fingernail, thinking he could do the same with his blood.

They'd checked on him, once. In the morning of day two, when the worst of the fever had claimed him. Orpheus had thought it a dream when a cool palm touched his overheated forehead. Whatever comfort he may have wrenched from that simple touch was stolen in his next breath, the hermit slipping from his bedroom on fleeted feet, door clanging shut behind them as a lock Orpheus didn't know existed clicked into place.

The others had arrived, after. Had crowded into his tiny room, a gaggle of wide eyes and hushed voices, the hiss-spit of their whispers crackling like lightning in his head. Orpheus hadn't been able to do anything more than curl into a ball and await whatever came next. Hadn't even struggled when the hermits picked him up and carried him to their laboratory—to the dark flame they kept hidden away there—the crack in the floor where violet twilight wept.

He'd slumped to the floor as they'd donned their robes: white plastic layers and domed helms and the black-blazoned sigil of their secret sect inscribed across their backs. While Orpheus had never been one to fight, he wanted to then. Wanted to beg the hermits to let him be—let him sleep—let him stop hurting and stop aching and stop being the subject of their constant need to inflict agony. But as they'd lifted him up and carried him towards the flame, he'd closed his eyes and escaped.

He thought of the story *Frankenstein* when they'd laid him out atop an examination table and began hooking him up to their machines. Had wondered if this violet light was the same source of power the Doctor had used when he'd brought his creature to life.

Regency England had never been his favorite era, but he'd read that book with a certain delight. History was not kind to monsters, he had learned quickly—but the doctor's creature had always seemed nice. Innocent. Deserving of more than the misery the world dealt out.

A scraping sound had torn him from his thoughts. Two of the hermits carried a large stone cistern to the crack, laying it across so it balanced across the edges, and Orpheus flinched as the flames boiled over, fire filling the bowl in a glowing pool of violet. He'd tried twisting out of their arms when they lifted him over it, but the fever had made him weak, and the hermits' hands were too many—their will too great—and he began to cry softly when he realized what was about to happen.

The hermits lowered him to the flame, and all Orpheus could do was scream.

Sparks flared when it touched his skin, ice tearing through his veins and making his breath catch. But the pain he expected never came. And when the machines still attached to him didn't wail out a warning, Orpheus wasn't sure if he should be more scared of that or the excited whispers the hermits traded while all the fire in the crack drained to nothing.

Orpheus couldn't remember how long they'd left him there. He'd laid in that cistern for hours or possibly days, the light slowly dimming as time passed on until the violet glow of the dark flame had been replaced by the shadows in his head and a deep, dreamless sleep. When he would wake again it'd be to that barred window and gray light—the pile of food on his floor and the echoing, distant throb of icy twilight in his veins.

Now, he pushes the door open to the library, looks up at the gloomy stripes of pale morning bleeding through the bookcases and allows himself to get lost.

Lore finds him after minutes, rather than hours.

She looks harrowed and Orpheus flushes, thinks she must be relieved to see he's okay, because he's never been apart from her for this long before. He offers his food up with a small smile, an apologetic lilt to his voice when he manages to say: "Sorry I was gone so long."

THE CRACK AT THE HEART OF EVERYTHING

Lore frowns as she lifts a hand and smacks the food away. It clatters to the floor in a loud crash, cold broth splashing across Orpheus' hands and then his feet when he leaps back. He doesn't get far. Lore's mouth is a downward quiver, her grip unforgiving when she grabs his wrist and squeezes.

Against the white of his skin, the scar is silver.

"Do it," she snaps, and Orpheus desperately tries to ignore what she means, looks into her eyes and shakes his head.

It's not—it doesn't *matter*.

She squeezes harder. Hard enough he can feel his bones strain.

"How," he breathes, voice catching. His wrist aches as Lore lets up a little—enough to bring his itchy fingers together, instinct seeking and finding the place where it's the strongest, the collection of cold fire there in his veins.

He knows without thinking. Feels without seeking. And while his wrist still aches his fingers itch enough to sting, the urge comes naturally.

He doesn't get it on his first try. His fingers are wet with broth, his skin cool and clammy with leftover fever, and he's not sure if it's that or the heat of Lore's stare that's the reason he begins to sweat. Nerves on fire, he tries again, gets enough pressure, the stickiness of the drying soup giving him the traction he needs.

His fingers *snap*, and violet fire erupts between them—dark flame the color of twilight.

His eyes widen and his mouth goes dry, and his stomach threatens to come up for one fleeting second before his mind catches up to his body and it's awe uncoiling in his chest.

Magic, his mind fills in when he cradles the flame, a dancing ball of possibilities hovering over his palm. Like the wizards in his history books, the men and women who could craft something out of the limitless nothing: Merlin and Morgana and Medea and Rasputin and Gandalf and all the other sorcerers he can name. And Orpheus reels with the potentiality of it all—the amazement, utter and consuming, that he feels when he lifts his hand and stares at the little lick of violet flame.

Lore immediately reaches out to take it.

Her fingers pass through, as if it doesn't even exist. She tries again, and again, and *again*—

"Lore, I don't think—"

Her hand finally falls to his side and there are...there are *tears* in her eyes. Orpheus has never seen Lore cry before. He's watched her edge the brink of starvation and sickness and pain but never has he seen her shed a single tear. His heart pounds a hole into his chest as the flame sputters dead and he reaches for her.

She slaps his hands away. Her face transforms, a wretched pull of emotion he dares call grief. He wouldn't realize until decades later that it wasn't pain he saw in her expression, but the covetous brutality of desire—something dark and twisted that coiled under her skin like the ice did under his. But right then, all Orpheus sees is the friend he has hurt—the only person on this hells-damned planet that hasn't yet hurt him in return—and as he falls to his knees before her, he promises to keep it that way. That of all the things his magic can do, helping Lore is the most important of them all.

CHAPTER XVI

RETREAT

He found Achates in the stable behind the hotel. From there, leading him to the garage was a simple matter of navigating the alleys. Those he passed barely paid him any mind. A sorcerer with his amalgam must not be the strangest of sights these people had encountered, and Orpheus counted it a blessing when he arrived at the garage alone and un-hassled.

Nothing could keep his hands from shaking when he pressed them to the locked bay door. The spell he whispered slurred his tongue, the grinding squeal of the latches coming undone rattling his bones. When the bay door rolled closed behind him and Achates, Orpheus stood in the darkness, staring at the sleeping vehicles and racks of guns, remembering the last time he had been there, running from the reality of what he had begun to feel for Fenrir Rawkner.

He never cared about me. Not really.

Not when he came for him that first time, dragging Orpheus from his dungeon before Ohm had its chance. Nor when he'd put his hand on his knee at Ole Patsy's and called his magic beautiful, despite the devastation it had caused. Not even when he'd held him in the alley after everything changing had become too much, offering comfort like the secrets Orpheus harbored were mysteries Fenrir had already discovered, precious things that were his to protect.

He pretended to care because I'm his best chance at stopping Lore.

Like Lore even needed to be stopped. Or could be. Ohm or not, Lore had always possessed the uncanny ability to get her way. It was part of why Orpheus had been drawn to her in the first place. If anyone was going to change the world, it was Lore. Not Fenrir. Not Red. Certainly not himself.

"He's lost his mind," he said to Achates, leading him towards the corner where a dim violet glow bled out from under an old tarp.

Achates snorted when Orpheus tugged the tarp back to reveal the Netherflame engines Farris had been holding onto all this time. Any one of them would work, but Orpheus chose one of the newest engines, a design he'd based off a vehicle Fenrir himself had dragged up the mountain and dumped in his workshop so many moons ago.

A motorcycle, he had called it. *A death trap, more like it,* Orpheus had replied.

He could still remember the beautiful lilt of Fenrir's laugh.

"I never should have trusted him."

Something velvet-soft touched his cheek, huffed hot breath into his hair. Achates nosed at his head gently, and some of the tension inside him dissipated. He spent a long time standing in the shadows allowing Achates to chew on his hair before he reached up and pushed the horse's face away.

"We have a long journey ahead of us, friend. It's time to get serious."

Achates flicked his ears. It may not feel the same as having Fenrir at his back, but Orpheus would be lying if Achates hadn't become a comfort over these past few weeks.

He would make it to the Keep, one way or another.

His hands shook as he unlatched the compartment that held Achates' combustion engine, the tools he took from Farris' workbench both familiar and strange in his hands. He worked through the engine swap without a blueprint to guide him, relying on years of experience reverse-engineering the tech Lore and her soldiers had recovered. Like hell Orpheus would get caught cold in the wasteland's wilds with an empty fuel tank. If he was going to make the journey to the Keep on his own, he may as well do it with tech he could fix in the case of an emergency.

Grease streaked his hands, got caught under his fingernails. By the time he lowered the gasoline engine to the floor, he'd stopped thinking of Fenrir altogether. There was a familiarity to this work that Orpheus fell into, the feel of the Netherflame engine coming to life under his hands a welcome reminder that not everything he touched turning into poisonous devastation.

He fit the Netherflame engine into the empty cavity before Achates' eyes could do more than droop, tightening the bolts into place and then re-fitting the electrical contacts that would link Achates' artificial vascular system into his newly upgraded heart. When Achates' eyes lifted, Orpheus wasn't prepared for the spark of violet he saw behind them, but there it was, Netherflame coursing through Achates' mechanical veins. A fuelless energy source that wouldn't fail at the first sign of an empty tank.

This was it, then. No more excuses. No lingering reasons. The Keep waited, and Orpheus needed to go.

Then the bay door squealed open, and someone said his name.

"Sparks?"

Red stood in the open rectangle of the bay door, hair backlit by the Stack's blinding fluorescence like a lit match.

"Red," he said, voice strange in the thick quiet.

"Are ya leaving?" She closed the bay door behind her, as if to seal off an escape route. Orpheus wasn't entirely sure he would ever leave the Stacks again—not with the way Red looked at him.

"Are you here to stop me?"

Red met his eyes as she came to stand before him. There was no gentle emotion in them, and for the first time, Orpheus saw in her the woman from Fenrir's stories—the one who had watched her friends die by Lore's hand, and then gone on to build one of her most monumental achievements.

Lore had never mentioned Red. Lore had never given the

impression that the grid was anything more than another one of her army's many technological rediscoveries.

"Fenrir told me," Red continued, "about y'alls conversation. I made assumptions that were wrong."

Orpheus swallowed, glanced back at Achates. "I'm not going to go running off to tell Lore, if that's your concern."

Something in Red's energy shifted. For the first time, Orpheus wondered if she wasn't somehow utilizing magic—nothing in her outward expression or body language changed, simply a shift in the atmosphere surrounding her. A tension he could have touched that was no longer there.

She shook her head while meeting his eyes. "Fenrir can be thick but he's a good judge of character."

So, I assumed he trusted you and told you everything already, he read between the lines.

Orpheus understood, now, why Red and Fenrir's conversations gave off the impression of so much left unsaid. Red didn't bother him with that same level of secrecy. What she said next was as frank as anything anyone had ever said to him in his entire life.

"He told me a lot about you, over the years. Who you are. What you can do."

"Did he," Orpheus tried to say, it came out a whisper.

"That you and Lore were close, y'all have always been together."

It wasn't a secret, but it wasn't something either of them went around broadcasting either. Lore had never said much about her history to anyone, let alone regarding him. They were considered close because he'd been a part of the war effort since the very beginning. The rest of the story had fallen into place, and if anyone knew the real details, they must not have thought they mattered all that much. It certainly hadn't mattered to Lore. And he'd never questioned that. He'd never asked many questions at all, for so many reasons. It was easier that way. It always had been.

Easier, when he'd had the Gilded Palace to shelter him. Protect him. Isolate him within a narrative of his own making. Blind him to the truth of what was really happening under Lore's banner.

He didn't have the same excuses protecting him, now.

So why should he protect Lore?

"I've always wanted to meet you," Red said, voice quiet. "An actual mage, can ya imagine? For a girl growing up in the wasteland, that sounded like something straight from a story. One of them campfire tales we'd tell each other as kids. Magic, *real* magic. That's probably why I got good at tech. It was the closest a kid like me could get. But then I grew up, and I realized magic was part of the reason our lives were such utter shit in the first place. Hell beasts are after more than you, you know. I've run from my fair share over the years. Enough to keep me awake at night more often than not."

Orpheus shook his head, unsure where this was going—why Red was here talking to him at all, unless she meant to stop him from leaving—from running back to Lore.

Then Red got to the heart of the matter, and it was so much worse than what he suspected.

"You do know that the Gilded Palace was originally a fallout bunker, don't you?"

Orpheus froze, the axis of the world tilting wrong.

"I do," he somehow managed through the static.

"And you know the rumors about what went on there. The scientists who holed up inside after the Incident, who were working on a way to reverse all the damage it had done."

Orpheus swallowed air, choking a little when he tried to speak. "Yes."

"And the children," she said. Quietly. Knowingly. A memory Orpheus had buried deeper than anything else—had in fact never spoken of to anyone, to the point he didn't think anyone could possibly know, let alone guess. "The children they took, to experiment on. You know of them, don't you?"

The words were painful to hear, needles lodging in his brain and making it impossible to speak. But Red didn't make him say it, because he didn't need to. The truth had always been there, just as it had been in all those stories and tales and fables he'd escaped into.

Orpheus let out a sob he had spent a lifetime holding in—a

broken acknowledgment of the childhood he had suffered, that he'd gone so out of his way to forget.

Not anymore.

Achates shifted beside him, big body pressing close. Sturdy. Steadfast. Orpheus leaned into him as he closed his eyes and remembered.

Heat, hot and piercing. Weeks of agony and pain. And a growing emptiness in the pit of him, a starvation for something he couldn't sate, let alone name. Then cold, nothing but cold. Ice so frigid it numbed the pain—became an escape.

He should feel angry right now, but all Orpheus felt was grief.

"Is she like you? Do you think she can change?" Red asked in a soft voice, ignoring his tears. "I would help her, if you think we can."

The answer to Red's question had been burned into his soul a long time ago: help wasn't coming, would never come, for neither him nor Lore, because the only people they could depend on were each other.

Except Lore had turned her back on him when he needed her most, and then every truth he believed about the world had been stripped barren and raw.

He reached for his wrist, clutched it, fingernails digging in.

"I don't know," he whispered, fist twisting tight enough to burn. "I just don't know."

"Okay," Red said, voice gentle. "That's okay."

Red didn't leave him, not when he turned his face into Achates side and quietly cried, nor when enough time had passed that the light bent low, blue edging towards violet, nighttime fast approaching. She stayed with him in the shadows, another child of the wasteland, where survival meant sacrifice, and what lines they crossed were never clear until they were left behind in the dust.

When Orpheus pushed away from Achates he found Red had carried a work bench over. She sat there patiently, hand patting the wood beside her when Orpheus met her eyes.

"This is for you," she said once he sat. "Didn't want you heading out without a plan, and a map is always a good place to start." The piece of paper in her hands was well-worn, reinforced by a kind of translucent seal, a little yellowed where the glue had aged and then begun to peel. "It covers most of the area between here and the Rim. Some stuff has changed, but it will get you to the Pit and I've marked the Keep just in case."

She smoothed the map out over her lap and pointed at a place with a small red circle.

"You'll want to stick to the woods around here. Keep the ruins on the horizon but don't get too close, don't know what's hangin' around out there. Once you reach the river you're not far, about an hour's ride south. I've not been down this way for a couple years but there's some places where the water is low enough to make your way across. Gets deep in parts though so if you don't see a way across keep heading west. There's a bridge, a good place to cross if ya can find it. It would have been right around here—" Red pointed at another place on the map, already marked with faded blue ink. "—but last I heard it was impassable. Finally collapsed I think but could be worth a shot."

She spoke as if Orpheus had traveled on his own before—which he hadn't—and the idea of his independence was even more terrifying now than it had been weeks ago. He knew what waited for him. What kind of world had been built out of not only Lore's war machine, but also the ashes of history itself.

"Not asking ya to leave, Sparks," Red said after the silence had become cumbersome. "Just thought ya could do with some agency in your pocket. I know what it's like to feel trapped by your circumstances. And ya gotta know you'll always have a place here, curse be damned."

"Thank you," he said, because it felt like the right thing to do.

Plus, it was easier than goodbye.

He watched Red fold up the map, tried to keep his hands from shaking when she held it out to him.

"At least wait for morning light to set off," Red said when he slid the map into his pocket alongside the spell page. "And say goodbye to Fenrir. I'll never hear the end of it if you don't."

"I can't be what he wants me to be," Orpheus admitted, the words quiet in the night.

Red looked at him for a long time before saying, "Do you really believe that?"

"I can't fight Lore."

"You know that's not what I mean."

Orpheus met Red's eyes and held them while he swallowed.

"Talk to him, Sparks." She reached out and touched his hand, then his cheek. "You owe yourself that, at least."

He spent a long time in the garage before he returned to the hotel, letting the night ebb on without him, hoping winter's cold might numb the pain in his heart. It didn't. The ache remained, growing larger as he led Achates back to the stables, through the throngs of people who laughed and cajoled and smiled and breathed. Who lived in this place Lore had never mentioned, leading lives she didn't think worthwhile enough to protect—a place she had ignored, turned her back on, like she had him.

When Orpheus finally swept through the revolving hotel door, he felt far more alone than he ever had before.

He missed Fenrir.

CHAPTER XVII

THE EMPEROR

Evening ambled on in the quiet revolution of the hotel lobby's door.

Orpheus rolled his wine glass around the edge of its base, watching the light play through liquid, the barest hint of red clinging to the sides of his glass. He'd never been much of a drinker, but tonight he made an exception.

Fenrir wasn't here. Fenrir wasn't coming back.

Orpheus put the rim to his lips and took a long sip.

The wine tasted sharp, dry like the peeled skin of an unripened grape. It sat on his tongue like sandpaper, heavier in his belly than it was in his mouth. He took another sip and swallowed before the sting had a chance to linger, watching Jack wipe down the counter again despite no one but Orpheus drinking at his bar.

If he hadn't already known he had a taste for self-inflicted emotional trauma, tonight would have sealed it. Nursing a bottle of hooch Jack tried to pass off as wine while wondering if Fenrir would surface and then asking himself what the hell would he say if he did was probably scraping the bottom of his self-pity barrel. It didn't help that from the corner of his eye Jack looked like Fenrir. Or that when he slid a plate of food in front of Orpheus, he said it was on the house because he was Fenrir's *friend*.

Not even a plate of freshly prepared food could remove the sour taste from his mouth; Orpheus chose to blame the wine.

"You look like a man with a broken heart," Jack eventually said, a dirty little hand towel hanging off his shoulder. Orpheus stared at it, his excuse for not being able to meet Jack's eyes.

"A broken heart is the least of my concerns." Lore. The Keep. A death Curse. Orpheus had a verifiable *list*—even if, currently, Fenrir was at the top of it. "This wine, for starters. It tastes like piss, you should know."

Jack laughed, leaning in, arm atop the bar, his grin wide. He was handsome. Tall and broad. Not nearly as big as Fenrir, but big enough Orpheus noticed.

Inside his chest, Orpheus' heart stuttered, an open pulsating wound.

Stop spiraling, Fenrir's voice echoed in his head.

"It's still young. *Beaujolais* is the term." Jack smiled when he spoke. His teeth were a little crooked; Fenrir's were perfectly straight. Orpheus took another sip of his wine, shoving Fenrir out of his head. "Anything I can age gets sent up the mountain."

"That must be lucrative, selling wine to the throne?"

Jack raised an eyebrow at him, fingers drumming atop the bar, frown tugging at his smile.

"I couldn't say, haven't gotten paid for a barrel yet."

Orpheus blinked at Jack, then slid his gaze to the wine.

"Not that I'm complaining," Jack continued, voice stiffer than it had been. "It's an honor to...to *serve*." The word sounded strange even without Jack's forced inflection.

Oh, hells—did *everyone* hate Lore?

More so, did everyone think he was her loyal dog?

Orpheus' face went hot right before his blood went cold. He looked away, staring down the bar at empty seats that *should* be filled will patrons. Travelers. Merchants. People from across the Empire arriving to celebrate the peace Lore had finally won.

Instead, the dim lights of the bar created ghostly shadows where people should exist.

"It's good," Orpheus sputtered, holding his glass close. "The wine up at the palace. It's good."

"Thanks." Jack's smile returned. "What's it like up there? As fancy as the rumors go?"

It's awful, he couldn't bring himself to say. "They like to throw parties," wasn't supposed to light up Jack's face the way it did, but here they were.

"I bet they're a sight to see." To be fair, the gaudy excess of Lore's court was good for an evening of people watching. "My cousin headed up there beginning of autumn. Got conscripted as a scout and then transitioned to court messenger after the war. Those parties were all he talked about before he left. Think that's why he accepted the position. Haven't heard from him since he headed up there, so the rumors must be true."

"A...messenger?" Orpheus' mouth went dry for reasons that had nothing to do with the wine.

"Yeah, none of us could believe it. Kid has an awful stutter. Get him nervous and he can hardly say his own name." Jack laughed; Orpheus thought he was going to be sick.

A smear of blood, a wretched scream, and a cacophony of whispers: *He's going to get us all killed.*

"I'm sorry," he breathed, hands shaking when he placed his glass atop the bar. Jack's frown returned, eyes trying to meet Orpheus', but he was too busy staring at his hands. "I'm— I should go. Sleep. I need to sleep."

Jack's eyes followed him when he shoved away from the bar, the weight of it lingering long after Orpheus rounded the corner and started up the stairs.

He returned to his room, only bothering to kick off his boots before climbing into bed. Above, the ceiling stared down at him in white-stuccoed silence, shadows rending its surface like claws. Even so, it was a better sight than what greeted him when he closed his eyes.

A twitching body, a dissolving leg, a streak of red trailing him, a bloodied path that followed him still.

Maybe Fenrir's plan had been to use him against Lore but wasn't that the fate he *really* deserved? Certainly, it was more fitting than a death curse. At least Fenrir's way, Orpheus could pay the world back for some of the damage he had done.

A pain existed inside Orpheus that hadn't been there before today. A crack at the heart of everything that he wasn't sure could be fixed—that he thought Fenrir had put there when he'd taken Orpheus' heart and crushed it in his big, stupid fist—but that he now realized had been there long, long before then.

Orpheus rolled over, pulled his spare pillow into his chest, and smothered a sob in the fluff. Somehow, he dozed off like that—pillow wet, the room empty, the night cold.

He drifted in the emptiness, a dreamless nothing that came as close to sleep as Netherflame came to fire. Until a sound cut through the quiet. The clatter of a key, the tumble of a lock. Cool air touched Orpheus' skin and he shoved the pillow away, blinking into the darkness because— *because—*

"Fenrir?"

"*Shh,*" cut through the dark, followed by a hand over his mouth. Orpheus' scream died in his throat when Fenrir loomed into view, all Rim-pale eyes and that wild, thick hair.

Orpheus gasped into Fenrir's palm as relief slammed home.

Fenrir was *here.* He had come back for *him.*

Hand shaking, he grabbed Fenrir's wrist, torn between pushing him off so he could breathe and never letting him go again. Fenrir didn't budge. He leaned down, so close Orpheus didn't have a choice but to look at him.

Everything he wanted to say lodged in his throat—the apology he wanted to give, the explanation he needed to demand. But mostly the questions he ached to ask. Like why had Fenrir served Lore so long if he hated her that much? And could they stay together if Orpheus agreed to help?

Would Fenrir still care for him if Orpheus wasn't strong enough to take Lore out?

Orpheus whimpered, a strangled sound that shattered through the quiet and then cut off. Fenrir dropped atop him, a crushing weight that pushed the air from his lungs.

"*I said shh,*" Fenrir hissed, thumb and fingers gripping his face, body pressed so close it was more than the heat of his hand Orpheus felt. His stomach tossed, a sharp little twist that bottomed out somewhere deeper, heat rising despite the anger he knew he should feel. And when Fenrir's breath hit his cheek in a shaking exhale, Orpheus knew he wasn't alone.

Under the cover of darkness their eyes met, and time held still. Like they were back in the alley again, at the cusp of everything Orpheus couldn't resist.

So why are you?

Orpheus grabbed Fenrir's wrist, pried his hand off his mouth and said—

Every word Orpheus knew died in his throat when something enormous crashed into the building, shaking it to its foundation, spidering cracks across the ceiling as it dragged itself across the roof.

Broken plaster rained down from the darkness, Fenrir's hissed "*Fuck*" the precursor to his entire world turning over.

He hit the floor in a tangle of blankets, was kept there by the weight of Fenrir's body on top of his. Orpheus could feel him, smell him, so much and so close. But the tension from before was gone, panic replacing the fluttering feeling inside his stomach, because through the gap between the floor and the bed, Orpheus could see the window, and what filled it made him want to scream.

One massive golden eye peered into the darkness, split pupil dilating, hunting the shadows for its prey.

A dragon. *The* dragon. Red had been right, and it was *here*—for *him.*

The darkness wouldn't hide him, not anymore.

"*Fenrir,*" Orpheus whispered, voice gone thin. The eye snapped towards the sound—pupil narrowing when it found him; Orpheus couldn't look away.

The world shifted again when Fenrir hauled him to his feet.

"Run," Fenrir breathed, and then he shoved Orpheus out of the room at the precise moment the whole world exploded.

Bricks shattered inwards, cut into his skin. Fenrir grabbed him past the doorframe, out of the worst of the debris, Orpheus tripping over his own feet when a bellowing shriek turned his thoughts liquid. He stumbled, half-blind, half-deaf, the tough grain of old carpet scraping under his bare feet—trusting that wherever Fenrir dragged him would be safer than here.

They rounded a corner, out of the dust, hallway coming into focus, electric lights flickering overhead. Their room was on the top floor of the hotel, the lift that could have taken him and Fenrir down closed off by an ancient-looking "Out of Order" sign. But it wasn't down they were headed. Orpheus went stiff when Fenrir grabbed his wrist and dragged him away from the main staircase.

"But the stairs—"

"There's no time!"

A utility door groaned on its hinges when Fenrir threw his shoulder into the metal. The deadbolt gave way, revealing a short span of steps up, towards what Orpheus assumed was the roof.

"Why are we—" he dug his heels in, resisting Fenrir's forward momentum, "—you want to get on the *roof?*"

"You want the whole building to come down on top of us when that dragon tears it apart to get to you?" Fenrir asked, pulling on him again, one hand already reaching for the door handle. But Orpheus wasn't thinking about that anymore.

"Why did you come back?" he breathed out, eyes finding Fenrir's and holding.

"*Seriously?*" Fenrir made a face Orpheus had never seen before, somewhere between panicked and crushed. "You think I'd abandon you *now?*"

"I don't know if I can fight Lore," Orpheus admitted, unable to meet Fenrir's eyes.

"*What?*" Fenrir blanched, hand loosening around his wrist, then tightening again. For maybe the first time Fenrir visibly struggled to compile the shattered pieces of Orpheus into something that made sense. "Orpheus, is that why you think I'm here? To make sure you live long enough to fight Lore?"

THE CRACK AT THE HEART OF EVERYTHING

What else am I supposed to think? Orpheus didn't say. He ground his teeth together and looked away instead, unable to answer.

"Orpheus." Fenrir's hands cupped his face, dragged his head up so he had to meet his eyes. "That's not why I'm here."

And like all the words Fenrir left unsaid, Orpheus heard these too. And he believed him, because what was more terrifying than Fenrir using him like Lore had, was that he *wasn't*—that he had helped Orpheus, simply and without reservation, because he *cared*.

Orpheus didn't have time to reflect further. The building rocked, and then Fenrir released him, spinning around to shoulder the roof door open. In a blast of cold air, the starless sky spilled open and exposed. Orpheus locked up, whole body frozen, legs unwilling to work even as Fenrir dragged him forward anyway.

"I'll protect you," didn't sound as reassuring when it was a *dragon* after him instead of some pathetic little Brainrotter wiggling into his head.

One final push and Orpheus stumbled through the doorway, the cold bite of night stabbing straight through his robe and into his skin. Gravel slipped under his bare feet, left over from when the rooftop's asphalt had been poured, goose pimples creeping up his exposed ankles as he slid to a stop. But it wasn't the cold that had Orpheus shivering, it was the sensation of the entire building trembling, rocking on its foundation as if it were made of sticks rather than bricks. He couldn't see the dragon, but he heard it grappling its way around the outside of the hotel's facade, the great huff of its breath a second before a set of claws arose from beyond the roof top's edge.

A talon as large as he was small ascended, a momentary illusion of time standing still before it came down in one great arc.

Gravel sprayed, the rooftop rippled, and Orpheus scrambled backwards as the dragon tore into the asphalt and hauled its way over the edge. The night was already dark, but the shadows became suffocating when one enormous wing swept overhead, venous in refracted city lights, the serrated edge of its spined crest framing a trachea swollen with glowing dragonfire. Scales the size of Fenrir's chest covered the dragon from nose to tail tip, rusty red like the color of old blood, shielding a mass of muscles that rippled like waves in a tumultuous sea.

But it was the eyes that nearly brought Orpheus to his knees. Those enormous, gold-gilded eyes that slid to him and stilled, pupils narrowed now, like he was a target caught in a sniper's sight.

Time slowed as Orpheus watched the dragon hover at the roof's edge, mortar and bricks and asphalt giving way as twenty tons of muscle and bone and scales dragged itself upright, and Orpheus realized with sinking dismay that this wasn't just any dragon. This was an *Emperor Dragon*—the king to crown them all—something even those heroes from history had struggled to take down.

This was it, then. This would be how the curse got him. This would be how he *died*.

Fenrir shoved him backwards, one hand on his chest, the scream of drawn steel shrieking through Orpheus' skull a moment before the dragon's roar tore open the air. Saliva stretched to snapping between its teeth, the coil of red-orange light deep within its throat a promise of even more pain than its jaws threatened. Which was why he couldn't make sense of how *huge* Fenrir's grin was, or the raging fire that ignited in his Rim-pale eyes.

"Fucking *finally*," Fenrir growled. "Let's go, you hells-damned bastard!"

Then the whole roof quaked when the dragon lunged.

Steel met scales; man met dragon. With nothing but the flat edge of his sword Fenrir deflected the first strike, a bone-shattering impact that should have turned Fenrir's arm into putty. Instead, he confronted a dragon one-hundred times his weight class as if strength were a matter of sheer willpower rather than muscle and bone. Orpheus' whole world narrowed in on the impossibility of exactly what he was witnessing, heart hammering into his throat as Fenrir danced around the dragon like it was *nothing*, sword slipping between scales with every opening he was given, fluid and easy and unlike anything Orpheus could have imagined.

He'd never seen Fenrir fight. Not really. There'd been moments in the palace barracks when he'd caught some of the soldier's training—practice sessions when Fenrir had spent more time leading a young recruit through their sword forms than any actual engagement. This was nothing like that. This was reckless and illogical and profoundly, remarkably *incredible.*

When a curdle of smoke expelled through the dragon's nose, Fenrir was ready. When its tail lashed out to sweep Fenrir's legs out from under him, he was already out of its way. And when the dragon decided to ignore Fenrir entirely and focus on Orpheus instead, Fenrir's arms were tight around him, sailing through the sky like a raptor with its prey, landing neatly atop the opposite side of the roof, sword arm waving in the air as if to say, *"come on, we're over here!"*

"Shouldn't we—" Orpheus could barely breathe, let alone speak. Not because of shock, but because Fenrir's chest was shoved firmly against his nose. Somehow, he got his face to the side and gasped, "—run? Shouldn't we be running?"

"Never ran from anything in my life," Fenrir said through bared teeth. Then, he actually *did* call out to the dragon: "Hey! You! Yeah, that's right! We're over here!"

"You're insane," Orpheus hissed, shaking. His fingernails dug furrows into the leather of Fenrir's armor. "That's a fucking *dragon.*"

"Always wanted to fight one," Fenrir said like...like he'd been looking forward to this for far longer than the last ten minutes.

"What if I told you that isn't a normal dragon?" Orpheus tried, shoving at Fenrir while ignoring how fiercely the dragon stared at him from across the rooftop. "What if I told you that is an Emperor Dragon, and the only person on record killing one is a knight named Gawain from the fifth century?"

"You're such a nerd, Fifi," was Fenrir's baselessly simple response, his eyes warm and vivid when they met his.

Then fire boiled over them both, and it was Orpheus' turn to react.

It happened faster than a collider could split atoms, magic sparking between his fingers just as the dragonfire swallowed them whole. With a single snap, Netherflame roared to virulent life, a blast of ice-cold air that turned the air to muggy fog. It wouldn't last, heat was already building again, but Orpheus had everything he needed right here.

Sweat poured down his forehead and stung his eyes as he whispered the invocation, Netherflame flaring again as a delicate crystalline cocoon blossomed to life around them. A shield. And a good one. But it wouldn't hold long, not without a sigil to harness the incantation, and the only tool he had to work with was currently dripping off his nose.

His fingers slipped with sweat, Fenrir's chest heaving beneath his hand. Another wave of dragonfire rolled towards them, Orpheus' finger sparking with Netherflame a split second before it hit, fire tumbling overhead and around, the shield now locked firmly into place. Between them, the sigil glistened, wavering, a reckless gamble but one he'd called right because the dragonfire turned the air so molten that the heat would have consumed him and Fenrir both if not for the shield.

If the dragonfire had been a surprise to Fenrir, this was more so, because Fenrir looked at Orpheus as if he'd grown a second head.

No, that wasn't right. Fenrir was looking at Orpheus as if he'd just become the most delicious, expired meal pack he'd ever unearthed.

"Did you just *save* me?" Fenrir gasped, stars in his eyes.

"Shut up." Orpheus would later blame the fire for how hot his face grew. "If you're going to kill that dragon, now would be a great time!"

Inspired. It was the single word that came to mind when Fenrir let out a whoop and released him. Orpheus staggered, completely untethered, the single step he took unsteady even without the quake of the building beneath his feet. The mortar holding the brick building together cracked as the dragon closed the gap and landed before them with a massive crash.

And then the fight was on again. All Orpheus could do was watch as Fenrir deflected the swiping claws and snapping jaws of an immense creature. Hold his breath as the dragon shrieked, lurching sideways when Fenrir's sword sunk between two scales and came away dark with blood. It dripped an arc over the split concrete as Fenrir leapt back, barely avoiding the teeth that had gone for his head.

THE CRACK AT THE HEART OF EVERYTHING

"That the best you've got?" Fenrir laughed as he swung again, tearing through not scales or flesh, but the sinuous stretch of one massive wing.

The dragon roared, and the air shivered. Something close to a shockwave knocked Orpheus to the ground. His head throbbed and his teeth ached as pressure built and built, until it felt like his brain was going to leak out of his skull. Nausea twisted his stomach, the sound bleeding into a drone, vibrating through his bones and into his flesh so that Orpheus couldn't move, couldn't breathe—from his hands and knees he watched the dragon approach, slow and steady, Orpheus snared like a rabbit in its trap.

And maybe it should have been strange that the dragon didn't immediately tear into him. Maybe Orpheus should have taken the opportunity to cast another shield, or summon a column of Netherflame, launch some kind of attack of his own. But instead, his world narrowed in on those massive golden eyes, body held frozen as pupils blacker than night narrowed in an uncanny impression of intelligence Orpheus had yet to confront with any other hell beast.

The dragon stared him down, and Orpheus stared back, a precipice between them except for this invisible, intangible *question*.

Then, so fast that barely the glint of the neon lights catching steel gave him away, Fenrir dashed through his peripheral. There was no way for Orpheus to break whatever trance the dragon had cast upon him, but he didn't need to. Not when Fenrir did it for him. Orpheus held his breath as Fenrir sailed through the air, coming down in a deadly arc, the glinting blade of his sword sinking directly into one of the dragon's massive golden eyes.

The dragon shrieked, and the whole world turned to fire.

Faster than he could scream, Orpheus flung up a shield, but he was too slow to keep the edge of his robes from singing, or the asphalt beneath his hands and knees from softening into tacky mud. His hands shook as they carved the sigil into the half-melted ground, eyes squinting into the fire in a desperate search for Fenrir because how was Orpheus supposed to protect him if he kept leaving him behind? But Fenrir was nowhere to be seen, the fire too dense, too blinding to see through.

Tears stung Orpheus' eyes as he searched the blaze anyway, his swallow thick as he thought—*no*, Fenrir was *fine*. He had lived through worse—*Orpheus* had been the reason he'd lived through *worse*—But where was he? Where the fuck was *Fenrir*?

Tightness strangled his chest, choked out a sob. His fingers clawed at the asphalt around the sigil. If he could dig it up he could take the shield with him, go find Fenrir somewhere in this blaze, because he couldn't be dead. Orpheus would finally discover if necromancy was possible, just to bring Fenrir back and kill him himself, if Fenrir went and did something as stupid as *dying*.

But before he could rip the sigil from the ground, everything stopped. The shrieking and the fire and the heat and the fight. It all came to an abrupt end in a cyclone of wind when the dragon took to the air. One massive beat of its wings propelled it into the sky, the lift force flattening Orpheus where he knelt. He collapsed onto the rooftop, asphalt soft and sticky beneath his cheek, watching the dragon gain height as if...was it...was it *retreating*?

The dragon rose, and rose, and *rose*, until the smog swallowed it up, nothing but a churning shadow where it should be.

Silence descended, a disconcerting backdrop to the pounding in his ears. Orpheus shivered so hard he couldn't stand. Didn't think that really mattered because all he could focus on was the gaping absence of the dragon above, and Fenrir, who should be at his side.

Where was he? Where the fuck was *Fenrir*?

Orpheus struggled upright, determined to find out, when everything tilted sideways.

Decades of patchwork repairs came apart underneath his feet, twenty tons of Emperor Dragon more than enough to push the building past the point of no return. The echoing fracture of its roar would have shattered supports that had never been meant to hold anything heavier than a few feet of snow, the red-hot inferno of its dragon fire hot enough to melt the strongest of steel. And as the ground opened up beneath him, Orpheus thought it a wonder he had made it this far at all. He'd expected the worst when he'd been punted from the Gilded Palace's gates; in retrospect, the last few weeks hadn't been that terrible at all. His singular regret was that the curse had taken out Fenrir alongside him.

I'm sorry, he thought, world slipping out from under him. *Fenrir, I'm so sorry.*

Then the entire hotel collapsed.

A slow building roar, a deafening rush. Smoke and dust and the acrid tang of pulverized metal filled Orpheus' lungs. His feet treaded air in a slow-motion dash, gravity pulling at his robe, tangling around his body in a tight twist. He choked on a scream, throat filling with smog, the Netherflame rose from the darkness on a sweat-slicked snap. Without a sigil to hold it, Netherflame erupted around him, a wall of cold fire that devoured everything it touched. But that was all Orpheus needed. Clean air swelled his lungs for one precious second, the breath all he needed to shove his hands out and cast. Atmosphere pulsed, a pocket of safety that bubbled around him, channeling without a sigil by sheer force of will, until the moment he collided with the ground and the whole building came down around him.

Dust filled his nose, clogged up his lungs. Thoughts swam out of his head, emotions a tangle of juxtapositions. Terror and relief. Panic and an uncanny calm. The dragon had attacked but Orpheus was alive. Buried under a mountain of bricks and dust and the weight of his mistakes but *alive*.

Dim light shimmered through the cracks of the debris piled atop him, and he reached for it, shoving through bricks and mortar, following the light, and digging himself free.

The Stacks emerged from the wreckage, all dense dust and a distant, fluorescent haze. Orpheus sucked dirty air through his teeth while the world pieced back together, his thoughts making a bid for purchase before slipping through his fingers all over again.

He was— he needed to— find him. Fenrir. He needed to *find* *Fenrir*.

Reality slammed home, adrenaline propelling him to his feet. Gravel and broken pieces of brick skittered off his shoulders, skin scraping across the debris as he stumbled around in a circle. Looking.

Searching. He had to be *here—*

"Fenrir!" he shouted, voice drowning in dust.

His eyes stung with every blink, the sleeve he brought to his face too dirty to be the filter he needed. But he pushed air though his lungs while his feet scraped over broken brick, tripping over the rubble in search of the only thing that mattered.

Fenrir. *Where was Fenrir?*

A brick gave way under his foot, his chin hitting the brick because the hands he reached out with plunged through a collapsing hole. He felt it immediately. The softness of skin, the stiff give of muscle beneath. Warm, but not moving. Recently alive, very possibly dead. A ringing swelled Orpheus' head, all the spells he knew for maneuvering heavy objects fleeing his thoughts as he began throwing brick after brick into the dusty darkness.

He searched the shadows, eyes digging through the rubble alongside his now bloodied hands. He didn't stop until he saw it: the torn edge of a shirt, the pale expanse of a forearm, the tangled curl of tawny, brown-blonde hair.

He grabbed for the hand, blood slickening his grip. It slipped from his grip once, twice, he caught it on the third time, pressing his fingers into the soft place above the tendons and holding his breath—

Nothing.

Air choked in his lungs, caught on his sob.

He tried again, squeezing the wrist until his nails bit into flesh, the shaking in his body coming on hard and fast. Still nothing. Nothing but cooling flesh and his own blood slicking the skin. Orpheus dropped the arm, reached for the hair.

Voices rose in the distance, growing louder, the scraping slide of brick against brick emerging from the darkness behind him. But he was halfway inside the hole, shoving bricks to the side because his hands were too slick with blood to grip them. Unable to worry about the debris potentially collapsing beneath him because he had to— he had to *see—* one last time—

He shoved a bloodied brick to the side, freezing as sightless brown eyes stared up at him.

Brown eyes. Not blue.

…It was the bartender. Jack.

Jack was dead.

Relief and guilt hit Orpheus in perfect tandem, a one-two punch that left him reeling because how dare he feel anything but grief when *Jack was dead.*

It's not Fenrir, his mind screamed in manic glee. *You got Jack killed*, it spat out like venom.

He shoved away from the body, bloody palms scraping over the brick, a sob ugly tearing from his throat. He'd done this. He was the reason Jack was dead, the hotel in pieces, that the dragon had attacked the Stacks at all. His curse and his mistakes and everything that had come before. Everything Lore had done. All the power he'd given her. All the spells and archanics and weapons that had allowed her not to unite an Empire but strip it down to its bones.

I'm sorry, he wanted to say—to Fenrir. To the world.

Instead, he started into Jack's dead eyes and sobbed.

"Fifi?" tore through the ruined night.

Hands grabbed him—his shoulders—hauling him out of the hole. Through his tears, Fenrir's face swam through his vision, dirt and blood and that infernal scar marring his face, but he was whole. Hale. Very much there and more so *alive*. Orpheus shoved forward at the exact moment Fenrir dragged him in.

The relief—it was soul crushing. Too heavy for Orpheus' bloodied hands to hold. Jack was dead but *Fenrir was alive* and Orpheus should feel grief but all he really felt was grateful, because it was Fenrir's heartbeat beneath his cheek. Fenrir's chest that rose with every shallow breath. Fenrir's arms that were around him—holding him—clutching him so desperately that Orpheus finally felt like he had found his place in this awful cruel world he helped Lore make.

He grappled his hands into the back of Fenrir's shirt, buried his face in his shoulder and cried.

The sounds of the Stacks bled through the dust, building at a frenetic pace: the soft whine of an emergency siren, the gaggle of voices too numerous to follow. But Fenrir was safe against him. A living breathing anchor that Orpheus realized through the hysteria of his grievous solace, he was going to have to give up.

I nearly got him killed.

He had to leave. The Stacks, yes, but more so Fenrir.

"Jack is dead," Orpheus breathed into Fenrir's chest, voice rough, hands shaking. Finally, he pushed Fenrir away and clamored to his feet. "I can't stay here. I need to leave."

"Orpheus," Fenrir breathed his name, already standing and reaching for him again. Their hands brushed and Orpheus jolted back, shaken. "It's not your—" Fenrir cut off, face seizing, stricken with pain. But there was no hiding the truth anymore.

"It is my fault. I got Jack killed. I nearly got *you* killed."

Fenrir shook his head. "Plenty of things have almost killed me." Which was true, but it didn't make it hurt any less. "And that dragon's been hanging around a lot longer than you have. Tonight was inevitable. At least we were here to chase it off."

"You chased it off," Orpheus clarified. "I was little better than bait."

"Every good hero needs a damsel to save," Fenrir tried to joke, voice breaking. But Orpheus clung to it, wishing for some kind of return to normalcy, despite how far from normal his life had become. Because Fenrir was supposed to hate him, and everything that needed to come next would be so much easier if that were still the case.

Orpheus took a step back, the world rubble beneath his feet.

"It's going to come back, Rawkner. That dragon is going to come back because the curse won't give up until I'm dead, and what will you do then? Are you going to fight off every hell beast that comes for me? Am I expected to let you, all because you have some stupid obsession with playing the hero?" Orpheus meant to sound scathing, but it came out desperate, his voice high, strung out.

"Better than playing the villain, right?" Fenrir asked, and of all the truths Orpheus was confronting, that might be the heaviest, a weight Fenrir had also been carrying. Orpheus knew with complete certainty that Fenrir wasn't joking.

"I'm not playing," Orpheus whispered, "I'm just as guilty as her."

THE CRACK AT THE HEART OF EVERYTHING

Like the rubble of the hotel they stood upon, Orpheus watched Fenrir's expression crumble—a rare solemnity replacing his perpetual mirth.

"That's not true. You're a good man, Fifi," Fenrir said around the tremble in his voice, "You *saved* me. I could have fought that dragon while you saved yourself and then where would I be?"

Fried to a crisp atop a pool of molten asphalt. Orpheus knew, because it had nearly happened. But one good deed didn't overwrite a lifetime of devastation. Maybe Fenrir had been secretly working towards something better long enough that he didn't feel responsible for the damage Lore had done. But if Lore was the horseman, then Orpheus was her spear, and they'd reigned destruction across the world *together*.

Maybe he was worse, because he'd never even bothered to see it— the world he had dared to crush.

You might be a hero, but I'm anything but, was what he needed to say. Instead, all that came out was: "I don't want you to die."

"Well," Fenrir said, voice thin, a little broken, "good thing you have that snappy flame shield trick you do."

Then Fenrir reached out, hand lifting until his fingers brushed under Orpheus' chin, the lightest touch of skin on skin—gentle and careful, reverent and honest—and whatever impetus Orpheus was searching for was right there, staring him in the face.

"I can't do this," Orpheus tried to say; it came out as a whisper.

Fenrir's expression flickered, hands dropping to his sides like it was taking everything inside him not to reach out and grab him. "I told you; I don't expect you to fight Lore."

Orpheus closed his eyes. "You know that's not what I mean."

Fenrir's voice came out strange when he asked, "Say it."

It would have been easy to lie. Tell Fenrir it was the dragon or a Jackdog or a Brainrotter he wanted to protect him from, but he was tired of all his excuses, because Orpheus wasn't actually scared of any damned hell beast. It was himself—and the evidence was right there in the mark he had put on Fenrir, the only time Fenrir *had* been hurt, not by a dragon or a curse, but by *him*.

Fenrir's scar glinted in the scattered neon light, a reminder of Ohm and Lore and all the power Orpheus had handed her. The power to devastate a whole empire, all because of *him*.

Orpheus *was* cursed. Had *been* cursed, for far longer than the last few months.

"Lore may be wrong about a lot, but she was right to kick me out," Orpheus half said, half whispered. His voice was raw when he said, "I have to go."

"Please don't, Orpheus, I—"

But too late, the voices shattered the dusty night, reality crashing back into place as Red and a group of locals stumbled over the rubble behind them. Breathless and panicked, they descended upon him and Fenrir, and whatever they might have said next was swept away into the cold, starless night.

INTERLUDE
THE SEED

He finds her in the corner of the Library he knows Lore calls home. Orpheus doesn't come here often because it's always been Lore's private space. She moved out of the dungeons months ago, hiding where the hermits won't find her, and something about that makes Orpheus feel like he should give her space, too. But she hasn't emerged in two days, and he's become worried—though whether she is in danger or that she's upset with him, he doesn't know.

"Lore?" he calls into the shadows of one of the largest bookcases, "Lore, are you there?"

A rustle and a scrape are his answer. Orpheus shifts his weight, scuffs his foot, scratches his wrist and tries again.

"May I come in?" he asks into the near quiet, hearing how thick it becomes once the echo of his words leave the air.

"Yes," Lore finally says after what feels like forever.

Orpheus holds his breath as he slowly rounds the corner.

Lore has made this part of the library her own. There's a well-worn rug atop the stone floor he doesn't recognize, tightly woven wool in deeply colored patterns, red and black and blue and green that would have been fancy enough for a king before time got in the way. Tapestries hang from the wall, silky colors gone gray in the sun-kissed dust of the skylights. A handful of objects adorn the space, what looks like a bell-pull hangs from a heavily brocaded tapestry, and a brightly colored piece of stained glass has been propped against two stacks of books so light can shine through. And at the center of it all a low table sits, a pillow of patches providing a cushion for Lore to sit, though right now she is sat crossed-legged atop a pile of blankets Orpheus recognizes from his own room. She's drug what she could up from the dungeons, and though he can't see it he knows there's a lumpy mattress hidden underneath.

She juts her chin at the table and Orpheus interprets that as an invitation.

The rug is surprisingly scratchy against his bare feet and Orpheus flinches as he lowers down to the patchy pillow. His elbow knocks a lamp that Lore placed at the center of the table, and he reaches out to steady it. He feels a stranger in his body lately, growth catching him off-guard and making his already gangly limbs cumbersome. For all the months of sharing his food with Lore, his body is growing. He's going to be tall. Maybe he'll be big and strong too—like the heroes from his books.

"Sorry," he breathes as he cups the lamp until he's sure it's not going to topple over. The shade is pretty, frost-etched glass with a single crack running through the narrow base. It's as fancy as everything else Lore has collected in her little corner and Orpheus treats the object with the same kind of reverence he does his books. "This is nice. Your—your room, it's nice."

Lore looks at him with the same baseline regard that she usually does, and Orpheus counts that as a win. After what happened two days ago, he isn't really sure where they stand.

"That's for you," Lore says, and Orpheus feels like he's about ten minutes behind in their conversation. He looks at Lore and his confusion must be obvious because her eyes slip to the lamp he nearly knocked over.

"This is for me?" he asks, heart filling at the fact that Lore—Lore's giving him a gift? "It's beautiful, I'll treasure it for—"

"Light it up," she says before he can finish, and again Orpheus struggles to keep up. He blinks down at the lamp and thinks—how? It's an antique oil lamp and he knows the world hasn't had oil in ages because it all got used up in the—

"With your fire, *Orpheus*," Lore says his name like she always does, like it's a struggle for her to get the syllables right.

He stares at Lore, then at the lamp. He doesn't understand.

"What will that—"

"Do it," she snaps.

Orpheus looks at the lamp, all innocuous brass and a delicate glass shell, and he feels the itch in his fingers before he thinks about what comes next, the guts-deep need to free the icy fire that's spent days now infecting his veins. He brings his thumb and middle finger together and, like a tiny explosion, dark fire erupts in his palm.

He looks at Lore as he cradles it. Can't unsee that desperate grief he remembers from before.

"Now place it inside," she says in a voice so calm it shakes.

Orpheus reaches out, hand trembling as he holds the fire in one hand and takes up the lamp in the other. If Lore's instructions were supposed to be clear, they don't feel that way anymore. Orpheus doesn't know if he should dump the fire through the open top or press it against the glass or pry open the brass reservoir underneath. But like the instinct that's guided him this far, it seems sheer willpower is enough, because in an unlikely turn, a thin thread of glimmering violet light peels away from the ball of flame in his palm and fills the entirety of the lamp.

Orpheus blinks, concentration lost. And as the fire in his hand sputters out, the fire in the lamp remains, and he realizes with sudden incredulous disbelief that he's done something that shouldn't be possible. Bridged the gap between technology and whatever strange matter this fire in his blood is. The wheels in his head start spinning at the precise moment he acknowledges where Lore's have already gone.

"Good," Lore says, and it takes Orpheus a second to register she spoke at all.

He looks up, ignoring the thoughts in his own head as he waits for Lore's.

"They're going to try and take it," she says, "they're going to want it for themselves."

She doesn't need to say who. Orpheus has spent the last two days fearing the same thing. The hermits did this to him for a reason. There is something more that they want from him. And as the little light in the lantern churns on without fading, like one of those electric devices he's read so much about, he knows that what flows through his veins is pure and simple *power*.

"It's ours, they can't have it. I won't let them, I promise," he says in a fierce rush; his heart fills again when Lore looks at him with something close to satisfaction.

"You'll have to stop them when they try." And it's no longer a question of if but *when*.

He won't feel the disconnect until hours later, curled up in his bed staring at the closed door of his cell, waiting for *when* to come, the incongruence between what will happen and what he'll have to do suddenly real in the same way the magic he possesses is real: hard to imagine and impossible to believe, but a fact all the same. And as the gravity of that weighs on him, a part of Orpheus wishes he could give everything back—the magic to the hermits and the promise he made to Lore—go back inside the stories he'd escaped to and forget that his life is his at all.

But then the itch in his fingertips erupts with a tenacity he can't resist, and Orpheus thumbs a lick of violet flame into life. It's incredible and beautiful and perfect and *his*, and he knows Lore is right. He can never give this up—not for anyone, or anything.

CHAPTER XVIII

PATH AHEAD

Out there, beyond the Stacks, the stars were so much brighter.

Orpheus dug his heels into Achates' flank, encouraging him onward across a babbling creek. Stones slipped under his hooves, the water so black that all Orpheus could do was trust Achates' instincts rather than his own. Without Fenrir to guide him, Orpheus wasn't sure he was even following the right path, let alone the safest.

Stop, that voice snapped, *I thought you'd agreed—*

I wish he was here, slithered to the surface, as unwelcome now as it had been when he'd reached the edge of Red's oil fields and seen the desiccated bodies of six teenagers on pikes. And again when he'd ridden through her dying orchards, the dirt as dried out as those bodies, the wilting branches blackened by some unknown disease. But it wasn't until he'd crossed beneath the humming arcs of the electrical grid that the feeling really hit home, the silvered web of worked steel and stretched cable making him feel small, completely irrelevant.

If the refinery had been impressive, the grid was *magnificent*. Electricity hummed through the air, setting the tiny hairs on his neck on their end, as pure, devastating *power* drew out from the earth, all that geothermal energy from the crater powering a turbine that belched clouds of steam into the sky. A testament to the hard work of the hundreds of people who had given their lives for access to something so much larger than any one of them, Orpheus had looked upon that grid and seen not a network of steelwork and cable, but a sigil. Worked with singular intention, forged from the bed of wreckage that was the wasteland, raw power for a formless machine that could shape the future of the world itself.

Despite the Netherflame thrumming through his veins, Orpheus felt small in that moment. Had ridden away wondering what more there could be if this grid was the first step towards the future. What other mysteries could be uncovered, secrets lost alongside their ancestors—sacrificed, so it seemed, to the entropy history always tended to keep.

He'd wondered if that was what Fenrir had seen when he'd first looked upon the grid. If he'd envisioned the same future and found worth in it—if that was why he had protected Red and turned a critical eye on Lore. Because it was becoming clear to Orpheus that the world was on the cusp of what could be called healing, and something like that needed to be nurtured, not met with a bloodied sword.

And here he was, on a purely selfish quest to break a curse that only affected him, when the altruistic option was to let it have its way so the world could move on.

If Lore allows it, his mind whispered.

When he'd camped that first night and hadn't been able to ignite the kindling he'd collected, cold had crept into his bones. Without a fire he settled on the cool light of his Netherflame, spending a long time staring into the purple flame and feeling empty of the comfort it normally brought. Maybe it was the cold, or maybe it was the strange snuffling coming from where Achates grazed, but Orpheus considered again that he'd made a mistake leaving Fenrir behind.

He hadn't seen any hell beasts yet, but it was only a matter of time. What would happen when one inevitably attacked? What would he do if he got lost on his way to the Keep, stranded in a forest he didn't even know the name of, let alone where he might go for help? Who would guide him, protect him, make sure he remembered to eat and watch over him while he slept? Who would distract him from the thoughts in his head, or all hells, make him *laugh?*

I miss him, Orpheus quietly admitted.

I'm protecting him, made the loneliness a little less bitter.

He woke the next morning to frost, a shimmering second skin that set the world on fire. It would have been beautiful if twenty minutes into his morning that icy dew hadn't turned to cold damp, permeating every porous surface on Orpheus' body, including his robes. He tugged Fenrir's gloves on, the soft leather not warm but at least impermeable. Not even Achates burned hot anymore—the Netherflame engine he'd taken from Farris' garage pumping ice cold fire through Achates' guts, and as those strange snuffling sounds grew more frequent, Orpheus began to wonder.

Achates was struggling—the snuffling, yes—but more so the lethargic weight dragging his steps, an unsteadiness uprooting his footing, and most worrisome, the droop to his eyes. Things, all of them, that hadn't existed days or weeks before.

Orpheus knew Netherflame wasn't safe for long exposure, but he hadn't thought it'd be a problem for Achates. He wasn't fully alive, after all—at least in the biological sense. But in retrospect, Orpheus realized that for his half organic body, the Netherflame was poisonous. The engine was killing Achates, slowly, but surely, and Orpheus couldn't blame that on anyone but himself.

I can swap it out again, he told himself. *As soon as we reach the Keep, I'll find another engine and swap it out.*

He was three days out from reaching the Keep, according to Red's map.

The pine woods that overwhelmed Lore's mountain were thinner out here. Rock had been traded for soil, brown needles softening the trail. Bold green moss pushing through patches where the sun shone best, and Orpheus used it as a distraction, finding shapes in the patches like they were clouds in the sky.

It was strange how little life he encountered. There were a few birds in the trees and the rustle of fauna in the undergrowth, but no people. No settlements. The clearings he passed looked years aged, whatever structures had filled their voids stripped from time like they'd never existed. Not for the first time, Orpheus wondered what had happened. Had this been Lore or the work of people long since dead? Was the Incident to blame, or the panic that had arisen in its aftermath?

He'd never come across many books recorded in the years following the Incident, so he had pieced together a picture of nature reclaiming what it had lost to industry and enterprise. The pictures of cities and planes and highways had been overwhelming, and that was from the omnipotent vantage history tended to give. But the landscape he rode through, it didn't feel natural. It felt strange. Wrong. *Haunted.*

Where are all the people? He wondered, and if Fenrir had been there, he knew the kind of expression he'd don if Orpheus asked.

In the far distance, a familiar trill wavered over the soft *shush* of wind. Orpheus grit his teeth and clenched Achates' reins, keeping his head down as if, by ignoring the sound, he could hide.

Out amongst all this untouched land, he was exposed. Whatever roads Lore's army had taken weren't here. Perhaps he wasn't actually headed towards the Keep at all. Perhaps Red had sent him off to his death rather than risk him returning to Lore and divulging her deception. Or maybe she was worried that the damage the dragon could wreck on the Pit would be as great a loss as that to the Stacks, and she'd sent him towards the most uninhabited place she could think of.

East—the Rim—and whatever secrets it hid.

The gray hatch marks that carved out the map's eastern edge were no more or less revealing than the little weaving snake of a river that apparently laid ahead, their positions noted, their dangers presumed. Orpheus recalled Lore's war table and the positioning of the trenches, the ragged edge of the world where the land itself dropped off. Red's map looked different. The gray swath of the Rim was a little larger, the marking indicating settlements more numerous than those recorded on Lore's table. Orpheus chose to trust that Red's map was accurate, but it could as easily be nonsense. He didn't want to think Red would deceive him, but he was reminded again of how deeply entrenched he'd been with Lore—how Red may not believe he could overcome their connection.

Lore used me, the voice inside his head whispered. *Is she still using me?*

The thought settled uncomfortably, reinforcing Orpheus' choice to leave Fenrir and the Stacks behind.

The dark veil of night descended, stars glimmering high above, the path they walked limned in pale reflections, ghostly in the dense lifeless quiet of the pine woods.

"It's okay, we'll be okay," Orpheus murmured when Achates stumbled. He ignored the rock in his stomach, the needling impression that nothing at all was okay.

Ahead, the darkness split, the silvery trail of the path he followed sinking into shadows, stars falling towards a horizon he couldn't see. Once he urged Achates closer he realized the path hadn't split off into a divergence but fallen off into a massive chasm that cracked the earth in two.

He thought he could see, some two hundred yards down, the dim flicker of Netherflame. But he couldn't be sure, and he couldn't take the risk, not to cross the chasm or to try and find a way down. Instead, he shoved the map into his pocket beside the spell page, tugged back on Achates' reins and forged a path along the scar in the world.

He wouldn't find the reason for the chasm until morning. Wouldn't realize he'd discovered the river on his map until he heard the surge of a waterfall emerge from the bloated quiet.

He and Achates stumbled upon the river alongside dawn's gray embrace. Water rushed over the edge of the chasm, river emptying into a bottomless nothing, and at the opposite shore a piece of his machine speared up through the ground. Here, a hundred miles away from the mountain's dig site, the earth carved open, a literal hole into Hell where the river roared down, down, *down* until Orpheus couldn't see anything but shadows and mist and the dim dark glimmer of Hell's violet light.

You're not getting past that.

Suddenly, the Keep felt entirely out of reach.

He had no one to blame but himself. Couldn't help but think that had been the case his entire miserable life.

From deep within the chasm, the warbling trill of the dragon echoed, like it could sense he was there, alone and defenseless.

Fenrir's voice murmured in his head, an assurance of hope that Orpheus wished, in that moment, he could believe. But, alone in the empty pine woods, winter's strangled embrace beckoning, the curse a hound at his back, hope felt like a lie.

CHAPTER XIX

THE CROSSING

The morning of their fourth day, it became clear Achates was going no further.

Orpheus shifted his weight, staring down at where Achates lay. He knew horses would sometimes lie on the ground, but the way Achates' looked didn't feel natural, and when he knelt down beside him, he heard the strain in his lungs, saw the watery glaze in his eyes. Orpheus didn't need to put a bare palm on his skin to know it'd be cold, but he did so anyway, stroking down Achates' neck as he murmured half-empty assurances.

"I'm sorry, my friend." Orpheus offered his hand to Achates' snout and let him push into it. "I did this to you. This is all my fault."

Achates made that snuffling sound, the one he'd been making for days.

Like this, he could feel the Netherflame flowing through his blood, cold and prickly, like a river of barbs beneath his skin. Orpheus had never been good at healing spells, but at this point, anything was worth a shot.

From his pack he pulled out the little bowl and a vial of quicksilver, tools he hadn't touched in weeks, the longest he could remember having gone. He tipped the silver into the bowl, sparked a violet flame within the pot and unrolled his tool kit. The canvas spread across his lap was soft and well-worn, the tools it held so familiar as to feel like extensions of himself. From the array he selected a delicate needle—close to a paintbrush—the little tip at the end hollowed out to hold a thread of liquid silver. He dipped the tip into the still-flaming pot, thumbing the mechanism at the end that would draw the silver up into the reservoir hidden inside, then held the needle aloft.

The spell he had in mind was of his own creation, a sigil he had experimented with a number of times over the years before giving up and simply focusing on building more engines. The markings he inscribed were a series of simple commands, meant to lessen the wearing of delicate parts and relieve the stressors born of continuous work, but Orpheus modified them now, including within them a sort of portal into himself, a connection between him and Achates that would hopefully allow Orpheus' own body to act as a kind of filter for the Netherflame poisoning his body.

Could his immunity be passed on? Orpheus wasn't sure. Casting an untested spell probably wasn't the way to find out, but if Orpheus didn't try, Achates would die. It could work. It *should* work. Whatever doubt held him back was born of the shadows in his mind—the same ones that insisted he run back to Lore and beg for his old life back. But there was no going back. He needed to move forward, and if he wanted to help Achates—and himself—he needed this spell to work. He had to try.

Desperation made heroes out of some, cowards out of others, and Orpheus was tired of always feeling like a coward.

"This might sting," he murmured, placing the needle against Achates' shoulder. The horse snuffled again, softer this time, like he understood; a comforting notion.

The first prick went unnoticed, same with the second and third. Orpheus made it halfway through the first arc before he noticed the fever bubble up in his veins. Heat swelled through him, anathema to the cold he'd spent days traveling with. Was this what Achates felt? Was this what Orpheus had done to him? A creature he had dared to call a friend?

THE CRACK AT THE HEART OF EVERYTHING

He completed the sigil, gently stroked Achates while he watched the silver set. Physical contact would be necessary for the spell to take and he figured it'd be at least thirty minutes before any potential effect could be noticed. They would rest while they waited, and though Orpheus had never been the praying type, he figured it wouldn't hurt to try.

He dozed off under the soft light of a morning sun, Achates a cool balm to the growing heat in his flesh, his feverish dreams a welcome escape, only waking once afternoon grew too bright to ignore.

Orpheus fought through the swamp inside his head, blinking his eyes against a stickiness that hadn't existed when he'd fallen asleep. Achates stood over him, brown eyes clearer than they had been in days, the snuff of his breath warm rather than that strange, concerning cold.

"Is it working, my friend?" he murmured, hope sparking amongst the fever, the first he'd felt in days.

Hope did not come without a price. Now, it was Orpheus' turn to suffer. Gravity dragged at his eyelids and sensitivity scratched at his skin, every movement cumbersome for a body already exhausted from five days of non-stop traveling. His legs were sore from riding, and the perpetual cold of oncoming winter was barely tempered by his rising fever. He wondered again if he hadn't made a mistake. Of all the complications he'd predicted and contingencies he'd planned, disease had not made Orpheus' list.

He slipped twice when climbing onto Achates' back.

By the time he was seated in the saddle Orpheus was ready to collapse. Achates fared better. His pace evened and some of his strength returned, and though their pace was slow, by Orpheus' estimate, they were closing in on the Keep, if they could cross the river. He needed to find that bridge, but he'd been following the river for a whole day now and hadn't seen any trace of it. Maybe Lore had blown it up, or a storm had washed it down river—all Orpheus really knew was that he needed to get to the opposite shore before the curse found him again.

Five days now, without an attack. Five days of respite he hadn't earned, which meant something big was coming. Something worse than the dragon. Something dangerous enough to finally take him out.

"Come on friend, we'll get through this together." He petted Achates' mane while directing him forward along the reedy shore. The map sported several new folds from where Orpheus had been gripping it for days, and he smoothed it out over his thigh as he checked it again.

Close. They had to be close. He put their left side to the embankment, the forest thinner here around the edge where the water had receded from its original path. The river may be a little smaller, a little shallower, but the water still churned, angry white-capped rapids frothing over rocks and trees and what almost looked like one of Farris' vehicles, half-drowned several dozen yards in.

The farther west he headed, the more evidence he found. Like the abandoned encampment on Lore's mountain, there were memories here. Forgotten things the world had swallowed up, either left here by Lore and her army or three-hundred years prior, when reality had changed faster than anyone could have prepared for.

Where the earth eroded away cement broke through, the crumbled remains of some man-made structure Orpheus couldn't identify, clinging to a shape that once made sense. And there were clearings beyond the trees, large swathes of land that carved shapes out of the woods, the ground too infertile to grow anything even after all these years.

But whatever damage the Incident had caused, it was his drill Orpheus kept circling back to. Blackened trees, a dead forest, gray ground hammered thin, flaking like shale. Even here, miles away from the errant drill head, the forest struggled. Swathes of browned pines painted the landscape, the fallen tips strangely dusty and hollow, lacking the memory of life. And where the river calmed the water was gray, debris clogging in frothy dams, water flowing thick, a strange viscosity that shouldn't exist.

Perhaps that was what really kept him from trying to forge those waters. Something other than the foamy whorls and dead fleshy mounds he and Achates avoided on the shore. The cloying stank of rotting fish reached him in patches, most of the corpses he spotted long-dead. Strangely old, left alone to decay. Not even the forest's scavengers had any interest in what could have been a feast, and that made Orpheus worry. This far out, he didn't think the Netherflame would have that great an impact, but he wondered if the drill's path was somewhere down below, buried deep beneath his feet. A vein of Hell carved through the Earth's very crust, poisoning everything in its path.

He pushed out a breath and encouraged Achates onward.

They stopped once the sun began to dip behind the trees. Twilight had arrived and with it a hunger Orpheus had no desire to sate. His stomach tossed when he pulled out the half-empty bag of Red's trail mix. She'd given him enough to snack on for weeks, but he'd begun feeding Achates his food. Despite the fuelless engine in his guts, the horse always had an appetite, and some small, pathetic part of Orpheus had decided that keeping his horse well-fed was the least he could do to apologize. He'd run out of the freshest food, but some expired meal packs were left.

"Would you prefer curried yams and imitation lamb meat, or rice noodles in poultry parts?" He picked through what flavors were left, trying not to think about Fenrir and then blaming the fever when he couldn't stop himself.

Was he helping Farris in his garage or keeping Red company at the refinery? The hotel would need rebuilt and Fenrir himself admitted he liked manual labor. Maybe he'd been the one to bury Jack. Maybe he'd been able to dig survivors out of the rubble.

Maybe he was wondering if Orpheus had made it to the Keep. Or he was making plans to come after him despite Orpheus telling him not to. Maybe playing hero was something Fenrir couldn't actually resist, and he would show up in the nick of time, saving Orpheus yet again when the curse inevitably found him.

Or maybe Fenrir wasn't thinking about him at all. Maybe he had more important things to worry about. Like his coup or saving the world.

He washed out Achates' feeding bag with the water from one of his canteens rather than the gray stuff from the river. Then they set off again, cresting the ridge of the riverbed as the clouds above became bloated and dark. Wind brought ice along with the cold, carrying with it the threat of winter's first snow.

Not far in the distance, rising from the unnatural quiet, he heard it again. A warbling trill that made the hairs on the back of his neck stand on end.

The dragon. The dragon was out there. Looking. Searching. *Hunting.*

Orpheus ignored how his breath caught when he exhaled.

By the time night fell, Orpheus was certain he was going to die.

Cold chattered through his teeth, his body hunched over Achates' neck while the fever chewed through his brain. But Achates was improving with every hour, steadiness returned to his steps, that snuffling sound nearly completely diminished. Orpheus would have smiled if moving didn't hurt so much. But the pain wasn't as bad as the fever's heat. Sweat pricked his skin, ran rivulets down his back, and pulsed fire though his brain.

The rain began just as they came upon what Orpheus quickly realized were the remains of a bridge.

His hands shook as he pulled out the map, staring at lines that looked more like spirals with the way his vision swam.

This had to be it. This *needed* to be it.

Pylons arose from the river, fingers of water-stained concrete reaching towards a crumbling stone surface that had completely collapsed down the middle. Water foamed in angry whorls around the base, the fallen stone creating rapids as deep as he was tall, water sucking and spinning and churning below the surface, the winter storm coming down from the mountain bringing with it a flood of dark water.

He should have crossed a mile back, forgone his fears of the strange sludgy water and corpses and crossed when he had a half-decent chance.

Over the sound of rain and water, a trilling scream echoed. Close now. Getting even closer.

Orpheus swallowed down the bile that inched up his throat and tugged back on his reins, looking at the sky. He couldn't see anything. The clouds were too low and the rain too heavy and the sky too dark to reveal signs of the dragon. But he could hear something, a low whoosh that broke through the rushing river, like wings struggling to gain flight.

He wasn't ready. He couldn't do this. He never should have left Fenrir behind.

"What do you think, friend?" Orpheus asked Achates as they picked their way down to the river's edge. "If we keep to the pylons, could we make it across?"

He didn't know what else to try. Didn't want to risk doubling back and coming face to face with the dragon. At least here the bridge's ruins provided some kind of cover. A chance. They could hide under the still-standing arch where the bridge reached the shore and hope the dragon couldn't see them through the rain. Or perhaps, if they could get across, they might find some real shelter—a vehicle or an abandoned storehouse, something the military would have left behind that they could use in a fight.

A fight. It was becoming increasingly clear; he was going to have to fight.

Achates gave a snort, hooves clopping when they hit the solid pavers breaking through the smear of dirt and sand, the remains of what had once been a road however many years ago. Orpheus dismounted then, leading Achates on foot, feet and hooves shuffling down the embankment as they came upon the first of the pylons.

Embedded into the shore, the concrete was old and cracked, the blackened rebar underneath exposed in the places where the river had eroded the concrete away. Orpheus staggered as Achates came to a stop, placing his hand upon the pylon to keep his balance as he sighted across the river and tried to decide their best route.

His balanced swayed, achy joints protesting after sitting upon Achates for so long, the fever a miasmic buzz, making the world slide sideways every time he moved too fast. And his skin was hot, his breath shallow, nausea churning in his gut as violently as the water rushed down the river. Orpheus was sick, and there was no way he would make it across—not in his current state.

But when Achates took his first step into the water, he knew he was going to have to try.

The horse stopped, front hooves planted ankle deep in cold gray water, looking back with one dark brown eye.

Come on, Achates seemed to say, and it took all of Orpheus' strength to climb back into the saddle.

"Are you certain?" he whispered, bare hand on Achates' neck, sliding down to rest over the sigil. It was cold to the touch, the wave of ice against his skin a momentary relief. Then Achates plunged forward, strong despite the roaring water.

Water licked at Achates' knees and nearly touched Orpheus' toes. Barely five yards in and Orpheus was already looking over his shoulder, judging the increasing distance like it was a noose being drawn. He clung to Achates, thanking the stars that his spell was working and that Achates possessed a fortitude of will Orpheus had always struggled to claim.

He'd been beaten down by worse than a raging river—had survived months of attempts on his life by nearly every hell beast imaginable. And he'd lived through the dragon's attack once already. Had, for a moment, stood against it on his own two feet and came away unscathed. He could do this, if it came to it. He could fight for himself. He wasn't incapable, even if he often felt that way. Because no matter how weak Orpheus felt—how beaten—how scared and close he was to giving up—he knew he hadn't made a mistake.

Even if he died here—he had made the right choice. Because Fenrir was alive, and in the end, that's all Orpheus really cared about.

"Steady on," he murmured over the roaring water when Achates' hoof slipped.

His shoulder slammed into the pylon, knee crunching into the concrete as he took too much of Achates' weight. A pained sound escaped him, vertigo swimming through his head as Achates regained his footing. Then they were inching their way forward again, water splashing over Achates' haunches, swallowing Orpheus' calves, and when there was nothing but open river before and beside them, the edge of the pylon passing as they crept out into deeper water, Orpheus held his breath as Achates pushed off into open water.

Weightlessness blossomed, an unwelcome tide. Orpheus would have closed his eyes if he didn't think that unfair to Achates. They hadn't reached the rapids yet but that didn't keep Achates from drifting downriver, and for one harrowing second Orpheus thought, *this is it*, before Achates pushed against the current and dragged them onto the foundation of the second pylon.

They'd made it, this first step. One of six pylons between them and the far shore. It wasn't a lot to celebrate but what else did he have but hope? Maybe if Orpheus believed—if he trusted—Achates would see them both to safer shores.

Then the water rippled, and the wind kicked up, and the terrible scream of the dragon tore through the night above. Gray water glowed incandescent, dragonfire boiling hotter than the fever in Orpheus' veins.

The dragon had arrived, and with it, his curse.

And Orpheus...he wasn't ready.

But Achates was.

CHAPTER XX
DROWNED

In a crash of gray gloomy water, they plunged into the river.

Dragonfire rolled overhead, the surface of the water a ripple of glitter and gold. Orpheus clung to Achates, his hooves uselessly scrabbling across the loose rocks below the surface, lungs obviously still organic with all the bubbles of air clouding the surface above. Horses could swim but Orpheus hadn't been so sure—didn't know if Achates' half-metal body could even float or if his engine might flood and seize up. But Netherflame didn't have any need for oxygen, and for the first time Orpheus considered that he had actually made the right call when he'd swapped it out, because as they broke the surface of the water for some much-needed air, he saw how they'd cleared the distance to the third pylon.

They were doing it. They were forging the river. And if they could avoid the worst of the dragonfire they would likely make it across.

Achates pushed his flank up beside the concrete of the third pylon, Orpheus hunching over his back as they both caught their breath. Somewhere overhead, the dragon screamed. From what Orpheus guessed, it was some distance overhead, banking back around for a second pass. They were safe, for now. Possibly for a few seconds or a minute, but Orpheus hoarded time like he hoarded his breath, giving Achates space to make his own call rather than encouraging him back into the river. Even here, at the base of the pylon, their footing was uncertain. The rapids were ahead and with them the chance to get swept off with the current. All it would take was one foul step and they'd go down—get sucked into a riptide never to break the surface again.

But Orpheus didn't let those thoughts linger. He sunk his fingers into Achates' mane and kept their bodies close together, breathing air through his nostrils and letting it out through his mouth, calming his heart and seeking his center.

The first buffet of air hit them seconds before the dragon descended, but this time, he was ready.

"Close your eyes," he told Achates a moment before he cast.

The spell passed his lips, no more than a breath, the sigil a scratch against Achates' flank and then all the Netherflame he could summon rolled out of him and across the water in a bright, blinding flash.

Just like the shield trick, the blinding spell couldn't be sustained. He had nothing permanent to cast the sigil with, but he didn't need it—not for his plan. Above them, the dragon screamed, wings snapping in a whirlwind of air as it staggered mid-dive. Icy water stung Orpheus' face, kicked up by the gusting air, but Achates moved onwards, steadfast and committed. Orpheus realized, in that moment, that he'd misjudged Achates. He may be skittish and soft and a little bit uncertain, but he was stronger than Orpheus had ever given him credit for.

Something small and precious inside him coiled at that thought. Orpheus recognized the feeling because it wasn't the first time he'd sensed it. It was much the same to the feeling he got whenever Fenrir was near. Whenever they moved together, in sync with each other, like they had on that rooftop, or in the alley—how Fenrir knew him, understood him, on a level that went beyond anything on this physical plane.

I can't think about him right now. If he ever wanted to see Fenrir again, Orpheus needed to focus. Because if he could survive this, he actually might get the chance.

They reached the third pylon, current raging past them, capping the water white.

"Easy now, or that water will sweep us away," Orpheus said over the roar.

Achates' ears were tipped back, head high as he edged carefully forward. Orpheus could feel the tug of water over his thighs, a gripping, tearing sensation of ice dragging over his skin. He squeezed his legs tighter around Achates, hunching down over his neck and chancing a glance up at the sky. He couldn't hear the dragon but that didn't mean it wasn't there, recovering from the blinding spell, readying to strike. He sifted through his mental book of spells, fingers itching to cast despite the numbing water. Drops of ice speckled his nose, his cheeks, the water cold enough to freeze if not for the rushing current, and maybe that was why he didn't notice the skitter of rock coming down from the pylon—didn't register the dark stain of water dripping down the cement until it was too late.

He didn't need to look up to know the dragon was perched on the ruins of the bridge above them. Didn't need to look into that massive, golden-gilt eye to understand this was it.

Dragonfire erupted, molasses-thick.

The shield spell came up a second too slow. Orpheus's robes repelled some of the fire, the enchantments he'd placed weeks ago absorbing what they could, then crumbling under the overwhelming fire. Suddenly, every pocket of protection he'd sewn into the lining, every reflecting spell he'd embroidered onto the hem, every thread of silver and intersecting sigil came undone in a burst of burned-out power at the precise moment Achates plunged into the freezing, rushing river.

It occurred to Orpheus as his head went under, that this might be it. He may be a vessel for magic but he was still human—and Achates may be part machine but his flesh was still flesh, his mechanical body still able to break. And as the current swept them back up to the surface and past the bridge, it wasn't the vast open world that greeted him, but the dragon's open maw, and whatever fear Orpheus had been harboring for the unknown paled in comparison to this familiar horror—the realization that of all the horrible things that might kill him, it was his fear of dying alone and unloved that scared him the most.

I'm so sorry, Fenrir, Orpheus thought as dragonfire blossomed before him.

Achates plunged under the surface, taking Orpheus with him. Fire boiled overhead, a glimmering wave they barely avoided. The water surged, snapped up on a current or a rapid or one of those massive tangles of dead trees, the world tumbling around him as he clung to Achate's mane, water filling his nostrils, his lungs, his eyes and his ears so that he almost didn't feel it, when it happened. Wouldn't have noticed the snap-crack if not for the desperate hold he kept on Achates'. The rigid break not of waves crashing over him, but in the creature below him, Achates going stiff, and then still.

He knew the moment their bond broke. Felt the rupture of glass in his veins when the cold he'd drained from Achates' flesh snapped back through the sigil and out in a scream.

He couldn't tell who was screaming. Whether it was him or the dragon or the two of them together. The abrupt moment Achates' soul left his body echoed through Orpheus, well before he ever saw the strange angle of his neck. And then it was the crushing weight of guilt he struggled against, heavy enough that the churning water didn't matter—the weight on his heart was enough to drag him down.

That's all it took, one quick foul turn of fate, and that precious thing building inside him shattered—vicious shards of pain pierced through his guilt and tore it to shreds, something far worse bubbling up to take its place.

Rage tore through the darkness inside him, shadows receding, Netherflame taking their place. Power. Raw and sublime. It tore through him like an inferno. Bubbling and bursting and boiling until he couldn't contain it anymore—himself or his pain or the memories he'd spent a lifetime burying—the source of magic inside him not that silvery brand those scientists had clamped around his wrist, but the crack they had put in his very fucking heart.

Like the crack his machine had put in the earth. A source of devastation, but also, *power*.

A power he sensed running right there, right below him, the pocket of Hell he had carved through the crust of the earth, a sinuous, snaking pulse of poison that lived inside him, that Orpheus' own nature demanded he spread. All he had to do was touch it.

Touch. He *could* touch it, if he wanted.

You do. You want it.

Beneath him, the earth trembled, tear cracking wider as Orpheus reached inside and *took*.

Netherflame erupted, a blinding column of violet fire. He didn't emerge from the water so much as it turned to glass below him, a crystalline web of energy that transmuted the river into frozen waves of ice. He stood steady atop it, Netherflame pulsing from what could have been his very soul, a shiver of violet blossoming in the dark night, an aura of power like all the magic inside him was too much to be contained.

A familiar shape twisted in the frozen current, Achates' body encased in the ice, big brown eye frozen in perpetual horror—as if seeing Orpheus for the first time.

Teeth bared to his grief, he looked to the sky.

This was the power the scientists had given him. And he thought, suddenly, this was what Lore had been trying to drag out of him. Why she had given up on him, when she failed to do more than drive it further away.

Why she had let him loose in the world, hoping it may force it free.

The dragon trilled, and Orpheus tasted its fear.

"Get back here, you bastard," he snarled, lifting his hand towards the sky.

The sigil emerged, threads of power tangling, not in the air or the ice but right there, in his mind's eye. He didn't even need to work it. It manifested, wholly formed, his body an avatar for the Netherflame in his veins—in the earth—a rapture of fire that wouldn't consume him but everything else in its wake. And when his eyes settled on the dragon banking hard east, he had his target.

"Fuck you," he breathed, the Netherflame contracting—a coalescence of pure raw power he willed at the hells-damned beast.

Light shattered, faster than his scream.

Violet pierced the night, a strike of light through the velvet swath of sky, clouds limning gold when dragonfire boiled out on a fiery scream, coiling, curling, churning—explosive, like the hydrogen bombs of old. Thunder clapped a half-breath later, the force cracking the ice below his feet. Water burbled up to lick at his boots, but it didn't matter, not anymore. Orpheus whispered again, a second strike severing the sinuous flesh of one of the dragon's wings, the same one Fenrir had snagged, but this time there was no way for it to recover. The dragon screeched, a spiral of violet ice and broiling flame spinning down into the needly claws of the pine woods, disappearing into the shadows like they would finish what Orpheus had started—drag that damned beast back down to Hell and then keep it there, where it belonged.

But it wasn't enough. It wouldn't be enough. Not until this pressure in his chest was gone and his eyes didn't sting and his soul no longer seemed like it was breaking. Not until he felt that thread of life-force flee the dragon like he had Achates, saw the light leave its eyes as fear overwhelmed it—convalescence found in the trade of one life for another, the absolute decimation of everything he could possibly blame for all this pain.

Orpheus staggered forward, fingers curled at his side as one last spell tore through him.

The pine forest erupted into violent, violet flame.

Orpheus watched it burn. He stood atop his crystalline river, dripping ice from his fingers and tears from his chin, hunched over and shaking, feet spread wide as the power coursing through him thinned and his rage faded, like a wound that hadn't healed so much as bled out.

If anything was left inside him, it was a burned-up husk of what had existed before.

Achates was dead. But so was Orpheus, in all the ways that counted. Like the earth he stood atop—the carved-out flesh of the world poisoned by an infection he had put there, that would, eventually, spread across the whole of the planet like a virus, like a cancer, like a hells-damned *death curse* that was coming for all of them—Orpheus realized, even with all this power, nothing inside him had been fixed.

He hit the water with a choked wail. Let the rapids take him under as he closed his eyes and found those shadows, let them pull him close as the river did, ice dissolving into a cold dark embrace that had been waiting so much longer than the curse ever had.

He could feel it clearly: the beat-pulse of the wounded earth below. There was a pain it ached to heal, an echo of the crack in his heart. But Orpheus had never been good at healing spells, and some wounds were far too cataclysmic to mend.

Orpheus sobbed, rotten river water flooding his nose and mouth. Above, a light shimmered. Too small to be the sun or the moon or even dragonfire, but a beacon, nonetheless. Orpheus stared at it as his body tumbled in the current, following the golden light like if he watched it long enough it might come for him.

Some spoke of a light at the end. A bastion to guide them safely in death. Like a lighthouse atop a grim shore, it waited for Orpheus, and he reached for it, kicking his feet and paddling his hands. But he couldn't get any closer. The current was too strong and the water too gray, and soon the light grew smaller, until the flickering ember of its hope extinguished at the precise moment Orpheus' head broke the surface.

He gasped in an inhale, choked on a mouthful of river water.

You're alive, his mind thrilled, and Orpheus realized not everything inside him had died.

Because, despite the damage he had caused, despite the river rushing around him, despite the grief in his gut and the ache in his heart and the heavy guilt dragging him under, there was still something light and warm and good within Orpheus—and he wasn't ready to give that up too, not yet.

I don't want to die, Orpheus thought to himself, eyes straining to see past the descending veil to the light above. *I don't think I deserve to die.*

Everything inside him cracked as he let go of something important—a tether of his own creation—a fear and a sickness that had poisoned him for an entire lifetime. And like a weight lifted, he broke the surface in a spray of water, light dispersing into a fracture of waves and sound and cold and ice. Orpheus choked in a breath, then another, arms reaching and feet kicking until he broke from the current and reached the opposite shore. He crawled onto solid land, fingers slipping through sand and mud, and then finally, the gossamer-pale blanket of freshly fallen snow.

Winter had arrived while he drowned, and Orpheus lingered a moment at its edge, staring down at the little white snowflakes, so many stars amongst the death-blackened land. And for a moment he thought this had been the light he'd seen, the beacon he'd been drawn towards, the moon to his tide and the limitless possibilities of the vast in between, until the sound of boots atop pine tips filled the quiet winter night.

Almost drowning had left him weak—accepting the nature of his pain had left him crippled—and like the wick of a candle that had run out of wax, awareness flickered at Orpheus' edges as he looked up and found that golden beacon once more.

No. Not a beacon. A torch.

It was Fenrir.

He almost didn't recognize him. Gone was the confident smiling man who had hounded Orpheus for weeks, the ghost in his place stricken with grief, as if everything Orpheus had survived, he had lived through too. And when Fenrir didn't immediately drop to his knees and gather Orpheus up into his arms he feared for one awful, terrifying second that something more important than he realized had changed inside him. That the person he'd become wasn't someone Fenrir recognized, because the shadows he'd been hiding within had been too dense for even Fenrir's light to reach.

But then Fenrir's voice reached his ears, a barely-there "Fifi?" that fell soft as snow.

"I'm sorry," he whispered, looking up at Fenrir, knowing he didn't need to explain.

The torch tumbled to the snow, Fenrir descending into Orpheus' darkness like a sun come to set. His hands were impossibly warm when they pushed through Orpheus' hair to cup his face, fingers curling, holding, only a breath between them for the second it took for them to align together again.

Then all Orpheus could feel was the softness of lips against his, a riotous sensation that at another time, in another place, would have been terrifying. Now, it felt right. Orpheus gave into it. Let his mouth open on a sigh while the parts of himself not critical to survival shut down. And when the darkness came for him this time, Orpheus knew he'd be alright because he wasn't alone anymore—hadn't been in some time—and didn't need to be again. Not even when the curse inevitably caught up, because Orpheus didn't have to face it alone.

He'd fight with Fenrir at his side.

INTERLUDE
THE HERMITS

It's warmer than he expected, but then again, not everyone has ice for blood.

Orpheus scrubs his hands in the basin, hoping this third pass will be his last. The robe he wears is too big, but his clothes are ruined, and he doesn't have the stomach to return to the lab and find something better. Not yet. Not so soon. Hours or minutes could have passed. He's lost track of time, mind skipping backward every odd second so that he can't keep straight the timeline of events. The hermits aren't dead but then why all this blood? Why all this blood if the hermits are already dead? Why are they dead at all when this morning they were fine? How can they be fine when Orpheus knows they are dead? How does Orpheus know they are dead unless he—did he—he didn't—

He sinks his fingernails into his wrist, burrowing in, tearing it open. His blood runs cool and lazy, making murky little swirls out of the water in the basin. He doesn't stop until the water's gone cloudy, feeling a tightness release in his chest now that he has an explanation for all the blood on his hands.

The guttural whine of creaking hinges nearly propels him out of his skin. Water makes dark stars out of the concrete floor when Orpheus spins around to face the door, but it's only Lore. Her expression is always unreadable but right now Orpheus gets the impression of a mask. She's looking at him...not cruelly, but carefully, as if wondering if he should be considered a threat. The idea hurts and he stumbles over the few steps it takes to put some distance between them. The robe is slipping from his shoulders, and he pulls it close, hands shaking as he wraps himself up as if he could hide—like it's Lore who's the dangerous one and not—no—that's not—he's not—

"Stay here," Lore says and then the door creaks again when she closes it behind her.

Orpheus sinks to the ground and shakes.

She returns what could be minutes or hours later. Time pulses strangely when she washes her hands in the same basin he had used. Orpheus watches blood that must be his rinse away with every swipe of her palms. She's calm where he is not, and he finds comfort in that. Like whatever has happened here isn't deserving of his worry. He's safe. Lore's taking care of him in a way she has never bothered with before and he's grateful when she dries her hands and squats down to look at him.

She cocks her head, dark eyes hooded, pale skin veined purple where his is blue. A moment passes when Orpheus thinks—if he asks—Lore might hold him, but he knows he doesn't deserve it, not after what he's done.

But Lore doesn't leave, and for that Orpheus is grateful.

He doesn't want to be alone. Didn't realize just how alone he was until it was him and all those—those bodies—

"It's over now," Lore says, shattering the silence, "you've done well, Orpheus."

He—he *has?*

Orpheus feels the gravity of the world shift as he looks into Lore's eyes and clings to the satisfaction he sees there.

"Thank you," he breathes without thinking, the spell over him breaking alongside Lore's praise. He feels the shaking in his hands subside a little, calm rising where before there was panic and pain. Whatever happened here was scary, but it couldn't have been bad, not if Lore doesn't hate him for it.

THE CRACK AT THE HEART OF EVERYTHING

That night, it's Lore who gathers their meal and brings it to the library where he's holed up. He doesn't want to go back to his room in the dungeons though he knows he can't stay here. This is Lore's space, and he is a guest. But she's arranged her room for two, rug cleaned and table clear and a new box of books and texts she must have gathered stuffed under the pillows at the far side of her bed. It's a tidy little space she's made up for what feels like a celebration. And as Lore arranges the food on the table between them, Orpheus feels the balance between them rearrange. Ever since Orpheus gained his magic nothing has felt right, but as Lore places her lamp at the center of the table and the light of his magic tinges everything in cool violet, that changes.

Orpheus has done well today, despite how terrified it left him. But what is there to be so scared of now that he and Lore are finally safe?

"A toast," Lore says, lifting a chipped crystal goblet she must have dug out from storage. "To freedom."

"To freedom," Orpheus repeats, voice a little weak, brain parsing through all the ways in which his freedom could take shape. Incredible, marvelous shapes that leave no room for the memories of what had to happen to achieve it, and when Orpheus gathers up his robe and heads down the steps towards his little dungeon bedroom with the tiny window and lumpy bed, he stops in the laboratory first.

It's clean. Everything in its place, properly put together. But empty. Cold. Abandoned.

The hermits have left; he doesn't know where they've gone. But in their absence Orpheus sees an inheritance, freedom in the tools they have left behind, and all the potential they offer. And when he steps into the room and closes the door behind him, it's not memories Orpheus confronts, it's possibilities.

It's his future.

CHAPTER XXI

GOOD MORNING

It wasn't the slow creep of sunlight across his face that woke Orpheus, it was the sudden absence of warmth and the trickle of cold that took its place.

Memory came together in pieces, a puzzle assembled by the aches in his body and the stickiness in his eyes, the comfort of heavy blankets and the impression of drowned robes, in a drool-damp pillow and tear-stricken cheeks, of the loss of a friend and the grief that still echoed. Of hands cupping his face and lips touching lips and of someone holding him, comforting him, at a moment when nothing in his life was close to okay. Impossible things that he'd gone his whole life without, so that when Orpheus opened his eyes to the stacks of books surrounding him—things immediately familiar and all at once not the same—for a moment he was certain he wasn't dreaming but had actually gone ahead and died.

He hadn't died. Fenrir had found him—saved him—and then must have brought him here.

The Keep. He was—he was in the *Keep*.

Orpheus shoved up from where he lay, hands pushing through the pile of blankets as he sat up and stared.

THE CRACK AT THE HEART OF EVERYTHING

Bookcases stood tall all around him, row upon row of stacks that stretched back as far as the eye could see. Hundreds and thousands of spines were lined up in meticulous sequence, fingers of brass beneath each shelf denominating sections by author name, number and title, all beneath a domed arc of a mosaic ceiling, tiers of banisters lining the walls where more shelves lived, story upon story of books—of words—of history and legend and folk tales from what must be every corner of the world.

Behind him, snow tumulted, a blizzard of white that spilled bright and brilliant through the window at his back, his makeshift bed tucked away into a shallow alcove, so the full splendor of the Keep sprawled out before him like a stage dressing set and waiting.

For him. Like it was waiting for *him*.

A hitching laugh breathed through him a moment before Fenrir's voice did.

"You're awake."

Orpheus twisted around to find Fenrir standing beside the window, sunlight liming him in gold. Fenrir reached for him, fingers pushed through Orpheus' hair as Fenrir came around the side of the bed and sat down, cupping the nape of his neck as he put the back of his free hand to Orpheus' forehead. Their eyes met. Their bodies close, but not as close as they must have been. Orpheus understood now what the absence of warmth he'd woken to meant. Fenrir was dressed in soft clothes, long pants and an unlaced shirt, both of which were wrinkled from a long span of sleep, and the only bed Orpheus could see was the one he was currently tucked into.

His breath went thin, his heartbeat fast. He held perfectly still while Fenrir leaned into his space. Comfortably, like Fenrir had spent hours or days touching him just like this. All hells, Orpheus wished he could *remember*.

"Fever's gone down," Fenrir said, holding Orpheus' eyes as he turned his hand over to cup his cheek. Fenrir's thumb rested right there, at the corner of Orpheus' mouth, and another memory came to him—that of Fenrir's lips on his, a brief coming together under a falling blanket of snow.

"Am I dead?" Orpheus asked, just to be sure.

Fenrir laughed, and the sound moved through him like an earthquake.

"Not dead," Fenrir said, voice warm but quiet, hands steady and firm—holding on like he was afraid to let go. "But I thought you were close for a second there."

"Achates." He hadn't forgotten, but he hadn't been given the chance to remember either. His chest clenched when he said, "He was swept away during the attack."

"Yeah, I saw," Fenrir's voice lowered with the admission. He squeezed the back of Orpheus' neck before his hands fell away, an airy cold left in their absence. Fenrir looked unsure when he said, "I was already across the river, I couldn't get to him in time."

Across the river?

He saw then, the bruises creeping up out of the open collar of Fenrir's shirt. The fresh cut across his cheek, and a matching set down his chest. And a wound on his forearm, tightly wrapped, the wet seal of the fresh bandage leaking past the folds of the dressing—a burn—a bad burn—

"I was hunting that dragon. Thought I could get to it before it got to you," Fenrir said without saying.

"So, you decided to hitch a ride across the river on a dragon?"

Fenrir grinned, a half-sized thing that made the fresh cut on his cheek pull at its scab. "Bridge was out, figured it was faster than doubling back for the plane. Course' Nightmare got across fine without me, but I've always had a flare of the dramatic." Fenrir shrugged, a little sheepish.

Orpheus closed his eyes for a moment, tried to stop his head from spinning. When he looked at Fenrir again his expression was open, ready for whatever admonishment Orpheus had to give.

"I'm not even going to ask about the plane," or why Fenrir had named his horse Nightmare, "but I told you not to follow me."

"Technically, I was following the dragon."

"Semantics," Orpheus breathed. Then, "Thank you."

Orpheus watched Fenrir swallow, saw how the smooth glide of

his throat was framed by the open collar of his shirt, and he suddenly missed the weight of his hand on his neck, the warmth of his palm on his cheek. The feeling of Fenrir's skin against his, alive and well and in one piece. Fenrir had nearly died again, and Orpheus wouldn't have been around to save him—all because he'd insisted on pushing him away.

We're good together, Fenrir had told him once. Oh, how naive Orpheus had been.

"You got it pretty good," Fenrir eventually said, pulling Orpheus out of his head.

"When it killed—" he cut off, tried to steady his voice again and utterly failed, "When it killed Achates, I—" Lost it? Lost control? Went into a bloodthirsty rage? Orpheus swallowed all of the words, closed his eyes. He didn't want to relive it, but he needed someone to hear, to remember with him. Fenrir would have seen it all. Seen him turn into the monster Lore had sought. Have borne witness to the real power inside him—something so much more devastating than a silly flame shield trick that had saved their lives.

It'd been inside him, all along. All that power. That magic. That poison that had rent the world asunder, far before he'd even been put on this Earth.

"Fifi, you're—"

"—Spiraling, I know," he laughed, the sound strained. "Maybe let me, a little bit, this time?"

Fenrir's expression broke, mirth lost, replaced by a vulnerability Orpheus was finally able to say he understood. He saw a mirror to himself, a need that reached through the both of them—of someone who understood but was also as much to blame. Because if ever there was equal ground between them, it was here, confronting the failures of their flaws and the repercussions of their poor choices.

But Fenrir had changed. He'd committed to doing better. And Orpheus...he could too, if that was what he wanted.

What he wanted.

The truth was...what he wanted...well, it was already here, sitting right in front of him.

Orpheus looked at the empty space separating him from Fenrir, the wrinkled sheets and cold mattress, a no-man's land Fenrir had dared to cross—a feat more unimaginable than bringing down a dragon, and Orpheus wondered if Fenrir understood the extent of what that meant. Then he thought of the last thing he could remember. The last clear memory he had, in fact.

"You saved me," Orpheus stated like it wasn't something Fenrir had done over and over again for the last month.

Fenrir met his eyes when he said, "Yes."

"You *kissed* me," Orpheus whispered.

"I did," Fenrir confirmed, voice quiet. Then, like he could read Orpheus without any words, he reached out, hand returning to Orpheus' neck, large and warm, settling in and remaining there. Orpheus shivered as a thumb stroked behind his ear, a slow, gentle circle. He liked it. It felt good. He never wanted it to end.

Orpheus choked up with the feeling of it. Safety, yes, and an impossible impression of trust.

Is this what it was like? How it felt to be loved?

"Can I, again?"

Orpheus' breath went ragged, his heart a pounding mess. He looked up at Fenrir and was confronted with everything he wanted, right there, on offer.

"Again?" he asked, breathless.

"Kiss you," Fenrir said, voice raw, "Can I kiss you again?"

The pressure on the back of his neck let up, not because Fenrir was moving away, but because Orpheus was leaning in. Then it was momentum carrying him forward, the silent urge to close the distance—align, as they'd been trying to for weeks.

Fenrir hesitated there, lips almost touching, the moment hanging, an out silently offered—as if Orpheus was going to stop this now that he finally had it.

"Are you sure?" Fenrir breathed as if they were on the brink of something so much greater than a kiss. Maybe they were. It certainly felt that way. And when Fenrir's breath shook over his lips, Orpheus knew he wasn't alone in his suspicion.

He tipped his chin up, closed his eyes, and submitted to it—the feeling inside—this beautiful compulsion.

Skin met skin. Breath met breath. A gentle pressure greeted him, warm and wet. It wasn't like any kiss Orpheus had read about. Soft, where he expected hard. Careful, where he expected confidence. Fenrir's breath sounded as shaken as his and something about that emboldened Orpheus. He put a hand to Fenrir's shoulder and tilted his head, mouth open, pressed close, almost tasting.

Fenrir made a sound against him, a muffled moan that had Orpheus shivering.

He pulled away. He had to. His breath was coming too fast and his whole body was on fire—like the fever had returned but this time, Fenrir was the infection. He didn't get far. That hand returned, tangling into Orpheus' hair at the exact moment another cupped his jaw, and then Fenrir dragged him forward, into a kiss nothing like the first.

Fenrir kissed him like it was their first time and their last—like he was only going to get one chance and he needed to make it count. Lips slid over his, from one corner to the other, a careful mapping, the hand in his hair holding, the thumb curling into the hinge of his jaw firm, pressing, until Orpheus understood and opened up for him.

The kiss was different than he expected, Fenrir's mouth warm and soft—possibly the only soft place Fenrir had besides his big stupid heart—the hand he had tangled into Orpheus' hair holding fast as if this might all get torn away at any moment. The idea made his heart ache, because he had put that fear there when he'd pushed Fenrir away, and Orpheus desperately wanted to take it all back—to have pursued this the first time it had become clear that whatever existed between him, and Fenrir was so much more than rivalry or hate.

Fuck. He'd almost fucked this up. He'd come so close to fucking this up.

As if reading his thoughts, Fenrir broke the kiss.

"Are you okay?" breathed over his lips, the hand on his neck steady, the palm on his cheek firm.

"I'm sorry," Orpheus had to say. "For pushing you away, for

wasting so much time, for not—"

"Fifi," Fenrir said, voice so raw it broke, "I would have waited until the world ended all over again if that's how much time you needed."

"You would—" he choked out, leaning into Fenrir. "Why would—"

"Because I love you," Fenrir said, gentle as the falling snow. "I've been in love with you for ages, and I hope that doesn't scare you, because if we're going to do this, I need you to know the truth."

Orpheus laughed—he *laughed*—the joy flooding his heart brilliantly impossible, too luminous to contain. He likely sounded crazy, but at this point, he was pretty sure Fenrir already knew that about him, so he didn't think it too strange to say, "so that's why you shot me with a crossbow."

Fenrir jerked, breath puffing out in an indignant kind of snort. "That was an accident."

"Cupid used a recurve, to be clear. And his love arrows were tipped with gold. Steel made people aversive to him," Orpheus stated, matter-of-fact, relieved by the glimmer of mirth he saw in Fenrir's eyes—thrilled to know he had put it there—that he had possibly always been the one to put it there. "And you missed. Cupid had very good aim."

"Well," Fenrir pushed out, fighting a smirk, pale eyes crinkled at the corners, a spider web Orpheus was caught up in, "that certainly explains everything."

They were kissing again before either could say anything else, Orpheus unsure who had closed the distance and deciding it didn't matter. The world shifted as Fenrir wrapped an arm around him and dragged him in, Orpheus steadying himself with the hand he had on Fenrir's shoulder, the other sliding into his hair. And then the arms around him tightened and tipped him backwards, down to the bed and the blankets and the bracket of his body—shadows thrown in shallow dips as Fenrir moved over him, between him, Orpheus' legs parting as Fenrir found his place against him.

Heat met heat, soft and hard in equal proportion, nerves firing with a fever that had nothing to do with the Netherflame running through his veins.

He'd never been this close to anyone, but that didn't mean he hadn't spent a lifetime wishing he could be. The truth was there, exposed by words unspoken—or perhaps Fenrir had already known, because he'd always handled Orpheus like this: gently, carefully, respectful of his boundaries, cognizant of his limits.

"Too fast?" Fenrir pulled away to ask, breath warm against Orpheus' lips.

"No." Orpheus' entire body flushed as he said, "I've simply made this too easy for you."

"Nothing," Fenrir breathed, voice actually shaking, "has been easy about you, Orpheus."

Orpheus flushed, but then, so did Fenrir.

"I've thought about this for years. I'm sorry for anything I ever did that made you think I hated you."

"It's not your fault," was Orpheus' own kind of admission. "I went my life without any attention, so I didn't know what to do when one person suddenly gave me all of his. You had to be up to something."

Fenrir grinned, eyes sparkling. "To be fair, your instincts weren't wrong."

Their laughter sounded good together. An even ground that made what was happening here feel easy, rather than years in the making.

Orpheus was outright shaking when Fenrir leaned in to kiss him again, the tangle of his fingers with his own a moor he clung to. There was no stopping what they had started, for either of them. Orpheus felt it again, the hard line of Fenrir against his thigh, the beat of his pulse throbbing with every shift of his pelvis, riding the same edge Orpheus was at.

And it was—it was *so much*. His hips rolled into Fenrir's thigh as he gasped against his mouth, squeezing Fenrir's hands while his body spiraled higher, clinging to some unimaginable precipice for one precarious moment before everything he knew about the world came apart.

Fenrir kissed him, hard and possessive, a greedy claim upon everything that was happening—holding Orpheus to it, so escape wasn't an option—not that Orpheus would have run away again even if it was. Then it was his turn to unravel, Fenrir panting, arms trembling, hair a halo of tarnished golden light, made blinding by the tumbling snow beyond the glass window of the Keep.

Fenrir loved him. He *loved* him, and Orpheus had never known such complete happiness before in all his life—had given up hope he'd ever find it—certainly not now, when so much of himself had been given up to the cursed darkness.

But here Fenrir was, him and all his brilliant light.

Maybe they were as good together as Fenrir claimed. Maybe this meant something. Maybe, despite the curse hunting him and the decades he'd spent sequestered away from the world—the damage he'd inflicted and the people he had hurt—there was still hope for him. For them. For a future where they could both fit together.

Breaths hitched in his chest, one after another. The sting in his eyes was already turning to tears so when Fenrir found his hand and brought it to his mouth. He held his eyes when he pressed a kiss to his scarred wrist, and that's all it took for Orpheus to break.

There in Fenrir's arms, Orpheus cried, soft and unmuffled.

"Oh, Orpheus," Fenrir breathed over his skin, one more kiss, "everything's okay, everything's going to be okay."

Inexplicably, Orpheus found himself agreeing. He reached up, tangled his hand into Fenrir's hair and tugged. Fenrir came to him willingly, nearly collapsing atop Orpheus before he got an arm under him and rolled them over. By the time Orpheus had burrowed into Fenrir's chest he'd already made a mess of them both, the taste of salt and skin and the sharp tang of half-healed wounds potent in his mouth. Fenrir held him through it. Drew the blankets over them both and then tangled their legs together, locked one arm around Orpheus' waist and buried a hand in his hair. And when Orpheus' tears finally ceased and the snow had eased into a light flurry, they stayed there, together, and nothing else but that seemed to matter.

CHAPTER XXII

HEALING

This time, when Orpheus woke, it was to the feeling of Fenrir tucked into his side.

Like a furnace set to high, Fenrir bled warmth into the layers of blankets, the arm he had slung over Orpheus a brand of heat that would have put his fever to shame if he still had one. He didn't. He felt good. Better than good. The exhaustion was there, along with the aches and pains of riding for days and then fighting off an Emperor Dragon, but as Orpheus inched forward into Fenrir's chest, his eyes slipped shut again, smile pulling at his lips as he sunk into the not-sleep of a late morning doze.

He didn't rouse again until Fenrir moved against him.

He kept his eyes closed. Pretended to be asleep when fingers slid into his hair and stilled—a light touch, not meant to wake him—like Fenrir was simply affirming that he was there at all. But Fenrir's self-control must have been in tatters because Orpheus fought a smile when the arm around him dragged him in, Fenrir's face burrowing into his hair at the precise moment his hips rolled into Orpheus' thigh.

Well, how was anyone supposed to sleep through *that*?

"Fine, I'm awake," Orpheus pretended to snarl. Against him, Fenrir laughed.

"Morning, Fifi." Fenrir whispered the nickname, and it sounded like stars in the sky. "I think I need to get up."

"Why," he muttered into his chest, flaring his nostrils and breathing him in. Fenrir's scent pulled heavy, leather and sweat and that heavy unnamable thing that Orpheus now identified as purely Fenrir. All of it tinged with something else, something sharp and atmospheric that Orpheus dared to think was his own scent on Fenrir's skin.

Oh. That was—that was *nice.*

Fenrir hummed like he could hear his thoughts, the fingers in his hair scratching over his scalp. It'd be easy to stay right there, amongst the blankets and the books and the safety of Fenrir's arms. But like Fenrir said, they'd have a thousand more chances at this, to wake up in comfort with one another, tangled limbs and sex-stained skin and all.

"Can't stay in bed forever. Maybe I could tempt you with a shower?"

"Possibly," Orpheus sighed, "does this place have hot water?"

"Got the generator going." Fenrir shifted, pulling away far enough to look Orpheus in the eyes. "This is it, you know. The—"

"The Keep," Orpheus finished for him. "Yes, I presumed as much when I woke to all these books."

"Well..." Fenrir grinned, eyes glinting. "You'll be especially pleased when I tell you this is only a portion, much smaller than the main library. The student's stacks are another thirty stories up."

"Thirty—" Orpheus choked off as his eyes slipped from Fenrir to the window behind him, seeing now how the blizzard had died down, and that they were—they were at least twenty stories as it stood.

And there, not so far in the distance, arose a city.

He shoved up from the bed and crawled over Fenrir, nearly knocking himself over when his under robe tangled in his legs as he scrambled close enough to the window to press his nose to the glass. Snow blanketed everything, like an overexposed photo, but there was no denying what Orpheus could see.

The pit—as Red and Fenrir had called it—was anything but a *pit.*

It was massive. Sprawling. A jagged edge of steel stretching across a horizon of soaring towers and glinting glass, woven with highways and bridges on a scale that put the pictures in all those history books to shame. This was nothing like the dilapidation of the Stacks, the smoking remains of the crater, the wasteland surrounding the grid. This was the future, perfectly preserved in a place untouched by time.

"Lore left it mostly alone," Fenrir said from behind him. "But the army used this and the museum across the street as barracks when we were clearing out the—" Fenrir didn't call them bandits or the resistance, he swallowed around whatever word he wanted to use, saying instead, "—the pit."

"The pit?" Orpheus asked. "You keep calling it that."

"It's what we call it, the city."

"This city is not a pit," Orpheus said carefully, like the obvious needed explaining. Once upon a time, Orpheus would have thought as much when it came to Fenrir, but he'd learned weeks ago his skull wasn't filled with the muscle he'd always assumed he kept up there.

Fenrir sighed. "It's what the locals called it."

Fenrir didn't need to say who the locals were or why he chose to refer to them in the past tense. Orpheus was capable of conflating the two without any help.

All hells. If Lore had bothered to kill everyone who had been living in the Pit and then left it be, then she must have also been responsible for the bridge being out, and that meant she wanted something to stay hidden within this place—something not even Fenrir had been privy to. Something that had nothing to do with the curse, or the spell book it had come from.

"Where is the spell book?" He asked anyway, because he didn't know where else to start than the obvious.

"Shower first." Orpheus sensed the heat of Fenrir's hand before it ever touched his hip. "Then we can spend all day reading your precious books."

He didn't fight when Fenrir drew him back from the window. Didn't resist when Fenrir's other hand joined the first on his hips, drawing Orpheus into his lap and then into a kiss. The flutter-thin warmth of his breath came slow and steady now that they had tempered some of the heat that had spent weeks building between them.

Orpheus closed his eyes as their mouths touched. Smoothed his hands up Fenrir's chest and gave into the simple urge to touch him.

"Good morning, by the way," Fenrir murmured against his lips, teeth catching as he smiled. "A very good morning to us both."

Orpheus responded by deepening their kiss.

The showers, it turned out, were hidden below the main atrium— a massive four-story tall entry hall of stone masonry that put the Gilded Palace to shame. Like something built from the gothic cathedral blueprints he'd studied, the Keep lived up to its name. Flying buttresses arched four stories overhead, the marbled columns so massive it would take five men fingertip to fingertip to reach around.

Though centuries of disuse had left portions of it in disrepair, the bones were solid—the steel and stone of the mostly modern architectural practices of the nineteenth century ensuring it had lived on well past its original builder's intentions. Acutely demonstrated when Fenrir led him down a utility staircase lit by the humming whine of fluorescent lights, the "employee bathroom" as he called it a nearly pristine room of tile floor and porcelain sinks.

"Shower's here," Fenrir said as he stepped around a wall and the *squeal-bang* of old pipes clattered to life. "Let's get naked."

Orpheus choked on air as his face turned red.

Fenrir winked as he pulled his shirt over his head, tawny hair falling around his shoulders in wild waves. This wasn't the first time Orpheus had seen Fenrir nearly naked but now it was different. Now he knew what all this blasted heat in his body meant, and having Fenrir on full display was like an advertisement.

Fenrir's face softened when he realized Orpheus was at a loss for words before even he did. And Fenrir was kind enough to keep his pants on when he came over and slid a hand into his. Orpheus obediently stepped forward when Fenrir gave him a tug.

"I'm incredibly attracted to you," Fenrir said when Orpheus was close enough to feel the heat coming off his skin. "But I don't have any expectations for this. I meant it when I said I'd wait as long as it takes, and as far as I'm concerned that hasn't changed. This is only a shower unless you say otherwise."

Orpheus nodded his head because he didn't trust his voice yet.

"Okay, good." Fenrir's thumb slid over the back of his hand, tracking close to the scar hidden away under his sleeve.

Then, Fenrir was moving away, releasing Orpheus' hand and shimmying out of his pants.

Muscles shifted under golden skin, scars silvery under the unforgiving lights. And he was still beautiful. Orpheus hadn't really allowed himself to look before, not openly like this. But now that he could there was no denying that Fenrir was everything Orpheus had once resented him for—tall, broad, and beautiful in those masculine, virile ways Orpheus was not.

Orpheus fingered the edge of his under robe, coming to a conclusion not even he could name, and immediately threw it on the floor and headed for the shower. He avoided his reflection in the mirror because if he looked now, he'd lose all his nerve.

He kept his eyes averted as he stepped into the steam, clenched his teeth when water hotter than he was used to hit his skin. Fenrir must have noticed because he felt the temperature dial back a few degrees. But it took a long time of the spray hitting his chest before Orpheus had enough courage to meet Fenrir's eyes.

"Can I wash your hair?" Fenrir asked when Orpheus finally looked up. Something hard and cold inside him melted at that simple, self-indulgent request.

Also, it gave him an excuse to not have to look at Fenrir's beautiful nude body.

He turned around and put his hands on the wall, ignored how this must look to Fenrir who hovered there behind him, getting a full view of what might be his one good asset; running up and down his dungeon workshop's stairs had done wonders for his butt.

True to his word, nothing happened. Fenrir washed Orpheus' hair, then his own. Orpheus made an excuse to touch Fenrir out of fussing over his burn. The bandage sat in the drain, flooding the stall and very nearly the rest of the bathroom because Fenrir hadn't bothered wrapping it in plastic, the pinked skin angry under the warmth of the shower.

He dragged Fenrir out of the shower then, pushing him down onto an ornate bench that someone had obviously brought down from one of the floors above. They were still naked, but at this point, Orpheus' mind wasn't on anything but Fenrir's stupid wounds. He grabbed the medical kit from the supply closet, dug through it until he found some clean bandages and long-expired topical analgesic.

"There are better-stocked kits up in the entry hall," Fenrir said as Orpheus ripped open the packet of analgesic and smoothed it over the red, blistered skin.

"How is this not a third-degree burn?" Orpheus muttered. "This was caused by dragonfire, right?"

"Could've been worse," Fenrir shrugged, and Orpheus smacked his shoulder when it caused the analgesic to smear. "Just got lucky. You get used to it when you're me."

"Luck," Orpheus drawled, "you attribute your skills to luck."

"I mean, you can make literal magic come out of your fingers, I'm not sure what's so unbelievable about having really good luck."

Orpheus' mouth twisted because it wasn't like Fenrir was wrong.

But it also wasn't like he'd been born with that magic, either.

"I wasn't born able to," came out of him before he could stop himself. The room slipped away as the gravity of what he'd admitted hit him fully.

Red had tried to talk to him about this and he'd been unable to. Why he had decided to admit this to Fenrir out of the blue he didn't understand. But being here, in this literal Keep of infinite knowledge, it seemed important. What had been done to him—he didn't know why it had happened, but it had, and as Fenrir said—if they were going to do this together, he needed to know the truth.

"The Gilded Palace wasn't always a palace," he began, hands moving away from Fenrir's arm as he reached for a bandage, "it was a bunker in the mountains, meant—I believe—to withstand the Incident."

THE CRACK AT THE HEART OF EVERYTHING

Fenrir made an agreeable sound, soft in his throat as if what Orpheus said was common knowledge. Maybe it was. Maybe it always had been—to everyone but him.

He smoothed the bandage over Fenrir's burn, running his fingers over the adhesive edges slowly, dragging time out. When he finally began speaking again, the bathroom was so quiet he swore he could hear the snow coming down outside.

"I lived there since a very young age. I don't actually remember anything from before, but I don't believe I was born there. I wasn't the only child they—" he cut off, eyes flicking up to meet Fenrir's as the worst of his memories gnawed at his edges. His breath was quickening and whatever words he wanted to speak were lost to the miasma of the shadows that clogged his mind. He knew what he wanted to say but the words wouldn't come, and Fenrir must have realized something was wrong because his hand was on Orpheus' before he realized what was happening.

Fenrir raised Orpheus' hand—his wrist—into the space between them.

"They. Whoever did this." Fenrir said what Orpheus could not.

"Yes," whispered out on a shaky breath, eyes on where Fenrir held his scarred wrist. "They did that to me, and whatever they did caused the magic in me. The Netherflame—" he cut off again, fighting himself this time, pushing past grinding teeth: "Netherflame. They put Netherflame inside me, and I think they'd been trying to do that to children for years, but I was the first one they were successful with."

"How old were you?" Fenrir asked, the grip he kept on Orpheus' wrist tight but not painful—possessive—protective.

Orpheus tore his eyes away, looked back up into Fenrir's. "Ten or eleven, if I had to guess."

Fenrir's Rim-pale eyes held his. "Lore was another one of those kids."

It wasn't the most illogical conclusion, but Orpheus wouldn't have called it obvious either.

"Yes," he said, voice weak. "For her, the magic didn't take. But we'd...we'd become friends. Or the closest thing to a friend I had."

"Orpheus," Fenrir said with so much weight Orpheus flinched. "What happened to the scientists?"

Scientists. Not mages. Not wizards. Not sorcerers or priests or hermits or any of the names he had given them. Scientists. People who—according to Red—had been working on a way to fix the world after the fallout of the Incident—who he had—he had—

"I killed them," he breathed out, voice a barely-there whisper. "I killed all of them."

Fenrir dropped his wrist, and it felt like the world falling out from under him. Like gravity had lost its pull and Orpheus was going to spiral out of atmosphere—out of orbit—straight into the empty void of space itself.

Then Fenrir's arms were around him, and he was dragged into a hug before he got any further than the solar system's sun.

"Fifi," Fenrir said, voice soft but close, right there at his ear. "Fifi, you were a kid, and they hurt you."

"Did they?" he asked, voice shaking alongside the rest of him. "They gave me magic, and I repaid them with death."

"They were experimenting on you. They were hurting you—and they killed all those other kids—" now it was Fenrir's turn to choke out something Orpheus could not have predicted, "—we all knew. Everyone not locked away in that damned bunker knew. The rumors had been spreading for years. Kids disappearing from the wasteland, parents who couldn't afford to feed themselves leaving an infant at the foot of the mountain like some infernal sacrifice. I don't care if people thought those scientists were trying to fix things, whatever the fuck was going on up there was awful and it wasn't until Lore came down after a decade of silence that anyone put two and two together. I think we all thought it was her who had been their success, but then—"

Fenrir cut off, holding his breath long enough that Orpheus put a hand to his chest to make sure his heart still beat.

"—Then I joined her army, and she gave me a place at her side, and I went to that stupid fucking bunker she called a Palace, and I met you. And I *knew*. I knew before you ever flung a spell at me or heard a lick of rumor from the court. You were the success. You were our hope."

"Hope," Orpheus repeated, voice sounding far enough away to feel unmoored from his body.

"Nothing has changed," Fenrir said, "except that we found hope in other places, too. But back then, back before, people were barely surviving. And we may have all been terrified of what those scientists were doing, but we also believed they were at least trying to...to fix things. Lore...she's like those scientists. Working for something good even though her methods..."

Fenrir trailed off, like even he didn't believe what he was trying to say. Orpheus understood why. Fenrir had joined her cause under the assumption he was going to help people. Be a hero, and Lore...Lore had tried to turn him into a monster. Just like Orpheus.

"I don't think her intentions were ever to do anything good," Orpheus whispered.

Fenrir swallowed, hung his head. "No, I don't think so either. Not anymore."

But Orpheus, unlike Fenrir, didn't believe they were bad either. Lore was Lore. The world Lore lived within was insulated from far more than Orpheus' had ever been—and of the two of them he'd been the one always escaping into the books he loved so much. Lore was only trying to protect herself. Protect her sanity. And Orpheus understood why.

"Why did they make me?" Orpheus finally asked the question that had been burning a hole inside him his entire life. "What did they want me to do?"

Why had they done this to him—cursed him—to a life of poison and death?

"How is this—" he lifted his hand, rubbed his fingers together, chased the itch beneath his skin and gave into the urge. Netherflame flickered, small and deceiving, a hungry little ember he balanced on the tip of his forefinger, that no man should have the power to wield, "—how is this supposed to help anyone?"

"I don't know, Fifi," Fenrir breathed, "I really don't know."

"Is that why you wanted my help?" he asked, pushing away as he spoke, ember burning out as his hand dropped to Fenrir's bandage. He smoothed his thumb over the softness and asked, "Is this why you thought I would help you?"

Fenrir didn't say anything right away. He looked at Orpheus, face drawn into an indiscernible neutrality, as if he understood whatever answer he gave meant more to Orpheus than he knew. So when Fenrir did finally speak, Orpheus knew he was getting the truth.

Fenrir had always given him the truth, one way or another.

"By the time I realized Lore wasn't the kind of person I thought she was, I was in too deep with her. But by then I also had Red and her grid and the refinery was on its way to being built and whatever hope I might have been chasing up that mountain was eclipsed by the very real horror of what Lore's empire had become. That's why I wanted your help, not because I thought you were some ill-begotten savior of the world. And I think..."

Fenrir trailed off, eyes lowering to Orpheus' hand where it rested over his bandage. Fenrir's hand was warm when he laid it on top.

"I think I just wanted to get you out of there. Away from her. From everything."

Heat swelled in Orpheus' chest, warm and welcome.

"My hero," Orpheus nearly laughed, voice edged with an emotion he couldn't name—relief, but also grief. For the time they'd lost, but also all they'd gained. And despite what the future with Lore might hold, at least Fenrir didn't expect to level him with the inane title of *world savior*. "And it should be known, I am complete shit at healing spells, let alone any that could possibly fix this wasteland of a planet."

Orpheus felt better when Fenrir relaxed against him—realized, in that moment, that his response to Fenrir's answer had meant just as much to him as Fenrir's had to Orpheus.

They remained like that for a long time, loosely entangled, Orpheus taking his time as he dressed each of Fenrir's new wounds, as if the healing that really mattered had nothing to do with the planet or the Incident or the scientists up that infernal mountain. And when Fenrir drew him into a slow kiss and a murmured *thank you*—as if the simple act of bandaging him up had been as monumental as Orpheus saving his life—Orpheus wondered if he wasn't as awful at healing as he'd always thought.

CHAPTER XXIII
THE KEEP

Sixty-three stories up a tower that made Lore's mountain feel small, Orpheus felt more out of depth than he ever had before.

"This is it?" His hands shook when he lifted them, palms up, unable to cross the precipice without a little help.

Fenrir carefully placed the heavy spell book in his hands.

"Want me to show you?"

Orpheus nodded, no longer able to speak.

The leather spine creaked when Fenrir opened the cover, the yellowed parchment curling with time-worn edges. Spells scrawled across the heavy paper, sigils an animated image of circles and marks as Fenrir let the pages fall from his thumb. He stopped nearly halfway through, palm coming up beside Orpheus' to balance the book in both their hands, turning each page carefully as he sought out the missing spell.

Orpheus saw it before Fenrir did—the ragged tear at the spine, the familiar ridge of parchment a mirror to the page in his pocket. He didn't need to pull it out to confirm this was it: the part of the book that documented both the existence of an army in Hell, and the way for a person to summon it.

He didn't need to skim more than the two adjacent pages to know there was no mention of a curse.

"It's not here," he whispered, grief churning his gut.

"Let's take a closer look before we say for sure." Fenrir took the book from Orpheus' shaking hands, stuck a thumb between the pages and then slid an arm around his waist.

Hope felt as out of reach as the snowy drifts creeping up the side of the Keep's enormous walls.

Six hours later, the spell book sat off to the side of the large mahogany table Orpheus and Fenrir sat at, the shadow of a Skullmoth falling long over its ancient leather spine. Orpheus ignored the ring of teeth chewing fruitlessly at the glass, the wings beating a dull rhythm as the Skullmoth tried—unsuccessfully—to eat its way through the window.

"Have you ever read this one?" Fenrir's Rim-pale eyes met his, so much larger than Orpheus was used to.

In the quiet of the library on the sixty-third floor, the only secret Orpheus had uncovered was that Fenrir Rawkner needed *glasses* to read.

Fenrir used one finger to push his glasses back up his nose while sliding a book under Orpheus'.

He knew this book. A big, black-bound leather tome by one Aleister Crowley that Orpheus determined had been written in a fugue state by a man who had convinced himself *angels* would speak to him if he took enough opium.

He looked up at Fenrir while pushing the tome to the side, enjoying how the thick black spectacles magnified his eyes.

"If I had access to unlimited psychotropics I may have been able to make more sense of it, but yes, I have read all of Crowley."

"I couldn't make it past the first chapter," Fenrir admitted with a grin. "But if it's mind-altering substances you're after, Red has these mushrooms you'd really like—"

"—Rawkner," Orpheus cut off, "you've read these?"

"Not all of them, obviously. I have a—" Fenrir's mouth closed, eyes blinking. Magnified by the glasses, he looked like some overly muscled owl; it was cute, and Orpheus knew his face was turning red.

Fenrir didn't seem to notice, too caught up in a realization Orpheus had dealt with weeks ago. "—well, I *had* a job. Think Lore's mad I skipped out on her?"

"And what, precisely, would she do if she was?" Orpheus asked as he closed the cover to the book he had been skimming—an interesting take on Morgan le Fay and Avalon he'd never read before, as accounted by one Marion Zimmer Bradley.

Fenrir shrugged. "Send Ohm after me, I guess."

"Well, good thing you have me here." Except... "There's nothing in that book about how to send him back to Hell, you should know."

Fenrir looked back over the rim of his glasses, face carefully neutral.

Orpheus sighed. "You shouldn't fight Lore." He reached for a book—any book—something to excuse his eyes not meeting Fenrir's. "At least, you shouldn't without a plan."

Fenrir's chair creaked when he leaned forward. "Fifi, that's insurrection speak."

Yes, it was. And despite Orpheus' loyalties lying with Lore all his life, there was no denying something important inside him had shifted. He still wasn't sure he'd ever be able to fight Lore—whether he wanted to, let alone thought he could—but he could no longer deny she was a threat to the progress her empire was supposed to represent.

Orpheus chewed his lip. "Your coup won't get far with Ohm in play."

Fenrir didn't push him. He simply asked, "You think he can be killed?"

"How can one kill that which is already dead?" Orpheus muttered, opening the book he had grabbed, a hand-written journal recorded sometime after the Incident. He recognized the author—a woman who had discovered silver and gold as modalities for Netherflame. He'd read another of her works. A book he'd found in the hermits'—scientists'—laboratory years after their death. This volume was around a decade older, written from the author's deathbed, if the foreword was to be believed. Outside their library, the scientists hadn't kept many books, something Orpheus had always found strange, and that one had been hidden behind a storage bin, discarded, or possibly forgotten.

"I've killed plenty of hell beasts. They can die like anything else, and you killed that dragon."

But was Ohm like any other hell beast? He was summoned through a spell after all—a spell that, whether documented or not, had cursed him to die.

Orpheus swallowed, turned the page and dragged his eyes through words that made little sense. Maybe it was the dozens of volumes he'd read over the last two days, or maybe it was the fact that none of them had gotten him any closer to breaking his hells-damned curse.

"You don't think the dragon survived, do you?" Fenrir pushed, head cocked to the side, arms crossed over his chest.

"I don't know." Orpheus chanced a glance out the window, past the slobbering Skullmoth to the ruinous Pit in the far distance. "If it is alive, I'm sure it will find me again, eventually."

"Or it's tucked tail and run because it's terrified of you now," probably wasn't intended to make Orpheus feel sick, but the feeling was there all the same.

Slowly, he closed the cover of the journal. Slower yet he pushed it to the side. When his forehead touched his palms, he didn't even think, just sank into a hunch and let out a long, shaky breath.

"Fifi?" Fenrir's voice came quiet over the sound of his own breathing.

"I don't like the idea of anyone being terrified of me," came out steadier than Orpheus expected it to.

There was another memory here, one of voices raised and a puddle of blood under his knees. He pushed it away, letting out a held breath as he did.

"I'm sorry," Fenrir said, quietly. Then, "I'm not scared of you. I thought it was pretty fucking great. Never seen anyone fight like that before. You were incredible."

Orpheus grimaced—was grateful Fenrir couldn't see. "You would get off on barbaric displays of power."

"Not barbaric. Capable. I liked seeing you stand up for yourself. Protecting yourself."

Something Orpheus thought long dead inside him twisted at Fenrir's words. "I protect myself all the time."

I've always had to protect myself, until you, he didn't say aloud.

"Maybe," Fenrir said, "but I've been in that position before—have seen other people in that position before—when the pain is so great that the odds feel insurmountable, and that's the point most people give up."

Orpheus didn't say anything. Couldn't say anything. Because he was back there, back in that river, Achates' dead eyes staring up at him through a churning current, the shriek of the Emperor Dragon tearing through his head. And then he was somewhere further away, further back through time, curled up in a cistern surrounded by those hermits, Netherflame burning a literal hole straight into his soul.

The idea that he'd been ruined long before the curse emerged again, and no matter how much Orpheus may have wanted to live, that small dead thing inside him made him feel like he was already too late.

"What if there is no cure?" He finally asked. "What if there is no stopping the curse? How long will it take me to reach that point, when hopelessness catches up and I lose the—" he looked up, met Fenrir's eyes and wished they were anything but the pale, steadfast moor they were. "—I lose the will to keep fighting?"

"Then I'll fight for you," Fenrir stated, as if this really were all that simple.

"How do you do it?" His hands dropped to the table, palms up, like he was begging for something more substantial than—well, he couldn't honestly call Fenrir's offer an empty platitude, but right then, it felt like one. "How do you keep going, after everything? How has it not beaten you down yet?"

"Because I've always had something worth fighting for," Fenrir said without hesitation, Rim-pale eyes holding his as he unfolded his arms and leaned in—like Orpheus was supposed to know what that meant. He'd never had anything to fight for. Had never thought further past the simple fact that Lore needed him. Usefulness was all that had ever mattered to him, not some greater goal for the world. The idea that he'd been working towards anything let alone *something* was as obtuse and intangible as the reality of a whole world existing beyond the Gilded Palace's walls.

And look at him now, sitting atop a veritable tower amongst towers, that very world sprawled out beneath him, looking at a man he had fallen desperately in love with, debating what, precisely, he had worth fighting for.

Orpheus pulled in a shuddering breath. "I don't want to die. I don't want to be cursed. But I—" he cut off, giving his heart a moment to race as he stared down at Fenrir's big warm calloused hands, remembering how they touched him. How good they had felt. How alive that had made *him* feel. "But I'm tired. And I'm—I'm scared, Fenrir, that I'll die before I get the chance to live."

Because for the first time in his life, Orpheus had something to live for. Really live for—Fenrir, but also his freedom, and a whole world to discover, that he'd been kept from.

A well-worn itch crawled over his skin, wrist twinging with a reminder of the one thing in his life that had ever felt serendipitous. He brought his fingers together, the crack of his snap loud in the quiet. Netherflame crawled up his hand, flame balanced over his fingers, rolling across his knuckles.

"Fifi." Across the table, Fenrir stared at the Netherflame, eyes flicking to his and back again. "What if there is no curse?"

...What?

Orpheus looked up, mouth opening over silence. In his hand, the Netherflame fizzled out, a curl of pale purple smoke the only evidence it had ever been there at all.

Fenrir reached out, took his empty hand. "Humor me, okay? What if you're not cursed?"

"I—" the possibility for anything else hadn't ever occurred to him because what else was he if not cursed? "—I don't understand."

"Hell beasts, we know they're attracted to Netherflame, right? And if what you said about the scientists is true, then you've got a pretty substantial amount of it within you." The physics of the world went strange as Fenrir spoke, his words chasing the shadows in his mind, the ones where his memories hid, dark secret things he'd stowed away for safe keeping. Of a violet flame in a hidden laboratory, snuffed out when he—when he had—he had *absorbed* a crack.

"So, what if that's why they're attracted to you." Fenrir's thumb tracked his wrist, a steady press. "What if they see you as another—"

"—another crack into Hell," Orpheus finished, voice breathless and thin. He raised his hand, stared at it, then at the gnawing Skullmoth slobbering across the glass.

Everything Fenrir said clicked into place.

"I'm just another crack." If Orpheus' heart had been racing before, now it was in an outright sprint. "When did the dragon show up at the Stacks? Eight, nine weeks ago?"

Fenrir nodded, "Around then, yeah."

"And when did I summon Ohm?"

Fenrir's face grew grim. "Nine weeks and six days ago."

The timeline was right, but the dragon could have been drawn by the crack in the mountain his drills had created.

"Fuck!" Orpheus swept up, chair grinding against the floor as he shoved away from the table and headed for the bookcases. There was a section he'd ignored because it hadn't contained any spell books, a shelf of first-hand accounts of survivors of the Incident, something that hadn't been relevant when he thought he was hunting for a counter curse—

"The Gilded Palace," he said over his shoulder, Fenrir following him down the aisle. He picked through the books, looking for something earlier than the journal he'd pulled before. Something from soon after the Incident, anything that would give him a clue— "The Gilded Palace was a bunker before it was a fortress, but what were they guarding against?"

"Fallout from the Incident?"

"Possibly, yes, but what were the enchantments for? All those sigils? What were they trying to keep out?"

"People?" Fenrir tried. "So, they could experiment in peace?"

"Also possible," he said, eyes snapping to a slender, leather-bound journal he'd passed over thoughtlessly earlier, "but what if it was hell beasts?"

Fenrir's eyes went wide, blinking down at Orpheus in...well, *shock* was a good way to describe it.

"You're right, Fenrir. Hell beasts become territorial around Netherflame, and they—the scientists—they—" Orpheus cut off, heart pounding, voice low in the shadowed stacks. He didn't know whether to cry or scream, it was all beginning to make so much *sense*. "They needed to keep the hell beasts away so they could have access to the dark flame. And then when it worked and the pathway was put inside me, I never left that fucking palace, did I?"

He could hear the shake in his own voice, the way his mind snagged over what he was saying—what he was about to say.

"And then Lore began renovations." Fenrir followed the path of Orpheus' thoughts and met him in quiet revelation.

"She began those hells-damned renovations," Orpheus confirmed; it was so absurd he could laugh.

"Fifi," Fenrir said softly, eyes wide in the dark, catching the light, "you're not cursed."

"No," he whispered, "I don't think I am."

They stared at one another, the darkness of the stacks growing shallow, as something like relief dawned on them both.

"You're not *cursed*," Fenrir repeated, the relief so tangible on his face Orpheus realized in that moment how much this had been weighing on Fenrir. He may have done a convincing job playing Orpheus' curse off like it hadn't mattered, but seeing Fenrir now—eyes wet, smile trembling, carefully hopeful—Orpheus realized it had always been a ruse.

Orpheus wasn't cursed. Nothing was trying to kill him. There was, in fact, a perfectly logical explanation for the hell beasts' attacks, which meant there was an equally logical solution—one Orpheus didn't quite fully grasp yet, but he knew had something to do with the cracks in the world—the crack in his heart—the crack the Incident may have—

"Orpheus." Fenrir closed the distance, hands reaching for him before he had a chance to open the book he'd located. It fell to the floor with a muffled thump when Fenrir cupped his face and hauled him into a kiss.

For all the excitement, the kiss was soft, gentle, a careful press of lips that Orpheus laughed into. Fenrir grinned against his mouth, pressing close, teeth closing over Orpheus' lower lip, the arm around his waist a vice locking their bodies together.

The world fell away, the books on the shelves a distant lure—all Orpheus cared about was the sensation of Fenrir against him and the reality that *this* was all his. Would remain his, now and forever.

Happiness, he thought to himself, *is this what it feels like?*

"I love the sound of your laugh," Fenrir said, voice pitched low, breathless and honest. Inside Orpheus' chest his heart clenched, throbbing, like that crossbow had actually found its mark.

It should have been easy to let the world fall away and follow Fenrir where he was so obviously headed. But Orpheus had always struggled against his curiosity, and he fought the same compulsion now, toe brushing the book he had dropped as Fenrir's mouth found his in another slow kiss.

Orpheus lost himself to it for precisely three-and-a-half seconds before breaking away again to ask, "Fenrir, what's out east, beyond the Rim?"

Against him, Fenrir went rigid. Where his breath touched Orpheus' lips, he felt it stagger.

"The edge of the world," Fenrir said ominously. "It leads to Hell."

Orpheus pulled away enough to look into Fenrir's face. Even in the shadows, there was no hiding his fear.

"What does it look like?" Orpheus asked as gently as he could.

Fenrir's voice went soft, small. "It's a chasm."

It was both what Orpheus hoped to hear and feared.

He should have known. How had he not *known?*

"The edge of the world is a chasm into Hell?"

Fenrir nodded, unable, it seemed, to say much else.

He put a palm to Fenrir's cheek and, this time, it was he who kissed Fenrir. Like every kiss they'd shared, this one seemed different, Fenrir searching now, instead of offering, seeking the comfort he was always so ready to give Orpheus. Fenrir never hid that whatever lay east of the Rim scared him, and now Orpheus had an inkling of why. They'd both seen the damage one small crack into Hell could make. What could have resulted from the damage the Incident inflicted? Orpheus wasn't sure he could imagine it, but the book might help.

He broke the kiss, palm to Fenrir's cheek, eyes on the journal at his feet.

Back at the table, he was proven right.

These new bombs decimated the east coast, from Boston, Massachusetts down to Richmond, Virginia. New York, Philadelphia, and the District of Columbia taking the brunt of the impact, the initial fallout reaching as far west as the Appalachians. But the concern our team has isn't the bombs or the fallout, but what has been revealed to our discovery drones. There is a crack in the Earth's crust, some two-thousand miles long and another three-hundred-and-twenty miles at its widest, which has reached an impossible depth our sensors cannot register. The most reliable readings we can get reveal an infrared bleed that appears violet on the visual spectrum, and a drop in temperature that reaches zero Kelvin—the maximum negative temperature our sensors are capable of recording—which is impossible for the planet's core to maintain let alone produce within its physical structure.

What lay east wasn't the edge of the world—it was just another crack into Hell. An enormous, incomprehensibly cataclysmic crack—but a crack all the same.

Like the one he'd made when he summoned Ohm. And the one he had tapped into, then *torn apart*, when he'd fought that hells-damned dragon. The one the scientists had put inside him, so many years ago, for a specific purpose.

Not to open cracks—but to *close them*. Close the biggest one of them all.

"I can close it," Orpheus said, voice catching on his breath as he looked up at Fenrir. "It's what they made me for."

Across the table, Fenrir's pale eyes went wide. The fear Orpheus had seen in the shadows of the bookshelves looked closer to terror here, exposed to the light of the sun. Fenrir shook his head while leaning in, hand reaching out to cover Orpheus', the eyes that met his wet and pleading. Suddenly, it was like the hero inside Fenrir had only been a front, the man in front of him torn open with a fear Orpheus fully understood.

Heroism never came without its price.

Fenrir knew that. Orpheus knew it too. And as they looked into each other's faces, the reality of what Orpheus was proposing settled on them both.

"I can close it," Orpheus repeated, a little less sure. "I should close it," coming out weaker, but closer, to the truth inside his heart.

INTERLUDE

FAREWELL

They meet in the courtyard an hour after dawn.

She's dressed in dark trousers and a gray coat, the seams stitched neatly with the silvered thread he'd spun weeks ago, his weather resistance spells woven smartly into the structure of the fabric itself. It's some of his best work and he's glad it's going with Lore. This is an important mission—a critical next step. Orpheus doesn't like to think about how he'll be alone, but he has his workshop to distract him and there's the gardens that need tending as well. The hermits may be gone but they've left behind all their loose threads alongside their ghosts.

"Is that it?" Lore asked as she tugs on a pair of leather gloves he'd dug out from one of the dungeon's supply rooms.

"Almost," Orpheus breathes, fingering the smooth metal surface of the one last gift he has for Lore. It's warm under his skin, sharp too. He imagines he can hear the blade ringing as he slides his thumb over the edge. "Here," he pushes out as he carefully draws the knife from his robe. He holds it out to Lore without explanation.

"A weapon?" she asks, plucking the knife from his hand and immediately holding it up to the sun. "Is it enchanted?"

"No," Orpheus says, shifting his weight, "but I made it based off a technique I read about in a fourteenth century Japanese—"

"—Right," Lore interrupts, pocketing the knife and with it, whatever Orpheus was going to say. "Thanks."

"You're welcome," he sighs, shoulders dropping like carrying the secret of that gift around for the last week had been a burden. "Are you sure you want to do this, Lore?"

"Of course," she snaps, sneering at him like he'd asked something stupid. He didn't think he had; now he wasn't so sure.

"Why?" he asks anyway. He doesn't question Lore often. There hasn't been much reason to in the past. But Lore is leaving and the loneliness he already feels is growing by the second, and he doesn't understand why she insists on doing this alone.

"I have to," she snaps, then her voice softens, just a little. "I'll be back," the edge isn't completely gone but Orpheus is grateful for the affirmation that, despite whatever worries he may have, this isn't the end. Lore gives him a firm look when she says, "Keep the palace safe."

"Palace?" Orpheus asks, squinting up at the towers and the wall and the lookouts along the perimeter—the sigils and their swirls and the way they catch the sun every morning and the moon every night.

"What else is it?" Lore sniffs as she hefts her bag and shifts her weight. She's looking past the open gate when Orpheus turns back towards her, head held high, profile strong, the lines of her body straight, aligned, sure.

A palace, he thinks, *one fit for a queen.*

Orpheus stands upon the ramparts and watches her go. He stays there until she's a spot in the distance, the vantage of height feeling more like a curse when the wind picks up and drives cold into his skin. He descends the steps quickly, putting his back to the door once it's closed like it could somehow dampen the feelings stabbing through his chest.

He's alone again, and Orpheus doesn't know what to do with that.

"You're fine," he says into the quiet, talking to himself like his brain is all the company he needs. It's served him this long, hasn't it? Lore's his friend but she's never been the best conversationalist—it's part of the reason he loves books so much. Inside a book, he has hundreds of friends.

THE CRACK AT THE HEART OF EVERYTHING

But when he reaches the top of the stairs leading to his workshop, it's not friends he's thinking about, it's ghosts, because from the shadows memories whisper, and without Lore he's not sure he's strong enough to fight them off on his own.

You have to be, his brain snaps, *she gave you a mission.*

"I'm okay," Orpheus whispers into the quiet, hand pale against the darkness, the violet light that emerges chasing the shadows away.

CHAPTER XXIV
THE TEST

Cold kissed his face as he clung to Fenrir's back, the bleached-white sparkle of untouched powder putting tears in his eyes and a flush on his face. Fenrir was a wall of heat against him, armor traded for a heavy woolen coat that did nothing to keep Orpheus from feeling every shift of muscle and inhale of breath. Fenrir's horse—Nightmare— cantered through the snow as if it wasn't even there.

He couldn't help but think of Achates. He would have struggled through the nearly two feet of unpacked snow, his stout legs and barrel of a body too cumbersome to be called graceful on a good day. But Nightmare was big, and he was strong, and Orpheus supposed he had to be both those things to lug Fenrir back and forth across the wasteland all these years—let alone adding Orpheus into the mix.

"Northeast still?" Fenrir asked over his shoulder as he nudged Nightmare towards a gap in the woods. There wasn't a path to follow, but if Orpheus closed his eyes and concentrated, he could feel the seam where the world split, the cracked-open pit where Netherflame—and Hell—bled through.

"Yes, it can't be far from the bridge, I noticed it while crossing." And he knew they were getting close when the pine trees began to turn black, needles growing thin, the tall, spindly branches too ragged to hold the freshly fallen snow. In the near distance, he could hear the rushing gurgle of the river, the woods silent despite the bright sun and clear day. The poison had driven the fauna away, and Orpheus imagined that the hell beasts didn't care much for the cold of the snow—preferring, likely, the warmth of the wasteland—the crater that would always burn hot—so different from the Netherflame they were used to.

Orpheus wondered again if this would work. If the scientists had been right—had been working towards precisely this—and whether he would live up to those, to be frank, impossible expectations. The world had spent over three-hundred years recovering from the Incident, and the progress Red and the Stacks had recently made couldn't be an isolated achievement. Was he even necessary to the healing the world needed? Would he be causing more harm? Upsetting a balance that had taken nature years to achieve?

But then the woods turned dark, and the trees began to wilt, and little pockets of purple began to bleed through the pale fluffy snow— and it became clear that the vein of poison running through the world was not going anywhere without his help. That the planet and its people, no matter how hard they struggled, could never close the cracks he and those ancient cataclysmic architects had made.

"Do you see that?" Fenrir's voice came quiet as he slowed Nightmare to a trot, and Orpheus knew what he was talking about when he turned his head and saw the crushed clearing of recently charred trees.

"The dragon," Orpheus breathed, "where is it?"

"Not here. Think it, like, got scavenged by a bigger dragon?"

Orpheus sure hoped not.

"Shit," Fenrir hissed, "look at the snow."

A swept-out depression that, at first glance, could have been a snow drift had buried half the downed trees at the clearing's eastern edge. Like Fenrir, Orpheus knew immediately what it meant.

"It survived, somehow."

"Those fuckers really are hard to kill, huh?" Fenrir groused, and Orpheus knew without asking that he was thinking of Gawain.

"Well, now you'll get another chance to make it into the history books."

"That an offer to write about me? Bet I'd make a pretty good poem. Personally, I think I'm more of a Hercules than an Odysseus, but I might settle for an account the length of the Aeneid."

Now it was Orpheus' turn to grouse. "I'd rather burn at the stake than write anything in dactylic hexameter."

They passed the clearing without incident, snow crunching under Nightmare's hooves as they slowed their pace to a walk. Orpheus kept his arms around Fenrir's waist, fingers curling over his abdomen while his head tipped forward against his back, breathing him in as his eyes closed and his senses reached out in a careful, nascent search.

With very little effort, he could feel it. Not so far below, Netherflame burned, the icy crust of snow nothing in comparison to the bone-deep chill of Hell. It would have been easy to lose himself to it, that tide of violet flame and cold that swept him up nearly as easily as the river's current had. But then the warm slide of skin on skin tugged on his senses—two of Fenrir's fingertips slipping under the edge of the worn leather glove he'd borrowed over a month ago, resting atop the back of his wrist as if Fenrir knew what kind of anchor he was providing.

It was the most innocent of touches, but no less arresting; Orpheus struggled in a breath as he shivered against Fenrir.

"Okay?" drifted over Fenrir's shoulder as those fingers began to move.

"You're going to get frostbite," Orpheus breathed as he relaxed, the slow slip-slide of skin making him feel grounded, the physicality of Fenrir's touch keeping him there, in the present, rather than lost in the timeless current of Netherflame below.

"Well, too bad I gave my gloves away to some cute homeless sorcerer."

"I'm not homeless," came out of him before he could think straight. Fenrir's fingers stalled, didn't begin moving again until he took in a big breath. "We're close," he said when Fenrir didn't say anything else.

"How can you tell?" Fenrir asked. "What does it feel like?"

Orpheus turned his face into Fenrir's shoulder, closed his eyes and focused. "Like being caught up in that river. A current that wants to pull me under."

Fenrir's fingers became a palm when he closed his hand over Orpheus' wrist. His grip was firm. A claim upon Orpheus, like Fenrir actually was afraid he might get swept up and away. He liked the feeling. Liked being the subject of Fenrir's possessive need to be the strong one—his compunction to protect. Because he realized how easy it would be to give himself up to the power inside himself. How easily he'd tapped into that vein of Hell and used that power for his own desires.

"Here is good," he breathed into Fenrir's shoulder, eyes still closed, shivering against his coat.

Fenrir slid off Nightmare in a smooth dismount, feet sinking a foot deep before the packed snow caught him. His hands were steady as they smoothed up Orpheus' thighs, the grip he took on his hips strong as he guided him around in the saddle. Orpheus ignored how his hands shook when he put them on Fenrir's shoulders, pulled in a shaking inhale as he tipped forward and into his arms.

Neither spoke as Fenrir lowered him down, the closeness they kept saying more than any words possibly could right then. The gravity of what Orpheus was about to try was not lost on either of them, and if it worked how he hoped—how he feared—the balance of everything they knew about the world was about to shift.

Orpheus was self-aware enough to know he wasn't ready for that yet—but also that he never would be ready—just as he'd never been ready to leave the Gilded Palace and look at what that had gotten him.

Fenrir's eyes were nearly gray against the cold snowy backdrop of the pine woods when Orpheus looked up at him. The corners crinkled as Fenrir's lips quirked up into a smile.

"Ready?" Fenrir asked, hands moving from Orpheus' hips to his waist, not tugging, but holding, ready to go wherever Orpheus took them.

Orpheus closed his eyes and took a breath. "Ready."

Behind him, Nightmare snuffed loudly, snow crunching underfoot as Fenrir helped him through the snow and to a small clearing where the sun reached uninterrupted. Here, Orpheus knelt. Snow crept cold underneath his outermost robe, but beneath it all was that ice, the bite of magic that he had sensed beneath the river—in that mountain valley—under the electromagnetic pulse of the grid Red had erected. And if he closed his eyes and focused far east, to where the wound in the world festered, a massive infection that put this child's scratch to shame pulsed.

"I can close this vein here, but it's not connected to the one out east," Orpheus murmured, trance-like. "I'll have to go east to reach that one, if this works."

"Are you sure?" Fenrir asked, snow crunching as he shifted.

"I'm sure, this is from the drill I made," Orpheus nursed the memory with a soft, gentle thought, trying not to let the guilt sink in any further. "It runs under the Stacks and up the mountain. If I close this, it should make the Stacks safe again. No more dying orchards, possibly no more dragon."

"Just...be careful, Fifi, please," Fenrir said so quietly Orpheus nearly didn't hear the catch in his voice. Fenrir was scared, and Orpheus...he was too.

"If you see Netherflame that is not mine, run," he warned as he tugged off his gloves and smoothed his bare palm over the snow. "Here I go."

The sigil was large, but delicate, the same that'd he'd drawn into Achates except tethered to the world itself. Oxygen for the air they breathed. Iron and aluminum for the rock they stood upon. Silicon for the sand. Hydrogen for the water. And carbon for the trees, the birds, the mice and the hares and the ants and the humans—the single most important element for the composition of life on their planet—the only tether Orpheus could think of that would touch the world in a way that mattered—that could heal that which those before them had so ignorantly almost destroyed.

And me, Orpheus thought as he rubbed the melted snow from his fingers, closed his eyes, and snapped.

THE CRACK AT THE HEART OF EVERYTHING

Netherflame flared through the sigil, through his body, connection forged in the thing those scientists had put inside him, the push-pull of cold fire lancing through his heart and into the vein of hell below.

All around, infection bled, the necrotic earth surrounding the crack pulsing with a poison he'd first found in Achates. The sigils flared, like the stitches of a suture finding compromised flesh, and Orpheus sensed that infection draw into himself. Fever came upon him in tumultuous, nerve-searing force. Like a live wire stripped of its housing, he felt open and exposed, the current of Netherflame below making a new connection, an infinite vessel that could take and take and take.

And Orpheus realized, in that moment, precisely what was happening. Saw in his mind the network of tunnels—no, the beat-pulse of an entire nervous system—a pathway into Hell that his machines had burrowed through the earth like a flesh-eating bacterium, spreading and consuming and bleeding its poison everywhere it touched, and how far it had grown in these last few months. How it would never stop—could never stop—entropy demanding what only an exponential return could give, until decay became death and life as they knew it would end, and how infinitesimal it all was in the face of what lay east.

Massive. Monumental. Not a crack but a gorge. A whole stretch of the world that lay open and weeping, unhealed and untreated and festering with the gangrenous infection that would consume them all if not purged.

Hell on Earth, Orpheus dared to think, and then it was instinct that guided him.

Through the heady fog of fever, Orpheus located the vein, sensed the connection, and from the furthest point out, he willed the break to close. It could have been minutes or hours, but when the valley of Lore's mountain—the largest of the wound—shriveled and collapsed, he followed it along the errant path that curved round the Stacks and under the grid, the whole of it going dim, then dark. And for all his inability to craft a half-decent healing spell, a smile spread across

Orpheus' face as he closed this last leg of the vein.

Maybe that was why he nearly missed it. Why he didn't think twice about why the connection didn't break the moment the last of the vein closed, the spell still working, the whole of his body going from feverishly hot, to icy cold.

"Fifi!" tore through him a moment before the spell did. Orpheus' reeled where he knelt, gasping in a breath as his concentration broke and the sigil before him went dim.

"Fenrir," he gasped, white blinding in the absence of violet, vertigo tipping the world sideways as he collapsed forward into his sigil.

Hands grappled him upright, pushed snow from his face. Orpheus trembled as his heart hammered a hole through his chest, body frayed thin as fever pulsed through every nerve-ending, and realization dawned on him.

He'd nearly closed his own connection to Netherflame. Nearly snuffed himself out like a candle left too long to burn. And he hadn't even realized. Hadn't registered the point of no return because he knew that wherever this was headed, if he wanted the world to recover, the crack inside him would have to heal too.

And that wouldn't just take away his magic. It would kill him. Orpheus...he would *die*.

A pained sound tore out of him, wretched and filled with a lifetime of lonely aching. From a distance he sensed Fenrir maneuver him around, the brand of his touch somehow hotter than his fevered skin when Fenrir took his hands into his own.

"Hey, hey, I'm here, you're safe, you're okay," came out of Fenrir in a rush.

I'm not, Orpheus thought. *I'm really, really not.*

He shook when Fenrir pushed in, sucked in short shallow breaths as Fenrir got an arm around him and dragged him close. A hand ran through his hair, cradled the back of his head, directing Orpheus' face into the crook of Fenrir's neck and holding him there. Beneath his mouth he could taste Fenrir's skin, breathe in his scent, familiar, grounding things that at any other time would have calmed his breaking heart. Instead, a sob tore out of him, grief catching up with a momentum Orpheus couldn't stop, because whatever happened next, he couldn't tell Fenrir about this.

"I'm fine, I'm fine," he lied through his tears, shaking, trembling, gripping and clutching at the man he—he *loved*. "It worked. The spell worked. It will work."

And as Fenrir buried his face in Orpheus' hair and hauled him impossibly closer, he knew, with all the same certainty he had that moving forward meant accepting his death, that Fenrir would stop him. That for however much Fenrir might see himself as the hero of his story, he would never give up Orpheus' life for the benefit of the greater good.

Far in the distance, violet flame flared, Lore's mountain erupting in a herald of smokeless ash, klaxon lost to the howling wind as Hell stirred, and not Lore's, but Ohm's army came awake.

CHAPTER XXV

THE PLAN

"Wake up, Fifi, you've been sleeping all day. Yeah, good. Come on, drink this, I've got you."

The sensation of hands on his shoulders stirred Orpheus out of his half-sleep. Inside the Keep, violet-tinged twilight bled through the window, as cool as the water Fenrir tipped into his mouth. He swallowed in slow sips, eyes drifting over the snow-limned landscape of the city beyond while fever burned under his skin.

Orpheus had thought he'd get the chance to explore the Pit. Help Fenrir and Red bring it back to its former glory. In the days spent inside this Keep he'd read so many books—manuals and guides and theories regarding everything from civil engineering to politics to economics to religion and more—and from them had birthed a universe of ideas about the potential of what the world could look like moving forward that he'd begun dreaming of it at night. And he wouldn't get a chance to be a part of any of it, because in days or weeks or possibly hours, Orpheus would be dead.

"Found a thermometer that doesn't need a battery in one of the kits downstairs," Fenrir continued on when Orpheus had finished half the glass of water. His body was warm, but Fenrir's was warmer, even if the way he was looking at Orpheus made every cell in his body go icy cold. "This happen every time you overdo it with your magic?" Fenrir asked without asking.

Orpheus was awake enough to recognize that Fenrir had reached his own kind of edge. Worried didn't begin to encompass what Orpheus knew Fenrir was feeling. Disturbed possibly came close, and Orpheus felt both naive and guilty at the secret he was keeping. Wondered why he was doing it at all. If he even had to. Why he thought he must.

"Sometimes." Orpheus leaned into Fenrir, for once taking what he needed rather than waiting for fate to take pity of him; obviously, that wasn't happening anytime soon, if ever at all. "It's a new spell, I wasn't prepared for the amount of power it would take."

"The hole out east is a lot bigger," Fenrir said, coming close to the question Orpheus desperately did not want to answer.

What if you can't close the hole east?

There was a distinct possibility that Orpheus couldn't. Clearly, that was the worst possible outcome Fenrir could think of. Otherwise, Orpheus didn't have a doubt that he'd be tied to this very bed, unable to leave the Keep let alone entertain the notion of heading east, saving the world no more than a distant nightmare they'd both briefly entertained.

It wasn't a terrible option. Certainly better than the one he was currently struggling with.

"I'll be fine," he sighed, pushing away from Fenrir to slouch against the wall. Head tipped to the side, Fenrir stared out the window at the Pit and the setting sun and maybe the whole waiting world beyond.

If anyone knew if the world was worth saving, Fenrir did, so maybe Orpheus was scared of the wrong reaction. Maybe he should be terrified that Fenrir would be okay with him offering his life up in exchange for the greater good. After all, Fenrir had been gambling his own over and over for the last dozen years; what made Orpheus' any different?

Except, then Fenrir slid his fingers to Orpheus' wrist, a gentle touch that said everything neither of them seemed able to in that moment, and Orpheus knew he wasn't wrong. Fenrir may be a hero, but he wasn't an idiot—as inseparable as those two concepts might have once been.

Orpheus turned his palm up and their fingers entwined. A gentle grip that was slow to build, Fenrir also took something that had been out of his grasp for longer than Orpheus would ever understand. Here was something Fenrir wasn't prepared to give up yet. Not that Orpheus was, he just didn't know if he was capable of living with himself if he walked away from the alternative either.

They sat like that for a long time, the lanterns Fenrir had lit glowing brightly, the sun slow to set. By the time Fenrir drew his hand away, Orpheus was more awake than he had been in days. But he didn't stop Fenrir from digging out the thermometer he'd found, watching with precious fondness as Fenrir squinted at the ticks of numbers and measurements on the strip of metal encased inside the tube. Orpheus reached out and tapped the glasses that were currently propped atop Fenrir's head.

Dark frames settled low on Fenrir's nose, Rim-pale eyes leveling on Orpheus as Fenrir twirled the thermometer between his fingers.

"If this—" he lifted the thermometer, pointed it towards Orpheus like he was—well, to blame for all this, "—doesn't indicate any improvement, I'm building a sled and personally dragging you back to the Stacks."

"Yes, doctor," Orpheus whispered, forcing a coy smile. He didn't feel the humor but that didn't matter; Orpheus watched some of the tension release from Fenrir's face.

"If you can crack jokes, I'll assume the fever hasn't boiled your brain yet," Fenrir muttered and then abruptly slid the thermometer past Orpheus' lips. "Put that under your tongue and keep it there, I'll count."

His teeth clicked as he spoke around the glass, "Are yeh shure? Sixshy ish ra'er high—"

"Asshole," Fenrir snipped back, but the tightness around his mouth was receding, the slope of his shoulders becoming less severe.

Sixty seconds felt more like ten, but Orpheus attributed that to the yet-to-be-known timeline he was working with that had never really stopped counting down towards his death. One fate traded for another, it seemed. A curse wouldn't kill him, but that didn't mean something else couldn't.

"One-oh-two point one," Fenrir read off, frown tugging back into place. "What does the book say?"

Orpheus didn't need to thumb through the *Mayo Clinic Textbook of General Practice* to know his fever was high, but no longer dangerously so.

"Anything below one-oh-three is considered safe for the average adult. I'll be okay, Fenrir," Orpheus repeated again, not exactly lying.

Fenrir's eyes narrowed as if he knew Orpheus was withholding something important from him. When he spoke next, there was a bite to his voice Orpheus wasn't used to.

"I want it under one-oh-two by the morning." As if Orpheus had any kind of control over what was currently happening to him.

Nausea that had nothing to do with his fever churned his stomach.

He'd expected the fever. When he'd used the spell on Achates, the amount of Netherflame he'd flushed had been a fraction of what had seeped from that vein, and that had left him sick for days. All things considered, a few days of fever was nothing in comparison to the centuries of disease the world had been subjected to. So, while Fenrir may be worried, that wasn't what disturbed Orpheus the most.

No, what disturbed Orpheus the most was that if he closed his eyes and concentrated, he could feel every dimensional break into Hell within a five-hundred-mile radius—the massive wound that was east so blisteringly powerful as to nearly drown out the sensation of his own internal flame. If Orpheus hadn't had confirmation before, he absolutely had it now.

He wasn't simply a vessel for Netherflame, he was fundamentally connected to it.

All that power. Right there, surging alongside the fever, the itch under his skin to unleash that which he'd tasted, like he'd done with the dragon during their fight. He might have closed one vein, but he'd opened himself to something far more dangerous, and Orpheus didn't need a textbook to tell him what that meant.

Oh, what Lore would have done had she known.

For the first time in weeks, Orpheus thought of his workshop—the safe place he'd hidden away in for so many years, where the truth couldn't touch him, let alone this insidious responsibility he now felt for the world and its future. He could walk away from this. There didn't have to be a what comes next. If Orpheus told Fenrir he thought their plan was too dangerous, that would be the end of it. And as the crossroads he approached grew nearer, the temptation to do precisely that grew stronger.

Orpheus wasn't a hero. He'd never been fool enough to think himself one even before he'd understood the full scope of what he'd participated in. So, he didn't understand the ache in his heart that insisted he become one *now*.

"Are you sure we have to do this?" Fenrir was so close to asking the question Orpheus desperately wanted to avoid. But neither of them seemed able to give up their loosely assembled plan of: *"Head east, Heal Planet."*

"Have you ever read about blood sepsis—" Orpheus gestured at the textbook, didn't have the strength or desire to flip to the corresponding chapter, "—once bacteria have entered the bloodstream through a wound, it's there whether that wound remains or not."

Fenrir's eyes drifted to his, expression masked, unreadable.

"When I left the Stacks, I passed through Red's orchards." Orpheus said instead of answering outright, cracking an eye open to regard Fenrir, "Her irrigation system is impressive, so why did this season's crops fail? What else could taint her ground water if it wasn't the drilling?"

Fenrir's expression didn't change, but Orpheus knew he understood.

"And the wasteland, it's expanded, hasn't it? That's why so many people flooded into what is now Lore's lands. What started all the fighting so many years ago: limited resources, a growing population. Lore needed to cull the masses, build her walls, maintain her borders.

But those people didn't come from just anywhere. They were fleeing something. Escaping what lies east beyond the Rim."

The picture Orpheus was painting may have been an exaggeration, but the reasoning was sound. He'd read enough of history to recognize what had happened, even though it had taken this long to become clear.

"In physics there's the law of exponential growth. It's the snowball effect of something small growing to the point of something massive. I believe that is what we're experiencing now in regard to the Incident. The crack may be hundreds of miles away now, but where was it thirty years ago? Where will it be in ten, twenty years' time?" Orpheus asked, voice quiet but firm, like he'd already made up his mind about what he was going to do, even if he hadn't.

"And only you can stop it," Fenrir said, too soft in the cold wintery quiet. "And look at what closing one portion of it has done to you. I don't like it, Orpheus. I don't like it at all."

"Lore will like it less," landed like the blow both of them had been expecting.

Fenrir held his eyes and refused to let go.

"We may not be able to defeat Ohm, but I can seal up every crack of Netherflame he can feed off of."

"Orpheus," Fenrir breathed, "that's a terrible plan."

Closing off Netherflame from the world—stirring the hornets' nest that was Lore's mountain. All for what?

Isn't this what you wanted? He didn't ask.

Neither did he beg, *Ask me not to do it.*

The truth was, why should he? What had the world done for him other than dump its problems onto his shoulders? He didn't owe those scientists anything, let alone everyone else who didn't even know the planet's future lay solely with him. Who was to say life wouldn't go on one way or another? Perhaps the crops were failing, and the wasteland was expanding but it would take at least another few hundred years for it to fester to the point of an event horizon.

He'd be dead by then—curse or no curse, fever or no fever—so why end it all early when he'd finally found something worthwhile to live for?

Silver moonlight bled through the window, highlighting Fenrir in gilded edges. Magnified by his glasses, starlight collected in Fenrir's pale eyes in the same way tears might have, if given the chance. Fenrir didn't give it. Instead, Orpheus watched him fight off everything he felt, the stiff ledge of his shoulders the only hint that something was amiss. Orpheus ached to comfort him, but it felt wrong to lie to Fenrir like that.

Time passed in long, meandering minutes. And when Fenrir didn't say anything else, Orpheus gave in and broke the silence.

"We should head for the Stacks in the morning, before another storm comes through and we're stranded here," Orpheus said, voice somehow steady.

Fenrir pursed his lips, continued staring out the window. Orpheus knew that look; Fenrir agreed, even if his concern for Orpheus' health stood in opposition. They must be running out of supplies. Food, maybe. More likely fuel.

Time, his mind unhelpfully supplied. Orpheus closed his eyes and pushed the thought away.

Tomorrow came too soon when Orpheus awoke feeling the best he had in nearly a week, tucked into Fenrir's warm body. He took his time in the shower, letting the drain fill with suds as he squished his toes against the smooth tile, listening to Fenrir's electric shaver buzz as he trimmed his beard down to stubble in the bathroom mirror. They made a lazy breakfast out of Fenrir's meal packs and some of Red's leftover trail mix, dividing up the remainder of their food into three days' worth of rations because Fenrir promised he could get them to the Stacks faster than it had taken Orpheus and Achates to get to the bridge.

"Please promise not to hate me," Fenrir had said ominously, and Orpheus wouldn't realize why until they were six hours into their ride.

The fallen snow had reduced down into a blanket of crunchy ice, not quite melted but far from the fluffy down that they'd trudged through a week ago. The ruins rose from the trees, the crackle of Nightmare's hooves sinking into the frozen snow nearly enough to drown out the static building in Orpheus' head.

Here weren't the three-hundred-year-old ruins of an abandoned small town, but the site of a more recent altercation. Fresh burn marks trailed the half-shingled rooftops of the brick and wooden buildings that had obviously been pieced-together from the detritus of some older, more ancient devastation. The ghosts were all around them: the tire-tracks that collected ice in patterned puzzles; the tattered plastic of makeshift windows; the debris of everyday objects that spilled from the doorways, pieces of someone's former life stripped of the merit they'd once held. Discarded, it seemed, in favor of whatever search had gone on here, whether that was for useful supplies or simply the souls that had, once upon a time, called this place home.

That was one of seven towns—settlements—communities—they would pass through. Each one identical but for the map of their town square or the size of their outbuildings. Orpheus couldn't smell the bodies, but he knew the remains must be out there. Somewhere in those clearings he saw from Nightmare's saddle, the parts of the woods burned down not by Netherflame's eternal fire, but pure and simple gasoline.

Keep the ruins on the horizon, Red had said when giving him his map. *Don't know what's still hangin' around out there*, had meant something entirely different back then.

Yet, who was he to say that what Fenrir had been a part of out here was wrong? What line could Orpheus possibly draw when in his trembling hands rested the fate of the whole planet, and he wasn't even sure that was enough to convince him to help?

Orpheus wrapped his arms tighter around Fenrir, held him close while the world around him slipped through his fingers, then closed his eyes, and cried.

CHAPTER XXVI
THE RETURN

They smelled the smoke before they saw the fire.

He hadn't really thought about it, before—the scent the crater gave off. For all its three hundred years of fire, there was very little smoke—little smell—besides the sulfuric tang of hot minerals on the back of his tongue.

This was different. Soot clogged his nose, visible in the air, heavy and dark and obscuring the neon lights that illuminated the main strip. Orpheus couldn't tell where the smoke was coming from, not with the tower bellowing steam or the crater within sight, but he knew it was close. Knew it was fresh. Sinuses stinging with the acrid stab of seared carbon with every breath he took, his mouth watering because, if he was honest, it smelled like cooking meat.

"I don't have a good feeling about this," Orpheus whispered into the night.

"Something's up," was Fenrir's quiet reply, the two of them falling into silence as the wind kicked up in an icy cold gust.

They were about a quarter mile outside the Stacks. Close enough to see but not be seen—at least Orpheus hoped. Because as the minutes ticked by and the situation became clearer, there was more than the change in smoke to alert them to the fact that something was not right.

THE CRACK AT THE HEART OF EVERYTHING

Bandits? Orpheus thought to himself, placing his cheek to Fenrir's back and gazing up at Lore's mountain. Had Lore finally been attacked?

But as he stared up at the black wedge of the horizon where Lore's mountain slept, another thought edged into place. Maybe it was instinct which compelled him, but it was his newfound connection to Netherflame that warned him, because when Orpheus closed his eyes and reached, he couldn't feel the crack he knew lay within the mountain, but he could feel another source of Netherflame. One that hadn't—shouldn't—exist here at all.

There, throughout the whole of the Stacks, he could feel it. Feel him. Feel Ohm.

"Lore's on the move," Fenrir said at the precise moment Orpheus breathed, "Ohm is here."

Under the cover of darkness, their eyes met. Orpheus' saliva went thick as he stared into the shadows that made up Fenrir's face, body swaying with the pull of Nightmare's body as Fenrir edged them away from the Stacks. The quiet of the night became suffocating, fear a prowling monster hiding behind every shadow, between every breath.

For the first time in his life—the curse that was not really a curse be damned—Orpheus felt death closing in. This wasn't just some hell beast. This wasn't even disease or fever or a raging river trying to drag him under or a dragon tearing him apart. This was the general of Hell's own army, and the only possible, potential, *conceivable* reason he might be here, was because Orpheus, in both his greatest and most ill-fated achievement yet, had gone and closed up Ohm's fucking source of power—that crack.

"He needs a source of Netherflame," was the simple part of this fucking equation, "they have likely put two and two together that it was me who sealed up that vein."

"We need to leave. It's not safe."

"With no supplies? Have you lost your mind?" Orpheus snapped without meaning to, immediately regretting his choice of words. "I apologize, that was—"

"—Fifi, it's fine," Fenrir slid a hand over his as he spoke. "There are other places. A town north of the mountain, at the other side of the pass. We could make it there in four days if we head west. My parents would love to meet you. We can find water on the way, hunt for food. And there's always the lab—"

But whatever Fenrir might have said next was drowned out in a bellow of sound, the klaxon call of Lore's herald descending from the sky like a storm, setting Orpheus' bones to rattle and his mind...his mind to *work*.

"He needs a source of Netherflame," Orpheus breathed when the second of the klaxons died out—the command, Orpheus knew, to rally forces. "He needs *me*."

"Fuck. Fuck, fuck, *fuck!*"

In the near distance, shadows churned. Orpheus clutched Fenrir's waist as Nightmare fell into a trot.

"We can't outrun them, can we?" Orpheus asked as Fenrir pointed them west.

"No," Fenrir breathed through his teeth, "we can't."

"We need to go east."

Fenrir lifted out of the saddle, Orpheus following as Nightmare broke into a canter.

"Fenrir, we have to go east!" Not because he wanted to go through with the plan, because at least east, he would have the Incident's crack to drown out his own.

"Plan's scrapped," Fenrir snapped, "we have to get far enough away from the Stacks that Ohm doesn't level the whole place when he catches us."

"You're giving us up?" Orpheus shrieked.

"I'm going to fight!"

Wait. What? *No*—Fenrir couldn't fight *Ohm*.

"Let me down—" Orpheus panicked, shoving away from Fenrir with a sudden burst of adrenaline, scooting towards the back of the saddle so he could dismount. The fall would hurt but he'd be fine—fine enough to face Ohm himself, which would likely also turn out fine if all he needed was a replacement source of Netherflame. Ohm wouldn't want to kill him, right? "He's after me, not you, you can escape—"

"Sit down!" Fenrir roared, twisting in the saddle and reaching for him. A fist closed over the front of Orpheus' robes as Fenrir hauled him to the front of the saddle. At any other time, the display of brute strength would have had Orpheus swooning, but with an army from Hell at their back he barely managed a squeal.

"Listen to me!" Orpheus gasped, twisting around to bang a fist against Fenrir's chest. "You let me down and Ohm comes after me while you head for the Stacks, find something—anything—supplies or a—a—" he thought of Farris and his garage and the tarp in the corner and that massive machine it hid, "—a vehicle. Something fast. Something Ohm can't catch—"

Ice bit his cheeks as fog rolled out of the night, Nightmare's hooves banging cracks into the rocky wasteland as the ground turned to ice and fractured. But they had slowed, and Fenrir was looking at him as if he'd grown a second head, pale eyes edged white even out here, where the light of the Stacks hardly reached.

"Fuck, Fifi, you're a genius," was all Fenrir said before he launched himself off the back of the saddle and into the night. Orpheus reeled as he grabbed for Nightmare's reins and tried to turn him around, losing track of Fenrir while nearly falling off the saddle himself.

"Keep running! Cause a distraction!" Emerged from the darkness as Orpheus jerked at the reins, "Don't let him catch you! Give me ten— fuck, no, fifteen minutes, then head for the garage!"

"You're leaving me?" Orpheus shrieked like he hadn't just suggested this very thing. To be fair, it felt entirely different when you were the person being abandoned. "With your stupid horse?"

But Fenrir had already disappeared into the fog, nothing but the shattered prints of his boots evidence that he'd been there at all.

"Bastard!" Orpheus snarled into the shadows a moment before the klaxon rose once again.

It must be yards—no—feet behind him, so close his teeth rattled in his head and made his vision go funny. Nightmare was at an outright gallop now, heading off towards the crater at a speed that would kill them both the moment they hit one of the uneven patches of concrete or—hell forbid—a sinkhole. Orpheus clutched at the reins, hunching low over Nightmare's neck, finally remembering after the horse's sweat hit his face that that was precisely what you did to make one run *faster*.

"Easy, easy!" He breathed into the ear Nightmare tipped back towards him. "We need to kill time, not ourselves!"

Lore was about to take care of that for him, after all.

From the darkness, a shape emerged. Black against the pale fog crawling across the cracked ground, Ohm's hulking figure charged out of the night, the distance between them closing in one short, terrifying breath. But it wasn't Ohm Orpheus was looking at, it was the person perched atop his shoulders. Black hair, pale skin, stern face. Lore looked all the world like the Empress she claimed to be, the gracefully gilded armor he'd spent nearly a year crafting catching the Netherflame of Ohm's hollowed skeleton in familiar shapes. But when their eyes met, there was nothing in them he recognized.

Gone was the woman he'd watched ascend a throne of her own forging—absent was the little girl he'd found hiding behind a dusty bookshelf. The person perched atop Ohm was a stranger to Orpheus, and the part of him not currently fighting for his life was clever enough to realize that had always been the case.

A sword reached out, level with Orpheus' neck as Ohm charged in.

Nightmare whinnied when Netherflame erupted in a shield around them, the blast of violet light blinding them both for the moment it took the spell to settle into place. Orpheus' hands shook around the reins, the little sigil he'd scratched into Nightmare saddle crude but enough to deflect Ohm's passing swipe. He almost imagined he could feel the brunt of the hit passing through him, the clean sweep of his blade more than enough to have taken Orpheus' head clean off his neck. It was a dizzying realization; one made all the more real when Ohm pivoted around for a second try.

"Run!" Orpheus shrieked as Nightmare launched into a gallop straight for the crater.

Warmth bled up from the ground, threads of fire illuminating their path from below. Orpheus didn't know what to do other than run. His body ached, his legs were weakening, the effort required to stay balanced on Nightmare's back draining what little energy he'd recovered. But as the crater stretched out before him, an idea took shape. Like the vein he had closed days prior, perhaps he could achieve the opposite—open, for lack of a better term—the shattered earth below them.

"Can you make a sweep around them?" he breathed into Nightmare's ear, closing his eyes for a moment and imagining the sigil he needed. He'd never tried this before, but if it worked... "a wide arc, like a wall?"

Ear angled back, Nightmare said nothing, but Orpheus thought he understood when their weight shifted and Ohm and Lore bled back into Orpheus' peripheral. He cast quickly, hand reached out over his hip, eyes half closed while the sigil burned to life inside his head. When Netherflame curled out from his hand in a perfect mimic of that image, he took a second to steady himself, glancing out over the broken earth to where Lore and Ohm were closing in—committing, he acknowledged, to whatever came next.

His escape, yes. But also his death.

Orpheus bit his lip, smothered the urge to scream, and cast.

The sigil flared, a searing, violet fire that blasted from his hand directly into the ground below. One sigil down, Orpheus quickly focused on another, forging a series of marks directly into the ground they tore across, Lore and Ohm right there at the edge of his vision, getting closer with every second.

He didn't know how much ground they covered, could hardly see anymore past the blinding flares of his magic and the encroaching fog that followed Ohm everywhere he went. By the time Lore was close enough again for Orpheus to see her face, Nightmare was frothing at the mouth, his own strength nearly spent.

He needed to end this. And he needed to do it now. But he hesitated, looking at Lore as the distance between them fell away, like this time he might see something different—*someone* different. And for a moment time slowed its passing, a fractioned second between when the final sigil was cast and the spell went off, when their eyes met and Orpheus thought he could. Because from atop her hell steed, Lore looked at him with all the gravity fate had dumped upon her shoulders, and Orpheus understood in complete and sudden comprehension how heavy a weight she carried—felt the mirror of it in his very soul—and how he could help her—stop her—*save* her—like her fate truly was tied to his own.

Then cold hatred washed clear over Lore's face, Ohm's sword raising in a mimic of the knife in Lore's hand, and Orpheus knew it was either her or him.

The last sigil flared from his palm and struck the ground, and Orpheus understood how Lore had done what she did—brought the world to its literal knees—because not an ounce of fear broke over her face when his spell suddenly swallowed her and Ohm whole.

"Faster!" Orpheus screamed at Nightmare as Netherflame erupted across the crater, a massive explosion of dust and debris and steam and fire. The world turned molten, fire engulfing everything, Nightmare's hooves beating orange-violet-tinged cracks into the fractured terrain beneath them while the ground began to collapse. Fire boiled through the shattered concrete in hissing snaps a second before everything solid disintegrated into an inferno, the network of caves and pipes and sinkholes crumbling all at once as his spell tore through the ground in a massive sweeping arc.

Orpheus didn't look behind when Lore's klaxon called out again. He gritted his teeth and hunched his shoulders, closing his eyes against the heat and the tears and the terror as Nightmare tore off into the darkness, the skittering, scraping, crumbling earth close enough on their heels that Orpheus knew, if they slowed, it would gobble them up too. It didn't. And when Orpheus finally twisted around to look, he witnessed the arc of damage he'd created, an enormous sickle-shaped tear in the earth that wept bloodied fire, a near quarter mile's worth of damage placed between him and Ohm and Lore.

At the far side of the crater, Lore watched, perched atop Ohm's shoulders, a shadowy silhouette amongst what, Orpheus admitted, was all his own wreckage.

CHAPTER XXVII

TAKING FLIGHT

By the time the Stacks were within reach, Orpheus was sweating alongside Nightmare. He could feel his body systemically shutting down, adrenaline draining and taking with it whatever strength he had left. A week of fever had left him exhausted; running for his life from Lore had left him nearly catatonic.

But he made it to the alley, and by extension, Farris' garage.

"Orpheus," Fenrir hissed from the shadows, then hands were on his, prying the reins from his locked-up fingers. "Are they close? Are you okay?"

He tumbled out of the saddle and into Fenrir's arms. Fenrir caught him, easily, all strong arms and steady hands.

"We need to—" Orpheus broke off, sucking in a rattling breath. Fenrir's shirt was soaked with sweat when his fingers curled into the fabric. "—go. We need to leave—"

"Yeah, I know, I've got you," Fenrir said, gentle as he lowered him to the ground and put his hands on his waist to keep him standing. Fenrir gave him a smile once it became clear Orpheus wasn't going to collapse. "Got us a ride, come on, it's inside."

Fenrir led him through the open bay door, towards the far corner of the garage where the tarp along with Red and Farris both waited. Red came forward, face stern, while behind her, Farris looked like he was about to be sick. He stared at Fenrir like it was he who was the threat here and not Lore and Ohm.

"He's fine, see, just like I promised," Fenrir announced, steering Orpheus towards Red like he was passing him off. Maybe he was, because Red reached for him, clapping a hand on his shoulder while Fenrir ducked away under the tarp. Orpheus didn't miss the sharp-toothed grin he shot Farris.

"Are yeh sure..." Farris trailed off, hands wrung in front of him, face looking rather gray.

Orpheus drew a long breath and dared to meet Red's stare.

"Heya, Sparks," she said, voice sounding like she'd swallowed rocks. Orpheus grimaced.

"I'm sorry," spilled out of him before he could stop it. "I didn't know—I didn't mean—"

"No, this isn't your fault," Red said, face tight. "We've been anticipating something like this for a while now. Lore was never going to let peace last."

"But I—" he choked off, seeing, for the first time, the bodies littered across the garage. Most wore uniforms similar to Farris'—soldiers, ones loyal to Fenrir and Red—two others the skeletal remains of Ohm's own soldiers. The gun cage was open, and a section of the racks emptied, and beyond the garage he could hear everything. The roar of a city block on fire, the shouting of voices, the clap of gunshots echoing off brick. The garage must have been taken when Fenrir arrived, this contingent of soldiers giving up their lives so that Orpheus could get away safe.

Running. They were *running*, while the people here were dying because of *him*.

Something small and tenuous inside Orpheus twisted. "I'm sorry," he repeated, "This is my fault. I closed the hole—the one Ohm came through. Lore's on the move because of me. She's done all this looking for me."

Red shrugged. "Not gonna let her get ya, Sparks."

THE CRACK AT THE HEART OF EVERYTHING

How could she think that way? How could she *care* like that? How could she not be doing everything in her power to turn him over to Lore, to keep her from destroying everything she'd devoted her life to building? Orpheus didn't understand it. Wondered what all needed to change inside himself so that he could. But the grace of time had passed him over, and now Orpheus wouldn't have the chance to find out.

He had to close the chasm. But what should have been a monumental turning point of his character had instead been reduced to, yet again, basic survival. Something about that hurt. It felt wrong. Like another opportunity stolen from him. One more choice made on his behalf.

But at least Fenrir might survive. Along with Red and Farris and everyone else on this hells-damned planet.

The weight inside his chest lightened when he turned to Red and said: "Listen, in a day—maybe two days' time, everything running off Netherflame is going to fail. Anything left in the Stacks still depending on the archanics I built or the spells I cast are going to come grinding to a halt so you need to prepare. I don't know who else out there—"

"—North," Red said, "there's the settlements north, who haven't been hooked into the grid yet."

"Warn them, if you can," Orpheus breathed. "I'm sorry this is so last minute."

Red barked out a laugh, clapping him on the shoulder. "Sparks, if you'd been here for some of the last minute drama I've lived through you'd know this is nothing. I'll get word up north and make sure everything critical here is hooked up to the grid. Simple as a morning shit, we'll get it done."

"Thank you," he breathed, and then, "also, I may have caused the crater to collapse."

Red actually raised her eyebrows at that, a long whistle singing through her teeth. "Well, that is impressive." Then she let out a long peal of laughter, the sound rising to the roof, echoing through the rafters. Orpheus found himself smiling despite himself.

"Alright, we should be good!" Fenrir announced as he emerged from under the tarp. Orpheus didn't have a chance to ask what he meant before Fenrir grabbed the worn plastic and hauled it off in one mighty flourish.

From his memory the pamphlet emerged, the silly little safety demonstration suddenly no longer silly now that Orpheus was staring up at what was, very clearly, an airplane.

Beside him, Farris whimpered, a sad lonesome whine. "Y'all aren't taking her east, are ya?"

Beside Orpheus, Red groaned. "Worse things than ghosts out east, Farris."

"And unless that skeleton can sprout fucking wings this should get us where we're going faster than Lore can follow." Fenrir actually had the audacity to grin. It only faltered when he looked at Farris. Something like commiseration crossed Fenrir's face.

"That isn't—can you even—I'm not—" *flying in that thing,* Orpheus' mind finished because his voice failed. He glanced at Farris, somewhat validated at the shared expression of panic reflected back at him.

"Already fueled it up and ran through the pre-flight checks. Everything's—" Fenrir cut off and shrugged, close enough that Orpheus could see the laugh lines around his eyes. "I was going to say fine, but figured I should warn you. I've flown twice before and crashed both planes, though, not to the point of—" Fenrir broke off again, made an explosive gesture with his fingers. "—low altitude stuff, ya know. Landing is hard."

Orpheus thought he might actually be sick.

"Does it have to be old Bowie, Sir?" Farris finally cried, voice high and thin. "Last time you promised to bring Bessie back safe and she—" he choked off, an actual tear rolling down his cheek.

"It's true, I was there. He definitely should be a skid mark," Red unhelpfully added.

Orpheus closed his eyes, sank into the wall. Well, at least dying in a plane crash was bound to be infinitely more merciful than whatever Lore and Ohm had planned for him.

"Here, take this."

Red leapt up into the cabin and grabbed something from above, tossing it at Orpheus. It hit his chest with a thunk—a sack with enough straps to put that transport they'd ridden in to shame.

"What is it?" he asked, arms full.

"A parachute," Red said, over the sound of Farris' quiet sobbing. "Just in case."

A sound like a deflating balloon came out of Orpheus.

Inside, the plane was all weld lines and aluminum panels, mesh netting, and a web of interlocking straps. Orpheus identified what looked to be more parachutes stashed in one of the nets above, along with something Orpheus immediately recognized as a gun.

He'd seen plenty of guns before. He'd watched them be fired, there at the range in the barracks courtyard. Long, slender, strangely angular yet equally graceful things that looked harmless at first glance. This one was nothing like those guns. This one was also ten times the size of those guns.

"We call it *The Papa*," Fenrir said from where he was closing the door to the compartment overhead. "Because it makes this pop-pop-pop-pop-pop sound."

"Very clever," came out of him like a scratch as Red cackled. Fenrir grinned as he put a hand on his shoulder and directed him to a cracked leather seat.

"We found this and the others about six years back." Fenrir's breath touched his ear, hand heavy on Orpheus' shoulder. The leather cushion creaked when he sank down. "Some old airfield up north near the labs. Place was untouched but I think this thing was old even before the Incident." Fenrir's hands moved over Orpheus, taking his time to buckle him into the safety harness.

It helped, a little—the calm voice, the steady hands—the tightness of the straps where they cinched across his chest.

"We were pretty amazed we got the engine to turn over let alone put it back in the air." Then, quieter, possibly so Farris couldn't overhear, "It's Farris' baby, so help me get it back safe. From the ghosts, you know."

Fenrir winked and Orpheus laughed, a strange, strangled sound he couldn't stop when Fenrir cupped his cheek and leaned in, forehead to forehead. Time stretched, a moment of gentle connection that Orpheus clung to because it could very likely be their last.

His eyes met Fenrir's, recognized a mirrored sentiment, and ignored the way his chest ached.

"I'll leave y'all to it, then," Red announced in a low drawl. "Don't worry 'bout us, just stay safe and out of trouble."

"Always do, Red," Fenrir agreed, dropping into the seat next to Orpheus and beginning to strap himself in.

"And take this walkie, just in case. Range isn't great but I'll see what I can do about putting together a team to tail y'all. Not much for reinforcements left but may be able to help in a pinch."

Red passed Fenrir the same kind of device he'd seen in the transport, the antennae on this one longer and thicker than the other's had been.

"Thanks Red, for everything," Fenrir said, voice low, steady. Serious.

"Always, my friend." It wasn't an endearment Orpheus had heard her use before, and the gravity of the sentiment was not lost on him. Orpheus watched Red swoop in for a hug that Fenrir eagerly returned.

Then she waved them off, swinging out of the plane and closing the door and sealing them in with a metallic whine, Fenrir flipping a sequence of switches that caused the lighted panel to sing and the garage to fill with a flood of light. A roar descended from the retreating darkness, the building clatter of two massive prop engines coming to life.

Outside the window, Farris and Red were at the bay door, hauling it wide open so night spilled thick and frothy into the garage.

"Here we go!" Fenrir shouted over the noise, hand pulling back on a lever, the plane creeping forward.

The smoky smog of the burning fires rolled into the garage, sucked in by the prop engines so the working lights of the plane cast strange shapes amongst the shifting shadows. Red waved at them, an urging gesture, plane creeping forward through the smoke, the expansive wasteland emerging from the darkness, the brilliant glow of the collapsed crater bleeding across the horizon.

Fenrir whistled, "Damn, you really did crack that thing wide open."

"You told me to cause a distraction."

"Bet it'll look pretty wild from up in the air," was all the warning Orpheus got before Fenrir pushed forward on the lever and the plane kicked into gear. The whining roar of the engine filled the cockpit, the plane picking up speed, neon lights streaking across the cracked windshield.

Leather bit into his palms as Orpheus clutched the armrests, the open gash of cushion under his butt digging in painfully with every uneven jolt of broken pavement. In far less distance than the plane had any right to claim, the nose began to lift, the whole world tipping as the wings caught air and the windshield tinted white, icy fingers crawling up the glass as a klaxon howled louder than their engines. Orpheus grimaced, resisting the urge to cover his ears.

"Hold on!" Fenrir shouted, pulling back on what almost looked like a steering wheel, the plane gaining more of an angle while shaking like the whole thing was going to come apart.

The sound of screaming metal rippled through the cockpit, a shockwave that pulsed cold air into the compartment. When Orpheus twisted round, he understood why.

An enormous sword speared through the side of the plane, two feet away from the fuselage, instantly recognizable as Ohm's.

"It's fine, he missed! Boney bastard's always had shit aim," Fenrir laughed, whooping out a string of expletives Orpheus wasn't entirely sure he'd heard before. "Eat my jet fuel, you fleshless prick!"

And then the rattling stopped. All that awful shaking gave way to a buttery ascent as the plane left the ground behind and soared into the sky. Maybe it was gravity or maybe it was Orpheus' shock, but he sank back into his seat and fought to control his breath, watching the clouds and smoke and smog roll across the windshield for the longest thirty-six seconds of his life before suddenly, the plane leveled out and all he could see was clear sky.

Space unfolded before him, a velvety swath of inky black and glimmering stars. Light smeared between each pinprick, the arc of the Milky Way cutting a speckled furrow through the vast of night. Orpheus' breath caught and released in a quiet whimper, harness protesting when he leaned forward to take it all in.

Beside him, Fenrir laughed, and it sounded how his smile must look—small and gentle and impossibly enamored—special, meant only for him. Orpheus tipped his head and looked over his shoulder, found Fenrir watching him.

"Pretty impressive, huh?" Fenrir said.

Orpheus held his eyes. "I would say beautiful."

Fenrir actually blushed.

A quiet moment passed between them while the adrenaline of the last hour bled away. In its wake existed a familiar reminder: the reason he was here wasn't because Orpheus was running from Lore or off to save the world, but for Fenrir. Because if he approached what happened next under the scope of what really mattered, the conclusion Orpheus came to was the same as it had been when he'd realized his curse had only existed in his head. There was so much more than death that he could offer the world.

Fenrir had said that. Fenrir had *shown* him that. And however terrified Orpheus was of the approaching unknown, Fenrir had proved that that too could be something worthwhile.

"Look, down there."

Orpheus followed the line of Fenrir's gaze towards a scar of blazing red amongst a web of violet.

The crater, and his spell—another crack in the earth he had made.

Another crack he needed to fix.

"We need to head east," he said, breath casting fog across the icy cold glass, "we need to fix this."

And as the plane tilted and the Earth bled red, Orpheus knew he was making the right choice.

INTERLUDE

HOMEBOUND

The day Lore returns feels like a page pulled from a story that isn't his.

Orpheus watches with wide eyes as person after person limps in through the palace gates.

Blood blackens a path of churned-up mud, the hundreds of bleeding people—fighters—warriors?—dragging themselves into the courtyard. A beast is led inside, what Orpheus recognizes as a horse, knobby legs and barrel of a body far stranger in person, uncanny when all he's ever seen are pictures in his books.

Still, the people don't stop coming. He eyes the gates suspiciously, wondering if he should climb the ramparts and scope out how many more are left, because the courtyard has become crowded, and Lore still isn't anywhere to be seen.

These have to be her people. They have to be here because of her.

"Where's the well?" a person snaps at him like he's in charge, and Orpheus reels as he tries to find his voice and fails. It's been two years since Lore left, and the only person Orpheus has spoken to since is himself.

"Water, man. We need water, food, and whatever we can use for bandages and—" the person pauses, looking at Orpheus through narrowed eyes. "—Wait. You're the mage, aren't you?"

Is he? Orpheus resists the urge to look over his shoulder and see if there is someone else this person could possibly be speaking to. But he knows better—knows the truth. It isn't a word he's used for himself but, to be fair, he hasn't used many words at all over the last two years.

"I am," rushes out like a scratch. Orpheus clears his throat and tries again. "Yes, I am a mage."

Something like relief pours over their face. "Great, fuck the bandages then, healing magic, am I right?"

Orpheus' head swims as the person—warrior—*soldier*—leads him up the steps into the main hall like it's *their* home and not Orpheus'.

"Got the worst of them here, for morale. Don't need the others—" they gesture behind Orpheus to where the sun bleeds through the open front doors, hundreds of voices drifting in from the courtyard. "Don't need them seeing, you know. How bad it can get."

"It?" Orpheus repeats, keeping his eyes off the bleeding bodies. Most of them are moaning, a handful are not. He ignores how pale and empty those bodies look.

"War," the person says, meeting his eyes.

War, Orpheus repeats in his head. Lore has started a war. He knows it has to be the truth. Gets confirmation when Lore herself appears in the open doorway.

"Mage," Lore snaps, and Orpheus nearly falls to his knees when their eyes meet.

"My Lady," he breathes like it's a long-learned reflex. It isn't. He's never said these words in his life, let alone to Lore. But if she's calling him *mage* it only feels fair.

Fair. Like leaving him here alone for *two years* was fair. Like not even sending so much as a messenger when Lore's collected hundreds of men and women to wage a war on her behalf is *fair.*

But she has returned, as she promised. And Orpheus realizes that fairness has nothing to do with what's happening here. Like the mission Lore gave him before she left, Lore's had her own—and she's back, seeking his help again.

Of course he'll help.

"I may be able to heal them," he says, somehow keeping the shake out of his voice. Behind them, the bodies have begun moaning. Quiet cries for help now that Orpheus had said the cursed word out loud.

Lore nods her head once, then waits, expectantly.

The person closest is a woman. She's lost an arm and probably needs to lose a leg too. Blood is pooling around her despite the tourniquets someone has tied above her wounds, and Orpheus thumbs through the triage texts that live inside his head. He hadn't studied the medical books deeply—there hadn't been many to begin with—but a first aid kit he'd discovered years ago had given some basic guidelines, and the tourniquets were a good first step.

But Lore didn't bring these people here for first aid. She brought them here because of him—her mage—because the tourniquet wasn't going to save this woman's life. Magic was.

"Could someone hold her?" he says, voice stronger than it's been yet, not a command but close.

Two soldiers respond, moving into place, one at her shoulders and a second at her legs.

Orpheus kneels down and considers. He's played around with alchemical sigils that turn things like air to water and iron to steel. Human flesh shouldn't be all that different. Oxygen, carbon, and hydrogen are the building blocks of every living creature. And while he doesn't think he can regrow limbs, he figures patching up an open wound shouldn't be impossible.

He takes a moment to construct the sigil in his mind, the weaving tangle of lines and arcs and loops. But he needs his Netherflame first, and as his fingers come together in a snap, a gasp runs through the people directly near him—everyone but Lore, silent at his back.

Orpheus opens his eyes, ignores the traded whispers, and looks to the woman on the ground. Her eyes are wide, mouth a little open, staring at the unworked flame in his palm like it's the gates of heaven itself. He doesn't stop her when she reaches up with her single remaining hand to touch it.

Her scream is like nails hammering into his ears.

"What is—what's happening—" The soldier holding her shoulders chokes off, the smell of decaying flesh hitting them all with the force of a punch.

Orpheus snatches his hand away, eyes widening when the woman's fingers begin to turn gray, and then flake, flesh turning to dust and then to liquid, infection swelling the palm of her hand, her arm, the whole limb, a momentary bloat that collapses in on itself, gasses releasing, decay spreading, crawling up her shoulder and then her neck and then finally her face—no, her *brain*—and as her scream cuts off into a lung-rattling exhalation, the whole room breaks into a panic.

"He's a monster!"

"Like one of those beasts!"

"Cursed, he's cursed!"

"Silence!" Lore roars.

Orpheus doesn't hear what happens next. The ringing in his head is too loud to allow anything else through. He thinks Lore must say something to defend him because the next time he looks up the room has gone quiet. Eyes avoid his while he kneels there in a pile of flesh and viscera. The injured woman is gone, a puddle in her place.

A shadow falls over him, less dark than the ones closing in on his mind.

"Orpheus," Lore says, and it seems like she's restraining herself from something. "Get up."

He follows her to a familiar set of doors. Shadows condense, dark and foreboding—the dungeons.

Orpheus doesn't look at Lore when he hesitates on the top step.

Doesn't need to hear the *"stay down there"* she leaves unspoken.

Over the next few weeks, he throws himself into his work, giving Lore and her people a wide berth while he loses himself in a new project. It'll do no good for him to dwell on the woman he killed so he focuses on what he can do well instead: mechanics, engines, power and light. He uses the horse as inspiration, improving upon nature's design to create something he calls an archanic.

Two months after Lore walked back into his life she is leaving again, and he presents it to her as another gift. A war steed, he calls it, powered by his Netherflame engine.

"The engine can power almost anything that a combustion fuel engine would have," he explains as Lore circles the mechanical creature, eyes half-mast. "I have schematics for vehicles, but not enough materials. This exhausted most of what was in storage. If you find—"

"I'll send it here," Lore says, and it's good enough. Orpheus has a use again. A purpose. Lore still needs him, and that is all that matters to him.

Lore leaves within the hour, riding out atop his archanic with her army at her back. Orpheus watches from the ramparts where he won't be in the way. By the time the last soldier has disappeared around the bend in the mountain path, the sun is low, the last two months a strange, blistering dream.

Orpheus wanders the halls feeling something close to relief. Those people are gone, and the palace is empty, and while the loneliness hurts, he can't help but think things are better this way—for him—for those people—for the world at large. Because there's a stain on the floor where that woman had died, and whatever Orpheus is, it is dangerous, and at least in the solitude of this fortress, he and the world remain safe.

CHAPTER XXVIII

EAST

Under the bright light of day, the chasm glowed brightest.

Darkness blanketed the horizon, a limitless nothing descending from the heavens, so black as to swallow the sun. And there in the far distance, visible by the vantage afforded by their incredible height, Netherflame burned. An unnatural bubble of smoky night limned strangely with each arc of violet: the crack, and the hellscape that had birthed from it, a dimensional rift that should not exist. Not here. Not like this. Not in such flagrant violation of physics, because like the Netherflame running through his veins, this crack was artificial. The result, Orpheus now knew, of some vile experimentation. The same kind that had put that damned dark flame inside him.

"Not too late to turn around," Fenrir said from the seat beside him. His voice came out rough, sleep-edged despite their inability to rest.

"And I would still choose *that* over Ohm," Orpheus said without much conviction. At least these hell beasts weren't trying to kill him—not yet.

He could see them. The hell beasts. Not well and certainly not to the point of being able to identify any, but even from here the movement below was obvious. A churning mass of creatures teaming at the edges of the darkness, black specs flying through the sky, others swarming the brightest parts of the crack. Orpheus didn't need to get closer to recognize what they were. Only hell beasts could exist that close to the scar—hell beasts, and him.

"Can you put us down there?" Orpheus pointed at a place in the near distance where daylight bled clear, a relatively flat expanse of land that Orpheus suspected must have, once upon a time, been what his books called a parking lot.

"Sure," Fenrir said, squinting his eyes, "Probably. When you say put us down, that really means don't turn me into a skid mark, right?"

Orpheus let out a long, slow breath, checked the straps of his parachute and decided this was still his best bet.

"I *mean*, don't make me throw myself from this plane and leave you to become a skid mark by yourself, Rawkner."

"Noted, I'll do my best!"

For the half minute it took Fenrir to adjust the plane, the crack disappeared, the pale gray wasteland of the Rim filling the windshield as the plane began its descent towards the ground. Orpheus spent the time working his jaw and swallowing saliva he didn't have. He was tired, thirsty, hungry and cold, and as the plane descended and the pressure in his head built, he used it all to distract himself from what was going to happen next.

This was it. This was the end. It had arrived in a fury and without a care for the life it was about to take. In all the books Orpheus had read, this moment had felt a lifetime in the making. In reality, it had come too soon. He wondered what had happened to the dramatic buildup, the weeks of plotting, the mountains of complications that should have gotten in his way? All he had gotten was a week of badly thought-out hope and a mad dash over a literal wasteland, running from a reanimated skeleton and his former best friend. There hadn't even been a fight—not a real one—just some stakes raised by a chase scene before the hero got away scot-free.

Hero. Orpheus nearly laughed at the idea he was this story's *hero.*

Heroes don't die, his brain reminded him, and it was enough for his thoughts to quiet again.

Fenrir landed the plane—mostly. The landing gear, in its heroic yet failed effort to remain attached to the plane, had, in fact, left a skid mark, but at least it wasn't either of theirs. It should have been a point of celebration, and for the brief few minutes between coming to a stop and stepping onto solid ground it was. But then the gravity of where they were outweighed the mirth of the moment, and like the gray that swallowed the landscape whole, Orpheus' mood turned bleak.

Now, Orpheus stood at the crest of a small ridge, looking out over the Rim towards what little he could see beyond.

Violet embers rose from the fractured chasms, tiny stars that speckled the gray expanse. There was a strange kind of beauty to the Rim Orpheus hadn't expected. A calm to the emptiness that made the distant darkness seem inconsequential.

Or maybe, that was the poison in his veins talking.

"Came this far east, once," Fenrir offered up from behind. Orpheus turned his head and met Fenrir's eyes. "About as close as this. Didn't want to become one of Farris' ghosts, you know?"

Orpheus forced a laugh; Farris didn't seem so crazy, not anymore.

They returned to the plane together, sorting through the packs of supplies Red had apparently kept ready for them—in case of an emergency—as if she'd known the moment Lore came down her mountain they would already be out of time. Fenrir held the walkie like he would have called her if they were within range. Orpheus understood a little more, then, of how close they really were.

Something like this would bring two people together. Shared trauma, he'd read once, was a forge for strong bonds.

"You came here with Red?" Orpheus asked, keeping his words soft. He couldn't completely hide the shake in his voice, but if he didn't say much it wouldn't be as obvious.

"Yeah. A few years ago, before we first marched south. Lore wanted to scout out how far the Rim went. Map the edge of the world, you know? We all knew it was out here—three-hundred years of history isn't wiped out from the collective consciousness that quickly— but we didn't expect this. All the gray. The dust. The emptiness. The death. Three hundred years is a long time, something should have grown in the Rim. But it hadn't. It'd kept expanding, eating up more and more land. And I think once I saw the magnitude for myself, that's when I began to really think about what I was doing. Who I was helping. Why Lore was the way that she was."

Fenrir picked at the zipper of the backpack he held, thumb smoothing over a flaw in the teeth the head couldn't get past. Orpheus resisted the urge to go to him, tell him everything was okay—that he'd done his best, even if his best had been killing the very people he now wanted to help.

"You said, once, that empires aren't built without bloodshed, and you weren't wrong. But the people I was fighting, the groups that had amassed against Lore and her self-inflicted prison, they were trying to escape this. They didn't want our land or our food or our grid, they were running for their lives, and if we hadn't been so scared of protecting what we had, we might have seen that. It's something I've thought about every day since."

It's why you're the hero, Orpheus thought to himself, *and not me.*

Because a part of him still insisted he turn back and run, hold onto this new life and future with Fenrir however long he could. But Lore was coming, and if Orpheus didn't strip the world of Hell and its power, it wouldn't be generations of strangers or the planet that would suffer. Fenrir would die, too. Because while Lore may fall to a sword or a gun, neither of them were naive enough to believe they could win a fight against Ohm.

"I think," Orpheus began when it became clear Fenrir needed him to say something, anything, "that what matters more than the perspectives we held, is what we do when they change. You didn't run from what you did, Fenrir, you worked towards fixing the damage you helped create. That's what matters, in the end."

It has to be, or why else was Orpheus here and not far away, somewhere safe, chasing a future with Fenrir?

Bitter resentment was an old friend, the only one Orpheus had left. When he looked into Fenrir's eyes, however, he knew he'd said the right thing.

"Thanks, Fifi," hung in the quiet.

They made a fire out of the dead wood they collected, multitudes of Incendiary Beetles skittering across the dusty gray landscape with each nest they disturbed.

Out here, so close to the site of the Incident, Orpheus was nothing to the hell beasts. Barely a blip on their Netherflame radar and he was grateful for the unlikely respite. Even knowing that the curse wasn't real, he was wary of the creatures. He'd spent so long fearing them and even longer isolated from them that to see them here, going about their business as if he didn't even matter, felt stranger and more uncanny than anything yet.

"Want me to crush them? Turn them into ash?" rumbled into his ear; Orpheus nearly jumped out of his skin. "For old time's sake, you know."

"With our luck, we'll piss one off and it will mobilize every hell beast in a hundred-mile radius against us," Orpheus muttered, grappling with the armful of firewood he'd nearly dropped.

"I could take 'em," Fenrir preened, following Orpheus back to the plane and the pile of wood they'd collected. "Wanna take a second shot at a dragon before you seal them all away for good. Life's gonna get real boring without any monsters to fight."

"As if you won't have enough to distract you. If you think Red is going to let you off the hook for us destroying her fancy new hotel, you're sorely mistaken."

"I do love some good hard manual labor," Fenrir agreed as he knelt beside Orpheus and began sorting out the kindling from their wood pile. "But I'm more terrified of what cockamamie idea she'll rope you into. Red is a genius, but you have that whole mad scientist vibe going on and I know how those kinds of stories play out."

Orpheus flinched. He couldn't help it. Beside him, Fenrir noticed.

"I didn't mean it, Fifi, it was a bad joke."

Orpheus glanced up, tried to smile. "It's quite alright." Even though it wasn't—though not for the reason Fenrir suspected.

I should tell him, except he absolutely couldn't.

Not unless he wanted to live to see the next day.

THE CRACK AT THE HEART OF EVERYTHING

Fenrir struggled to get the fire going, the little assembly of sticks he kept lighting sputtering out before the flames could take hold, and Orpheus couldn't help but think it was because Fenrir was distracted. Orpheus could feel his eyes on him, their wandering path pulling on him with all the unspoken questions they hadn't had the time to ask one another. They were supposed to have days in the Stacks, not less than an hour. They were supposed to have more time, not have already run out of it.

The fire crackled, smoke thin and white, burning through the desiccated bones of the wasteland with little resistance. Orpheus hoped that when his time came, he too would not suffer.

"I know, Fifi, what's going to happen, and it's okay."

Unlike the crossbow bolt that had missed him, this blow pierced straight through his heart. For the first time in over a week his wrist ached, and he stuffed his hands in his sleeves and dug his fingernails in.

"But losing your magic isn't the end of the world," Fenrir continued, and Orpheus' stomach churned as he realized what Fenrir really meant. "You're a genius, and I mean that. There's a whole world of lost tech out there that you can help us rediscover, and I think that's—"

"—I'm going to die," Orpheus breathed, voice shaking, heart breaking.

Neither of them said anything while a tremor rumbled underground. Before him, Fenrir had gone still—white—like a ghost. "You feel like it will kill you. Because you won't have your magic." His face was blank, his eyes empty, like he already knew the truth.

"Fenrir. When I close that crack, I'll have to close the one inside myself too."

Fenrir visibly swallowed, throat working a second before he spoke.

"Like I said, you'll lose your magic," he said, slowly, carefully, like Orpheus wasn't making sense. "That doesn't mean you'll die."

"It's a part of me. A fundamental part of who I am," Orpheus said, voice growing stronger, like all that was left to sustain him was this fight. "The scientists made sure of that. And that's why this will work—why only I can do it and some other half-baked wizard with a decent resistance to Netherflame can't."

"Then you're not doing it. We'll find another way. Period."

"I don't have a choice!"

Fenrir shook his head, eyes wide enough Orpheus could see the white that ringed them. "Of course you do!"

He wanted to laugh, he wanted to cry—he wanted to climb into that damned plane and fly it through time right back to Lore's mountain and crash it into that fucking bunker she'd locked him away in, where he was safe, hidden away, not living so much as existing, but at least without all this *pain.*

Instead, he had to *die.*

"What is our alternative? And don't forget Lore and Ohm are coming for me as we speak!" Orpheus's voice cracked as he gestured at the gray wasteland they were stranded in, the rising dawn of darkness that hovered like an approaching storm—the literal *world* being eaten away by the rift their ancestors had created straight into fucking *Hell.* "If we somehow manage to defeat them, there is still this—there will always be this! Maybe we'll live the rest of our lives without witnessing the world's end, but what of everyone else? You want to be a hero, Fenrir? Then this is it!"

Fenrir didn't say anything. Why wasn't Fenrir *saying* anything?

How could Fenrir sit there silent when this pain, this torment, was *all his fault?*

"You had to go and show me a world worth living for," Orpheus hissed, tears choking his throat—pain strangling his heart, "and then make it impossible for me to give up."

"Fifi," Fenrir was barely able to get out, "this isn't what I wanted."

Orpheus laughed, honest and brutal. "Well, I don't want to die, yet here we are."

If there was anything left to say, neither of them knew what. But maybe being stranded at the end of the world did that to a person—made the hard truths all the more accessible because out here, there wasn't any room for comfort, for softness. Maybe that was why

Orpheus was relieved to see tears on Fenrir's face, grateful either of them could feel anything at all when the core of him was so broken. Grief wasn't his ideal emotional state, but he'd take it over the numbness he'd been escaping into these past few days. At least the guilt was gone, even if...

I haven't told him I love him; and he knew to say so now would only make things worse.

Instead, he rose from his seat and closed the distance, the space between him and Fenrir so much bleaker than any wasteland they'd crossed.

Hands dragged him down before he had a chance to touch Fenrir. And while Orpheus had meant to be the strong one, he crumbled into Fenrir's lap, clinging to him as Fenrir clutched him back, a drowned embrace that felt too much like falling—like this was the closest they'd get to saying goodbye.

But when Fenrir kissed him, it was like they still had all the time in the world.

Warmth built slowly, the slide of Fenrir's tongue undemanding, like by dragging this kiss out he could put off the inevitable. But it didn't last. Orpheus wasn't sure who broke down first, the kiss dissolving into softly whispered words and grasping hands, false promises made under the pretense of a hope neither of them still held yet clung to anyway. Silent tears wet his face and Orpheus gave up trying to fight them, crying softly into Fenrir's shoulder, his hand a welcome weight on the back of his neck—heavy, possessive, protective.

Time passed in fragmented pieces, the one constant the sensation of hands on his skin and breath in his hair. Of a fire, warm on his back, anathema to the ice in his veins.

"I'm going with you," Fenrir said once the sun had set and their fire had turned to coals. "I know you don't want me to, that it'll be dangerous and probably kill me too, but I'm going. I won't let you leave me behind, Fifi, not again."

A better person would have told Fenrir no. Would have carved a stasis sigil into Fenrir's armor right then while he was distracted and left him for Red to find days from now after everything was over. But

Orpheus wasn't a better person—he wasn't even a good person—and if Fenrir wanted to follow him into Hell who the fuck was he to stop him? It wasn't how the story was supposed to go, but Orpheus knew enough to acknowledge they'd already lost the thread years ago when they'd both followed a madwoman into war.

"It's Orpheus who chases Eurydice into hell," was all he offered in protest.

"Well," Fenrir said into Orpheus' hair, arms strong around his shoulders, heart pounding against his chest, "good thing I'm not Eurydice."

CHAPTER XXIX

HELL

They didn't wait for dawn to rise. Under the cover of night, they packed their bags and set off, the fire's smoldering embers and the stranded airplane the final marks either would make on the world at large.

Orpheus took point while Fenrir brought up the rear. The drag of that massive gun Fenrir had ripped from the plane carved sound out of a dense silence, neither of them knowing what to say—as if words even mattered anymore.

Now, it was the weapons they carried: Fenrir's sword, the plane's massive gun, and Orpheus' magic. Against his hip his satchel bounced, the bundle of tools and bowl of silver heavier than he remembered, the sigils in his head small and pathetic compared to the sheer *power* of what he faced. None of it seemed like enough, but Orpheus knew it would have to be, because as they crested the top of the ridge, he saw exactly what they were up against—what the planet had been fighting off for over three-hundred hells-damned years.

"Fuck," Fenrir said; Orpheus could not disagree.

This far east, the world wept.

A crevice of rot so massive that it made the crater outside the Stacks look like a scrape glowed in the not-distance, enormous enough Orpheus couldn't even say how many miles out the light stretched. Left unchecked to fester, violet oozed sluggishly where the blackened ground came apart, the dilapidated structures still standing in the near distance proof that, once, this land hadn't been completely poisoned.

The infection was spreading.

The structures were familiar. Like those he'd seen days ago, when passing through the empty settlements on their way back to the Stacks. This place had been recently abandoned, and as the ground rumbled again beneath his feet, Orpheus watched in real time as a fissure fractured wider and swallowed one of the buildings whole.

"It's growing," Fenrir said as a pack of Jackdogs cackled in the distance. "I remember this town. Last time I was here, people lived there."

Orpheus couldn't say anything. He was afraid that if he opened his mouth he might start screaming. Here, where the Incident's crack was so close, he could barely smother his sense of it. The ties he'd made into the network of Netherflame were a body of nerves on fire. Fever prickled under his skin, and he hadn't even cast his spell yet. But then he recalled the sigils he had placed on Fenrir, and he realized exactly what was happening.

It was too fast—coming on too soon.

"Tell me if you start feeling sick," Orpheus managed, risking a glance at Fenrir, relief nearly overwhelming him.

Like the sun rising after a long winter's night, Fenrir stood out from the gloom. Healthy, strong, bold.

Alive.

His spell was working. For now, Fenrir was okay.

A beat of silence passed as their eyes met and held. Then, "How close do we need to get?"

"Right down there will be fine," Orpheus said as he turned in the general direction of the ruins. They needed to be close to the crack but not so close his sigils could crumble away with one of the tremors. The flat shale near the edge would do, but as Orpheus looked more closely, he saw something familiar enough to nearly turn him back around.

Scratches, dust swept out in a half-moon circle, and the icky track of old blood.

THE CRACK AT THE HEART OF EVERYTHING

"Is that from a dragon?" Fenrir asked, voice hedging rough. "Fuck, is that from *our* dragon?"

"Dragons are the least of our worries." Orpheus didn't bother pointing out who was the worst.

"I don't like this, Fifi," Fenrir said even though they both knew there was no turning back, not anymore.

"Well good thing you have that enormous gun to protect us," Orpheus said instead of something actually comforting like: *we'll be dead soon, won't that be nice?*

"Yeah." Fenrir didn't sound convinced. "I'll set up here, I guess."

Fenrir grunted as he put the gun down at the crest of the ridge. The sound of metal clattering atop solid ground was strangely muted, like the air out here possessed an unnatural density—perhaps not an entirely unimaginable consequence of having your planet split open into Hell. Orpheus didn't know enough to say for sure. He hardly knew enough to be sure, anymore, if this ridiculous plan would work.

Maybe the scientists would have known. Maybe he could have asked them, if he hadn't slaughtered every last one so many years ago.

Out in the snow-covered pine woods he'd been at an advantage, the world mostly whole and hale despite the damage the cracks had caused. Here, he had no such luck. With the massive wound in the distance and the poisonous rot at his back, Orpheus was surrounded by devastation, and if he had nearly snuffed himself out closing a fraction of this network before... he wasn't sure how he'd manage the undertaking that was to come.

No. He couldn't think like that. If he did, he might as well turn around, stomp right back over that ridge to the stranded airplane and wait for Lore to come find him.

As bad as this looked—going back to Lore would be worse.

All hells, it looked *bad*.

Orpheus swallowed a mouthful of saliva and ignored the tingly feeling running down his spine. His hands shook when he stuffed them into his sleeves, his fingers too slippery with a cold sweat to get traction on his wrist.

"Orpheus—" cut through his spiraling thoughts, "—wait."

Hands touched his shoulders and turned him around. Orpheus met Fenrir's eyes for a brief second, fearful that any longer would send him running off back the way they'd come. There was a smudge of ashy dust smeared across Fenrir's nose and the desire to reach out and wipe it away struck painfully mundane—a simple familiarity he wouldn't have a chance to experience again. The realization would have brought Orpheus to tears if they had more time. It *hurt*. But somehow, he stood his ground as Fenrir's hands moved from his shoulders to cup his face.

Fenrir's hands were warm, steady, strong. Orpheus closed his eyes when his thumbs stroked over his cheeks, unresisting when Fenrir tipped his face up. The kiss was slower than the desperate ones they'd shared the night before, lingering, like they had all the time in the world left rather than a few hours at most. If Orpheus' heart hadn't already been shattered into a thousand pieces, this kiss would have done it. Perhaps that was why he was able to meet Fenrir halfway— why he didn't break down where he stood when the kiss deepened, then stalled. The two of them stood frozen together as if time itself ticked only for them, the future held at bay as long as they never moved on from this moment.

Then the ground rumbled beneath their feet, and Orpheus shivered, kiss breaking when he gulped in a quiet sob.

Fenrir didn't say anything. Forehead to forehead, palms cupping his face, Fenrir held Orpheus while he struggled not to cry. Steadfast at the edge both of them had been heading towards their entire lives. Strong until the very end, like the hero Fenrir was—or had, at least, always wanted to be.

If this was Fenrir's way of saying goodbye, Orpheus was glad for it; he didn't know what he'd do if Fenrir broke down too.

Orpheus pressed his fingers into his lips as he descended the gravelly incline, ignoring the sound of Fenrir loading his gun that followed him down the ridge. When a clutch of Incendiary Beetles began kindling under a chunk of rock in his path, he hardly gave them notice. Once upon a time, he would have been running back up the ridge towards Fenrir, the curse a constant in his head. Now, Orpheus didn't spare them a glance, understanding that whatever curiosity he presented paled in comparison to the devastation fracturing the world's horizon:

Rippling violet, curdling shadows, the world black and inky in the places Netherflame didn't bleed. Violent. Powerful. Raw. A sundering words couldn't do justice, but Orpheus was expected to fix.

He still wasn't sure what would happen when he began closing the crack. Would the hell beasts put two and two together and understand their way home was threatened? Would they panic and retreat back from whence they came? Hopefully they wouldn't investigate the strange little human with all that Netherflame in his veins. Because if they did...

Well, good thing Fenrir had brought that stupid gun.

He chose a flat stretch of ground some ten yards from the nearest fracture—close to the chasm, though not so close that the ground felt unstable. His knees protested when he sank to the shiny, obsidian-hammered earth, but he ignored the pain in favor of focusing on the fever in his blood. The confirmation that his spell was working was a comfort to Orpheus, and as he unrolled his tools and swept aside the dust, that was what he focused on instead of the skitter-scrape of the Incendiary Beetles scurrying past, or the distant chattering packs of Jackdogs, or the quiet, low whine of some unknown hell beast that bled out of the chasm before him. If he began focusing on any of that he'd be as good as dead before he got started. So, Orpheus did the only thing in life he'd ever been good at: he ignored the brutal reality of his circumstances and escaped into his head.

The spell came unbidden, exhaled before his tongue had a chance to taste the words. He funneled Netherflame through the delicate torch tip of his iron needle. The tool was a familiar friend, drawing on his power like a siphon, the whole needle glowing violet by the time Orpheus touched it to the blackened earth. The spell's words stuttered on his breath, tripped over his tongue, but it didn't matter. The spell had been cast, the summoned power forged into the sigils he carved, and as Orpheus drew each into the hammered shale of this petrified earth, his voice tapered off, the calm quiet of the surrounding hellscape strange in the face of what was about to happen.

No, what was *happening*. Because as the last of the sigils were completed and the tip of his iron needle lifted off the final sweeping line, the spell slammed into him, full force.

He collapsed forward, sucking in a sharp gasp. Gravel bit into his palms as he caught himself, the tremor of the earth shivering alongside the whole of his body. Fever flared in his veins at the precise moment Hell yawned awake before him, sharp-toothed and hungry to consume, consume, *consume*.

Orpheus' muscles seized and he jolted where he knelt, a nerve-snap reaction to the compulsive terror of falling into that starving abyss. But there was nothing to fear, not really. Solid ground held him despite the mirrored chasm cracking open his soul. This must have been what he'd sensed days ago when he'd trudged out into the snow and connected to that smaller vein. The dimensional rift where Hell rendered into earth was so much more acute now that he was physically on top of it. What had felt monumentally massive before now felt infinite, and as Orpheus tried to wrap his mind around where to start, the impossibility of what he faced threatened to undo him.

What the fuck had he been thinking? How was he supposed to heal *this*?

You need to run. Everyone needs to run. Head west, as far as the sea. Build bridges or ships or whatever it takes to get as far, far away as you possibly can. Because Hell isn't coming, it's already here, and maybe the best thing you can do is let everyone know because if you fail—when you fail—you're going to fail—

Stop spiraling, his mind whispered, voice the same but different, the words not his but Fenrir's.

Fenrir, who was up on the ridge on the lookout, ready for any threat that might try and stop him. Fenrir, who had fought his whole life in the hopes of something better, having seen firsthand what both this crack, and all humanity had wrought. Fenrir, who believed in him when no one else had, who hadn't left him for death, but had shown him how to live. Fenrir, who had followed him here, into not just Hell, but oblivion, so that Orpheus wouldn't be alone when it was time to face it, because he loved him. Fenrir *loved* him. And if anything made the world worth saving, it was that.

Orpheus closed his eyes and got to work.

Palms flat to the earth, he focused his attention on the vastness of the crack, let the thread of himself that tethered into the sigils extend—reach, reach, *reaching* until he found it, miles or dimensions away, the tremulous edge of the furthest fractures, feathered and frayed like a black hole at the center of the Earth itself. Then further, out across the span of thousands of empires, tiny fractures that were older than time that had existed so long that Orpheus wondered if this wasn't what Morgana and Merlin and Imma and all the others had drawn upon.

And he took each, and he drained them, and the world itself trembled as the crack at the heart of everything began to close.

It was then that—for lack of a better phrase—all Hell broke loose.

He wasn't wrong, was the first thing Orpheus thought when the *papapapapa* of Fenrir's gun cut through the tangle inside his head. Gravel kicked up and scratched his face, whatever Fenrir was shooting at close enough to be a threat. Orpheus forced himself to ignore it. Sank further into his spell, clinging to the connection, the vast distance between where he knelt and where the wound opened up taking all his attention to maintain.

Another spray of bullets traced an arc around him a second before the warm splatter of what he assumed was a hell beast's blood hit his face. Orpheus hunched over, head tipping towards the hard shale of earth where his sigils burned. He knew, because he could see them there, floating in his head like they'd been burned into the backs of his retinas, the fleshy pulse of fever heady enough now he supposed he could be hallucinating.

But that was good. That meant his spell was working. That meant, if all else, that Fenrir was still alive.

Another round of bullets, and another spray of blood, and then a murky silence enveloped him once more.

In the far, far distance, another portion of the crack closed— another fracture into Hell healed.

It's working, he thought when after minutes or an hour had passed the edges of the crack began to feather inward. *It's getting smaller*, he acknowledged when the next tremor that tore through the earth didn't have the world yawning open beneath him, but rather contracting inwards.

Orpheus resisted the smile pulling at his face, curled his fingers into the ground and lost himself to his magic for what would be the last time in his life.

Behind him, he heard the *papapapapa* of Fenrir's gun cut off, sensed the murky dimness of a passing shadow across his face. But the tether of his core was tied to the crack now, and all that mattered was the magic flowing through his veins, the raw power crackling under his fingertips.

The ear-splitting scream of metal against a shield spell he didn't remember casting forced his eyes open, the shimmery violet shell held in place by sheer force of will rather than any sigil. It was an impossible feat, or so he'd always thought, except Orpheus had been wrong about a lot lately.

He might have laughed at the absurdity of going all his life without realizing this font of potential if not for the hulking hell beast looming over him.

Orpheus clawed through the sticky miasma of his spellcasting, meeting the open eye-sockets of Ohm's flame-filled skull, and then the pitiless stare of the woman perched atop it.

It wasn't the world's hell beasts who had arrived to stop Orpheus.

It was Lore.

CHAPTER XXX

THE CRACK

Here, where Hell's darkness was greatest, the light of dawn didn't even try to make a dent.

Orpheus didn't blame it. He understood on some vital, visceral level the desire to turn a blind eye to the trauma the world had suffered here. Isn't that what everyone did? Ignore the pain and go on with your life, every day, over and over, until the darkness consumed everything because healing was impossible. How would it feel to simply dissolve into the Netherflame like the landscape before him? How bad could the slow slip through time into desolation really be? Certainly far kinder than the fate that had befallen humanity after the Incident. Dying could be peaceful. Undramatic.

Or, it could have been, if *Lore* hadn't come along to throw a fucking wrench into everything.

"What do you want?" Orpheus snapped where he knelt.

"What are *you* doing?" Lore snarled in reply from atop Ohm, sword descending again to slide off his shield in an awful, teeth-grinding squeal.

His concentration flagged, torn between maintaining the shield or the connection to the crack. The *papapapapapa* of Fenrir's gun echoed across the hardened shale landscape again, a little clearer, a little shorter, like reality was finally converging upon them both and Fenrir had realized his gun meant nothing to a creature like Ohm. A theory proved true when Ohm lifted his arm and knocked the bullets out of the air with an absent-minded flick of his hand.

"I asked you a question," Lore hissed, and Orpheus saw her now, clear despite the imposing darkness, Ohm's violet glow illuminating her in strange shapes. "Answer me, Orpheus."

Despite over a month apart, some sad fractured part of Orpheus still thrilled at hearing her command.

"I'm fixing things," he said. It took every ounce of willpower to resist the urge to explain more than that. Lore may have discarded him, but that apparently hadn't eliminated the compulsion inside him to serve her every whim. And as his shield flagged and his connection to Netherflame waned, he realized how dangerous that could be. He couldn't let Lore interfere. He couldn't allow her to manipulate him again, despite however desperately his heart remained entangled with hers.

"There's nothing to fix, Orpheus," Lore said a little more calmly. She must understand the effect she had on him—had to, after she'd spent their lives wielding it like a sledgehammer.

"There's more to fix now than there was before you started your damn war," tore out of him before he could stop it. Ohm's body hardly made a sound as he and Lore jolted backwards as if slapped, the rush of wind through armored bones giving a strange whistle as the crack before him flared.

So, his connection held, even without his continued concentration. That night at the river came back to Orpheus in a rush—the power he had harnessed with only that little vein of Netherflame flowing under his feet. What could he achieve out here, with all of Hell cracked open before him?

That's not why I'm here, he thought to himself as Lore began a slow circle, the tip of her sword dragging over his shield in a sharp, reedy grind.

Orpheus ignored her. He closed his eyes again and got back to work.

"You're closing it, aren't you?" Lore asked, voice warbling strangely as the feverish miasma pulled at his brain again. "You think you can close the hells-damned thing."

Of course I can, he kept to himself, chewing on his lip as another shudder tore through the ground beneath his knees. In the far, far, far distance another fracture stitched together, a soothing thread of calm replacing that fevered connection he had made.

"And what will happen then, Orpheus?" Lore continued, sword continuing its slow circumference around the shield, now level with his neck. "You seal off this place, and what will happen to all your precious magic?"

It doesn't matter, I'll be dead.

Orpheus continued working, fever swelling to nauseating heights, his head beginning to spin. But the fractures continued closing, even the most distant portions that were not directly connected to this massive gorge. Orpheus realized, with sudden clarity, that some of what he could feel was *leagues* away. Small but bright little chinks in the armor of the Earth that were old enough to have existed for millennium. And it was just as he'd suspected—as Lore had threatened—Orpheus wasn't healing this singular point of infection He was closing every last pathway to Hell that the Earth possessed. Magic would be snuffed out, and along with it a history of heroes and mages and magic and—truth be told—a whole hell of a lot of drama it always seemed to fucking inspire.

He would have laughed if he hadn't felt nauseous enough to vomit.

"Give it a rest, Lore." A familiar voice rumbled through the ringing filling Orpheus' head.

"Oh, it's *you*," Lore said with about half as much vitriol as she'd thrown at Orpheus. "I suppose you're here to play hero?"

Orpheus didn't open his eyes to look at Fenrir, but felt him there anyway, a few meters back, the sigils he'd cast on him before they'd left camp glowing in his mind's eye. Through their connection he knew Fenrir was okay, body resisting the decaying effects of the Netherflame thanks to Orpheus' magic, but now it was the shield spell welded into his cuirass Orpheus thought about; the sigils he'd placed on the soles of Fenrir's boots for speed; the call to strength he'd forged into the tang of his sword; the bullets he had multiplied even though he had no idea how many Fenrir would actually need. All of it was a guessing game based on factors he couldn't predict. A last stand, a final hope, a valiant effort to stave off anything that could put an early end to his and Fenrir's plans.

And here they were, twenty minutes in and facing down the only threat that really mattered—the only one that could possibly stop them—because as the distant fissures closed up and the hell beasts they fed scrabbled back into the holes they'd crawled out of, it was only Lore who stood between them and victory.

Bullets wouldn't take her down. Neither would a sword or a spell. Not even a conversation could dissuade Lore from her own personal end game. Orpheus knew, because he'd spent his entire life watching Lore reshape the world in her vision. If Orpheus was ever going to stand up to her, it should have been years ago. The truth was this fight had come too late. Orpheus suppressed the urge to look at Fenrir in a panic, kept his eyes closed and his concentration focused and pushed through the fever in his veins to close what he could, while he could, before everything crumbled apart in his fucking hands.

He absolutely couldn't think about Fenrir. Couldn't allow himself to think any further beyond closing the crack, because the moment this came to head—and it would, it was here—Fenrir would be dead. And despite them both walking into this aware of that fact, to be faced with it was another matter entirely.

"I won't let you stop us."

Orpheus had never heard that voice from Fenrir before, the even cadence, the buried threat. And if Orpheus wasn't fully aware of the kind of power Ohm was packing, he might have thought Fenrir stood a chance.

"It's not up to you," Lore breathed, dismounting Ohm in a slick slide, "it's up to him."

And then whatever game Lore had been playing came to an abrupt end.

THE CRACK AT THE HEART OF EVERYTHING

A hand reached through his shield, as if it were nothing—a knife through water as Lore's fingers closed over his throat. Around him, his spell shattered, the connection he'd made to the fractured earth snapping like a rubber band reaching its limits. A scream tore out of his throat as Lore bared down, fingers squeezing as she lifted him off the ground, holding Orpheus aloft as if he were nothing—had always been nothing—a pawn in her game that she had decided to actually throw away—an idea that became all too clear when she twisted around to dangle him over the precipice of that massive, pulsating crack.

"How—" he choked out, clawing at Lore's wrists despite the armored gauntlets protecting them. From behind, he heard Fenrir's shout turn into a grunt, his eyes snapping over Lore's shoulder to see Ohm had knocked Fenrir to his knees, one massive hand shoving his face into the hard shale.

"They may have put the flame in you," Lore hissed, dark eyes glimmering behind the black fall of her hair, "but they made sure I'd never get to so much as *touch* it."

"You're immune," he gasped, and how had he never known? How had he not figured that out? "Netherflame doesn't—"

It doesn't hurt her, Orpheus realized with sudden, horrifying clarity. A world consumed by Netherflame wouldn't even matter to her.

He choked again as Lore wrenched him higher, the glimmer in her eyes transforming into something else. Something wrong. Like an acid that would burn through everything it touched. Orpheus couldn't hold her gaze, the pain physical now, throbbing from his neck to his head and straight into his heart. For all the awful heat in Lore's eyes it was Orpheus who was crying, the last threads of his spell spiraling out of his reach, the crack below becoming nothing more than some wide-open maw ready to swallow him whole.

"I always knew what they wanted," Lore continued, teeth bared as she spoke, tiny little things that looked sharp in the distended shadows. "The solution they were trying to create. I was close but the flame wouldn't take. A failure. But you. They got it right with you. But the fool that you were, always lost in your stupid stories, too idealistic to realize what was happening, you had no clue. And once you killed them all I made sure you would never find out."

Lore's face had gone strange as she spoke, emotion traded for a distant kind of placidity, like the memories she was lost in were a comfort to her—a safe place she could go to hide. But inside Orpheus' head was a pit of terror, dark shadowy memories he'd gone out of his way to forget. Now they all came bubbling to the surface, like a hallway of doors opening on a life he had forgotten ever existed.

One memory stood out from the rest. A box of notes and textbooks stashed in the corner of Lore's room, appearing that night after he'd slain the scientists. The meticulously put together lab that he had destroyed, cleaned of every reminder that those scientists had ever been there at all—no notes, no books, no texts or computers or hard drives or anything—because Lore had destroyed all evidence of their work. Had hidden from him a truth she'd long harbored, that she'd then use against the rest of the world.

The world spun as Orpheus struggled to breathe—to accept—to face the woman who had, more than those hermit scientists ever had, destroyed his life.

"But a door that closes must also open," Lore continued, a smile quirking up the corner of her mouth. "And every time you used your magic, the world grew a little darker, the cracks—*this* crack—a little bigger. I watched it expand over the years, didn't put it all together until that dog brought me that spell and you tore open Hell just for me. What else could you achieve if I let you loose on the world? How close could you get me to Hell if forced to use your magic to defend yourself, rather than create those stupid, childish inventions?"

"You—" Orpheus choked off, the pieces in his head assembling. Lore hadn't kicked him out because of the curse, or because she was tired of him. She had kicked him out so he could herald literal Hell on Earth.

"You understand, now," Lore murmured, voice gone strangely soft, almost regretful. "I should have just killed you. Instead, I tried to let fate run its course. It's not a mercy I will offer anyone again."

THE CRACK AT THE HEART OF EVERYTHING

Orpheus looked for Fenrir as it happened, desperate to find him as the pin-prick of Lore's knife dipping between his ribs, the scrape of metal against bone as it angled up and slid in.

Where was Fenrir? Wait—where was *Ohm?*

Like a page from one of his beloved books, all hell broke loose.

"Fifi!" roared over the teeth-grinding clatter of metal crashing into metal, the swept-up dust of the wasteland stinging his eyes as Ohm—*Ohm*—slammed into Lore from the side.

Air flooded his lungs as Lore's grip suddenly went slack, and the sensation of free-fall would have been nauseating if Orpheus wasn't so overwhelmed by relief, because even though he couldn't see through the churned-up dust stinging his eyes, when a hand closed over his wrist, he knew it was Fenrir's.

A sweep of motion, a gentle tug, and then the world tipped sideways as Fenrir hauled him out of the chasm, over his shoulder, and leaped.

Wind pricked his skin as they sailed through the air, dust clearing the moment Orpheus's eyes snapped to Lore's as she and Ohm tumbled over the side of the crack. Netherflame engulfed them, but he knew enough now to understand this wasn't the end.

"She get you?" Fenrir gasped once they landed, the glowing violet light at his back highlighting him in an ethereal halo. Orpheus crumbled against him, fingers curling into his armor, clutching, like this would be his last chance.

"Fine," he rasped, ignoring the pang between his ribs where Lore's knife had slid in—the even larger one where his heart somehow still beat.

"Don't sound fine." Fenrir pet through his hair, a grounding tether, then said, "Take a breath, a big one, come on."

Orpheus swayed as Fenrir manhandled him around, lifting his arm over his shoulder as his palm swept down his side and pressed in. He felt a stickiness where Fenrir's palm pushed, gasping instinctively and flinching when the muscles twisted, but as air swelled his lungs he didn't see the panic he expected in Fenrir's eyes. He saw relief.

Fenrir looked on the brink of tears when he said, "Just a flesh wound, you'll be okay."

As if any of this was *okay*.

"Lore, she—" he struggled to speak, head swimming as everything happening caught up with him, "—she knew about me. About the crack, how I could close it. She's known this whole time—"

"Yeah," Fenrir murmured, voice hard. "I overheard."

"This is what she wanted," he continued, like saying it aloud would make everything fall into place—understanding, finally, that it was never her empire Lore had been building, but Hell's. "She wants Hell to take over. That's what she's been working for all these years."

"But why?" Fenrir asked, and Orpheus didn't have an answer.

Red had asked him once if Lore was able to be saved. Back then, Orpheus didn't have an answer. His own identity had been too tied up in Lore's for him to be able to blame her and not himself for all that had happened. Two terrified children locked away in a mad scientist's bunker doing what they must to survive wasn't exactly the recipe for a healthy relationship with forgiveness. But now he knew the truth. Now he knew, those scientists had been working towards something good— the greater good—and Lore had known all along. Had, in fact, gone out of her way to impede just that.

But that still didn't explain *why*.

Orpheus met Fenrir's eyes as he shook his head.

A shadow that had nothing to do with the surrounding darkness descended on Fenrir's face.

"We have to stop her; this isn't the end. We've only bought ourselves some time. Can you cast?"

Orpheus closed his eyes, found the frayed threads of his connection—the distance of his sigils but also the integrity of their shapes—and he knew. He could continue. He had to, now more than he previously understood.

"I can," he affirmed, as the scrape-slip scratch of metal against shale echoed up from the chasm.

"Good," Fenrir said, hands steady upon Orpheus as he took a worrisome step back, hefting one of his swords—Ohm's sword—that had been strapped to his back.

THE CRACK AT THE HEART OF EVERYTHING

Orpheus knew what was coming. Despite all his revelations, nothing that actually mattered had changed. And when Fenrir held his eyes, that understanding was reflected right back at him.

Fingers touched Orpheus' cheek, time balanced on a pin prick of a moment, within a world outside both their grasps, and Fenrir's voice came thin when he said, "I'll hold them off as long as I can," then turned away, and leaped.

CHAPTER XXXI

LORE

The temporal distension of time during high-adrenaline moments was a phenomenon he'd read about in a book. *The Matrix Effect*, the researcher had called it—a clever name for the suspension of linear time within a non-linear universe, as demonstrated by the film for which the theory was named. After everything, Orpheus wasn't sure if the researcher was credible, but as Fenrir faced off against Ohm and Lore, the first-hand experience of such a phenomenon was irrefutably *real*.

Fenrir moved through time like it was his to bend, catching Ohm's sword with the edge of his own, deflecting Lore's knife like he knew exactly where she would strike. What could have been seconds seemed like hours as Fenrir dodged and parried and took hit after hit. And it would have been remarkable if Orpheus wasn't privy to the reality that, eventually, Fenrir would slow. Ohm may be an undead magical nightmare from Hell, but Fenrir wasn't. And Lore didn't need to expend the same amount of energy Fenrir did, not when she had Ohm whittling down Fenrir's defenses until each moment she could slide in with that damned knife.

Orpheus could only watch while Fenrir's shield began to crack, fractures spidering out with every hit he took. The fluttering wave of distortion each time Lore slipped through revealed one secret, though: her immunity extended as far as the knife in her hand. She had to risk getting close to strike. An advantage Fenrir took each time his greater strength knocked Lore away. Regardless, the signs were clear. Fenrir would fall. And the cost for the time he bought Orpheus was too high for him to ignore—not when it was no longer his own life he bargained with.

Beneath him, the chasm in the world inched smaller. He couldn't say for sure how much was left, but with every passing second the power within him exponentially grew. He was working faster, more efficiently. Netherflame pulsing alongside the fever, the heated burn of his flesh a balm to the ice-cold fire pumping through his veins. And in the distance, darkness receded. Sunlight swelled over the shadowy horizon, a golden halo that felt so much like hope.

Just a little longer, Orpheus thought when he watched Fenrir stumble. Lore broke through with a quick dash, shoulder jamming in where Orpheus knew Fenrir's armor was badly cracked, knife slicing air to trace a line that barely missed his neck. Fenrir stumbled, then Ohm charged in, and the whole world seemed to shake.

Orpheus forced his eyes to remain open when Fenrir bowled over, armor taking the brunt of the hit but not everything—not now that the shield spell was hanging off him in tatters.

Only then did Orpheus look away.

Heat stung his eyes, a fist closed over his heart. Maybe Red would call him a coward, but it was either that or lose any nerve he had left. He had to finish this hells-damned spell. Had to make both their lives worth it, otherwise what was the point at all? Like all hells he'd die knowing he could have had the life Fenrir offered him, if he'd simply made a different choice.

A different choice. As if there had ever been a different choice— as if Orpheus had ever been given a choice at all.

It doesn't matter now, he reminded himself. The point of choice was long past. And the faster Orpheus completed his task the sooner everything would finally be over.

No more questions. No more what-ifs. No more hell beasts trying to kill him or imaginary curses nipping at his heels. He would be dead. And despite however many books he'd read that claimed otherwise, there'd never been an account of what happened after, so Orpheus was happy to presume he'd be suitably wiped from existence without any room for remembering all the things that had caused him so much pain.

Relief, he thought to himself, as he heard the strangled sound of Fenrir's shout carry across the chasm.

He dropped his head, smothered his sob, turned his attention away from the aborted choke of Fenrir's cry, and lost himself to his spellcasting.

Another tremble, another Earth-shattering quake, and Orpheus realized how close the epicenter had come. He didn't need to open his eyes to see the edge in the far distance—the closing in of everything that had harrowed humanity for the last three-hundred years—the literal detritus of their ancestor's poor choices. Incredibly, it was all coming to an end, all because of him. He certainly didn't feel like a hero while kneeling there regretting everything that had led to this moment, but history was written by the winners and Orpheus would be lying if this didn't feel like a win.

"Stop," sliced through his thoughts before the feeling could settle.

Across the chasm, Lore stood tall, her arm outstretched, Fenrir's body hanging limp from her fist. Their eyes met, Fenrir's Rim-pale in the violet light, nothing but the vast yawning maw of Hell's deepest pit between the two of them.

"I'll drop him," Lore said, and there wasn't a cell in Orpheus' body that didn't think she would.

"Please," Orpheus whispered, looking between the two of them. To Lore, he begged for Fenrir's life—to Fenrir, he begged for forgiveness. Both were true. Tears pricked his eyes as he said, "I have to do this."

"It's worth his life?" Lore gave Fenrir a rough shake and Fenrir flinched, pain in his eyes, and Orpheus thought—if he could only—stop. He could stop. In exchange for Fenrir's life. *He could stop.* The world would rot, and Lore would continue her rampage, but *he* could be happy. For once in his life, Orpheus could have what *he* wanted.

He wasn't a hero. He'd never asked for this power. All Orpheus had ever wanted was to find a shred of happiness in a world that had been cold and harsh. And he had. He'd found that in Fenrir and now he was expected to give it all up? For *what?*

You know what.

For Red and her engineers, working to make the world a better place for everyone. For Achates, who died to get him as far as he could, all because he asked. For Farris, who he had inspired to become a mechanic, despite his grief of losing his daughter to the Rim. For the patrons of Old Patsy's who hadn't seen his magic as monstrous, but a miracle. For the people Red's dead friends might have become had he not given Lore the means to start a war. For the refugees who had fled the Rim only to be met with the barricades of a society that didn't want them, that turned them away, sentenced them to this awful, poisonous death.

He swallowed, dragged his eyes back to Fenrir's and said, "Yes, his life is worth it. Along with mine, and yours and everyone else who died trying to fix this broken planet."

Lore sneered, a fire in her eyes when she snapped, "Fine." But Fenrir's soft, private, tear-filled smile was all Orpheus could see—the last thing he would ever see.

This time, Orpheus didn't look away.

Their eyes held until the moment they couldn't, Fenrir falling, swallowed up by that awful violet light.

Silence descended, suffocating, only the low howl of wind over the empty wasteland a reminder that Orpheus still lived.

Fenrir was gone. Just like that, he was *gone.*

No.

No no no no no—

Orpheus choked on his sob, heart wrenching out of his chest. The worn thread of his purging spell stretched to fraying, the fever in his body swelling his brain, a heady spin that had him hunching over the ground in an attempt to remain upright, to keep hold of the chasm and all the distance he had nearly closed.

He couldn't see it, but he could feel it—Fenrir falling farther into the Netherflame—into Hell. The amount of effort his sigil required quickly overwhelmed him, and Orpheus had to break that spell or risk everything they'd come here for.

He sobbed, clawing at the ground like he could reach through it to Fenrir. Shale tore at his fingernails, so when they found the soft flesh of his wrist, they couldn't even dig in. There was no release to be found in pain. Not anymore.

He had to do this. He had no other choice.

I'm sorry, Fenrir. I'm so sorry.

Orpheus let go of the connection, the spell slipping from his hands, and taking Fenrir with it.

Grief severed the quiet, a long, broken wail. Orpheus didn't care who could hear.

"You're next," Lore said simply, as if Orpheus cared about dying now. She took her time climbing atop Ohm's bony shoulders, like an empress assuming her throne, unhurried, because she'd already won.

All Orpheus could do was watch as Ohm gathered back on his haunches and propelled himself across the chasm. Somehow, he kept casting, racing to close off this wound that had poisoned everything Orpheus had ever loved.

Give me a few more minutes, then I'll gladly die, but time was something he'd run out of months ago when what he thought was a curse had come for him. Now, he knew it to be fate.

Lore slid off Ohm's shoulder and approached him casually, knife loose in her hand, knowing he wouldn't fight back—couldn't—not anymore.

All that he had left were questions.

"Why?" he gasped through his tears, looking up at Lore where she stood over him, his knees aching atop the shale.

"Because I can," Lore said in what may have been the most anti-climactic answer Orpheus could have expected. "Because they thought I wasn't good enough, a failure, and I hated them for that, though not as much as I hated you."

"Me?" Orpheus asked, not even buying time anymore—simply needing to know.

"You were their hope," Lore seethed, "their success. Pathetic weak-willed Orpheus was worthy in all the ways I was not. And back then, all I wanted was what you already had."

"Magic," Orpheus breathed.

"Power," Lore clarified. "The ability to impact the world in a way that mattered. Turn it into what you wanted it to be. And what you wanted? It was *pathetic*." She spat the word like it was poisonous. "Friendship. Love. For people to *like* you. You would have given up everything the hermits gave, all that power and magic, just to have— to feel—" Lore cut off with a disgusted snarl, but Orpheus knew what she meant.

Love.

"I loved you, and that could have been enough." Finally, he looked into Lore's eyes and saw something other than hatred.

It was pain.

"That wasn't love," she snapped, a waver in her voice—like the admission hurt, had left her raw.

"How can you say that? I *worshiped* you; I did everything you asked," Orpheus breathed, unable to believe that their experiences could be so fundamentally different. "I turned myself into a monster for you!"

"You were never a monster, Orpheus. That was the problem." Lore laughed, a caustic, burning scratch in his ears. She made it sound like *that* was a failure—like a monster was precisely what she wanted him to become. "You're weak. You've always been weak." She sneered, little teeth sharp in Netherflame's violet, though not as sharp as the knife tip she shoved into the soft place behind Orpheus' collarbone— right above his heart. She shoved in close. Orpheus tried to move away but Ohm appeared at his side, Lore closing in before him, the open maw of Hell behind.

Orpheus nearly choked when Ohm grabbed the back of his collar, holding him steady while Lore positioned her knife.

She held his eyes when she pushed it in. "Goodbye, Orpheus."

I'm sorry, Fenrir, Orpheus thought, eyes rolling closed.

He didn't see it, at first—but he heard it. A shriek echoing up from the cavern, the scraping drag of claws against shale. The world trembled, the pressure in his ears popping while the atmosphere turned molten, the column of dragonfire that tore from the chasm a precursor to the Emperor Dragon that burst from the Netherflame.

Orpheus reeled back, eyes going wide, the knife jerking in his flesh. From across the divide, the dragon's single slit pupil narrowed in on him, bleeding with a hatred that put Lore's to shame.

The dragon lunged, teeth bared, coming for him.

Lore snarled, knife tearing out of him as she dodged, leaving a clear path between Orpheus and thirty tons of hell beast descending upon his shield spell. His teeth ground as the impact jolted straight through him, shield a spiderweb of cracks. And as the threads of his spell frayed, as the chasm below him trembled, as dragonfire broiled over the ground where he knelt—where he bled—where he kept casting his hells-damned spell despite it all—Orpheus could have laughed.

Clinging desperately to the scaly ridge of the dragon's plume of spines was *Fenrir*.

"Do it!" Fenrir roared from the dragon's back, sword raised aloft like one of those heroes from Orpheus' books. Orpheus would have gone to him if he'd had the strength and the time. Instead, he met Fenrir's eyes and a swell of something other than fever or Netherflame burned through him.

Love. It was love. Of course it was *love*.

And how dare he tell Lore he loved her before he told *Fenrir*.

"I love you!" He shouted over the rushing whoosh of the dragon's wings. "Fenrir, I love you!"

Fenrir's smile could have been all they needed to heal the whole hells-damned world with how brightly it shined, but Orpheus knew there was more to do. He staggered to his feet and threw everything he had in Lore's face.

A whole Incident's worth of power tore from his very core.

Netherflame surged through him, drawing upon the chasm—this half mile of poison that simmered with three-hundred years' worth of unfettered destruction—a wealth of literal damnation there at his fingertips. But it wasn't lightning that cracked or a hail of flame that descended. It was the chasm, the whole torn-open seam of it zipping closed in a final rush of willpower, collapsing upon Orpheus, standing at its epicenter like he actually was some hell-begotten beast. Netherflame bled through his skin, burned in his eyes, clawed hands consumed in flames as all the magic he harbored inside himself came pouring out and into that hells-damned crack.

One-hundred feet—then seventy—fifty—only thirty left—

He heard, more than he saw, the dragon lash out. The telltale scrape of scales over shale sent gravel into his face, his shield falling while the ground below him tumulted. He stumbled to one knee as the dragon screamed, the boiling bellows of its throat convulsing as Fenrir sank his sword into the scaly pocket of flesh where the dragonfire glowed brightest.

The whole creature erupted. A blast of heat and flesh and the sticky-slick concoction of boiled blood and plasma nearly sweeping him off his feet and over the edge of the chasm.

Orpheus reignited his shield, held his ground, if barely.

Ohm was not so lucky.

Knocked off balance, Ohm stumbled, the crumbled edge of the gaping chasm buckling under his massive weight. And Orpheus might have missed it, the way Ohm's hand lifted towards Lore as she reached for him, fingertips brushing for one brief, tenuous second in their own kind of goodbye.

Then he was gone—tipping over the edge into the open maw of Hell.

"No!" Lore shrieked, voice tearing through Orpheus' fevered head. His vision swam, so he wasn't sure he saw right when he watched Lore fall to her knees and crawl to the closing edge.

Netherflame reflected off her tears, tracks of violet fire, and Orpheus couldn't blame her.

He understood exactly how she felt.

"You're immune," he breathed, unsure if his voice would carry over the roar of magic and fire. But Lore heard him. More so, she understood.

Their eyes met, and the last of the crack came together, ten and then eight and then six feet between Lore and everything in life she actually wanted. The same thing anyone wanted—not power or desolation or the end to everything that had hurt them—just a place and a person, somewhere to belong, to feel safe, to feel loved.

"*Go,*" Orpheus said through his tears.

Without another word, Lore followed Ohm over the edge.

Pain lanced through the fever crescendoing in his veins while violet bled from the world, the last of the chasm pulling at the hammered shale where he knelt, a final brilliant beam of Netherflame puncturing straight into his soul.

This is it, he thought as the ground trembled, and sun broke through the clouds. *It's over.*

Orpheus smiled, a laugh bubbling out of him as he closed his eyes and the crack inside him closed.

Heat and then cold tore through his body, a palpitation of fire and ice that dropped him to the ground. From a distance Orpheus felt hands on him, the levering grapple of Fenrir's arms as he dragged him off the ground and into his chest and then refused to let him go. Like he could stop what was happening inside him by sheer force of will. It wasn't an impossible concept, but without magic around to help Orpheus didn't think it likely. He didn't have the heart to tell Fenrir that, because it was clear now that one of them was going to survive all this.

With the last of his strength Orpheus looked into Fenrir's eyes and knew he was okay. In the end, Orpheus had been able to save the two people in the world he loved the most.

With that thought, Orpheus closed his eyes, and let go.

There were moments in Orpheus' life he thought about often, commemorations of the milestones he had achieved as both a mage and a servant to the Gilded Throne. And as those memories rushed through his mind, he found they hardly held a candle to everything else. Fenrir, Achates, Red and the rest. The Stacks and the Keep and the Pit and a curse that had driven him not to death, but straight into the world and a whole lifetime lived in a handful of weeks. Incredible, monumental memories that made the fear of dying seem less of an end because he'd filled what time he had with all the life he could, and how could he regret that trade when he'd received so much in return?

As the last of the ice drained from his veins, Orpheus was ready. He was no longer afraid.

He was okay.

Sun kissed his cheeks, warm and inviting. The wind that tugged at his hair bit cold, but with the edge of winter's approach. They were familiar things, a comfort if there was one in death. Orpheus sighed and allowed himself to feel, not quite ready to open his eyes, not when the memory of Fenrir's embrace felt so viscerally fresh.

"Orpheus," a voice called, gentle as the wind.

A smile pulling at his lips. How could Fenrir be here already? Perhaps time really did work differently when consciousness was no longer tethered to a physical body.

"*Fifi,*" landed with an affectionate urgency, "open your eyes."

What could be so urgent that eternity couldn't wait? Orpheus frowned, blinking into the light.

Above him, bloodied and bruised, the scar on his cheek now joined by a second, hair an absolute nest of filth and gore, eyes sparkling with sunlight and tears, was Fenrir.

Wait. What— *how*—

"You're so dramatic," Fenrir laughed through a sob, "you're also alive."

"But I—" Orpheus gasped, throat sticky with blood, ribs and collarbone aching where Lore's knife had nearly punctured his heart, his whole body wrecked and exhausted, like it'd been drained of something vital, but not to the point of taking his *life*. "—How?"

"Guess you were wrong," Fenrir's teeth caught his lower lip when he grinned, thumb stroking Orpheus' cheek, a slow slide down to his chin. "I'm so glad you were wrong."

Orpheus laughed, a broken, grateful sound that choked into a sob when Fenrir dragged him into a kiss.

It would be two hours before Red's panicked voice crackled over their walkie. Nearly two more before they were found, the dust plume kicked up by the entourage of transports churning like an oncoming storm with how enormous it'd grown. Red hadn't come alone. What could have been the whole population of the Stacks was piled into Farris' fleet of vehicles, guns and swords and pikes and any sharp tool that could be turned into a weapon held in every able hand—a veritable cavalry of reinforcements that Orpheus was relieved to say they wouldn't need.

"Fucking hell, y'all," Red breathed as she came forward, the tip of her gun dropping down to drag along the not-quite desiccated shale of what had once been the Rim. Beside her, Farris looked out, eyes searching the horizon for ghosts that would no longer haunt any of their dreams.

Color returned to the world. Gone was the gray, a dusty pale brown in its place, the blackened edges of the crack sealed up into a tight ripple, something like a scar though not as cleanly healed as any of Fenrir's. But it was the wholeness in Orpheus' heart that truly stood out. A lifetime of cold chased away by a warmth he had forgotten he could feel. There were still fractures inside him—guilt for the mistakes he had made, the half-truths that had driven him—but a path too, towards something good, something better.

And as he looked up into Fenrir's softly smiling face, Orpheus decided that for someone who hadn't ever been very good at healing spells, the results could have been much, much worse.

EPILOGUE

THE CROSSBOW

The Palace hums with the kind of excitement only Lore can inspire. Orpheus can feel it well before he steps foot into the receiving hall, his workshop isolating him very little, recently, what with all the people Lore keeps sending up the mountain in her stead—who haven't seen fit to leave.

Orpheus can't really complain. The supplies and plans and relics they've brought him are invaluable, components to research that, Orpheus likes to think, will win Lore her war. So, he holds his head high as he sweeps up from his workshop, striding through the Gilded Palace's halls with a confidence long earned by his position as Lore's closest adviser.

His steps falter when he turns a corner and comes face to face with what he can only describe as a threat.

Lore is there, fully armored, a small gaggle of courtiers hanging back in the shadows as the man at Lore's side laughs loudly at a joke Orpheus is not privy to. He comes to a halt well outside what could be deemed polite, heel slipping back as he considers the best route of retreat, because the man is still laughing, big booming voice and wild hair and a hack-job of a crossbow slung over one massively muscled shoulder, standing so close to Lore's side he might as well be hanging off it, Lore staring up at him with a kind of self-indulgent possessiveness Orpheus has never been able to inspire from her despite all their time together.

A spiral of panic blossoms in his gut, a sickening feeling of falling because he's—is he—has he been *replaced*—

"Orpheus." Lore's eyes level on him, pinning him like a moth to a board. "This is Fenrir Rawkner, my new general."

The man glances over his shoulder with a grin as sharp as that damned crossbow bolt. Their eyes catch and something inside Orpheus threatens to snap, because the man is looking at him in a way no one has ever looked at Orpheus before. Like he's a rabbit to be snared, caught in a hunter's trap, something that becomes painfully close to the truth when that sad excuse for a crossbow swings off his shoulder as the man turns towards him.

He hears the click of the mechanism and a sharp *whoosh* before a bolt lodges in the stone beside his head. Orpheus' face goes red as the world begins to narrow, and then goes violet.

"Oops," the man says while the courtiers gasp and flee, the Netherflame engulfing Orpheus' hand more a reaction than an intention. Lore gives him a look that clearly says it should stay that way, but Orpheus has eyes for no one but this man—Fenrir Rawkner—who'd just tried to *kill him*.

Except, Fenrir—he's—why is he *walking towards him?*

Netherflame sputters out, a curl of pale purple smoke obscuring Lore from his peripheral as Fenrir closes the distance and reaches for him.

Orpheus' back hits the wall a moment before Fenrir's hand brushes past his cheek to grab the bolt lodged in the stone beside him.

"Sorry 'bout that," Fenrir says, cocking his head, eyes sweeping down Orpheus and back up again, taking a measure of him that makes Orpheus feel much smaller than the two fingers of height separating them. "You're the mage, right?"

"Master Dark Wizard Orpheus Zon Ziffler of the Empress'

Exalted Court," Orpheus manages in one single breath.

"Okay," Fenrir says, pale eyes crinkling at the corners as a smile too soft to be trusted spreads across his face. "It's nice to finally meet you, Fifi."

The world turns red before it has the chance to turn violet, but by then Fenrir is walking away, bolt held loosely in one hand, that infernal smile cracking deep inside Orpheus' heart.

ACKNOWLEDGEMENTS

There are a specific few and a wider many I need to thank.

To my grade schoolteacher who told my parents: "Fiona is a great student, but sometimes they go somewhere inside their head. I wish I could go where they go" (here is your chance).

To my fellow creators who have graced the internet with thousands of free, character-driven deep dives that prove there is space for the type of story I want to tell.

To Stephen and Christina, who provided invaluable feedback and much-needed cheerleading.

To Sarah, who knows more about the stories inside my head than possibly even me.

To my publisher, Tiny Fox Press, who didn't hesitate to give this story a chance.

And to my parents and family, who have always encouraged, believed, and accepted me, no matter the strange or bizarre places my obsessions took us.

ABOUT THE AUTHOR

Fiona Fenn is an author of adult fantasy novels that put complicated "heroes" front and center. A fan of villains, redemption arcs, and intense explorations of healing in all its forms, their debut novel, The Crack at the Heart of Everything, is a love letter to all of those told they're too damaged to save.

ABOUT THE PRESS

Tiny Fox Press LLC
11782 Little River Way
Parrish, FL 34287

www.tinyfoxpress.com